VITALS

GREG BEAR

VITALS

HarperCollins*Publishers*

HarperCollins*Publishers*
77–85 Fulham Palace Road,
Hammersmith, London W6 8JB

www.harpercollins.co.uk

This paperback edition 2003
1 3 5 7 9 8 6 4 2

First published in Great Britain by
HarperCollins*Publishers* 2002

ISBN 0 00 712975 0

Set in Meridien

Printed and bound in Great Britain by
Clays Ltd, St Ives plc

Dedication

For Poul Ander
my friend, who d
long ago not

Our bodies are made of cells. Mitochondria are the parts of our cells that generate the energy-rich molecules we use every instant of our lives.

Billions of years ago, mitochondria were bacterial invaders, parasites of early cells. They joined forces with their hosts; now they are essential.

'My mitochondria compose a very large proportion of me. I cannot do the calculation, but I suppose there is almost as much of them in sheer dry bulk as there is the rest of me. Looked at in this way, I could be taken for a large, motile colony of bacteria, operating a complex system of nuclei, microtubules, and neurons, for the pleasure and sustenance of their families, and running, at the moment, a typewriter.'

– Lewis Thomas, 'Organelles as Organism', 1974

'We love Comrade Stalin more than Mommy and Daddy. May Comrade Stalin live to be one hundred! No, two hundred! No, three hundred!'

– Song sung by Soviet children, early 1950s

part one
HAL COUSINS

CHAPTER ONE
San Diego, California
May 28

The last time I talked to Rob, I was checking my luggage at Lindbergh Field to fly to Seattle and meet with an angel. My cell-phone beeped and flashed *Nemesis*, code for my brother. We hadn't spoken in months.

'Hal, has Dad called you?' Rob asked. He sounded wrung out.

'No,' I said. Dad had died three years ago in a hospital in Ann Arbor. Cirrhosis of the liver. He had choked on his own blood from burst veins in his esophagus.

'Somebody called and it sounded like Dad, I swear,' Rob said.

Mom and Dad had divorced ages ago. Mom was living in Coral Gables, Florida, and would have nothing to do with our father even when he was dying. Rob had stood the death watch in the hospice. Before I could hop a plane to join them, Dad had died. He had stopped his pointless cursing – dementia brought on by liver failure – and gone to sleep and Rob had left the room to get a cup of coffee. When he had returned, he had found our father sitting up in bed, head slumped, his stubbled chin and pale, slack chest soaked in blood like some hoary old vampire. Dad had died even before the nurses checked in. Sixty-five years old.

It had been a sad, bad death, the end of a rough road on which Dad had deliberately hit every bump. My brother had taken it hard.

'You're tired, Rob,' I said. The airport, miles of brushed steel and thick green-edged glass, swam like a fish tank around me.

'That's true,' he replied. 'Aren't you?'

I had been in Hong Kong just the night before. I hadn't slept in forty-eight hours. I can never sleep in a plane over water. A haze of names and ridiculous meetings and a stomach ache from French airline food were all I had to show for my trip. I felt like a show dog coming home without a ribbon.

'No,' I lied. 'I'm doing fine.'

Rob mumbled on for a bit. Work was not going well. He was having trouble with his wife, Lissa, a blond, leggy beauty more than a few steps out of our zone of looks and charm. He sounded as tired as I was and even more confused. I think he was holding back about how bad things were. I was his younger brother, after all. By two minutes.

'Enough about me,' he said. 'How goes the search?'

'It goes,' I said.

'I wanted to let you know.' Silence.

'What?' I hated mystery.

'Watch your back.'

'What's that mean? Stop screwing around.'

Rob's laugh sounded forced. Then, 'Hang in there, Prince Hal.'

He called me that when he wanted to get a rise out of me.

'Ha,' I said.

'If Dad phones,' he said, 'tell him I love him.'

He hung up. I stood in a corner of the high, sunny lobby with the green glass and blinding white steel all around, then cursed and dialed the cell-phone number – no go – and all his other numbers.

Lissa answered in Los Angeles. She told me Rob was in San Jose, she didn't have a local number for him, why? I told her he sounded tired and she said he had been traveling a lot. They hadn't been talking much lately. I spoke platitudes in response to her puzzlement and hung up.

Some people believe that twins are always close and always know what the other is thinking. Not true, not true at all for Rob and me. We fought like wildcats from the time we were three years old. We believed we were twins by accident only and we were in this long road race separately, a fair fight to the finish, but not much fraternizing along the way.

Yet we had separately chosen the same career path, separately become interested in the same aspects of medicine and biology, separately married great-looking women we could not keep. I may not have liked my twin, but I sure as hell loved him.

Something was wrong. So why didn't I cancel my flight and make some attempt to find him, ask him what I could do? I made excuses. Rob was just trying to psych me out, as always. Prince Hal, indeed.

I flew to Seattle.

CHAPTER TWO
The Juan de Fuca Trench
June 18

We dropped in a long, slow spiral, wrapped in a tiny void as shiny and black as a bubble in obsidian, through eight thousand feet of everlasting night. I had a lot of time to think.

Looking to my right, over my shoulder, I concentrated on the pilot's head bent under the glow of a single tensor lamp. Dave Press rubbed his nose and pulled back into shadow. It was my third dive this trip, but the first with Dave as pilot. We were traveling alone, just the two of us, no observer or backup. Our deep submersible, *Mary's Triumph*, descended at a rate of forty-four feet every minute, twenty-seven hundred feet every hour.

Dave leaned forward again, whistling tonelessly.

I narrowed my vision to fuzzy slits and imagined Dave's head was all there was. Just a head, my eyes, a thousand feet of ocean above, and more than a mile of ocean below. For a few seconds I felt like little black Pip, tossed overboard from one of Ahab's whaleboats, dog-paddling for hours on the tumbling rollers. Pip changed. He became no lively dancing cabin boy but a solemn, prophetic little thing, thinly of this world, all because of a long swim surrounded by gulls and sun. What was that compared to where *we* were, encased in a plastic bubble and dropped into the world's biggest bottle of ink? Pip had had a bright, cheery vacation.

One hundred and eighty minutes to slip down into the trench, two hundred minutes to return, between three hundred and four hundred minutes on the bottom, if all went well. A twelve-hour journey down to Hell and back, or Eden, depending on your perspective.

I was hoping for Eden. Prince Hal Cousins, scientist, supreme egotist, prime believer in the material world, frightened of the dark and no friend of God, was about to pay a visit to the most primitive ecologies, searching for the fountain of youth. I was on a pilgrimage back to where the fruit of the tree of the knowledge of good and evil had taught us how to die. I planned to reclaim that fruit and run some tests.

This blasphemy seemed fair exchange for so many millions of bright-eyed, sexy, and curious generations getting old, wrinkled, and sick. Turning into ugly, demented vegetables.

Becoming God's potting soil.

A mile and a half below the surface of the Pacific Ocean, humans are unexpected guests in a murky and ancient dream. Down there, nestled in the cracks of Earth's spreading skin, islands of heat and poisonous stink poke up from shimmering chasms flocked with woolly white carpets of bacteria.

These are the best places on Earth, some scientists believe, to look for Eden – the Beginning Place.

I zoned out. Napped for a few minutes, woke up with a start, clonked my head on the back of the metal-mesh couch. I was not made for submarines. Dave tapped his finger on the control stick.

'Most folks are too excited to sleep down here,' he said. 'Time goes by pretty quickly.'

'Nervous reaction,' I said. 'I don't like tight places.'

Dave grinned, then returned his attention to the displays. 'Usually we see lots of things outside – pretty little magic lanterns of the deep. Kind of deserted today. Too bad.'

I looked up at the glowing blue numbers on the dive chronometer. One hour? Two?

Just thirty minutes.

All sense of time had departed. We were still in the early stages of the dive. I sat up in the couch and stretched my arms, bent at the elbows. My silvery thermal suit rustled.

I liked Dave. I like most people, at first. Dave was in his late thirties, reputedly a devout Christian, short and plump, with stringy blond hair, large intelligent green eyes, thick lips, and a quick, casual smile. He seemed a steady and responsible guy, good with machinery. He had once driven DSVs for the Gulf of the Farallones National Marine Sanctuary, part of the National Oceanic and Atmospheric Administration, NOAA. Just a month ago, he had signed on with the *Sea Messenger* to pilot Owen Montoya's personal research submarine, his pricey and elegant little toy, *Mary's Triumph*.

It was cold outside the acrylic pressure sphere: two degrees above freezing. Chill had crept into the cabin and the suits barely kept us comfortable. I avoided brushing my hands against the two titanium frame beams that passed aft through the sphere. They were covered with dew.

Dave grunted expressively and squirmed in his seat, not embarrassed, just uncomfortable. 'Sorry.'

My nostrils flared.

'Go ahead and let it out,' Dave suggested. 'It'll clear.'

'I'm comfy,' I said.

'Well, you'll have to put up with me. Rice and macaroni last night, lots of pepper.'

'I eat nothing but fish before a dive. No gas.' That sounded geeky and Boy Scout, but I was in fact comfortable. Be prepared.

'I'm trying to lose weight,' Dave confessed. 'High-carb diet.'

7

'Um.'

'A few more lights?' Dave asked. He toggled a couple of switches and three more tensor lamps threw white spots around the sub's controls. He turned their focused glare away from two little turquoise screens crammed with schematics and scrolling numbers: dutiful reports from fuel cells and batteries, the onboard computer, transponder navigation, fore and aft thrusters. When we were at depth, a third, larger overhead screen – now blank – could switch between video from digital cameras and images from side-scanning sonar.

All we could hear from outside, through the sphere and the hull, was the ping of active sonar.

Everything nominal, but I was still apprehensive. There was little risk in the DSV, so Jason the controller and dive master had told me before my first plunge. Just follow the routine and your training.

I wasn't afraid of pain or discomfort, but I anticipated a scale of life that put all risk in a new perspective. Every new and possibly dangerous adventure could prematurely cap a span not of fourscore and ten, but of a thousand, ten thousand, a *hundred thousand* years . . .

So far, this was just an itch, an attitude I was well aware needed adjustment. It hadn't yet reached the level of phobia.

At twenty-nine years of age, I worked hard to avoid what Rob had once called the syndrome of Precious Me. I could always rely on Rob to provide sharp insight. In truth, part of me might have welcomed a little vacation. The void might be a pleasure compared to the anxious, egocentric perplexity of my recent existence: divorced, cell-phone guru for radio talk shows, semicelebrity, beggar-scientist, mendicant, dreamer, fool. Prince Hal, my coat, my vehicle, for ever and ever.

Spooky.

'You look philosophical,' Dave said.

'I feel useless,' I said.

'Me too, sometimes. This baby practically drives herself,'

Dave said. 'You can help me do a routine check in ten: Then we'll make our report to Mother.'

'Sure.' Anything.

I rolled and adjusted the couch to lie on my stomach, Cousteau-style, closer to the chill surface of the bubble. My breath misted the smooth plastic, a spot of fog in the surreal darkness. Experimentally, I raised my digital Nikon, its lens hood wrapped in rubber tape to avoid scratching the sphere. I looked at the camera screen, played with the exposure, experimented with pixel density and file size.

'They also serve who sit and wait,' Dave said, adjusting the sub's trim. Motors whined starboard. 'Sometimes we play chess.'

'I hate chess,' I confessed. 'Time is precious and should be put to constructive use.'

Dave grinned. 'Nadia warned me.'

Nadia Evans, the number one sub driver on the *Sea Messenger*, was sick in her bunk topside. A rich, creamy pudding past its prime had made eight of our crew very unhappy. Nadia had planned to take me on this dive, but a deep submersible, lacking a toilet, is no place for the shits.

Best to keep focused on where we were going and what we might see. Dropping into Planet Extreme. Eternal darkness and incredible pressure.

Still more than a mile below, at irregular intervals along the network of spreading trenches, massive underwater geysers spewed roiling plumes of superheated water, toxic sulfides, and deep-crust bacteria. Minerals in the flow accreted to erect chimneys around the geysers. Some of the chimneys stood as tall as industrial smokestacks and grew broad horizontal fans like tree fungi. Sulfurous outflow fizzed through cracks and pores everywhere. Magma squeezed out of deeper cracks like black, grainy toothpaste, snapping like reptiles in combat. Close by, at depth, through the hydrophone, you could hear the vents hissing and roaring. Wags had named one huge chimney 'Godzilla.'

Gargantuan Earth music.

Down there, the water is saturated with the deep's chemical equivalent of sunshine. Hydrogen sulfide soup feeds specialized bacteria, which in turn prop up an isolated food chain. Tube worms crest old lava flows and gather around the vents in sociable forests, like long, skinny, red-tipped penises. Royal little white crabs mosey through the waving stalks as if they have all the time there is. Long, lazy, rat-tail fish – deep-water vultures with big curious eyes – pause like question marks, waiting for death to drop their small ration of dinner.

I shivered. DSV pilots believe the cold keeps you alert. Dave coughed and took a swig of bottled water, then returned the bottle to the cup holder. Nadia had been much more entertaining: witty, pretty, and eager to explain her deep-diving baby.

The little sphere, just over two meters wide, filled with reassuring sounds: the ping of a directional signal every few seconds, hollow little beeps from transponders dropped months before, another ping from sonar, steady ticking, the sigh and whine of pumps and click of solenoids.

I rolled on my butt and bent the couch back into a seat, then doubled over to pull up my slippers – thick knitted booties, actually, with rubber soles. I stared between my knees at a shimmer of air trapped in the sub's frame below the sphere. The silvery wobble had been many times larger just forty minutes ago.

Two thousand feet. The outside pressure was now sixty atmospheres, 840 pounds per square inch. Nadia had described it as a Really Large Guy pogo-sticking all over your head. Inside, at one atmosphere, we could not feel it. The sphere distributed the pressure evenly. No bends, no tremors, no rapture of the deep. Shirtsleeve travel, almost. We wouldn't even need to spend time in a chamber when we surfaced.

The sub carried a load of steel bars, ballast to be dropped when we wanted to switch to near-neutral buoyancy. Dave would turn on the altimeter at about a hundred feet above the seafloor and let the ingots rip like little bombs. Sometimes the

DSV held on to a few, staying a little heavy, and pointed her thrusters down to hover like a helicopter. A little lighter, and she could 'float,' aiming the thrusters up to avoid raising silt.

An hour into the dive. Twenty-seven hundred feet. The sphere was getting colder and time was definitely speeding up.

'When did you meet Owen Montoya?' Dave asked.

'A few weeks ago,' I said. Montoya was a fascinating topic around the office water cooler: the elusive rich guy who employed everyone on the *Sea Messenger*.

'He must approve of what you're doing,' Dave said.

'How's that?'

'Dr Mauritz used to have top pick for these dives.' Stanley Mauritz was the *Sea Messenger*'s chief oceanographer and director of research, on loan to the ship from the Scripps Institution in exchange for Montoya's support of student research. 'But you've had three in a row.'

'Yeah,' I said. The researchers on board *Sea Messenger* fought for equipment and resources just like scientists everywhere.

'Nadia's trying to keep the peace,' Dave added after a pause.

'Sorry to upset the balance.'

Dave shrugged. 'I stay out of it. Let's do our check.'

We used our separate turquoise monitor screens to examine different shipboard systems, focusing first on air. *Mary's Triumph* maintained an oxygen-enriched atmosphere at near sea-level pressure.

Dave raised his mike and clicked the switch. '*Mary* to *Messenger*. We're at one thousand meters. Systems check okay.'

The hollow voice of Jason, our shipboard dive master and controller, came back a few seconds later. 'Read you, *Mary*.'

'What's going on between Nadia and Max?' Dave asked with a leer. Max was science liaison for the ship. Rumors of their involvement had circulated for weeks. 'Any hot and heavy?'

The question seemed out of character. 'Nothing, at the moment,' I guessed. 'She's probably spending most of her time in the head.'

11

'What's Max got that I haven't?' Dave asked, and winked.

Max was twenty-seven years old, self-confident without being cocky, handsome, but smart and pleasant to talk to. His specialty was Vestimentiferans – tube worms. Dave was not in Max's league, and neither was I, if it came right down to it.

'Enough about women,' I suggested with a sour look. 'I'm just getting over a divorce.'

'Poor baby,' Dave said. 'No women, no chess. That leaves philosophy. Explain Kant or Hegel, choose one.'

I chuckled.

'We've got lots of time,' Dave said, and put on a little boy's puzzled frown. 'It's either read or play chess or get to know each other.' He fiddled with the touch pad mounted at the end of the couch arm and once again punched up the atmosphere readout. 'Damn, is the pressure changing? It shouldn't be. My gut's giving me fits.'

I cringed.

Four thousand feet.

'I met Owen just once,' Dave said. Everyone in Montoya's employ called him Owen, or Owen Montoya, never Mr Montoya, and *never* 'sir.' 'His people trust me to keep his expensive toy from getting snagged, but when he shook my hand, he didn't know who I was. He must meet a lot of people.'

I nodded. Montoya seemed to enjoy his privacy. Best not to divulge too much to the hired help. Still, I felt a small tug of pride that I had spent so many hours with this powerful and wealthy man, and had been told we were simpatico.

I had met all sorts of people rich and superrich on my quest for funding. Montoya had been the best of a mixed lot, and the only one who outright owned an oceanographic research ship and DSV.

He was a whole lot more likable than Song Wu, the sixty-year-old Chinese nightclub owner who had insisted I try his favorite youth enhancer – serpent-bladder extract diluted in rice wine. That had been an experience, sitting in his living room, six hundred feet above Hong Kong, watching Mr Song

12

squeeze a little sac of the oily green liquid into a glass while I tried to keep up a conversation with his sixteen-year-old Thai mistress. Mr Song refused to spend a single square-holed penny until I gave snake gall a fair shake.

All the while, a withered feng shui expert in a gray-silk suit had danced around the huge apartment, whirling a cheap gold-painted cardboard dial over the marble floor tiles, babbling about balancing the forces of past and future.

'You know Owen personally?' Dave asked.

'Not well.'

Mary's Triumph leveled and alerted us with a tiny chime. Dave adjusted the trim again. The sub's thermometers had detected a temperature rise. The sea map display clicked on between us and a small red X appeared, marking where we had encountered warmer water. We had just crossed into a megaplume, a vast mushroom of mineral-rich flow rising over a vent field.

'That could be from the new one, Field 37,' I guessed. I looked at the printed terrain map pasted between us, dotted with known vent fields in green, and six red vents roaring away along a recent eruption.

'Maybe,' Dave said. 'Could also be Field 35. We're four klicks east of both, and they swivel this time of year.'

The world's seawater – *all* the world's seawater – is processed through underwater volcanic vents every few million years. The ocean seeps through the sediment and porous rock, hitting magma sometimes only a few miles below the crust. Deep-ocean geysers spew back the water superheated to the temperature of live steam – well over 350 degrees Celsius. But at pressures in excess of 250 atmospheres, the water stays liquid and rises like smoke from a stack, cooling and spreading, warm and rich enough to be detected this high above the field: a megaplume.

'Nadia tells me you're looking for new kinds of xenos,' Dave said. 'Ugly little spuds.'

'Interesting little spuds,' I said.

13

Nearly every dive in these areas found xenos – xenophyophores, the single-celled tramps of the seafloor, some as big as a clenched fist. Xenos are distantly related to amoebae and resemble scummy bath sponges. They use sand as ballast, glue their waste into supports, and coat their slimy exteriors with debris as they roll around on the ocean floor. Their convoluted, tube-riddled bodies hide many passengers: isopods, bacteria, predatory mollusks. True monsters, but wonderful and harmless.

'What's so interesting about xenos?' Dave asked.

'I have a snapshot taken by some postdocs two months ago. They found what they called "sea daisy fields" north of the new vents, but they didn't have a good fix on the position because one of the transponders had stopped sending. I examined a frozen specimen two months ago at the University of Washington, but it was all busted up, membranes ruptured. A specimen in formalin was nothing but gray pudding.'

Dave had already gotten a briefing on our dive. This was telling him nothing more than what he knew already. 'Yuck,' he said. 'So what's it to Owen?'

'Right.' I smiled.

Dave lifted his eyebrows. 'I'll just mind my own business and drive,' he said, and rubbed his finger under his nose. 'But I do have a master's in ocean biochemistry. Maybe I can render some *expert assistance* when the time comes.'

'I hope so,' I said.

'Is Owen interested in immortality? That's what I've heard,' Dave said.

'I really don't know.' I closed my eyes and pretended to nap. Dave didn't disturb me when he ran his check at five thousand feet. I don't think he liked my attitude any more than I liked his.

Owen Montoya wanted to be a wallflower at the Reaper's ball. That's what had brought us together.

Set the Wayback machine, Sherman.

CHAPTER THREE

Three weeks before, a slender little blue helicopter, bright as a fresh bug, had buzzed me over Puget Sound to Anson Island. It was six o'clock on a Northwestern spring evening and the weather was gloriously lovely. I felt more alive than I had in a year, since the divorce from Julia.

I am normally a nervous flier, especially in choppers, but the young, square-jawed pilot, his eyes wrapped in metallic blue shades, was reassuringly deft, and I was too busy enjoying the view.

'I was wearing my powder-blue suit,' Philip Marlowe tells us in *The Big Sleep*, 'with dark blue shirt, tie, and display handkerchief, black brogues, black wool socks with dark blue clocks on them. I was neat, clean, shaved and sober, and I didn't care who knew it . . . I was calling on four million dollars.'

I wore a black cotton sports jacket and pants, wrinkled white-cotton dress shirt with black tie, high black socks, shiny black brogues – that much was the same – and I was calling on forty billion dollars. Owen Montoya could have bought and sold the Sternwoods a hundred times over, even accounting for inflation.

I had worn that same outfit when visiting other angels, financial backers visionary enough or cracked enough – sometimes I had a hard time telling which – to spend small fortunes on a microbiological Ponce de Leon. I hadn't done too badly; my fancy footwork had kept me funded for the past five years.

I was no fraud. If the angels were smart, they sensed that I *almost* had the goods. If they were stupid – like Mr Song – they bought futures in snake-bladder extract.

I was very close. Just a little cash and a lot of very hard work, and I could jump the wall around Eden and find the ultimate treasure: vim and vigor for a thousand or ten thousand years, maybe longer, barring accidents or geological upheaval.

It was an amazing thought, and it never failed to give me chills.

The chopper performed a smooth bank to the north, and we flew over Blakely Point on Bainbridge Island. East of our flight path, midway between Bainbridge and Seattle, a cruise ship posed like a serene and well-fed lady on the fine ripples of the blue sea, her bow nosing into a bank of golden fog. Passengers gathered on a glassed-in observation deck below the soaring bridge, swam in three sparkling silver pools, spun around an open-air dance floor amidships. The kind of vacation Julia loved. At the end, she had started going on vacations without me.

Julia had ultimately found my talk about as exciting as a course in colonics. She had hidden her boredom for a few years, excited to be married to a young tenure-track comer at Stanford, a guy who regularly published little letters in *Nature* and longer discursions in *The Journal of Age Research*. But the gap in our minds, our educations, eventually wore her down. She complained she could not –

Enough of *that* shit. No way to spend eternity, moping over the past.

Two white-and-green car ferries plied the waters with more purpose and energy, their wakes crisscrossed by sailboats, catamarans, and cabin cruisers. Rich and powerful sailors everywhere, but how many had heard of *me*? How many would even care to listen to my ideas? Not many. They were like sheep running toward the slaughter chute, happily shaking their woolly heads, baa, baa.

I gritted my teeth and tried to enjoy the sunset doing a King Midas on the sound.

Thirty minutes out of Seattle, the chopper dropped a few hundred feet to circle a medium-sized island, lightly dotted with big, old, frame houses. We rounded a thinly wooded point to hover above a wide, deep cove. I squinted to riddle the mystery of a square, flat-topped floating object anchored a few hundred feet from the shingle-and-sand beach. Not a houseboat . . .

The golden glare off its white deck dimmed as we circled, and I made out a landing circle. It was a helipad, mounted high above the water on immense pontoons.

'It's a hundred feet on each side,' the pilot told me, smiling with impersonal pride. 'Equipped with refueling tanks, an automated weather station, and a repair shed. Impressive, isn't it? The island association refused Owen permission to put a landing field on his property.' He winked at such antiprogressive attitudes. 'Owen floated one instead.'

I clenched my fists, but the pilot expertly, and with barely a judder, brought the little dragonfly down in the precise center of the landing circle. He waved to an attendant and switched off the engine. The blades slowed with a disappointed trill as two men in gray overalls clamped the rails to the deck.

The pilot released the passenger-side door and pointed to the edge of the pad. 'Elevator and stairs over there. I'll wait,' and he smiled as if I were the most important man in the world. Next to his boss, of course.

As I walked toward the stairs, a breeze pricked the hair on my arms through my sleeves. Over my shoulder, I saw the pad crew, hooding the craft against salt spray.

Walking along the floating bridge to the beach, I had my first clear view of the house. Montoya's mansion faced the cove with a thirty-foot-high window-wall. Six Dale Chihuly chandeliers hung behind the tinted glass, spaced evenly across the lobby like frozen purple and blue fireworks.

I had not spotted the house on the chopper's approach, and now I understood why – the top was covered with patches of low forest, indistinguishable from much of the rest of the windswept island.

Betty Shun, Montoya's personal assistant, walked across the beach as I reached the end of the bridge. About my age, give or take a couple of summers, she stood five and a half feet high. She had a pert, sensual, but not very pretty face capped by a mushroom of thick black hair. Her body was her prime asset and she knew it. A clinging black shift revealed many attractions, sculpted by much working out and, judging from the adipose structure of her round face, dietary determination. I sussed a fellow traveler, ready to grab life, shake it, and ask a few hard questions.

'Dr Henry Cousins, I presume?' Shun asked with a lovely lilt.

'Hal,' I corrected.

'Hal. Welcome to Anson Island.'

The wall of glass and the mansion that lay hidden behind it bespoke a tasteful elegance that cared little for outward show. Montoya was no Trump or Vegas kingpin. Only from the cove did you know that a rich and powerful man spent time here.

'Last week Owen hosted Gus Beck,' Shun told me as we made the beachfront walk. 'And Philip Castler the week before. He didn't like what they had to say.'

'Really? I'm shocked.'

Shun smiled. 'So many wiseasses in this business,' she said. 'Be nice.' I could sense her intelligence, competitive and fierce, like heat. I idled a stray masculine thought about conquest, then shut it off. Something about that face, that body. Shun, for all her charms, would be too spirited to stay with any man for long. At least, any man worth less than a billion dollars.

'Gus was full of talk about uploading,' she said. 'You know, into silicon brains. I've never been much persuaded by that, have you?'

'Not much,' I agreed.

'Philip was brilliant but far too vague. And he kept asking about money. That's rude, and unnecessary. If Owen's visionaries have their feet planted firmly on the Earth, money isn't a problem.'

That was something I had learned long ago when going forth, hat in hand, to visit the Sternwoods of the world.

'Owen and Philip had a bit of an argument, I'm sorry to say. Mr Castler went home red-faced and empty-handed.' She smiled cheerfully, as if tallying sports scores.

Montoya had made his money off paper clips, or the equivalent in the cybernetic age: TeraSpin memory drives for home appliances, smaller, faster, cheaper, and denser than any others. Ten years ago he had been worth about a million dollars in stock – a few thousand in cash – and had lived in a ratty old Wallingford house west of the University of Washington. Now he was one of the richest men in a territory that on any financial map lay just a few degrees north of the Sultanate of Brunei.

I had never met so rich an angel, and I wondered what Montoya would be like. The last picture I had seen had been at least five years old. It is so easy to confuse the rich and the powerful with gods. Both can make or break you at a whim. The main difference is that our modern gods like to be called by their first names.

Shun reached up and straightened my collar as the tall glass doors slid aside. An odor of anise and crème de menthe filled the moist evening air.

CHAPTER FOUR

'Almost there.' Dave shook my shoulder and waved his hand at the pinging depth gauge, then switched on the bottom-scan sonar. We were about a hundred feet above the seafloor. A sound-etched picture of the terrain danced in ghostly blue waves across the display. The screen showed a stack of parallel lines between two walls of rock. The lines vaguely resembled a long rib cage.

'Is that a dead whale?' I asked, shifting right and reaching out to touch the LCD screen.

'I doubt it,' Dave said. 'We're coming down right over it. Let's take a look-see.'

'Dead whales are cool,' I said. 'They're like gas stations in the desert. Propagules move from corpse to corpse on the seafloor. Some get to the vents and set up shop for good.'

'That's one theory,' Dave allowed. 'But I still don't think it's a whale.'

He pulled a graduated lever and the DSV shuddered as we dropped most of our steel ballast. 'We'll try for ten pounds below neutral. "Dance like a butterfly, sting like a bee."' He pushed compressed air into the ballast tanks until we reached neutral buoyancy. Then he aimed the thrusters down and slowed our descent.

We hovered at about fifty feet, the sonar pinging insistently. He turned off the thrusters to avoid raising a cloud of silt.

'Get that bottom light bar,' he suggested.

I flipped the switch that turned on a bank of lights mounted directly below the pressure sphere.

'I'm going to move some ballast forward.' Dave pitched the nose down thirty degrees, giving us a wide-angle view of the bottom, and propelled us forward in controlled 'flight,' much more precise than weighted free fall. The DSV frame was equipped with a little railway system of steel weights that could be shifted fore and aft, or port and starboard, to adjust trim. This saved the sub from using thrusters, conserving power. The more power we kept in reserve, the longer we could stay on the bottom.

Dave thrust his hand into the data-glove box, a plastic cage containing a wire-lined black glove. With his left hand, he touched the instrument display and switched control of the lights to the glove. He expertly wriggled and pinched and twisted his fingers. The lights burned through a thin, whirling cloud of debris and flung brilliant white ovals on a small wooden fishing boat.

Not a whale after all.

'It's the *Castle Rock II*,' he said with a dry chuckle. 'An old wreck.' The boat's cabin thrust upright, intact after its long drop through the night, but the windows yawned broken and black like empty eye sockets. The crushed and splintered deck and hull showed the boat's wooden ribs. 'I thought I recognized it, but it's been a couple of years. Field Number 37 should be a few hundred meters north, if we follow this shallow canyon. A little current today, but it seems to be on our side.'

I looked over the shattered hulk, lost in cold and perpetual dark, and wondered about the weather above. Would our recovery go smoothly? Last trip, we had spent three hours in foaming, choppy sea, our beacons flashing, before being hauled aboard the *Sea Messenger*.

All around us, the seafloor was covered with broken sheets of lava like lost pieces of a giant's puzzle. The canyon walls, no more than fifty feet to either side, were not visible in the murk. The side-scanning sonar revealed that we were surrounded by what looked like columns in an ancient temple. Once, a lake of magma had pooled in the canyon and crusted over. Splits in the cap had allowed seawater to seep through and solidify the columns. The lava beneath the crust had then drained. As the molten basalt retreated, the sea had crushed the cap. Only the columns remained.

Dave pushed *Mary's Triumph* backward with a few spurts of the thrusters. I could make out the fishing boat's name, just as Dave remembered it, painted in a broken arc on the smashed stern.

'Let's go east,' Dave said. 'And up a bit. The boat dragged a few lines behind her when she went down.'

CHAPTER FIVE

We met in the mansion's Great Room, as Betty Shun described it, almost sixty feet long and thirty feet wide. This was the room that smelled of anise and crème de menthe. Skylights hidden in the forest above dropped the day's last filtered green light on a broad mahogany desk covered with magazines, newspapers, and a small laptop computer. Couches upholstered in rich yellow fabric awaited our attentions, like the laps of generous houris. The furniture floated on a velvety-smooth mauve carpet accented by white moons and antique yellow suns.

Betty Shun introduced us and gave Montoya a packet she had printed out a few minutes earlier. Then she left, wagging her finger and saying, with a smile, 'You boys be good.'

Montoya held out his hand. I gripped it and judged it, which is always unfair and completely natural: skin moist, pressure light. A polite handshake. He was good looking in a rugged way, with a short, pushed-up nose and probing black eyes. His cheeks had been pocked by youthful acne and a thin black nubbin of beard adorned his chin. His smile was quick but shy. His clothes fit loose but well, and his sandals were old friends, worn and comfortable. Montoya would not have impressed anyone had they met him on a street corner.

He invited me to sit at a long, ornate brass and maple bar.

'Welcome to the Fortress of Solitude,' he said. 'I'm the butler. Betty is really Supergirl. Coffee now, wine with dinner at eight, Madeira for dessert, and late-night chat, if you'd care to stay.' He went behind the bar. 'What's your jolt?'

'Latte,' I said. 'Please.'

Montoya had sold TeraSpin three years earlier and spent most of his time serving on the boards of charities. He had given grants and funded scholarships for more than sixty universities around the world.

He stood before the professional espresso machine and hummed the theme from *The Empire Strikes Back* as the valve roared and spat. Having my milk steamed by one of the world's wealthiest men was intriguing. I thought there was a touch of *ennui* in his eyes, but it's easy to overanalyze the rich. Maybe he looked that way because he had been disappointed so often.

'Did Betty tell you about Gus and Phil?' Montoya asked as he poured foam and hot milk from the small steel pitcher.

'She did,' I said.

Being around Gus Beck made me nervous. He was twitchy and far too brilliant. I never knew when he might erupt in

22

a fit of righteous technical criticism. Phil Castler was just the opposite – old-world gracious, fierce in debate but otherwise mild and self-effacing.

Montoya sprinkled cocoa over the peak, handed me my latte, and came around the bar carrying another mug filled with plain black coffee. He sat on the stool next to mine. 'And?'

I smiled. 'Uploading into cyberspace, living in a computer or a robot brain, immortalized in hardware, in silicon . . .'

'Makes you laugh?' Montoya asked, sipping.

'No. I just don't think it'll happen in time for me and thee.'

'Tell me why,' Montoya asked primly.

'The devil is in the details. The mind *is* the body. Gus is still back with Descartes in believing they can be separated.'

'Explain.'

'Downloading the brain's patterns isn't enough. Everything you know and think is embedded in your neurons, but your consciousness is in the cells of your entire body. Your mind is really a complex of brains, with major contributions from the nervous and immune systems. The flesh is intelligent, all flesh, and all of it contributes to your personality at one level or another. Take the body away, and you become near-beer, bitter without the kick.'

Montoya chuckled and looked away, rubbing one hand on his breast. 'Why not capture the state of each cell, each neuron, in a computer? A super MRI machine could do something like that, right?'

'Each one of our cells is like a huge factory with thousands of machines and workers. What the cells do, the decisions they make, how they live, contributes to what you think and how you behave. We won't capture that much detail in any artificial memory in our lifetime. Even if we could, one human being would probably fill all the computer capacity on Earth.'

Montoya nodded. 'What about Castler – sending in nano-machines and cleaning up an aging body?'

Easy questions so far. 'It's a good scheme, quite possible, but how old are you, Owen?'

'Forty-five,' he said.

'You'll be ninety before nanotech is proven and safe. Fifty years creeps up awfully fast.'

I was playing down the prospect of Phil's success a little; thirty years was not unlikely.

'You're not just saying that to get me to fund you?'

'I think Gus and Phil are brilliant. I encourage you to fund them both. But their ideas are longer-term.'

'They hate being told that,' Montoya said. He looked at me squarely. 'How are your theories any more convincing?'

'I won't turn you into a corpsicle and hope somebody knows how to fix you in a hundred years. I won't shave you down neuron by neuron, then upload you into some memory bank no one has even begun to design. I can begin to increase our life span in the next few years, with minimal intervention. If you and I want to stay young and healthy longer,' I said, closing in, 'our only hope is medical maintenance, keeping our bodies vigorous. Specifically, mitochondrial chromosome adjustment.'

'Beck turned red when I told him I was meeting with you,' Montoya said. 'He said you were insufferably arrogant. He said you were re-hashing theories proven wrong back in the nineteen twenties. I thought about asking Betty to fetch him a spit-cup.'

'There's a lot of passion there,' I said. Gus and Phil were my rivals and might have called me a fool once or twice, but they deserved a modicum of respect, even from a man as wealthy as Montoya.

'I agree, they're way off track,' Montoya said. 'They'll never see the promised land. I've read your papers. I like them. Tell me more.'

CHAPTER SIX

'That's new,' Dave said, swiveling the DSV and shining our upper bank of floods on a clump of tube worms. Beyond the worms, the sub's lights shimmered through white clouds like old, chalky paint: a bacteria-rich spring, small in diameter but productive.

'Let's see.' He sidled the sub in a few meters. I pulled down my data glove, feeling the plastic limiter box click into place, guided a sensor-laden mechanical arm, and pushed a probe into the spring outflow.

'Shove it, shove that old rectal thermometer right into the Earth's fundament,' Dave said with another leer. He wasn't funny. 'Eighty-six degrees Celsius,' he said.

'Congratulations.'

'I'm just the pilot,' he said matter-of-factly. 'You're the researcher. You'll get the credit.'

CHAPTER SEVEN

Montoya listened to my presentation for two hours. We broke for a quick dinner – crab cakes and stir-fried vegetables, served with an excellent Oregon pinot gris. We were studying each other, and neither of us was willing to reveal too much. Looking a little glazed, he called a break at ten p.m. Betty Shun appeared to take me on a tour of the house while Montoya fielded some phone calls.

The glass wall fronted the east wing. The west wing ended in a boat launch built into the native rock of another cove. It easily doubled what had at first seemed merely huge. The floor plan of Montoya's Fortress of Solitude had to total a hundred thousand square feet – two and a third acres, topped by wind-winnowed forest, the air-conditioner vents camouflaged as tree stumps and the condensers as moss-covered boulders.

'Don't try to take this tour on your own, Dr Cousins,' Shun warned me on the clay floor of an indoor tennis court. 'Without a permission wand, you'll be locked in the first room you enter.'

She held up a tiny plastic bar. 'Security will have to come and save you.' She looked at her wristwatch. 'Owen doesn't need a wand. The house recognizes him on sight. His steps, his voice –'

'His DNA?'

She smiled and tapped her watch. 'Owen should be ready now. We are exactly a hundred and fifteen feet from him, as the laser flies.' She gave me a look that might have spoken volumes, but I was unable to open, much less read, any of them. 'Why were you let go from your last research job?'

'At Stanford?'

She nodded.

'Money ran out in my department. I was junior.'

'Wasn't there some dispute?'

'A few of the faculty disagreed with my work. But my papers still get published, Ms Shun. I am still a reputable scientist.'

'Owen is fond of oddball thinking, and even fonder of tweaking academic whiskers. But I hate to see him disappointed, Dr Cousins.'

'Hal.'

She shook her head politely; keep it business. 'Owen needs something to commit to. Something solid.'

Betty Shun left me with Montoya on the west wing's biggest porch, overlooking the boat cove. It was eleven-thirty. We talked pleasantries for a while and listened to the splash of the waves, blankets over our legs, sipping from chilled glasses of draft beer, our heads warmed by radiant heaters. Did I like baseball? Montoya owned a baseball team in Minneapolis. I conversed as much about baseball as I could, having read *USA Today* in the Hotel W that afternoon.

Then Montoya drew back to our main topic.

'You don't say much about reduced caloric intake,' he said. 'According to most experts, that's the only antiaging technique proven to work.'

'It's just the tip of the iceberg,' I said.

'You haven't sunk your harpoon yet, Hal. I need to know more – much more.' He smiled wearily. Make or break.

I put my glass on the center table and leaned forward. 'The real problem is that we breathe. We respire. We accumulate poisons over time because of the way we burn fuel. We're part of a vast biological conspiracy, billions of years old, and we have to shake ourselves loose and grab the reins.'

'You've experimented on yourself, haven't you?' Montoya asked.

'I'd rather keep some things confidential until we firm up a relationship.'

'You *have* experimented,' he said, brooking no dissent. 'You've injected yourself with virus shells delivering modified genes, but nobody knows which genes, nobody on my payroll, anyway.'

'I've taken one or two things beyond the theoretical stage,' I admitted.

Montoya lifted his eyes to meet mine. 'And?'

'Obviously, I didn't screw it up too badly. I'm still here. But it's just the beginning,' I said. 'Until I know why individual obsolescence took hold a few billion years ago, I'm still going to grow old and die. And so will you.'

I was still being vague, and I knew it. The sweat under my armpits chafed.

'So far we've been dancing around the center. It's been a great dance, but I need something more. I've signed your NDA, Hal.' Montoya smiled, putting on the patented charm that had brought him so far in the business world. 'Give me a hint what's behind door number one. It'll be worth a few days on my ship, gratis. I'll put that in writing, too, if you want.'

'No need,' I said, swallowing.

'I'm all ears. I have all night.'

'It won't take that long,' I said, mentally arranging my cue cards. This was probably going to be the most important speech of my life. 'I start by altering a few genes in E. coli, common gut

27

bacteria.' I tapped my abdomen. 'Then I modify a few of my own genes . . .'

'Radical gene therapy,' Montoya mused.

'Some call it that,' I said. 'But it's just baby steps to solving an ancient murder mystery. Who designed us to die, and why? It turns out we're being betrayed by cellular organelles, little organs, called mitochondria. Mitochondria make ATP. ATP is the molecule our cells use to store and release energy. Once upon a time, mitochondria were bacteria. We know that because they have their own little loops of DNA, like bacterial chromosomes.'

He watched me intently. 'Respiration . . . seems pretty important. Breathing, using oxygen, right?'

I nodded.

'So why do we let old bacteria do that for us?'

'Mitochondria used to live free, a few billion years ago. Then they invaded primitive host cells, became parasites. Eventually, the hosts – our one-celled ancestors – found that the invaders had a talent. They were eight times better at converting sugar molecules into ATP. We formed a symbiotic partnership. The mitochondria became essential. Now, we can't live without them.'

'And mitochondria tell us when to grow old and die?'

'They have a big say.'

He pinched and tugged his earlobe. 'Explain.'

'The mitochondria turn state's evidence. Kind of a fifth column. They monitor our stress levels, track our physical and mental health, and pass that information on to tiny bacteria hiding in our tissues.'

'We have germs in our tissues?' Montoya asked, frowning. 'Doesn't the immune system clean them out?'

'Some bacteria burrow deep and hide out for years. They trigger diseases like atherosclerosis – clogging the arteries.'

'So what if I just spend my life relaxing? No stress.'

'Everything we do causes different kinds of stress,' I said. 'You can't stay healthy without some stress. But if we fail at our job, if we're unlucky in love, if we get sick, if we're feeling angry or frustrated or sad, our bodies fill with stress hormones. Bacteria and viruses mount challenges to our immune system, and the immune system is more likely to fail. But even if the immune system doesn't fail, over time, for some reason, we don't recover as quickly. We accumulate genetic errors in our cells. We deteriorate. We get weaker. The mitochondrial network reads these signs and reports to the deep-tissue bacteria, and the whole conspiracy tattles to the bugs in our gut. The bugs, in turn, tell the mitochondria to work less efficiently. That's the ultimate cause of aging. Together, they act as judge, jury, and ultimately, executioner.'

'That's a lot to swallow all at once,' Montoya said. 'I'm skeptical about bacteria communicating and cooperating. Don't they just grow and eat randomly?'

'What kind of toothbrush do you use?' I asked.

Montoya shook his head, puzzled. 'Does it matter?'

'Just tell me.'

'A Sonodyne. I've got a big investment in the company.'

'It uses high-frequency vibrating bristles, right?'

'Yeah.'

'There are over five hundred different kinds of bacteria in our mouths,' I said. 'Not all of them cause cavities. Some repel or destroy their disease-causing cousins. A healthy mouth is more like the Amazon jungle than a Listerine commercial.'

Montoya puffed into his palm and sniffed the result. 'Do I offend?' he asked, smiling.

I smiled back. 'Not at all. But some of them stick to each other and cement themselves to your teeth. After a while, they build up layers of bacterial architecture on your enamel. Dentists call it plaque. It's a community of cooperating bacteria of many different kinds – a biofilm. The Sonodyne vibrates the biofilm until it falls apart – breaks the cement the bacteria use to fasten to the teeth. In essence, you're demolishing their houses and shaking them up so bad they can't even talk.'

'Look, Ma, no cavities,' Montoya said.

'Other bacterial communities colonize your skin, your mucus membranes, and, of course, your gut, where they perform essential digestive services.' I could sense myself overstepping the bounds of what my angel might want to hear. 'There are so many bacteria in your intestines that even people who are starving excrete feces – made up mostly of bacteria.'

'Wow,' Montoya said. 'Gossip in the big germ city. But if we're so important to them, why try to bring us down?'

'A herd of antelopes sheds the old and tired to make way for the young and fit. Lions prune the herd like a rosebush. The lions may act like killers, but actually they're partners with a big investment in the health of the herd. Bacteria are more than just important partners – they're the most successful predators of all. We're their herd. Aging and death is one way to keep the herd fresh and healthy.'

'So, how do bacteria cause aging?' Montoya asked, leaning forward and moving his tongue over his lips.

'Bacteria in our gut produce quantities of a tiny protein I call *hades*.' Now I was really sweating. 'Our tissues open special receptors, coded for in genes I believe once came from mitochondrial chromosomes. *Hades* creeps in. It winds up a molecular clock days or weeks after we're born. With each tick of the clock, the bacteria increase the amount of *hades* they import into our tissues. *Hades* alters the way mitochondria work – jams them up, makes them convert ATP with less efficiency. We accumulate the resulting oxidants and free radicals, byproducts of respiration that damage our DNA. Our cells can't repair the damage. We start to lose our youthful resilience. We grow old.'

Montoya held up his hand and rubbed a few small, liver-colored patches on the back. 'Age spots,' he said. 'And I'm not that old. So what's in it for the bacteria?'

'There's a pot of gold waiting for them. Eventually, we get so weak, so full of genetic errors, that disease or cancer finishes us off. Then, the bacteria have an orgy. They feast like retainers eating a dead king.'

'Jesus,' Montoya said, and clenched his hand into a fist.

'That's the work I'll be publishing in a few months, communication between *E. coli* and mitochondria in human intestinal cells. I'm leaving out the news about *hades* for now.'

'We could just kill all our bacteria. Wipe them out with radiation or something. Live in a sterile environment.'

'They tried that in the nineteen twenties, and it didn't work,' I said. 'The fact is, we're designed to die. The molecular clock also acts like a deadman switch. Without bacteria, we go on aging anyway – only faster. A certain amount of *hades* may serve double duty – if we're active and productive, it may even reset the timer on the clock. It may also help repair genetic damage. Without *hades*, old viruses in our DNA start popping up and antagonizing our immune system. We become more prone to cancer or autoimmune disease.'

'Like a time bomb,' Montoya said. 'Awful. I assume you've found a way to defuse it?'

'I'm close. The solution isn't simple, but it involves training bacteria to pump in just the right amount of *hades*, at the right times – not too much, and not too little. And we have to jam the tattletale signals from our mitochondria. I'm pretty sure I can fool our bacterial partners into turning back our clocks. We live longer – maybe a lot longer.'

Montoya flexed his fingers and compressed his lips with something like satisfaction. 'Why go against the wisdom of nature?' he asked softly, fixing me with a limpid stare. 'Why live longer than the "judges" want us to?'

'We're big kids now. We made fire. We made antibiotics. Did the bacteria give us permission to go to the moon? We're ready to take charge and be responsible for our own destiny. Screw the old ways.'

Montoya grinned. 'I've never tried to think like a germ.'

'I do it all the time,' I said. 'It's enlightening.'

Montoya made a face. 'A whole new view of human existence,' he said. 'Makes me dizzy.'

'Not entirely new.' I reached into my satchel and pulled out a list of the researchers whose work had helped me. 'There are going to be a lot of Nobel prizes for these people in the next decade.' I was taking another chance, but I would not work for a man who was always sniffing for someone more famous. Montoya had to believe that I really had the goods.

'How about *your* Nobel?' he asked.

I shrugged. 'Not important,' I said. 'I'm in it for the long haul.' Sometimes I whispered that phrase to myself to get to sleep at night, like counting sheep. *The Long Haul. The Really Long Haul.*

A butler – Swedish blond and about sixty years old – carried a tray of glasses and a bottle of 1863 Malmsey Madeira. He poured, and Montoya handed me a crystal glass.

'Nobel prizes won't be half of it,' Montoya murmured. He narrowed his eyes as if about to fall asleep and leaned his head back. Here it was. My angel was about to pull out his flaming sword. 'You have a compelling vision. How can I help you to get on with your work?'

I took out the pictures shot by the *Alvin* crew the month before. Montoya thumbed through and reversed them to look at my notes.

'There are some deep places I'd like to visit,' I said, 'and some problems I'd like to solve. I'd like to do it in secret . . . Until I find out whether I'm a major-league idiot, or whether I'm really on the edge of a revolution.'

'What will I get out of it?'

'Nothing all to yourself,' I said. 'My work is for everybody. No patents, no marketing exclusives. I'm pretty hard-headed that way. But maybe – just maybe – you'll get a crack at living a few hundred years longer. Or a thousand. Or ten thousand.'

Montoya lifted his finger and seemed to wag it in time to unheard music. His eyes got dreamy. 'Eternity means for ever without time. Like standing still for ever. Did you know that?'

I shook my head. Philosophy has always been my weak point. Why argue about printed words when there are thousands of proteins and enzymes, the verbs and nouns of living biology, to memorize and understand?

'You know what I want to do, Hal?' Montoya asked. He stared out over the Plexiglas shield at the end of the porch and lifted his golden Madeira to the breaking waves. 'I want to build a huge starship. I want to travel to other star systems, stand on new worlds, and party with all my friends on my millionth birthday. I want to dip my feet in the waters of unknown shores and help lovely, enthusiastic women become mothers.'

Montoya finished his glass in one big gulp. 'I have all the money I need, Hal. I just don't have enough time.'

By ten the next morning, I had a pledge from Owen Montoya for three million dollars.

CHAPTER EIGHT

The *Mary's Triumph* had managed to cruise between three massive chimneys. Outside, hydrogen sulfide had leaped from a stinking trace to levels toxic to humans. Where steam-boiler temperatures did not scald, life flourished. Tube worms gathered in weird bouquets between the chimneys. White crabs crawled through like ants in grass. No alien city would ever look so strange or so weirdly beautiful.

For a second, I spotted something gray and serpentine just beyond a nearly solid wall of tube worms. I tried to call it to Dave's attention, but by the time he turned to look, it had faded like smoke. A current? A ribbon of bacterial floc scalded loose by a geyser?

'We have about two hours,' Dave reminded me. 'Those chimneys have to be eighty feet high.'

'That could happen in a few months down here.'

'It's still pretty damned wonderful. One of the biggest fields we've found.' Dave shook his head. 'But you're not interested in tube worms.'

'Not right now.'

Tube worms are born empty, then suck bacteria into their hollow guts and rely on them to process sulfides and provide all of their nourishment. They live about two and a half centuries, three at the most. Impressive, but they still take their marching orders from germs.

I wanted evidence from earlier times, when the host was still putting up a good fight and the bacteria were still flying their true colors.

'Under the plume,' I reminded Dave. 'Let's go east about a hundred yards. The walls seem to open up, and there are already fewer vents.'

'So there are,' Dave said, comparing the image from our forward-looking sonar with a terrain map made several months ago – a map, incidentally, that did not show Field 37.

He rechecked our position, triangulating between the pulses from the mother ship and the transponders on the seafloor, then pushed the stick forward. Two, three, four knots; a gentle glide through the forest, over tube worms and around spewing, roaring geysers.

We passed near enough to look up at a flange thrusting almost six feet from the side of a tall chimney. The bottom of the flange was painted with rippling, silvery pools. Superheated mineral-rich water, refusing to mix with the cooler local fluid, gathered under the flange's rough surface and reflected our lights.

'I get nervous around these puppies,' Dave said. 'Had one almost topple over on me when I was working for NOAA. Just clipped it with a manipulator arm, then, wham.'

'That's not common, is it?' I asked.

'Not very,' Dave admitted. 'But once is enough. Well, shit – I mean, dog poop – on it.'

That just didn't sound like reliable Dave the Christian man, the steady pilot of NOAA DSVs. I gave him a concerned look, but he was too busy to notice.

We made our way between the long, winding canyon walls,

pushing along at half a knot. The vents were behind us now, but wooly bacterial clumps fell all around, flashing in the lights. Bacteria coalesced into floc, carpeting the seafloor or being blown up into the megaplume, where they could be carried for miles, then sprinkle down like fake snow from an old Walmart Christmas tree.

'Looks promising,' Dave said. His arm twitched. The little sub tilted, and he corrected. 'Poop.'

'Focus,' I said. The view outside was getting interesting. A thin, viscous silt covered the floor of the canyon. Ideal.

A long, segmented ribbon like a thick blade of grass floated in our lights. 'There.' I pointed. Dave had turned the thrusters to reduce our forward motion, and the ribbon greeted us with a frantic, gelatinous shimmy. Then – before I could take charge of the data glove on my side and extend the manipulator arm – the organism tore itself into spinning bits of jelly.

I watched the bits get lost in the floc.

'Sorry,' Dave said.

I was furious, and with little reason. How else could we slow down? How else could we maneuver to pluck this singular and interesting anomaly off the seafloor?

'Some sort of cnidarian?' Dave asked.

'I don't think so. Let's rise a bit and descend on the next one with the thrusters up.'

'All right.'

'Just focus, please.'

His lips moved silently. I shifted my eyes from his face to the illuminated field beneath us, then back to his face.

We rose twenty feet and drifted down the narrow canyon. The walls dropped off. We passed a lava column, lonely and rugged. Everything was covered with silt and floc. There was no motion except for the fall of bacterial snow; still and empty, lost in a billennial quiet.

My hand twitched inside the glove. The manipulator responded with a grinding outward push.

'Careful,' Dave said.

I wanted to tell him *screw you*, but he was right. Easy does it. Focus.

Dave let rip with a long and heartfelt fart.

'Jesus, I'm sorry,' he muttered.

His stink filled the sphere. It was lush and green, like a jungle, but gassy, like corpse-bloat. I had never really smelled a fart quite like it, to tell the truth, and I wanted to gag.

'I don't feel very good,' Dave said. 'This is nothing like rice and pepper.'

My tickle of anger became a nettlelike scourge. Little sparks of resentment and frustration came and went like stinging fireflies. I could not focus. I glared at Dave, and he shot me a screw-faced look from the corner of his eye that totally grounded me.

We both turned away. We had been homing in before a fight. We couldn't get up and circle and bristle in the pressure sphere, so we had just glared – then agreed to back down.

Sweat soaked my armpits.

The sub crept over the sea bottom. I took control of the lower bar of lights and fanned them out.

Something big, round, and long came into view, lying horizontal on the seafloor like a toppled ship's mast. 'What in hell is that?' I asked, startled.

Dave practically jerked control of the lights from me, then chuckled. '*That* is a condominium dropped from heaven. Take a look.'

Clams, boring worms, polychaetes studded the mystery shape like maggots on a corpse.

'It's a *log*,' Dave said. 'We're not that far from some big forests, the Olympic Peninsula, Vancouver Island.'

'Right.'

A few tens of meters east, we came across another log. A chain drooling rivers and ponds of orange rust tied the log to at least seven more, all thick with life, all broken loose from a raft who knows how many years or even decades ago. It takes a long time for deep scavengers to move in on such riches, but when they do, organisms gather from miles around to share the feast.

We churned our way east a few more yards, following the rust rivers until they faded into the silt. I lifted the bar and spread the lights again. Dave did not object.

Ahead, dozens of little blobs wobbled on the ooze and sediment like dust bunnies under a kid's bed. I rotated the entire light bar, flooding the seafloor with daylight glow. 'There they are,' I said. Xenos by the dozens cast long shadows. The DSV glided over them, lazy as a well-fed manta. Our lights picked out hundreds more, then thousands, jiggling on the silt. I could barely make out the blurred tracks of their slow, rolling movement.

'Got 'em,' Dave said. 'What next?' Everything was fine again. The smell was going away or I was able to ignore it.

I kept moving the lights. Dave gently precessed the submarine.

'See those?' I asked. 'Those fans . . . and over there, gelatinous mounds – way over there.' I drew back the manipulator and armed its claw tip with a revolving suck tube. 'What do they look like to you?'

'Sea daisies?' Dave asked, as if eager to confirm my hopes.

'Some would call them that. A little yellow tinge in the lights. But they are *not* siphonophores. They're something else.'

I sucked my lips, afraid I might just be looking at loose debris, deluding myself. But they were not debris. They were real.

'I've never seen anything like them,' Dave admitted. 'They look like little squashed balloons.'

'Swim pillows,' I said. 'Bubble wrap.'

Dave's eyes were perfectly normal for this situation: wide with speculative interest. 'They aren't jellyfish or corals. And no algae – not this far down.'

'Rack your brain,' I said, giddy. 'Think back. Way back. Think living fossils.'

'Ediacara?' Dave asked, and immediately shook his head: *couldn't be.*

'You got it,' I said. My hands trembled.

The earliest known large fossils, from tens of millions of years before there were shelly or bony animals, are either lumpy bacterial colonies called stromatolites, or the peculiar formations that Adolf Seilacher named the Vendobionts. Another group name is Ediacara, from the Australian outcropping where type specimens were first found. These ancient life-forms had sat on the floors of shallow seas about six hundred million years ago. All they had left behind were sandy casts, impressions, little more than ghosts in stone. Until now.

I noted large chambers arranged radially or in grids, some rooted, some floating just above the seafloor. Mushroomlike bells; graceful, waving fronds; jointed blades; gelatinous air mattresses spreading over the silt. And all around them, perhaps their cousins and successors – possibly even their larvae, their propagules, the form which they assumed while spreading themselves to favored habitats – the xenos.

I was just guessing. I did not know whether xenos had any connection with these ancient marvels. But there they were – cozy chums at the bottom of the sea, just around the corner from Eden. If these were indeed the last Vendobionts, they had found a safe niche away from six hundred million years of evolution. Metazoan predators – our ancestors among them – had driven these ancients into hiding, forcing them into the ocean deeps.

I was getting way ahead of myself. Too much leaping and not enough looking, not enough science.

'Is that a jellyfish – on a stalk?' Dave asked.

Our lights were heating up the area, forcing some of the organisms to expel fluid and contract into wrinkled little raisins. 'Dim the lights,' I suggested.

Dave cranked down the rheostat. The seafloor became suffused in a golden glow, absolutely spectacular for mood. I wanted a room that color to sit and dream in. To dream of the Garden of Eden.

Nobody knows what the Ediacara organisms were, precisely,

and where there is mystery, there is speculation, and where there is speculation, scientific careers can be made. Colleagues can debate, friendships can dissolve in argument. Wonders come and go and theories die a dozen deaths only to be resurrected and win the day. A possible connection between xenophyophores and the cushiony Vendobionts had hardly escaped notice. But nobody had crawled out on a limb as far as I had.

It certainly looked like a garden, *an octopus's garden*, I started to hum, *in the shade . . .*

'Are we there yet?' Dave asked, tapping me on the shoulder.

I jerked, my reverie broken, and said breathlessly, 'Yeah. Let's circle – with the thrusters up. They look delicate. And let's start the documentation.'

'Video has been on for several minutes,' Dave said. 'I'll get the Hasselblad. You blanket the scene with the digital camera. Here – let me lay down a photo grid.' He paged through to the camera control display on the LCD, and squares of red light pulsed over the scene outside the sphere. Our cameras coordinated with the flashing grid.

We circled the garden, taking pictures for almost fifteen minutes.

'Ow,' Dave said, clutching his stomach.

I barely heard him.

'Dog poop.'

'Let's collect,' I said.

'Okay,' he said.

We moved into position to capture some of the smaller organisms. Somehow, breaking up the fans and bells seemed a sacrilege – but one we would no doubt commit.

I reached into my data glove and extended the manipulator arm, now tipped with a revolving suck tube. This was a special version of a tool used by earlier collectors to draw up specimens. Ours spun a small fan with variable pitch blades to pull water into a transparent acrylic tube.

I nudged the small tube up against a xeno in front of the

DSV's skids and fingered a small trigger. The fan spun. When the xeno crossed a photo detector, the fan cut off before it could squash the sandy blob against a mesh screen. Valves closed and capped the tube, and it rolled out of the way like a spent round in a gun.

Another tube was chambered, and, seconds later, another specimen – a segmented stalk – kinked and slipped neatly into the plastic prison. A third tube, and I had a small sea flower, each petal a separate cell covered with tiny hairs, like an arrangement of sea gooseberries.

Their jewel-like translucence gave me the final clue. These were not made of the tiny-celled tissues found in more familiar organisms. The sub's golden light warped through thick cellular membranes with a peculiar refraction, like interference between two layers of glass. Lovely, oily little rainbows.

The *Sea Messenger* had eight pressurized drawers for keeping specimens alive. Recording temperature and pressure for each tube, I ejected them into the drawers.

Samples of ambient seawater were analyzed by a miniature NASA chemical lab, the data stored for transmission on the next uplink. Labs on board the mother ship would soon begin preparing aquarium inoculants.

'What are you going to do with them?' Dave asked.

I sucked up another specimen, chambered another tube. 'They're wonderful! I've never seen anything like them.'

Dave gave another groan. His face was pallid and green in the reflected light from the seafloor.

'Are you all right?'

'I feel really weird. I swear I didn't eat any dessert.'

For a moment, making an effort, I forgot the manipulator arm and the precious specimens and sat up. 'You look like you've got a chill.' I reached out to touch Dave's forehead. He batted my hand away.

'Son of a *turtle*,' he said.

'Goddammit,' I said, simultaneously, and I was suddenly, irrationally furious, as if a flashbulb of rudeness had gone off in my head. 'Are you going to screw this up because of something you ate?'

He cringed and clutched his stomach, eyes going blank under another wave of pain. 'Don't take the Lord's name in vain around me, buster,' he said. 'Grab your specimens and let's get out of here. Quick!' he growled.

I pulled back in my seat, jerked the arm toward the drawers, and spewed the last tubes out, one, two, three, into their receptacles. So many more to collect. But training and humanity beat science.

Dave looked bad. He drew his knees up in the chair.

A pungent, tropical odor filled the sphere. It wasn't flatulence. It came from Dave's sweat, from his skin, and it was starting to make me feel ill, too.

Topside was straight Up, eight thousand feet. Three hours minimum.

I took a last look at the Garden of Eden – what Mark McMenamin had called the Garden of Ediacara. Serene, untouched, isolated, downwind from the geyser spew, just as I had seen it in the photos – imagined it in my dreams – my triumph, the highlight of my exploring, perhaps the key to all my research . . .

'Let's go,' I said.

'Diddly,' Dave muttered. His eyes went unfocused, wild, like an animal caught in a cage. He rapped his hand against the smooth inner surface of the sphere with a painful *thwonk*. The sphere was six inches thick – no risk of cracking it with bare knuckles. 'It's too . . . darned *small* in here,' he said. 'Colder than a witch's tit,' he added, eyes steady on mine, as if to receive applause, or criticism, for a dramatic performance.

Clearly not an experienced blasphemer. I stifled a laugh.

'I can call you Hal, or Henry, can't I?' he asked, peppering the honey of sweet reason with sincerity.

'Sure,' I said. 'Dave, we have to go up now.'

'I got to ask you.' He held out his hand, and the fingers twitched as if grasping something in the air between us. A little to the left, and he would have been strangling me. 'I don't really give a . . . horse's patootie . . . I don't give a dung heap if you know Owen Montoya. But did he ever give you a phone call?'

'Yeah, I suppose he did. Dave –'

'Did he ever tell you what *to do* with your life?'

This made no sense. 'Maybe,' I said.

'Did your Dad ever call you, long after he was dead?'

'No,' I said. This shook me, and I started to get really scared. My brother had asked me pretty much the same thing. 'Why?'

'Dog poop on them all. All the *petty* little bosses out there making their *petty* phone calls and telling me, of all people, what to do. Well, I don't understand a *petty* word they're saying, but they're making me sick. Don't you think that's what it is?'

I didn't think it was the hi-carb diet. 'Dave, I can get us back. Just relax and let go of the stick.'

'You don't know *diddly* about this boat.' He shook his head, flinging stinking drops of sweat against the inside of the pressure sphere.

My mouth hung open. I was on the furry edge of braying like a donkey, this was so utterly ridiculous.

With a dramatic shrug and a twist, Dave wrenched back on the stick. The aft thrusters reversed with a nasty clunk and churned up the silt below. Backwash shredded the delicate little garden. The golden lights glowed like sunset through the rising cloud of silt, and a few sparkling, dirty little jelly balls – xenos and bits of other creatures – exploded in front of the pressure sphere.

'No! Dave, get a grip.'

'*Piddle on it,*' he said coldly. Then he let out a shriek that nearly burst my eardrums. He flailed, knocked loose the data-glove box – leaving it dangling from its connecting wires – and pushed the stick over hard right. The little sub started to respond, veering, but the autopilot kicked in.

A small female voice announced, 'Maneuver too extreme. Canceled.'

'*Poop* on you!' Dave screamed. He let go of the stick. His thick-fingered fist struck my cheek and knocked me back. I shielded myself with my arm, and he pounded that a couple of times, then grabbed it with both hands, torquing it like he wanted to break it off and get at the rest of me.

'Dave, Goddammit, stop!' I yelled, really frightened now. Should I fight back against my pilot, knock him senseless, possibly kill him?

Did I really know how to surface all by myself?

He let go of my arm and seemed to reconsider. Then, with a last, final grunt, he yanked his control stick out of its socket and swung it around his head. Before I could raise my hands again, he crashed the stick hard against my temple. I grabbed my head with one hand and the stick with the other.

Dave wrenched the stick loose and screeched it against the inside surface of the pressure sphere. The metal end dug a shallow white groove in the acrylic. Not satisfied with that, he jabbed the stick into the sphere, scoring a pentagram of divots. He gave a doggy grin of delight, like a kid scrawling on walls with a Magic Marker. Then he delivered a frenzy of gouging blows, spittle and sweat flying.

I pushed back, ignoring the blood dripping onto my arm. Watching for an opening, I straightened and swung. He saw the punch coming and leaned. We scuffled like two kindergarteners. I bruised my knuckles against the top of the sphere, then connected solidly with the side of his jaw.

My hand exploded in pain.

Dave dropped the stick. It rattled to the bottom of the pressure sphere. He curled up like a bug in a killing bottle and moaned. Then he flung his head back, mouth agape, and gave the pitiful howl of a disappointed child. His hands jerked and shuddered.

Dave stopped howling and lay stiff and still.

The smell got worse.

I watched him warily, ready to fight again, then lost control, doubled over, and retched. There was only a little sour fluid in my stomach. It dribbled between my knees and under the seat. I noticed that the silvery air pocket beneath the sphere, trapped in the sub frame, was no bigger than the bubble in a carpenter's level.

So much pressure.

I sat up, waiting for the sphere to split along the white gouge or punch through the divots.

The sub's polite female voice spoke. 'Please exert positive control to disengage autopilot.'

I did the calculations, weirdly precise in my panic. *Two hundred and forty-four atmospheres outside. Twenty-four million seven hundred and twenty-three Pascals. Three thousand five hundred and eighty-five pounds per square inch. A four-door sedan parked on every square inch.*

My head cleared. I wiped the blood from my cheek with the back of my hand and rubbed it against the fabric of my thermal suit. *Training. Think.*

I had my own control stick stowed beneath my chair. It could be pulled out, inserted into my chair's socket, and engaged. I could take over *Mary's Triumph.*

Dave let out a sigh and collapsed. He looked like one of those polyurethane foam mannequins ever-present in the galleys of ocean research vessels, carried to the bottom, squished in the deep and hauled back for laughs. I watched in horror. But he was just going limp, and that seemed worse: complete, total relaxation. His half-open eyes had a forgiving, indifferent gloss. They socketed in my direction as his head burrowed into his chest. Dave skewed over until the seat harness, still wrapped around his shoulder, brought him up short.

He looked dead.

Mary's Triumph rotated above the seafloor. I reached beneath my seat and felt for the stick, detached it from its clips, raised it to inspect the connector, then tried to insert it into the control armature. Sweat spilled into my eyes. The stick wouldn't go. I reached down with damp fingers and pinched the plastic plug away from the small socket. I was shaking so hard by then it took me almost a dozen tries to make the fit and push down hard enough to lock both the electrical and mechanical connectors.

I waggled the stick.

'Autopilot control relinquished,' *Mary*'s voice announced. 'Shall we begin the return to the surface?'

I hadn't been briefed on everything the autopilot could do; there hadn't seemed any pressing need. 'Sure,' I said. 'Yes. Please.'

I pushed on Dave with the tip of a finger. Inert. He had smashed the LCD screen and two of the smaller displays. It was the autopilot or nothing.

The sub still rotated.

'*Yes,*' I said, louder. 'Go up.'

'Answer clearly for voice activation.'

'YES!' I shouted. 'GO UP!'

'Beginning ascent to surface. Transmitting emergency signals.'

CHAPTER NINE

The water outside grew brighter. It was now a twilit gray. I wiped cold sweat from my eyes.

Dave stirred about ten minutes before we surfaced. I watched from my seat, ready to hit him again.

'I feel sick,' he moaned.

'Sit still,' I said.

He goggled at my bloody head. 'Cripes, what happened?'

The good Christian was back.

'You went nuts.'

His eyes looked sad, betrayed. 'I did *not*,' he said. 'You tried to hit me.'

'You broke your stick and gouged the sphere,' I said. I wasn't about to argue with the man, not after spending three hours trapped with him in a dark, stinking, wretched little ball.

Dave looked at the marks and divots. 'We were collecting specimens,' he said thickly.

'Shut up.'

'I can drive,' he said.

'You broke your stick. The autopilot's in charge. Just shut up.'

Dave's face showed guilt and disbelief.

We broke the surface and the beacons switched on automatically. Through the waves crashing over the sphere – just our luck, a rough sea – I tried to spot the mother ship. I couldn't see a thing. Time to stand on top of the sub, by the mast, if only to get a breath of fresh air. I crawled back over the third, empty couch to undog the hatch.

'It's too rough out there,' Dave said.

'Screw you,' I muttered, and crept into the tunnel, an L-shaped pipe barely two feet wide. Swearing, I knelt in the usual small puddle of water at the base of the tunnel, got to my feet, and crooked my arms to twist and spin more levers and wheels.

The hatch sighed and my ears popped. Spray showered down. I sucked in the cold sea air, incredibly sweet and alive. I searched for the *Sea Messenger* and found her at three o'clock, well over a thousand yards away.

I yelled into the wind and waved my arms. I didn't dare crawl out any farther – Dave could close the hatch on me and take the sub down again. Lodging my leg, I held on to the mesh deck behind the pressure sphere.

Dave glared up at me through the bubble, still in his seat. He looked frightened. He was calling on the radio. That made sense, but I still wasn't ready to forgive and forget. *Sea Messenger* should have been almost on top of us, responding to our emergency signal with her H-shaped crane lowered for retrieval and the rolling ramp extended like a tongue.

'They aren't answering,' Dave shouted up through the tube. 'Come back in and shut the hatch.'

'No way!' I shouted. 'I'm staying out here.'

'Look,' he said, his voice hoarse and crackling, 'This is a rough sea. If you're staying out, get *all the way out* and shut the hatch or we'll ship water and sink.'

The waves were pounding stronger than ever and the wind blew stinging spume off the whitecaps into my eyes. The ship's lights were out and it was dusk. All the running and rigging lights should have been on, and the searchlights jabbing over the water, looking for us.

Nothing. *Sea Messenger* looked dead.

'I'm going to bring us closer to the ship,' Dave shouted. 'And I'm closing the hatch, damn it!'

'All right,' I said. Reluctantly, I dropped down and dogged the top hatch. But I stayed in the tube, squeezing my back against the metal wall, still cold from the deep.

'I'm really all right,' Dave insisted, his voice hollow in the sphere. 'I swear, I don't know what happened.'

'You tried to kill us.'

'That can't be right! I swear.'

I let it go. Dave moved over into my seat and tried to disengage the autopilot. There was something wrong, and at first it wouldn't let him. He pulled up the touch pad and keyed in an override. The autopilot disengaged with a small chime.

Then Dave maneuvered with my stick.

The sub cut through the chop to avoid being overturned. We lurched like a bucket in a slow-motion paint shaker, with nauseating jerks and some rough slams. Standing in the tube in a rough sea could leave bruises for days. I climbed down into the sphere.

The sub bobbed up on a roller and we caught another glimpse of *Sea Messenger*. People ran along the upper deck toward the forecastle. The lights were still out. Another bob, and I saw a flash of brilliant yellow-orange near the stern, then five more, rapid.

'Did you see that?' I asked, as if once again Dave and I were partners trying to outguess the rest of the world.

'Muzzle flash,' he said. His face went gray. 'What in hell?'

'How do we get on the ship if they won't grab us?'

'We abandon the DSV, swim to the ship and use the stern ramp. More than likely a wave will wash us up.'

'Or brain us,' I said.

Dave did not disagree. 'There's a diving platform on the port side – if they have it down in these seas, which isn't likely. We need to be out of the water fast.'

That was important. Immersed in the icy waters for ten or fifteen minutes, even in our silvery thermal suits, could be deadly.

'It's important we let them know what happened,' Dave said.

'That you went nuts down there?' My teeth chattered.

The pilot seemed to accede to this scenario. 'Your brain is not in charge,' Dave said. He looked like a frightened little boy confessing something dire. 'They can just ring you up and it's all over.'

Dave Press's mind was heading south, then north; he didn't even know how to read the compass needle.

Abruptly, *Sea Messenger* lit up like a squid boat on parade: beacons, running lights. Broken ribbons of silver and red and green glinted off the waves. A searchlight beam swung out from the bridge through the moist air, and another switched on near the stern. They swept the water, then converged on *Mary's Triumph*. Dave shielded his eyes.

'Somebody finally woke up,' he said. He wiped his face with his hands and stared at the palms, shaking his head forlornly. 'That's it for me. You coming?'

Dave pushed himself out of his seat and gave me a look as if he were going for coffee, did I want some, too?

'You can't swim from here,' I said. Was that what he intended to do – abandon the sub and strike out for the mother ship? We were too far away, even for a strong swimmer, in this sea.

He grabbed an overhead bar and hauled himself upside down to the hatch, then, with expert grace striking in a plump guy, swung himself around and knelt on the third couch.

'So long,' he said. 'Take my advice, for what it's worth. Stay away from the telephone.'

Before I could react, he shinnied up the tube. I swore and went after him, but he was quick as a seal, out the hatch before I could grab an ankle.

That left me halfway in the tube, stuck at a precarious angle. My leg bent, and the sub lurched. For a moment, my upthrust knee jammed in the pipe and I couldn't move. I struggled to drop back, and when that didn't work, to crawl higher.

I had been tamped down like a cork in a bottle.

A wave washed in through the upper hatch and swamped me. Sputtering, I pressed on my thigh with both hands and shoved the knee down hard, painfully, past a welded steel join, then squirmed to grab a rung.

I poked up through the hatch. Twilight was leaving the western sky, a lovely orange fading into blue and then black. Stars filled the zenith, visible even through the spray from swooshing and bumping whitecaps.

Dave was nowhere to be seen. Another wave almost blinded me and spun the sub around. I palmed water from my eyes and blinked at the nightmare. The *Sea Messenger* had come about and was backing her screws two hundred yards to starboard, whipping the sea into dancing foam.

A flare shot up from the ship's deck and arced over *Mary's Triumph*. They knew where I was.

'Get Dave!' I shouted, and swung my arms over my head. 'Man overboard!'

Another wave loomed, a greenie so high I could see the last of the daylight through it. It smashed over the sub's tiny housing and slammed me against the metal lip. The hatch banged shut on my head and fingers. A bomb blast of pain brought on blind rage, and I slammed the hatch back once, caught it on the rebound, flung it back for a second bounce, and once more, with all my might.

Anger spent, fingers and head throbbing, I dropped and sealed the hatch. I wasn't going to take any chances with the open sea. I trembled so hard I thought I'd vibrate around the inside of the sphere. For a moment I saw Dave in the water outside the sub, thrashing and drowning, but it was only a fat little twister of bubbles.

It was finished – I was going to die.

I caught myself moaning like a whipped dog, then, hearing water slosh in the bottom of the sphere, I remembered the specimens, locked safe in their drawers. My reason for being here, the reward for months of working the angel circuit.

I had survived a maniac sub driver, I was afloat, I still had the prize, the putative Apple, the Golden Fleece of the Gods.

Nobody had said it was going to be easy.

I fumbled with the ship-to-ship, changing frequencies, and finally a breathless voice answered.

'*Messenger* here. Is that you, Dave?'

I recognized Jason, the controller and mission planner for the DSV. I pressed the mike switch. 'It's Hal. Dave flaked. He's over the side. Get a Zodiac out there – he might still be afloat.'

'Shit.' Jason held his mike open and I thought I heard sobbing. 'Are you driving the sub?'

'She's on autopilot.'

'Hal, we have a bad situation. Someone's shooting up the ship. We may have casualties. Hal?'

'I'm here.'

'Paul and Stan went aft about ten minutes ago. We can't go back to the crane until they check in.'

'Dave went nuts, Jason,' I said, eager to make clear my own tale of woe. That seemed too much for him to absorb, and I decided to skip it for the time being. 'Just get me back on the ship.'

'I don't know how long that will take. Hang on. We'll do our best.'

'Yeah,' I said, and braced my hand against the inside of the pressure sphere. The sub almost rolled over.

I buckled myself in and gripped the mike like a lifeline.

CHAPTER TEN

Nadia herself bobbed in the water next to the DSV and tapped the frame with a grappling hook. I waved, and she gave me a strong chin-nod back, wet black hair peeking out from under her hood, black eyes distinct even behind the mask. She made the hook fast on a lift ring and swam out of sight. When she was done with the other hooks, she clambered up on the frame. I peered up over my shoulder to see her. Behind her rose the dark stern of the *Sea Messenger*, and the outline of the big red crane mounted aft of the helicopter pad. I saw Jason step into a little booth out of the weather, which was getting worse.

Then the rain sheeting down made seeing outside impossible. I felt the submarine rise from the waves, felt the waves hold us back, and with a jerk, the sub leaped out of the suck of the sea and swung in open air. Paul and Stan waited for me on the sled and prodded the *Mary's Triumph* onto her skid. The sled withdrew into the stern with a grind of gears.

Nadia jumped down to help Jason fasten the sub to the docking frame. I climbed out of the hatch with her help.

'We can't find Dave,' she said, her lips almost blue with cold. 'Gary is out there now in a Zodiac.' She looked ill, but stood straight and spoke clearly. I fell in love right then and there, with relief and admiration and more than my share of near-death giddiness.

'I'm sorry. What happened?'

'We're a mess,' Nadia said. She climbed the ladder out of the well.

'Dave went a little nuts down there,' I said. 'He tried to kill me.'

51

She gave me a level look at the top of the ladder. 'How do you mean, nuts?'

'He tried to sabotage the sub. Ripped out the control stick and used it to punch the sphere.'

'Jesus,' she said, but she didn't sound surprised. Maybe she was in shock. She leaned against the bulkhead. 'Dr Mauritz slipped a gun on board. He killed Thomas and Sylvia. Paul and Stan tackled him right here, where we're standing. He's tied up in the sick bay.'

I had spoken with Mauritz for a couple of hours the day before yesterday. 'That's stupid,' was all I could manage to say. I looked around and saw dark red spatters on the deck and across the bulkhead under an emergency light. Blood dripped from the light cage. The sight knocked me off-balance and I groped with my outstretched hand to find a clean space on the wall.

Nadia grabbed a towel from a deserted lab, returned to the passageway wiping her face and hair, and threw me an odd, blameful look.

I felt like a Jonah.

'I can't find Max,' she said, and tossed the towel back into the lab. We both heard the helicopter at the same time. She turned away with an exhausted slump of her shoulders, eyelids drooping, and said, 'That'll be the Coast Guard.'

'Nadia, I have specimens,' I called out to her as she wobbled up the ladders to the bridge.

'Fuck the specimens,' she shouted. 'People died, Hal! Don't you get it?' She paused at the top and her red-rimmed eyes bored into me. 'Mauritz was looking for *you*. He wanted to kill *you*.'

CHAPTER ELEVEN

A 250-foot Coast Guard cutter pulled up alongside the *Sea Messenger*. The Bell helicopter strapped onto the pad had carried two FBI agents. They were currently gathering evidence and interviewing Stan and Paul.

Dr Mauritz was hauled up on deck in a stretcher, past the crew mess, strapped down securely and talking a mile a minute, trying to explain that he was all right, they could let him go now. Mauritz was big-domed and balding. He had a kind of aristocratic English accent, and frankly he looked like a mad scientist. But he sounded apologetic and confused.

He had put up a stiff fight. Stan and Paul had banged him around hard. His head was covered with bandages.

I didn't know how long the specimens would last in the sub. I knew they'd be kept pressurized and at the proper temperature for at least another four hours – unless something went wrong. I didn't want to take that chance, but I also did not want to seem an insensitive asshole. The mood on the ship, understandably, was not good.

I waited in the crew mess, sipping a Diet Coke.

The Jonah feeling is indescribable. It's about nothing you've done personally. It's about a shadow hanging over you, an unshakable association with shit that no one understands. There I was, the closest thing to an outsider on the *Sea Messenger*, right in the bull's-eye. Why would Mauritz want to shoot me? He hardly knew me. Why would Dave Press want to drown me and wreck the DSV? The DSV was everybody's baby. Pilots would cross swords for the privilege of taking *Mary's Triumph* down to the vents.

None of it pieced together. Without a rational explanation, even the smartest of scientists reverts to a tribal suspicion of bad juju.

Exhaustion slammed up against emotional shock. I couldn't keep myself from shivering. Alone in the mess, waiting for the agents to work their way down the list and talk to me, I worried about the specimens.

Jason came in and stared at me. 'You all right?' he asked.

'Fine.'

'Owen called Captain Burke and asked about you. He said

53

take care of you and your work. I moved your specimens over to the aquarium. They're okay, I think.'

Unspoken, Jason was saying that what Montoya asked for, he got, even in the face of a police investigation. But Jason did not have to approve. 'Owen knows about us, about the ship,' he continued. 'It's on TV. You sure you're all right?'

'Thanks for moving them,' I said, nodding like a fuzzy dog in a car's rear window. I could have hugged him just for bringing good news.

'What'd you find?' he asked, and bit his lip, nodding along with me. We wobbled our heads, matching rhythm, and that was too weird. I stopped.

'Xenos,' I said.

'Right. You were diving for xenos. Look like cnidarians to me, though. You sure you got what you were after? Dave grab them, or you?'

'I used the suck tube,' I said.

'Do you know Dr Mauritz, off the ship?' Jason asked.

'No,' I said.

'Why did Dave go overboard?'

'I don't know,' I said.

'You didn't hurt him and push him over, just to hide it? You didn't fight, I mean, and hurt him. Self-defense?'

'No. He did it all.'

'Did he say he wanted to kill you?'

'No, he just started . . .' I sucked in my breath. 'Trying to curse and not doing a very good job. Kind of funny, but scary, too. I better wait for the police. Don't want this to seem rehearsed.'

'Right,' Jason said. He got up and stuck his hands in his pockets. 'We found Max. He's dead, too. Nadia's severely shook.'

I just stared at him. 'I'm really sorry,' I said, as if it were all my fault.

'Yeah.'

Jason left, and a tall man in a blue parka came in. He was

forty or forty-five, dressed, beneath the unzipped parka, in a wool sweater and khaki cargo pants, damp with sea spray. He was an FBI agent out of the Seattle Bureau, he said. His name was Bakker and he asked a lot of questions, some of which did not make sense until I realized he didn't know I had been on *Mary's Triumph* when Mauritz flipped. As well, Agent Bakker had not been informed Dave Press was missing and presumed drowned.

The news seemed to confuse him, so he turned back his pages of notes and started over.

'What in hell is a DSV?' he asked.

By the end of the interview, I was ready to collapse. Bakker folded his notebook. None of the pieces fit for him, either. In his experience, scientists didn't just go around killing each other.

After he left, I stretched out on the long, padded bench behind the main dining table and blacked out. I should have dreamed of falling through ink, this time without the bubble, drowning in endless, stinking night. Instead, I dreamed of being out in the desert, walking beside a guy with bushy white hair, wearing a long gray shirt.

CHAPTER TWELVE
Seattle, Washington

The ship returned to the Port of Seattle the next morning and agents and Coast Guard investigators swarmed over her. Diligent men and women marched aboard and began stringing yellow tape and ribbon. A dozen agents with digital cameras and crime-lab kits took samples. We were instructed not to move anything, certainly not to *re*move anything.

Jason intervened with the agent in charge and he allowed Nadia and me to go down to the lab and check the specimens taken during the dive. We were accompanied by a young female agent, built a lot like Dave, I thought, her pant suit a size too small and stretched tight. She watched suspiciously from beneath a knit cap perched jauntily forward on neat cornrows, and asked a lot of questions.

She would not miss a trick, I judged.

Nadia did most of the talking. She had more color today, but her manner was cold and efficient, as if her emotions were running on a very low charge.

I was trying to figure out how to get my prizes off the *Sea Messenger*. The ship was likely to be impounded for days, and I had no idea what would happen to them over so much time. I just wanted to haul the containers off the *Sea Messenger* and get them over to the lab I was renting on southeast Lake Union. I was eager to get my critters stabilized in the proper inoculants, supplied with fresh seawater, and under reliable pressure.

Maybe it was a personal disconnect, like an emotional circuit breaker blowing, maybe it was shock. All I needed on this Earth, right now, was to document and describe the Vendobionts, if that's what they were. Perform a few tests. Count their little fingers and toes.

It was not that I didn't care about the rest. I just did not have a clue how I could help Nadia feel better, or do anything for Jason. I certainly did not feel responsible for what had happened, however strange the circumstances.

Maybe it was the *Sea Messenger* that was hexed.

I peered into my cabin. The plump agent in the too-tight suit stood there with two men in plain clothes – and I do mean plain, black suits and London Fogs.

My clothes, books, and computer were spread out on the bed, being violated.

'Hello,' I said.

The young agent had removed her cap and her cornrows were indeed perfect. She had the most intense and unreadable eyes, and the skin of her round face was an unblemished work of art.

'We're through with these,' she said, and indicated the

clothes on the bed. 'But we'd like to keep these.' She swung her hand – her whole upper body, as well – to indicate my computer and three textbooks.

'The books are available on Amazon dot com,' I said. 'The computer contains private information. Unless you have a specific warrant, I'd like to take it with me. I'm not under suspicion, am I?' I gathered up my few clothes and pointedly thrust them back into the travel bag, flopping over and pressing down sleeves and legs.

'We need to establish relationships and circumstances,' she said.

'Am I a suspect?'

'No,' she admitted.

'Do you have a warrant that lets you . . .' I looked for the right legal words, then gave up. 'Fumble through private documents?'

'No,' she said, eyes lidded with sublime nonchalance.

'I'll keep it neat and tidy, and I'm sure you'll let me know if things change,' I said, shaking a little at my presumption, and at hers. I tossed the computer and the books into the bag and zipped it shut.

I passed Nadia in the corridor as I rolled the bag on its wheels to the gangway. She was smoking a cigarette and looked dead on her feet. She glanced my way, then sharply looked aside and stubbed out her cigarette in a little can.

I had not seen her smoke before.

'I won't say it was a pleasure,' she said.

I stopped and regarded her sadly, still buzzing from my anger in the cabin. I switched the bag handle to my right hand. 'I feel like a goddamned Jonah,' I said, and realized my eyes were watering. 'Christ, what did I do?'

'Nothing,' Nadia said.

'I have no idea why Dave went crazy in the sub, or why Mauritz wanted to kill me. I really don't.'

She kept her face pointed toward the shadows and bleak gray concrete planes of the dock. I flashed on all the women who had ever stubbornly tried to put me aside or pigeonhole me, or blame me, with or without cause.

'This is nuts,' I said, and tugged my ridiculous little bag toward the gangway.

'Betty Shun wants to talk with you,' Nadia said, biting off the information like an insult. *You're being called to the principal's office.*

I looked back, eyes wide. She was lighting up another cigarette.

Our generation had taken up Dean Martin and Frank Sinatra, reading cheap paperbacks, wearing black suits, and smoking cigarettes, like all the war-weary lemmings of the nineteen fifties, but without their excuses.

I felt sick.

CHAPTER THIRTEEN

After a bad night's sleep on the fourth floor of the Homeaway, just blocks from the Genetron Building and my rented lab, I opened the curtains. Across Lake Union, morning fog slid over the rusty tanks and pipes and broad lawn of Gasworks Park. I stood there for five minutes, feeling fortunate.

I was no Jonah. It wasn't me that was hexed. I had survived, and that meant I was lucky, maybe even on the right track in this great scheme of things. Only the FBI and a couple of murders were in my way, and that pissed me off.

Rob would have recognized my mood instantly. Prince Hal was not getting his way.

A cell-phone rang on the nightstand. Data phones in the U.S. had been screwed up for weeks with viruses. I carried four with me, on four different systems, just to make sure: a PalmSec, an InfoBuddy, and two standard Nokias.

It was the PalmSec that was beeping. The pert little a.m. triple-tone told me two things, that I had a call, and that it was before noon. I flipped open the jacket, keyed in my unlock, and answered. 'Cousins.'

'Dr Cousins, Betty Shun. How are you?'

'Dandy,' I said, and regretted the flippancy.

'We're very sad here,' she said. 'We've lost a lot of friends.'

'Yes. I know.'

'We need to get together. I'll bring along a man who also works for Owen. He wants to talk with you.'

'When?' I asked.

'We're in a car in front of your hotel. We'll take you to the Crab Cart for breakfast.'

I had been given my marching orders. But I wanted to find out about my specimens. Time was running out.

As always.

CHAPTER FOURTEEN

Betty Shun stood in the lobby, dressed in a green-leather coat and green slacks. I turned and saw a blocky, balding man in his late forties push through the men's room door, blowing on his hands. He made sure they were dry before he offered to shake.

'Hal Cousins, this is Kelly Bloom,' Betty introduced. Shun, Bloom, Press . . . I was seeing a pattern here, all members of the Monosyllabic Verb club. Bloom wore denim all over – denim pants, denim jacket with brass buttons, a blue-denim shirt. And Air Jordans, old but scrubbed clean.

'Dr Cousins, first off, congratulations,' Bloom said. 'Let's get out of here and go someplace quiet.'

They escorted me to the drive. I had expected a limousine or at the very least a BMW, but the car parked in front of the hotel lobby, beaded with rain and speckled with mud, was a mid-nineties Ford Taurus, conspicuously purple, with a dented right fender and scrape marks all along the driver's side.

59

'Yours?' I asked Bloom. He grinned.

'It's going to be a long day, isn't it?' I asked Betty. She gave me a studied smile.

The Crab Cart was quiet and dark. In the back, under windows overlooking yachts at private moorings, the booths were separated by barriers of glass and wood. Betty ordered first, oatmeal and two eggs. Bloom had nothing, not even coffee, maintaining his ascetic posture. I ordered a bowl of Wheat Chex, toast, and a small crab omelet. Bloom smiled as I laced into my food. Betty ate half her oatmeal, both of her eggs, and patted her mouth fastidiously with the cloth napkin.

The questions began. Bloom spoke in a pillowy bass, with a gentle North Carolina accent. He kept his hands folded on the oak tabletop. 'Do you know why anyone would want to kill you?' he asked.

'No,' I said. 'You're a private investigator, aren't you?'

'We both work with Owen's security detail,' Betty answered. She cocked her head at my raised eyebrow. 'Did you think I was window dressing?' She laughed, a tinkling trill. 'Owen can afford much prettier, just not much smarter, or more cautious.'

'Okay,' Bloom said. 'You understand we aren't trying to go around the police investigation, and that we have no authority? You don't have to answer.'

'Decent of you to warn me,' I said. The corporate Seattle way – a shakedown without the hard edge.

'We try,' Bloom said. 'Owen wants to understand what happened. You were down in the DSV with Dave Press during the shooting on the *Sea Messenger*. Did you think Press was acting funny?'

'He was acting scary,' I said. 'Not in the least funny.'

'What did he do?'

'I told the police, he was trying to curse and not doing a very good job of it.'

'Was he asking inappropriate questions?'

60

'Yes,' I said. 'But that wasn't so bad . . . I mean . . .' I paused. 'I never mentioned that to the police.'

Bloom shrugged. His shoulders strained at the denim jacket. 'Did he talk about Mr Montoya?'

Bloom was new to Montoya's staff, I guessed.

'He asked how we'd met, like that. Nothing suspicious.'

'He wondered what you were doing with Mr Montoya?'

'He talked about my getting special privileges with regard to the dives, the submarine. Jealousy aboard the *Sea Messenger*.'

'Jealousy involving Dr Mauritz?'

'I suppose. But mostly it was just water cooler talk – you know.'

Bloom nodded, but he wasn't satisfied. 'Dr Mauritz did anonymous peer review on one of your scientific articles,' he said. 'He recommended it be rejected.'

'I didn't know that,' I said. 'But then, I wouldn't, would I?'

'Did he ever show any animosity?'

I heard it first as *anonymosity*. 'Not to my face. He seemed pleasant, but we had very little contact.'

Betty Shun broke in. 'This isn't going anywhere. Dr Cousins, Owen had your specimens taken off the *Sea Messenger* and sent to your lab.'

'You should have told me that right away,' I said.

'He made sure they were delivered to your postdocs and they're being well taken care of.'

'They're in special pressurized containers,' I said, my anger building. 'They should have been transported in a powered van. We agreed, the specimens are incredibly delicate – the temperature down there makes their membranes –'

'Everything was done according to your instructions,' Shun said. 'If you'd like, we'll drive you over there.'

'It's just a short hike. I can go myself,' I said through clenched teeth.

'A car is faster,' she said persuasively. 'And Owen –'

'Yes, yes. Owen *wants a report.*'

We drove to the old Genetron Building. It's in a former

power plant that was given a multimillion-dollar makeover when Genetron moved in. You can see the building, with its tall exhaust stacks, from the I-5 bridge. Genetron was sold to the Swiss-French pharmaceutical giant Novalis, which rented me lab space in the now-vacant facility for a good rate – and with guaranteed security.

The lobby was an expensive waste of blond wood and stainless-steel, with a cut-pile green carpet that matched Betty Shun's leather jacket. A security guard checked my card and gave Shun and Bloom temporary passes. I showed them the way to the ground-floor lab, at the end of a long hall on the north end of the building.

'Does he have to come along?' I asked Shun, waving my hand at Bloom.

'Yes.'

Bloom lifted his head as if sailing into a wind and winked at me.

'The specimens may have been in poor condition,' Betty said as we walked down the hall. 'We could not tell if they were dead or alive. We did our best, at Owen's request.'

'Did Nadia or Jason help carry them over?'

'No,' Betty said. 'Nadia is in police custody now.'

That took me completely by surprise. 'Why?'

'Under suspicion of tampering with the food on board the *Sea Messenger*.'

'That's stupid,' I said.

'We think so, too.'

'Tampering how?' Then I remembered the creamy pudding and its results. 'Some of them ate a bad dessert, but –'

Bloom interrupted. 'There was a lot of odd behavior on board the ship, from the very beginning of the cruise. Fights, arguments, irrational statements at odd moments.'

I had spent much of my time in my cabin. Not being very sociable – and having a lot of reading to catch up on.

'Somebody *could* have put drugs in the food or water,' Bloom concluded.

My lab filled two rooms, each about twenty feet square, connected by a white Dutch door. I had ordered special holding tanks for the specimens. Dan and Valerie, my two assistants, were pressurizing the tanks as we walked in.

Dan was a postdoc in oceanic microbiology, a tall, big-shouldered farmboy in appearance but a wizard with equipment. He looked up from the pressure gauge and gave me an unhappy shake of his head.

'The specimens are pretty traumatized, Dr Cousins,' he said.

I muttered under my breath.

Valerie stood back, arms folded across her bosom, hands gripping her shoulders, as if contemplating a relative's coffin. 'They look dead.'

I moved around Shun and Bloom and fluttered my hands for a moment, probably stuck my tongue between my teeth, trying to figure out where to begin. A steel box full of plastic tubes filled with foot-long core samples from our first and second dives was still on the loading cart. The metal tanks containing the specimens from the third dive had been stacked on the power bed and plugged in. They were still cold and seemed, at a quick glance through the fogged plastic panels, to be carrying Items of Interest.

Still, the damage was likely already done; how to minimize its effects?

'These creatures didn't look that alive to begin with,' I suggested, hoping to break the tension and help Dan and Valerie relax. 'They're sedentary.'

Valerie shook her head again, tears welling. I wasn't lying very effectively.

'All the specimens are here,' I said, checking the inventory. 'In that small tank – the one that's not at pressure – we have some shovel loads from the sediment that need to be analyzed. I doubt we grabbed any infaunal specimens intact, but we can preserve them and stain for cytoplasm and do some tube counts in the mud. Get some formalin and rose bengal.'

Dan and Valerie focused on the scoop samples and a couple

of shallow cores. I wanted them out of the way while I either silently mourned or, less likely, breathed a sigh of relief.

I wiped the panels on the big steel transfer tanks and peered inside with a pocket flashlight. Straight from the briny deeps: shadowy masses that might have been clouds of sediment. Or ruined xenos. I knelt and squinted. Some forms were more than just fragments.

Shun stayed, but Bloom slipped out to answer a phone call.

I checked out the stats in the lab computer and made sure the necessary conditions were being met: water at 3.5 degrees Celsius, high oxygen, 36 percent salinity, metal sulfides in medium traces.

'It's at 250 atmospheres,' Valerie said.

'If we reduce the pressure, the xenos break down into slippery mush,' I said to Betty Shun. 'Their cell membranes – mostly lipids – melt like butter on a hot day. Deep down, where it's cold and heavy, the membranes are gelid.'

I'd begun a culture of typical bacterial mats even before going out on the *Sea Messenger*, and now I harvested them from a container in the refrigerator and shot them with a plastic bottle straight into the pump chamber. I watched them spread in pale ribbons into the lab's central refrigerated tank.

'Very impressive,' Betty Shun observed, laying a hand lightly on the big tank's cold acrylic. 'I notice you just dumped in the bacteria. Why?'

'The bacteria adjust quickly. Their desaturase enzymes stop working under pressure, and that pumps up the unsaturated fatty acids in their cell walls, keeping them from getting too inflexible. Our larger specimens aren't so adaptable.'

I asked Dan to help me connect the first transfer vessel to the big lab tank. We carried it to the worktable and connected it to the delivery chute, making sure the lock seals were tight. I checked the pressure – the vessel had lost about three atmospheres – and I dropped the pressure on the lab tank to match. Then I opened the inner doors and mixed the waters. Small chunks of sandy, dirty jelly floated past.

Like the man praying that the bottle falling through the liquor store bag was vermouth, not gin, I hoped these fragments were common xenos and not our fancy Vendobionts.

'It's soup,' Dan said.

I looked accusingly at Shun. 'I should have moved them myself.' She did not react. No doubt she had dealt with personalities fiercer than mine.

I tilted the plastic baffle inside the transfer tank and gently encouraged more contents to drift past the small acrylic port. Dan switched on the main video camera and turned the monitor so I could see.

A frond undulated in the junction between the two tanks, still tinged with yellow.

'Alive?' Valerie asked.

'Probably not. At least the cells haven't ruptured,' I said. 'Let's salvage what we can.'

Bloom came back and posted himself out of the way, in a corner.

Eight hours passed. I can always lose myself in lab work. I become something lovely and serene, a disembodied Spirit of Science. Tech Zombie, Julia once called me. I don't even need coffee – there's something about discovery that pumps me full of my own natural caffeine.

Shun was more patient than I expected – not that I paid her much attention for the first seven hours – but Bloom began to fidget after two, pace after three, and made his excuses after three and a half and stepped out once more.

We had our work cut out for us. These celebrity living fossils were dying or dead, and all their secrets were fading with them. We had to move fast.

First, I performed triage and used the manipulator to gently push fragments and clearly defunct organisms back into a specially prepared transfer tank. I set Valerie to doing proteomics on a few cc's of mush that I could not otherwise identify. That occupied her for several hours. She used the

Applara Proteomizer – a machine the size of a large bread box, capable of doing whole protein analysis at the rate of five hundred amino acid components per minute.

I doubted these critters used more than a few thousand proteins. Your average protein is about a thousand amino acids long. In a few hours, we had a first-order list of the proteins in the mush, and some hints as to the kind of genes and byproducts we would find when we ran the nucleic acids through a sequencer.

While Valerie worked, I spent an hour just staring at the intact organisms in the main tank. Shun stood shoulder to shoulder with me during much of that time, but she wisely kept silent.

If I was a flaming and driven Spirit, she was an unobtrusive shade – or the sword-bearing arm of my angel, Montoya. I didn't care. Nothing scared me more than failure.

The largest of our specimens, the frond, was a rubbery feather with many compressed ribs, its greenish mud color tinged with yellow. It was about twenty centimeters long, ten centimeters across at its widest point, and it looked like a leaf made of bubble wrap.

It was clearly colonial, fairly hardy in comparison to its companions, but, most important, it was still alive. My first guess was that it was made up of xenolike protists. Each saclike bump of its anatomy was an individual cell, anywhere from a few millimeters to a couple of centimeters in size.

Most modern cells are microscopic and need only one nucleus, the central computer and factory that contains the chromosomes. These cells were much larger than most modern cells. I supposed, in my intensity of speculation, that each of the components would have many nuclei, as xenos do, to speed creation and delivery of the necessary gene products – ribosomal RNA, proteins, etc. – across its comparatively far-flung cytoplasmic territory.

That would be familiar. That would be expected.

But when we carefully plucked a cell from the feather-fan

colony, froze and micro-sliced it, then mounted it for the lab's little electron microscope, Dan reported that there were no nuclei whatsoever. The cell was a blob of jelly with unbounded circular chromosomes floating in a thick but simple membrane, and that in itself would make it a variety of bacteria or archaea, neither of which sequester their DNA in nuclei.

But the cell was supported by a microtubule cytoskeleton, looking like wads of glassy fibers under the microscope. Bacteria and archaea do not have cytoskeletons.

The sampled cell was as big as the tip of my pinky. Inspection of another cell showed us that there were bacteria of many different kinds living loose inside, screwing their way through the cytoplasmic gel. Some of these bacterial interlopers were large – millimeters in size, visible to the naked eye. They reminded me of extremophiles I had seen profiled in *Science* a few months before, the kind that clustered on the butts of ugly red Pompeii worms in vent communities.

The frond, then, was neither plant nor precisely animal, nor did it belong to any of the remaining three kingdoms of modern biology. Each big cell in my colonial critter was like an old-fashioned Western mining town. The bacterial hitchhikers were free to come and go, but mostly they stayed. I imagined they were like mine workers recruited from the town's ruffians, doing their jobs, but on occasion hog-tying the boss and his wife, threatening the engineers (my imagination was fevered by lack of blood sugar), and forcing the lucrative mine owners to pay out caskets of gold, and not a sheriff in sight.

Lots of free-range cooperation between characters who might at any moment pull out six-guns and start blazing away at each other, then turn around the next moment –

And share a drink at the bar.

I laughed. Valerie and Betty blinked at me, owlish and exhausted. I looked at my watch. It was seven-thirty in the evening. We hadn't taken any breaks.

We were due.

The machines could run themselves. The tank would keep whatever was still alive happy. I looked at Valerie's tentative list of proteins from the mush and pursed my lips as if coming in for a smooch.

'Wow,' I said.

'Good?' Betty asked.

'Phenomenal,' I said. 'There are no nuclei and no mitochondria in these cells. They are very primitive.'

'That's good?'

'It's what I've been dreaming about for years,' I said. 'The bacteria in the cytoplasm are commensal, but not symbiotic – they help the cell respire and metabolize its food. But they're a long jump behind becoming mitochondria. Maybe hundreds of millions of years . . .'

My arm flesh pricked up with goose bumps. 'Jesus,' I said, with all the reverence I am capable of. 'We could be looking at ghosts from the Garden of Eden. And they haven't taken the Fall.'

Dan had slumped over the Applara monitor. Valerie shook him awake and whispered something into his ear. He brightened.

'Dinner?' he murmured.

'It's on me,' I said. I looked at Betty. 'You should come, too. And Bloom, if he's still around.' I felt magnanimous. Hell, I was punchy with glee.

'Tell Owen,' Betty insisted.

I called Montoya on Betty's cell-phone. He answered on the second buzz.

'Betty, I'm taking a shit. What is it?'

'This is Hal,' I said. 'It's fantastic. I've got news. I think I have the final clues.' I took a deep breath. When tired, both Rob and I had a tendency to commit unwitting rhyme. *Shall we visit Dr Seuss?*

'*Good* news, I hope,' Montoya said. 'Because up until now it's all been terrible.'

'I've got a primitive cell. Primordial.' Now I went out on a limb. 'Of a kind we haven't seen for three billion years. With the blueprints for bacterial domination still fresh and all the players fairly naive.'

'Tell me what that means when it's at home, Hal.'

'I think I've got the list of RNA and protein products that bacteria use to take control of our genome.'

'And what will you do with it?' Montoya asked patiently.

'Break some of the pathways, interrupt cell receptors, create new bacteria,' I said, as if that were perfectly obvious. 'Our cells won't be told to shut down or age. They won't lose their ability to self-repair. They'll stay young.'

'Fine. So you know how to fix us?'

'Not yet,' I said. Miracles would take years, not days. 'Based on earlier work, I need to find the five or ten more proteins that are triggered by *hades* to shut down youthful cell maintenance. They could be on this list. I need to sequence the free-floating chromosomes – less than a few million base pairs. I want to do some Southern Blot, some PCR, run homology tests. I'm sure we still have the same genes, somewhere, highly conserved.'

'Congratulations, Hal,' Montoya said. He did not sound enthused, but as he had said, so far the news had been all bad. 'Put Betty on.'

Coming down off my high, I handed the phone to Betty. She listened for a moment, then shut it and turned to me.

'Owen insists that dinner is on him. And after dinner he wants to see you. He's flying into Seattle.'

Dan and Valerie high-fived me. Betty was more subdued, though I wouldn't learn why for five more hours.

Angels can be pipers, too.

CHAPTER FIFTEEN

Dinner at Canlis was elegant but quiet. The somber gray-stained wood and white tablecloths framed a terrific view of Lake Union. I could seldom afford to eat so well, but I was nervous and excited all at once, and the best I could do was share a champagne toast with Valerie and Dan and pick at my plate.

We shook hands and parted at midnight. Betty Shun drove me in her Lexus to one of Montoya's four Seattle residences, a penthouse apartment on the top floor of a complex less than five blocks away. I catnapped during the short drive.

Betty woke me when she set the emergency brake in the underground garage. I jerked up in the seat. She was staring at me. Her face glowed pale violet in the garage's cruel fluorescence.

'I have one question,' she said. 'Why do you want to live a thousand years?'

I cocked my head to one side to work a crick out of my neck. 'More is better than not enough,' I said.

'Life is full of pain and disappointment. Why prolong the misery?'

'I don't believe life is all pain and misery,' I said.

'I'm a Catholic,' Betty Shun said, still searching my face with her eyes. 'I know the world is bad. My grandmother is a Buddhist. She knows the world is illusion. I want to live a healthy life, a useful life, but I don't want to live for ever. Something better is in the wings.'

'I'm more of a Shintoist,' I said. 'I believe the living world is all around us, thinking and working all the time, and that all living things want to understand what's going on. We just don't live long enough to find out. And when we die, that's it. No second act.'

'You will push out others not yet born,' she said.

'If the world is full of pain, I'll be doing them a favor,' I said testily. I wasn't up to a sophomoric debate at midnight, not after a hard and enlightening day's work.

Betty Shun blinked at me with her patented empty face and opened her door to get out.

Compared to the mansion on Anson Island, the penthouse was positively demure. Less than five thousand square feet, vaulted ceilings throughout, bedrooms suspended above a

70

maple-floored workroom slash studio, with sixty feet of glassed-in sunporch currently fending off a spatter of early morning rain. It smelled of spearmint and tea roses.

Montoya met us on the sunporch and handed me a cup of very strong coffee.

'Explain it again,' he demanded as Betty left us. 'I've got five funerals to go to in the next week, and I can't keep it straight. I want to know where we're headed.' He bit off his words angrily but his face seemed calm. 'I'm afraid of death, Dr Cousins. You showed me a possible escape hatch. And I took the bait.'

I sat stiff as ice on the lounge. I had no idea what he was driving at, but I did not like it.

'Sometimes I sample every dish on the menu,' he said. 'I blow money just to taste all the choices. Understand?'

I regarded him through bleary eyes. 'No,' I said.

'I'm concerned – or rather, let's say some people are concerned for me. Concerned about your involvement. You're a mystery, Hal.'

His expression was one of wing-plucking curiosity. I wiped my damp palms on my pant legs.

'Betty told me about your tiff with Mauritz before you went aboard *Sea Messenger*. You had quite an argument.'

'We just said hello.'

Montoya ignored me. 'Murder is following you around like a cloud of smoke.' He gestured vaguely at my head with a crooked finger. 'Bloom recommended I not even meet with you again.'

I balled up my fists and stood. 'I've been completely straight with you, Mr Montoya.'

'Owen, please.' He scrutinized my fists with that same wing-plucking curiosity, then looked up at my eyes like a little boy wondering idly what this strange little package, so tightly wrapped, might contain.

'I don't know why Betty would lie to you.'

'I have to believe my people.'

'There has to be more. I deserve an explanation.'

Montoya seemed to lose all interest. I might have been fading to invisibility right on his porch.

I've never taken rejection well. Lies can drive me to fury. But something was deeply wrong, and if I were Montoya, considering what had happened and what his people were saying, perhaps I would feel the same way. I needed to get out of this rich man's playhouse and do some detective work of my own. But the meeting wasn't over, not as far as I was concerned.

'Our agreement specifies I complete substantial ongoing research if for any reason you decide to cut off funding.' I congratulated myself on getting that out without a single garbled syllable.

Montoya tapped his watch. 'Time to sleep.'

He walked off the porch and climbed the stairs to his bedroom. Bloom and Shun waited on the edge of the studio. Bloom was bent over examining an impressive collection of glass paperweights in a tall cabinet. Shun stood back a step or two with arms folded like a guilty schoolgirl.

'I'm being sacked,' I told them. 'I could give him what he wants, but he won't listen to me. He listens to people who lie.'

Bloom gave a comradely nod, lips turned down. 'Sorry to hear it. I'm to escort you downstairs.'

'The bum's rush,' I said.

'Whatever.'

Betty started to hurry off. I grabbed her arm and Bloom grabbed mine, forcefully. We stood there for a moment, a little triangle of tension, with Betty not meeting my eyes, and Bloom trying to compel me to meet his. His grip tightened.

'Who told you to lie?' I asked her.

'I don't understand you,' Betty Shun said.

'I'm just a Jonah, you can do anything you want to me?' Spelling it out like that, saying it out loud to others, shot the bolt home with knee-shaking strength. My voice squeaked.

'They found Dave Press floating in the water off Vancouver,'

Bloom said, as if discussing the weather. 'They said his head was bashed in. Maybe he hit something, maybe someone hit him.'

Betty Shun shook loose with a glare and Bloom pulled me, not very gently, to the door.

Aurora Avenue was black and shiny with rain. I had neither a coat nor an umbrella. I stood for a moment, watching the traffic dart past, hiss after hiss of wet tires on either side of the segmented gray-concrete barricade that divided the highway. I wasn't used to a cold summer night, and I hated it, hated the city. I felt sick to my stomach, what little rich Canlis food I had eaten balling up in my gut.

Shivering, I banged on the condo's glass door and asked the liveried doorman to call a taxi. He looked up from the copy of *Red Herring* on his podium as if I were one of the thin parade of homeless drifting north from Seattle Center. He returned his attention to the magazine.

I walked in the rain, making the fishhook around the south end of Lake Union, past the Center for Wooden Boats. I walked from there in wet silence the quarter mile or so to the glowing front of the Genetron Building.

Maybe, I thought . . . Maybe they had impounded the lab. I wouldn't be able to get in. But nobody stopped me. I strolled past the sleepy-eyed guard, who hoisted his mug of coffee in salute when I displayed my ID.

I keyed myself into the lab.

We wait until our body tells us what to think and feel. Even in the hall, I had smelled something sour and salty, but had consciously denied the awareness, the despair.

Seawater slicked the floor. The proteomizer and the Perkin Elmer had been removed. The computers were also gone. The walls of the big pressurized tank were no longer frosted with moisture. Someone had unplugged it, then pried up the top and stirred the contents with a mop handle. The mop lay on the floor.

The Vendobionts were ghostly mush.

I threw up in the lab sink.

My ghastly early morning was not over. I stumbled the few blocks to the Homeaway, feeling and probably looking like a dead man, and let myself into my room. The suite was bright and tidy and the bed was square and perfect, the pastel floral pattern on the coverlet like a hug of civility and kindness. The room smelled clean. The bathroom shone white and bright, all the miniature shampoos and soaps laid out in wicker baskets on little folded face cloths and the gleaming white toilet lid sealed with a paper wrapper that proclaimed it sanitary.

The hotel room welcomed me and believed in me. Safe.

I stared at my open suitcase, dirty clothes in a plastic bag beside it. Time to start all over again. I could not just give up. Too much was at stake. The Long Haul. I had my little list of proteins, pitifully small, but it could lead to a new beginning.

Automatically, I took the four cell-phones from my suitcase and laid them out on the bed. Scanned their displays. Maybe another angel had called – maybe Mr Song was tired of drinking snake gall.

I had two messages on my main Nokia. I dialed in to retrieve them. The first was from Rob. He sounded far away.

'Hal, can't say much now, got to go, just wanted to tell you how sorry I am. We should have pooled our efforts. I tried to keep you out of it, but now they'll probably try to get us both. We're too much alike. Peas in a pod. I've learned *silt* is after you, too.'

That's what it sounded like, digitally garbled, and that's how I wrote it down. *Silt*.

'Talk to K, please. I gave him a package for you. He's a poor fucked-up son of a bitch, but he knows more than anybody. The package explains a lot, if you're smart. Keep your eyes open.' He made a dry chuckling sound, like a sick dog's cough. 'What I don't understand is with all of the pain, why you're still sane. Did you armor your brain?'

He sucked in his breath, and said, for the first time in my

memory, 'We're not exactly friends, but I really do love you, Prince Hal.'

I balled up the counterpane with my clenching fist and dragged the three pillows against the nightstand.

The system told me I had a second message.

It was Lissa.

'Hal, please phone your mom, I don't have her number handy, and anyway I just don't have the heart. I'm so sorry. The police in New York say Rob is dead. He was shot in an alley. Oh, Jesus, Hal, I can't think straight, can't think what to do. I can't think at all.'

Think, think, think, like drops of silver on the tiny speaker.

She left her number and hung up. The system asked if I wanted to save or delete.

I clacked the Nokia shut. Stood. Turned left, turned right, surveying the room, the neutrality, the order. Fumbled for my PalmSec to look up Mom's number in Coral Gables. Sat down on the bed and let out all my breath until the room got black. I couldn't bring myself to make the call. What would I tell her? Did I really believe it, any of it?

That thing I had not done, tracking down Rob and finding out what troubled him, had come back to haunt me. Flesh is the unbreakable bond.

I sucked in some air and stared at the clock radio on the bed stand. It was three thirty in the morning and as I sat there, I wept like a terrified child in that clean and safe room, the world's most rotten lie.

CHAPTER SIXTEEN

I had nowhere else to go. I locked the room door, connected the chain, turned the dead bolt, pushed an armoire up against the door (after jerking out the TV), and drew the thick curtains on the window.

I have always had high hopes for humanity. I've never given in to despair, no matter how hard life became. I just thought I knew the way of things and how they could stand against you and your dreams.

Now I was swinging over to the opposite side. I had completely underestimated how bad things could get. I had a strong feeling they were going to get a lot worse.

I don't remember falling asleep. I awoke half on the bed, half off, and took a shower. First I checked the water, smelling it, rubbing it between my fingers, then letting it run for several minutes to make sure it wouldn't scald.

I thought my situation over pretty thoroughly and drew some grim conclusions. Someone was out to kill us, Rob and me. I was lucky to be alive. Rob . . . Not so lucky.

The brain will wander through a forest of explanations and sometimes climb the likeliest tree, however naked and ugly it is. I found my tree. Someone had poisoned the food on board the *Sea Messenger* – perhaps with hallucinogens. I had spent most of the voyage in my cabin and had missed my dose.

Dave Press had gotten his dose; that was clear. And Mauritz. Mauritz had gone mad and shot up the ship.

Maybe you did speak to Mauritz. Maybe you did get your dose and forgot all about everything – including killing Dave Press.

I shook my head in a violent quiver of disgust and pounded the wall. I was still naked and wet from the shower, and my hand left a damp print on the striped wallpaper.

In the opposite room, someone pounded back and shouted for me to sober up.

I rubbed my finger inside the Mr Coffee's water reservoir and sniffed it, then checked the Seattle's Best packet for pinpricks. Nothing suspicious – nothing I could see – but I decided against having coffee, anyway.

Betty Shun was involved, somehow, lying to her boss about my conversation with Mauritz. But why lie? She didn't seem the type, didn't seem to dislike me.

That made me wonder if the connective tissue, the center of it all, was actually Montoya, the rich god of Puget Sound.

I looked at the clock radio. One in the afternoon.

I pulled the armoire back into place, replaced the television, wiped the sweat out of my armpits with a wet washcloth, and got dressed.

Packed my bags.

Time to get the hell out of Dodge.

I opened the door, bags in hand, just as two men in suits lined up outside. The shorter and older had his hand in the air, balled into a knocking fist. He drew back, eyebrows raised, nostrils flaring. The other looked at me in some surprise and reached inside his jacket.

I watched this questing hand with somber fascination. They had guns. They had the look of sworn peace officers.

They thought I might be dangerous.

'Going somewhere?' the taller man asked, suddenly cracking a smile. To this TV cop wit, no good answer popped to mind. I stared back and lowered my suitcases.

'I'm Detective Tom Finn, Seattle Police Department, Homicide. This is Detective Keeper. Are you Henry Cousins?'

I nodded.

'Pleased to meet you, Dr Cousins.' Finn entered the room, gave it an innocent, hands-off once-over, saw nothing that interested him (though he did bend down beside the ripped-out TV cable and go *tsk*), and invited me to come downtown.

Keeper helped me with my bags.

CHAPTER SEVENTEEN

I've led a straight and narrow sort of life; I've never been arrested. No drugs, no shoplifting, no embezzlement. My worst sin has been bullheaded and egotistical stubbornness. Crime once passed me unseen in the night. I used to feel protected, even privileged. But in the last few days, I had dropped through an unseen trapdoor into a low place where nasty things happen all the time, and the police take an unwanted interest in your affairs.

If I had had any doubts about that before, I had none now.

Finn and Keeper drove me downtown and escorted me to an interrogation room at the end of a long, busy hall on the fifth floor of the Public Safety Building. The room was eight feet by twelve, pale vanilla and tan, with a sturdy wooden table and four plastic chairs. No half-silvered peep mirror, only an empty corkboard and a small, barred window. They left me alone for a few minutes while they gathered their papers. I looked around, sad and jittery, getting a headache from no breakfast.

I looked through the barred window onto a sunny stone plaza. It was dotted with courthouse workers on break, sitting cross-legged or with arms slung back on benches, reading newspapers and drinking Starbucks. Transients napped in rough but civic comfort on a minuscule triangle of lawn. The view through that window, minus the bars, was a postcard of peace and justice, if not equality, for all.

Detective Finn came back first and began with a little catch-up. 'The Kitsap County Coroner just ruled Dave Press's death an accident. He drowned. Head injuries occurred postmortem.'

Keeper entered with a can of Diet Pepsi and shoved it at me. No sugar, just caffeine to ramp up jitters. I had no idea what that meant: a little grilling, just between friends?

'Dr Mauritz shot and killed his wife before he joined you on the *Sea Messenger*.'

'I didn't know that,' I said.

'We found her last night,' Finn said. 'The shipboard murders are a federal problem, but this one's in our jurisdiction, and the FBI is giving us the reins. The questions keep piling up.'

Keeper took a seat and hunched forward like a gargoyle in a Haggar suit.

'Murder on a ship full of scientists doesn't make sense,' Finn continued. 'You were nowhere near the *Sea Messenger* when

Mauritz started shooting. But do you have any idea why Press jumped overboard?'

'He was acting strange throughout most of the dive,' I said.

'What sort of strange?'

'Trying to swear. Erratic behavior. Finally, he got violent.'

'Some sort of rapture of the deep? Both of you, maybe?'

'Just him. I don't know about rapture. I don't think so.'

Finn paced. 'Some of the crew claimed they were poisoned and that explains their irrational behavior. Were you poisoned?'

'Not that I'm aware of.'

'Is that a definite no?'

'I felt fine. I got mad at Press when he started acting weird, fought him off when he tried to sink the sub . . . but that's all.'

'You hit him?'

'He was landing the blows.' I pointed to the bandage on my temple. 'I brought the DSV back to the surface after he conked out. I was scared out of my wits, but I felt fine. Really.'

Finn kept staring. He rotated his hand, go on.

'Anyway, Press was unconscious or in a funk. I thought he could be dead, but he seemed to recover once we surfaced. Then he –'

'What did he say to you, Dr Cousins?'

I thought back. 'He asked if Owen Montoya had ever phoned me. He seemed to think it was significant.'

'Did Montoya talk to him, maybe tell him something before the ship left port?'

'I doubt it. What difference would it make?'

Finn smiled and tilted his head. 'Montoya's assistant said you exchanged angry words with Dr Mauritz. You deny that?'

'Yes.'

'Nobody else saw you talk with Mauritz until the second day of the voyage. Was that conversation friendly?'

'We said hello.'

'What do you know about a man named AY3000?' Finn

lifted a page on his small stack. 'That apparently is his legal name.'

'He changed it from Jack Scholl,' I said. 'He comes to conferences on nanotechnology and longevity research.'

'Why did he change his name?'

'A stunt. Philosophy, I guess. AY stands for Apollo Year 3000, dating from the first moon landing, approximating his hoped-for life span.'

'I see,' Finn said.

AY suffered from prostate cancer and had not looked good the last time I saw him. Still, he kept his hopes high.

'Nanotechnology . . . that's the little bitty stuff, electronics and such, isn't it?' Finn asked.

'Yes.'

'Sci-fi bull,' Keeper said with a superior smile.

'Was AY3000 an investor in your research?'

'AY has a little money. He was a small investor, until last year. I guess I wasn't moving fast enough. He found someone more convincing.' I looked at Finn through a short silence, then added, 'He's a gentle, intelligent old man.'

'Mr Montoya is also an investor?'

'He was.'

'This AY3000 made threatening phone calls to a number of colleagues, including Dr Mauritz, starting early last week. But he never left San Francisco. Is he still one of your professional contacts?'

'I haven't spoken to him in months. Are there other crimes I don't know about?' I asked.

'The little light finally switches on,' Keeper said from his corner.

'Quite a few,' Finn said. 'And no connection but the victims' interests. Biology. Genetics. Oceanography. Two in Woods Hole, Massachusetts, on June 7. Dr Mauritz's wife, June 8. One in Palo Alto, June 17. You used to live in Palo Alto, didn't you?'

'I left ten months ago.'

'Divorced?' Keeper asked.

'Yeah.'

'From the former Julia Merrivale,' Keeper said.

'Yeah.'

'She took you to the cleaners,' Keeper said.

'She got the house.'

Keeper whistled. 'In Palo Alto. Worth how much?'

Finn shook his head, and Keeper turned away with a smile. 'All the victims but Mauritz's wife were doing biological research, related one way or another to yours, as near as I can tell,' Finn said. 'But I'm no expert. To me, it's all buzzwords and jargon.'

'Biology can seem that way at times.'

'Coincidence?'

'I truly don't know,' I said. 'Do you?'

'And now your brother, shot to death in New York,' Finn said.

I cleared my throat. 'I still have to tell our mother.'

'What's going on, Dr Cousins?' Finn took a deep breath. 'Somebody trying to scare scientists, or discredit them, maybe? Radical Greens, animal rights freaks?'

'I don't torture kittens or puppies.'

'Any other threats you're aware of?'

'I've never been threatened,' I said.

'Nobody ever tried to *call* you?' Finn asked.

'Other than my brother, no.'

'He didn't threaten you.'

'Of course not.'

'Did he say anything unusual?'

'Yes.'

Finn's face filled with patient encouragement.

'He asked if our father had talked to me. Our father is dead. My brother seemed tired.' I looked from Finn to Keeper and back to Finn in the warm, stuffy room, a lump rising in my throat. It was certainly no place and no time to start crying.

Finn pulled up another sheet of paper and scanned it with his pale blue eyes. 'A lot of odd behavior. We're getting nowhere trying to find a motive.'

'I doubt Nadia Evans did anything,' I said.

'She *is* attractive, isn't she?' Finn said.

'Was Mauritz jealous of her?' Keeper asked.

Finn was not impressed by this question, either. He waved it aside, arranged his papers on the table, and pulled a chair close to mine before sitting. He clasped his hands earnestly.

'How would you induce coordinated, malicious behavior?' he asked. 'Surely not with food poisoning.'

'Hypnosis,' Keeper suggested, clasping his knee with big rough-skinned hands. Finn scowled ever so slightly and Keeper tilted his hands back, giving it up.

'Was there food poisoning?' I asked, trying to get into the spirit of this peculiar tête-à-tête.

'The FBI lab says no. The food on the ship was free of bugs or toxins. Besides, Mrs Mauritz was dead before you put out to sea.'

'Drugs?' I asked. I did not want to reveal my earlier line of thinking, so I played as if this were all new to me.

Finn didn't seem to mind my reversing the roles. 'No drugs we can find.' He faced the window, resigned to futility.

I began to feel for the first time that I might be more a source of information than a suspect. Keeper, however, was still trying to keep up the pressure with a baleful stare.

'The feds seem to have put this on a back burner,' Finn said. 'Our Seattle shoes walk us only so far. I can't be concerned with crimes at sea or in other states, except where they tell us something about our own single, lonely murder. Dr Mauritz, frankly, is a pitiful specimen, a mental case. No memory of what happened on the ship or at his house. We'll prosecute, and maybe the feds will prosecute, but I doubt it will give anyone satisfaction.'

'I wish I could help,' I said.

'So do I,' Finn said, and waved his arm in dismissal. 'You're free to go, Doctor. Sorry about your brother. It's a crazy old world out there. If you learn anything interesting, we'd appreciate a heads-up.'

'Live long and prosper, Spock,' Keeper cracked from his corner, with a wicked little smile.

CHAPTER EIGHTEEN
Coral Gables, Florida
June 27

Lissa threw her broad black sun hat on the dark maple dining table. 'God damn it all to hell,' she muttered, and lifted her fingers as if to drag on a cigarette. She tapped her lips, pink, with long nails a tasteful shade of pearl, and gave me a flicking, sidewise glance, to see what I thought of her manners, not that she cared. 'He deserved better. He deserved a lot better.'

I could not disagree. Never in my life had I felt the impact of mortality so strongly, not even when Dad died. I had just buried my genetic double.

At our mother's insistence, Rob had been encased in a ridiculous waterproof Aztec Bronze casket. At the funeral, under the hideous sun, we had watched the shiny sealed tub of pickled meat drop into a seven-foot pit backhoed from Florida limestone.

Mom sat in the den wailing gently into a black-rayon handkerchief, surrounded by her bridge club ladies with whom she shared soap opera gossip and grocery bags full of paperback romances.

I could not get out of my head the time I had punched Rob in the nose in the middle of a heated argument about who would get to date a certain girl. We had been eighteen years old. We had stood beside this very maple dining table, words getting hotter and hotter, each convinced the other was over the line and in need of severe correction. I had moved first and caught him completely by surprise. Rob had dropped like a sack of beans.

His nose had bled like a sonofabitch all over the floor.

Right now, I wanted to crawl into a deep hole and pull the hole in after me. But I could not help checking out Lissa.

Women complain that men are all alike. That's not true. We just share some common goals. In the middle of my shame and my grief, and with my mother sobbing in the other room, I appraised my brother's estranged wife, his widow, and knew that at twenty-six years of age she was about as prime as a beautiful woman could get.

It's useless reining in all the horses in one's herd. They just kick the fence harder when death is in the air.

'Have you heard anything?' Lissa asked, drawing back a pale wisp of hair. She seemed to want to keep her elbows crooked and her hands near her face. She had quit smoking, I guessed, some months ago, but the urge was on her with feline tenacity.

'No,' I said.

I had gone to the funeral home and signed the proper forms. Their driver had received my brother from air freight at the Miami airport, delivered him to the stainless-steel tables, and made sure all the proper chemicals were injected. There had been an autopsy in New York. No one had wanted an open casket anyway.

I would have given anything for a few minutes alone with a living Rob. I wanted one last chance to apologize for a few things not the least of them that sucker punch in the nose.

'I'd give anything to apologize to him,' Lissa said, making me jump at our synchrony. She looked straight at me. Brown eyes a little small, topped by squared-off and serious wheat-colored eyebrows in a head also a tad small in its average measurements, considering the dimensions of her body. These disparities, framed by that casual but orderly butter blond hair, made her even more sensual.

'Beg pardon?'

'We did some things to each other that weren't very kind, and I feel the need to confess. To him. How sorry I am.'

'I understand,' I said.

'Your mother . . .' she said, looking in the direction of the quiet sobbing in the other room. Lissa grimaced as if at the rasp of fingernails on a blackboard.

'Her son,' I said, defending our mother against this disturbing beauty, who had put Rob through the wringer in a way I never could.

'No arrests,' she said.

'No arrests,' I confirmed.

We picked from trays of finger sandwiches and vegetables on Rob's behalf and sipped punch, and when most of the people had gone and Mother was in the bathroom, tidying up, I cracked two cold beers in the shadowy kitchen and gave one to the funeral director, a black-haired guy with admirable cheekbones, younger than me by a couple of years.

Lissa had gone somewhere else for the moment. I actually did not notice her leaving.

'Funerals are the worst in hot weather,' the funeral director confided. 'We feel so alive in the heat. That hurts us in the twilight hours, when the air cools and we're reminded of the long, deep earth.'

I had little time to respond to his surreal burst of eloquence. Lissa came into the kitchen with Mother on her arm.

'Lissa tells me they were thinking about getting together again,' Mom said, as if it mattered, as if that peculiar, possibly kind little white lie could make any difference, stuck as Rob was in a waterproof Aztec Bronze casket in the long, deep earth.

We watched Mother thank the funeral director. I accompanied him outside to where the limo was parked, behind the garage.

He removed his jacket and slung it across the front bench seat in the Lincoln. 'Sometimes,' he said, 'mothers give me a tip when the service is over and the caterers have departed. I have to return it with graceful apologies.' He smiled and shook his head with sad understanding.

He must have thought I was a stronger sort, able to listen to his professional tales with amused objectivity. I hated his guts. He had seen Rob dead.

All I could do, lying in our old bedroom, the last room we had shared together, listening to the nighttime breezes blow through the backyard palms and dance invisibly across Florida, was imagine the very worst.

They cut him open and took out his mangled brain, then stuffed it back. Or maybe they didn't bother and his head is empty. Either way, the toy will never run again.

That boy will never run again.

In the early morning, I woke from dreams of impossibly devious plumbing in huge bathrooms and went down the hall to relieve myself. I saw my mother sitting with Lissa in the battered and frayed rattan chairs in the living room. They must have been up all night. They were talking about Rob. Mom had her back to me.

'How they fought,' she was saying for the ten thousandth time. 'Sometimes when their father was away, I didn't dare even reach between them, they were like two wildcats. When they were three, they loved for me to read to them. The only way I could make them stop fighting was take out some picture books. I'd say, "Break it up, cut it loose. Shall we visit Dr Seuss?" And they would come running like nothing was wrong and sit on my knees.'

Lissa looked up and saw me standing in the hall, my BVDs tented by a piss hard-on. I felt like a ten-year-old boy caught doing the rude. Her eyes widened a fraction, then, with a slow blink, she looked away and resumed her vigil with Mom.

Women do hang together.

CHAPTER NINETEEN
Berkeley, California
July

The requests for interviews stopped coming. The *Sea Messenger* disaster became old news, and old news without a juicy update is deeper than history, darker than forgotten. Mauritz had gone crazy and shot up a ship, crew members had acted strangely, Dave Press had drowned, a few biologists had been murdered, including Rob. Other than Mauritz, no arrests, no suspects. End of the trail.

I slipped quietly away from Coral Gables and returned to the West Coast. I cleaned out my small apartment in Oakland, a shabby, temporary place at best, and wiped away a few obvious traces. No forwarding mail, and I canceled my cell-phones.

I needed time and a place to think. Under an assumed name, I rented a mother-in-law apartment in Berkeley, which was, on any given sunny summer morning, literally in the shadow of the beautiful white Claremont Hotel. My landlady was an elderly artist who thought it lovely to have a scientist living and thinking over her garage. She shared the main house with two younger female companions with short hair and no patience for men. I came to her highly recommended by a professor of microbiology at San Francisco State University, a Fellow Traveler who had hidden radicals far more controversial than me in the nineteen seventies.

I called my mother now and then – from a pay phone.

I felt invisible. It was frustrating, but it was also reassuring.

My life became quiet for a few weeks, a breather before my first meeting with K, Lissa's return, and what I call Hell Week.

Reclining in a worn easy chair, looking through the apartment's tiny bay window at the banana trees spreading under the broken milky panes of the old greenhouse, I mulled over the suspect proteins from the Vendobionts.

The greenhouse sat cater-cornered to the garage, behind a big old 1920 half-timber house, hidden from my view by junipers and haunted by the staccato tap-and-whisper of the nice old lady's slippers.

I was slowly coming to the conclusion that what I had in my little list – and it was all I had – was enough. The list would guide me to where I really needed to look in the labyrinth of chemical pathways that constitute the biography of a human cell.

But whom did these proteins talk to when they were at work? What chemical messages did they intercept or promote over the decades of a human life? Without live specimens of Vendobionts, I had no solid way of knowing. I could guess at a thousand real possibilities, but guessing has never been my style.

When the view of the greenhouse palled, and peace turned to stagnant boredom, I walked across the street, between trash-can-sized concrete auto barricades, and a few blocks west to the University of California at Berkeley. I sat in the library and kept up with the journals. I used a library computer to log onto the Internet and look over the latest preprints.

But it was an uncharacteristically quiet month in my area of interest. Reading in the library was not the cure I needed.

I thought about Nothing too much, and sadness was no friend. I needed a lab, rigorous conversations with colleagues, connections with companies doing deep genomics. I needed more specimens. I needed to work with my hands, which have always guided and encouraged the deeper muses of my brain.

So I opened up again. I put in a phone, wrote letters, and took walks around the campus and the streets near my apartment. I put out a few feelers for lab space, through my microbiologist friend, and watched them all come back rejected. Lab space was tight and my résumé was too mysterious.

My paper on mitochondrial communication with gut bacteria was put through another peer review (so I heard) and rejected. All my ties to science were being cut, and my tracks erased.

I was finally reduced to wandering through the campus

biotech centers and the supercomputer lab, filled with longing, trying to imagine myself respectable, fully funded, with a nice complement of postdocs to fetch and carry and argue with me on my weaker points.

After a few weeks, my bank account was perilously low. I shopped and ate sparingly and imagined that by cutting back on food I was slowing my own senescence. For a few days, I convinced myself I was my own lab, my own experiment, and made notes to that effect – charting weight loss, ups and downs of mood. I counted shed hairs in the drain catch of the small shower.

Making thin lemonade out of old and bitter lemons.

AY3000 had starved himself for twenty years. His sex drive had dropped to zero. Bettina, his wife, had not found that a major inconvenience. Reduced caloric intake worked on rats and may have increased the life span of survivors of concentration camps. AY had been the crazy inspiration for so many of us. And now he was dying and calling up people and making threats – hardly an encouraging example as I went to bed hungry.

I was on the edge of losing heart. I had already lost perspective. My letters went unanswered, my phone calls got me nowhere.

Curing aging is not respectable in some quarters. We're only tourists in the land of the living, many believe. Living too long is against God's law. Who would suppose that liberal academics, even scientists, secretly fear the wrath of Jehovah?

I wondered what Rob would think of me now. In my solitude I was becoming gentler and more introspective.

I needed my brother to give me a good punch in the nose.

On one of my infrequent trips to the Star Grocery on Claremont Avenue, I saw two lean, wiry men standing near a bus stop. They wore gray sports coats and gray slacks. Their hair was dark brown and close-cut and their faces long and theatrical.

They looked light on their feet; they might have been actors or circus performers. One wore a beret. The other glanced at me through small, wire-rimmed sunglasses as I walked by, then nudged the other, who nudged him back. Together, they studiously ignored me.

Nothing unusual for Berkeley.

The grocery smelled of expensive fresh peaches in fir boxes and bags of bulk carrots and dish soap and a thousand other domestic necessities. I bought four apples, four bananas, two cans of frozen orange juice, a pound of turkey ham, two loaves of bread, a bag of rice, mayonnaise, and some olives. I sorted through my change and spilled a few pennies onto the dirty linoleum floor. I picked them up, straightened, and added the necessary six cents to my twenty.

As I extended my hand to the cashier for three dollars back, a small man with a pushed-in nose and thick black hair shuffled between the registers, bumping me in his haste. More of my change clattered on the floor.

The little man's desperate grip dimpled the soft plastic of an unmarked spray bottle, trailing drips of clear liquid.

A young and totally bald male clerk ran after him. 'God damn it, get out of here and don't come back!' the clerk shouted. He swung his booted foot, face drawn into a pimply mask of disgust. The boot missed, and the man skittered through the double door.

The clerk swung around to glare at the cashier, then at me. 'Sorry about the language,' he apologized. He was festooned with ear and nose rings. 'Now I've got to throw out all that lettuce.' He held up his hand as if gripping a pistol and disgustedly mimicked both the motion and the sound of *spritz-spritz*. 'Mrs Lo will kill me.'

'I've seen him here before,' said a plump red-haired woman in her fifties. She hoisted her canvas shopping bag onto the counter and pinched forth a lovely green head of romaine, as if it were a big insect. 'I thought he worked for you.'

'I never noticed him,' said the young cashier. She stood on

tiptoes to peer over the cigarette case. The little man was out of sight.

'Christ,' the young clerk said, and apologized again.

I shook my head, no offense. Just a normal day in Berkeley.

That night, I had a dream about the little man. He was spraying water on everything, and the whole town was shriveling up. The Claremont Hotel was ablaze, and the stately old houses of Berkeley melted like wax in the heat from the fire. Then I was back in the desert, walking beside the man with the white hair.

He was my father, and he was trying to tell me something important about Rob.

Hell Week began brilliantly. My friend at the University of San Francisco called and told me that on August 8 there was going to be a Promethean conference on the Clark Kerr campus at UC Berkeley. He had wangled an invitation for me from the directors, Phil Castler and his wife Frieda – the same Phil Castler who had not impressed Owen Montoya.

The Prometheans are visionaries, innocent in many ways, and wise beyond our time in many others. Castler himself combined a grave sensibility about larger-scale politics with a childlike enthusiasm for Progress, an enthusiasm I had once shared, and now long for desperately. They were devoted to listening and exchanging information and enthusiasms, and ideas were their common coin. They were my people, my friends, even when we competed for funding, even when we disagreed.

Castler's invitation, and a conference badge, arrived in the mailbox the next day, along with a quickly penned note from Frieda clipped to a collection of past newsletters: *'Wherever have you been? Phil and I are anxious to get caught up on news!'*

Never in my life had I looked forward to a conference so much. It would mark my return to the real world.

*   *   *

91

I spotted Phil on the tiled entrance portico outside the beautiful, mission-style Joseph Wood Krutch auditorium. He wore a Mr Rogers yellow sweater unbuttoned over a white shirt, loose gray slacks, and scuffed black shoes, and he was talking with a portly young man in jeans and a black-leather jacket. Their conversation was intense. The young man jabbed his finger in the air, and Castler rocked back and forth on his heels, absorbing every point as if it had real weight. At key moments, he nodded a professorial, even courtly nod I have observed in older scientists from Europe. Castler, however, was born and raised American; it was his personality that was old-world and courtly.

An armed security guard stood by the entrance, arms folded like a genie. That was a first for a Promethean conference. Too many scientists were dying.

As I drew near, Castler spotted me from the corner of his eye and paused the young man in mid-point, then spun about and marched toward me.

'Hal!' he cried, smiling and holding out his hand. His hair was longer than when I had last seen it, down to his collar, thick and flowing. The Liszt look suited him. 'How good to see you! It's been a hard couple of months – so many friends gone. We had feared the worst!'

At Castler's wide-eyed urging, I gave him a not very scary version of the last couple of months – severely truncated and minus key facts. He listened sympathetically, commiserated with me about Rob's death – a horrible loss, he said. He then launched into the Prometheans' difficulties. Memberships were up but corporate contributions were down. There had been a particularly vicious attack on his theories in the *Wall Street Journal*.

I listened with a strong sense of disengagement, like a soldier home from the front listening to a businessman's prattle.

'What did we ever do to the *Wall Street Journal*?' Castler asked with a world-weary smile. He stared at me intensely, and wrung a neck of air with his hands.

Another conference attendee distracted Castler, and he spun away to engage in a new debate.

I looked around the hall, admiring the dark oak Spanish beams supporting the high ceiling, the orange and white and blue Moorish tilework along the walls. I picked up my packet and booklet at the registration desk, chatted for a minute with Frieda – a fashion designer who deftly fit her humanities training into Phil's technocratic schemes – and read through the topics. Most of them were standard fare. Five single-track presentations and several break-out meetings would spread over two days. The keynote speaker was giving a talk on second-stage proteomics and the potential for identifying single-gene roadblocks on the highway to rejuvenation.

I felt an itch of irritation, reading the abstract of his talk. There were no single-gene solutions – that had been proven years ago. The bright-eyed enthusiasm was familiar, but the approach was also familiar, and the answers were no longer cutting-edge.

A flip through the membership list told the tale: eighty members attending, down from a hundred the year before.

We filed into the auditorium. I was one of the few in the audience not taking notes on a palm or laptop. The beeping and clicking of keys went on for several minutes as Phil and Frieda and their staff finished coordinating video cameras and digital projectors.

My restlessness crossed over into sadness. Around me flocked the people who had created the scientific approach to longevity research. Some of them had been working the ideas and exploring the possibilities for over forty years. But the conference had an air of been-there, done-that, musty backslapping rather than cutting-edge thinking.

I knew it was not Castler's fault. In part it was a result of most of the talent going into corporate biotech. The big corporations – and the small – seldom shared their hot-button results, certainly not with visionary pioneers. Visionaries could not be trusted to hold their tongues, and pioneers were often inclined to file lawsuits.

The MC, a molecular engineer from Stanford, was introduced by Castler. He took the podium, cracked a few jokes as the crowd settled in for the morning session, and challenged the audience with a restatement of the old theory that longevity was a function of sexual strategy – breed copiously and die young, raise fewer young and live long.

'And what do we say to that?' he said provokingly.

'Bring 'em on!' shouted a young woman in the back.

A young man with two knotted black pigtails rose. He had missed the MC's humorous tone and argued that this totally neglected the social aspect, so crucial to understanding human life span. Humans are part of a social tissue, the young man said, not wild-type animals breeding indiscriminately, flecked with sperm and yolk, red of fang and claw.

The MC politely reversed course, from humor to debate, countering that sex was more than just exchange of sperm, it was also an exchange of viruses and bacteria. An isolated monk might live longer not because he was celibate, but because he didn't swap spit. A forest of hands shot up.

'Hey, we're hot now!' the MC crowed. 'Now why don't we get started on the real program –'

But the small crowd was having none of that. Castler himself stood and asked a leading question, enjoying the debate for its own sake and the hell with decorum.

A tall, heavyset young man and a small, grandmotherly woman in her sixties took on the assertion that natural selection ceased after we stopped reproducing. In other words, we were out of the genetic game completely once we stopped bearing children. Half a dozen disagreed – good for them, I thought. That had been the standard evolutionary explanation of aging since Bidder came up with it in 1925, and it creaked.

Castler rode over the murmurs, conceding that while this was true, the health of the society – and thus of the individuals relying on that society as much as any bee in a hive – depended on elder wisdom. Retirement age typically occurs thirty years after one stops having children, and grand-parenting goes on for years after that. The health of a society is reflected in both the numbers of offspring, and the elder vigor that allows society to support more offspring.

The keynote speaker, already onstage, stood back with his notes, quite happy with the orderly trashing of the schedule.

I began to relax. These were my people. This was my meat and drink. This was *real*.

A discussion soon raged over the statistical fact that entropic maximum was reached at age twenty – that we consumed more, per unit of weight, and engaged in more activity and cellular growth, with the potential for genetic error, before most of us reproduced. Yet it was on the long slope of comparative entropic stability that aging and death finally caught up with us. Which genes kept us healthy during the time when entropy and hence error should accumulate?

It was an interesting question, several agreed, but very complex and quite beside the point. We did not want to get off in a discussion of entropy and closed systems when in fact we should be discussing information-binding and complexity.

Castler swiftly cut off debate between two would-be-physicists intent on exploring the differences between open and closed systems.

'May I speak now?' the keynoter asked. He was ignored.

Frieda Castler made an ingenious suggestion. Leapfrogging from a previous statement that longevity depended on how long it took to raise our children, she claimed we all deserved to live thousands of years. It was going to take that long to raise our real children – the coming silicon-based artificial intelligences. Clever, but it didn't make a hell of a lot of sense to me. I was a firm believer in slime, not silicon – and in that, differed from Gus Beck, the Castlers, and most of the audience in the hall.

But the conference was getting my juices flowing, and that was one of the reasons I had come.

We broke for lunch, before the keynoter had a chance to deliver his address, and at the back of the auditorium, picked up boxes stuffed with sandwiches, apples, cookies, and canned soft drinks. I chose my box from the bottom of the stack, then ate sitting alone on a bench in a courtyard, watching wind blow leaves around a dried-up fountain.

Nobody offered to join me. People walked by in small clusters and moved on.

I ate more slowly. Felt the gloom creeping back. Castler and Frieda had been glad to see me, but others had sharper instincts.

The belly of the whale had left a fishy stench.

AY3000 arrived in his wheelchair after the break was over, and was promptly surrounded at the rear of the hall by a crowd of well-wishers. To me, he looked like a rolling museum exhibit on mortality. His flesh clung to his skull. His pate was covered with thin patches of wispy white hair, and his brow beaded with sweat. He could barely raise his thin, knobby fingers to shake hands with well-wishers and students, his intellectual children. Still, there was a light in his eyes I recognized even from twenty feet away. The same glow of conviction that our birth certificates were not also our death warrants.

I could not imagine this venerable old man making crank phone calls.

His wife of thirty years, Bettina, pushed his wheelchair and wiped his lips with a linen handkerchief. Bettina was in her early sixties, and her hair stood thick and silvery white above a high forehead. She rolled him out of the press of well-wishers after ten minutes, giving AY the chance to take some air before the conference resumed. The hall would get stuffy and old men tended to fall asleep. The crowd parted politely.

Bettina propelled her husband past where I sat in the back row. AY turned his head and slapped his hand feebly on the chair's armrest. Bettina obeyed and stopped. He raised a withered fasces of fingers and pointed one at me. 'Rob Cousins. You're dead,' he said.

Prickles up my spine.

Bettina whispered in his ear. AY blinked in irritation.

'Forgive me,' he said. 'The worst part of this . . . is the loss of my memory, and for me, memory is soul. Your brother was a great man. Greater than you, and more powerful. He used to call and talk to me. Give me advice. Instructions.'

My face burned.

'Much greater than you,' AY persisted. 'Definitely the smarter brother.'

'Hush,' Bettina said.

'Why did you call Dr Mauritz?' I asked.

He rolled his eyes up and coughed gently into a handkerchief. Bettina gave me a fierce glare. *How dare you upset him. How dare you rise to the bait of a sick old man.* And she was right, but I had to know.

'I do not remember a Dr Mauritz,' he said when he had his wind back. 'But yes, I *probably* called him. I was told to call a number of people.' AY threw his hand back as his wife again tried to shush him, then pretended to wave at the enthusiasts taking their seats near the front of the hall. 'Why waste your time here? You don't belong, Henry. This is a meeting of gifted dilettantes. Go do your important work, while you can. This is old home week for me. They'll celebrate my influence and ignore all my warnings, my feeble . . . warnings.'

'Just hush,' Bettina insisted, more forcefully. He waved her off again, leaned over to push aside a folding chair, then rolled himself closer. Bettina stood back with arms crossed, tired of his obtuseness.

AY came within whispering distance. His breath smelled of bad teeth and poor nutrition. 'Do you have any idea what men of ill will can do? What they can take from you?' His voice sounded like two crackers rubbed together. 'I'm a dying old man, not worth killing. I'm just good for running errands. But you and Rob, you're the real thing. *They know what you're doing.*'

Four young Caucasian men in black jeans walked past, accompanied by two Asiatic girls. They were doubtless part of

Phil's cyberjock contingent. Asiatic girlfriends were de rigueur. They nodded to AY with admiring smiles.

He sat up, moving his lips silently until they were out of ear-shot. Then he focused on me, pleading. '*Listen* to Flora Ramone. She's speaking today at three. The rest . . .' He made a *pfft* noise. 'To think we could ever master the future without truly knowing the past. Don't take those calls. Don't take them.'

Another fit of coughing grabbed the patriarch of longevity. Bettina hurried him out of the hall, eager to get away from me.

Against all my instincts, I stayed and listened to Flora Ramone at four in the afternoon – the conference was running late.

She gave a painfully slow, detailed talk, with many diagrams, on social organization and the quest for cellular immortality in neoplasms – cancerous tumors. She warmed to her subject, eyes gleaming.

The cells went rogue. They cut themselves loose from the cellular police, encouraged the growth of knots of arteries, demanded resources beyond their needs. They reproduced wildly and refused to obey the signals that demand self-identification and, failing that, apoptosis – cellular suicide.

Tumors had a certain arrogance and presumption. They reproduced at will – *will* was one of the operative words. They exhibited *free will*, free of the larger body. The cells within the tumors tried to make their own society, but having cut loose from the sophisticated controls of the larger organism, they reverted to a more primitive and self-serving kind of biological 'politics.'

Tumors often failed to feed all their component cells, and cell death – necrosis – was one consequence. If they sent out missionaries to spread the gospel of freedom and liberation, death of the larger organism was all too often the final result.

'Tumors strive to break their bonds and live for ever. Freedom is their quest, but they bring disorder and death,' she concluded. 'How are *we* any different? If we, as individuals, strive to live past our natural lifetimes, what do we contribute to the whole of humanity? Are we smarter at one hundred and fifty than we were at forty? What if we stand in the way of the young? What if we demand all the available resources and starve our society, or go off on eccentric quests that ignore a larger wisdom? Are we then biologically any different, any less malignant, than tumors?'

Silence met her conclusion. Few liked what they had heard. Dr Ramone fielded a scatter of hostile questions, with little effect. The audience broke up into murmuring groups. Alone on the stage, she raised her eyebrows, sadly tapped her papers on the podium, and stepped down.

I watched her, gritting my teeth.

Castler approached me in a seethe. He shook his composer's mane and glared at the oak beams high above. 'She's put a damper on the whole afternoon. That was inexcusably myopic. What is she, a *Marxist*?'

I've always hated the naysayers, those who argue for an end to controversial research for the greater short-term good of the whole. But what made me really angry was that I had no convincing argument to refute Dr Ramone's quiet and persistent polemic.

AY's pronouncement and Dr Ramone's talk had sucked all the energy out of me. Going for a long trek around Berkeley before returning to my apartment seemed the best remedy for my funk. I walked toward the dark oak doors at the rear of the hall.

'Hal Cousins?'

A shadow in the corner broke free and approached. My first instinct was to back away, but there was neither room nor time. The shadow, as it emerged into the afternoon sunlight, became a short, handsome man in his fifties, with graying temples, a distinct hooked nose, and thick, perfectly formed, aristocratic eyebrows. He was shabbily dressed in a tweed suit with frayed cuffs, a once-expensive linen shirt with a collar worn through by too many pressings, and polished brown Oxfords snubbed high at the toes. He carried something under his buttoned coat – he seemed a little pigeon-breasted.

'You should never have come here,' he said. 'Far too obvious.' His accent was hard to place – English with a touch of Eastern European, I guessed. He had an Ace bandage wrapped around his left hand, wrist to knuckles, held by a metal clip. He noticed my attention and tucked the hand firmly in his pocket. 'Your brother might have mentioned me. I am K. Shall we leave – this?' He thrust out an elbow like a stubby bird's wing. 'Let's find some obscure place to talk. We'll toast your brother's memory and try to get drunk.'

CHAPTER TWENTY

'Hard liquor is the ideal,' K explained, and made a sour face as we took a seat in a back booth at Pascal's, a pub on College Avenue.

The dark room, illuminated by small yellow parchment lamps and a tiny skylight in the center of the pressed-copper ceiling, smelled of hops and sawdust sprinkled over the brick floor. 'Wine is acceptable,' he added. 'Beer . . . not very reliable. Water, forbidden, unless we buy it sealed and pick our store at random. Can you guess why?'

'Poison?' I ventured.

Again the sour face, a comment on my naïveté. 'I saw AY in the auditorium,' he said, as if to change the subject. 'Did he say anything to you?'

'He's dying,' I said, and gave a small shiver. 'Something about having his strings pulled.'

K made a snuffle of acid amusement. 'Did he mention Silk?'

'Silk?' *Not silt,* I thought.

'Silk,' he affirmed.

'No.'

'Then he doesn't know. They pull strings,' K said. 'The true Illuminati. I've spent the last fifteen years tracking down its history. The damned Jews blocked me every step of the way.'

I stared at him intently. Thought about just getting up and leaving the bar. One problem with libertarians, scientific elitists, and other rugged individualists is that a significant minority of them hold odd and sometimes pernicious views about races and religions other than their own. Think *The Bell Curve* and you'll know the type.

'Are you sure we have anything to discuss?'

'Your brother believed we did,' K said, his expression hardening. 'He recommended you talk to me, right?'

'My brother led his own life, and I lead mine.'

Our drinks arrived. I had ordered a Scotch, something I enjoyed but rarely indulged in. K slugged back his bourbon neat and opened a bottle of club soda, listening for the hiss of escaping gas, then swallowed that down immediately after.

'Oh, don't get me wrong,' K said, arching those dramatic dark brows in a way that suggested Errol Flynn. 'The Jews, too, have their strings pulled.' His features seemed to melt, as if he were a chastened puppy. A drifting sadness filmed his eyes and his lips twisted, the words were difficult to control. 'Forgive me,' he said. 'It's a nervous tic. You'll get used to it. It's dogged me for twenty years now. Ruined my whole, *fucking*, life.'

Just as quickly, the arch, self-assured face returned. The transformation was startling. 'We are going to do this in stages. Less cautious, sooner dead. You have no idea who I am?'

'Just K,' I said. 'Like in *The Trial*.'

'Your brother told you nothing more?'

'Nothing.'

'How close are you to your goal, Dr Cousins?'

I examined his face for a moment, wondering whether or not to lie. 'Pretty close,' I said. 'A few years, maybe less.'

'Rob was at Lake Baikal. He died in New York. Do you have any idea what that means?'

'No,' I said.

'There is a war,' K said. 'Your brother found himself in the thick of it – targeted because of his research.'

'Rob and I were – are – doing research in life extension. I know it's controversial, but how in the hell does it plant us in a war?'

'I am not a scientist, I'm an historian. Your brother told me to give you something. It was practically his last request . . . to me.' He lifted a package from under his jacket and laid it out on the table: a nine-by-twelve buff paper envelope, filled to bursting, wrapped in glossy cellophane packing tape. He pushed the envelope across the table. Scrawled across the front in Magic Marker, in Rob's blocky style, was *Prince Hal Only. Out of the jaws of defeat. For you, Brother. With true love and respect. Rob Cousins.*

The signature was definitely Rob's, with jaunty loops, though more ragged than I remembered.

'As you can see –'

'Please,' I said. My throat tightened, and tears welled in my eyes. I wiped them hastily and took hold of the package.

K watched me. 'It *is* from your brother,' he said softly. 'No contamination. His hands, to mine, to yours, and . . . as you can see –'

'Please,' I said.

'This is important, Dr Cousins. He made sure the document would not be opened by anyone but you.'

The envelope's flap had been taped over with embedded hairs the same color as my own, quite a few of them, arranged in a crisscross. Hairs protected the seams, as well. Paranoid. Driven. The wrapping matched the mood of Rob's last message.

'Do I look at it, then give it back to you?' I asked.

'It's yours,' K said, and withdrew a handkerchief to blow his nose. 'Do with it as you please. I suggest, however, that you don't read it here.'

'Thank you,' I said.

'Rob told me to look out for you. So be it. Things are getting rough. You must start training.'

'Training for what?' I asked. Despite the envelope, I was poised to get up and walk out and leave the mysterious Mr K to his clockwork aberrations. *I will not let Rob's delusions drag me down with him.*

'Survival,' K said. 'Do you have any money?'

I shook my head.

'I know someone in the City who is very good. She seldom takes on students as an act of charity. I hope we can find the money to pay her.'

'What sort of survival – wilderness, camouflage tents, eating grubs and lizards?'

K smiled with a paternal tolerance that I found more irritating than his nervous bigotry. 'She teaches people how to avoid extraordinary attempts on their lives. I'll make the appointment. Do you eat fresh fruit and vegetables?'

I looked up from the envelope. 'Yes,' I said, hoping I wasn't compromising some important secret.

K gave me a sharp look. 'Stop now,' he said. 'Canned food only, and supplement it with vitamins in sealed containers. Shop at different stores, widely spaced, supermarkets preferred. Avoid strangers, or friends who behave strangely. In time, you will avoid *all* your friends. Friends and lovers are our greatest weakness.'

I remembered the little man with the spray bottle. Surely if someone were poisoning the entire city, it would be in the news.

'Why should I do what you tell me?' I asked.

'Your brother worked hard to protect himself, and for a while, it seemed he was succeeding.' He pointed to the envelope. 'What he did not know, killed him.' K sidled out of the booth.

My Scotch was half full.

'I'll buy this round,' K said. 'Talk is medicinal.' I noticed for the first time that he was wearing a smooth beige glove on his unbandaged hand. He pulled money from his wallet. 'They can reach us through coins and currency, you know,' he murmured. 'But cash is better than being tracked through credit transactions.'

We walked out into the early evening. The air was sweet and mild in Berkeley, the sun filtered through a high layer of haze. I clutched Rob's envelope in both hands. Despite myself, I glanced at the people around us – a shuffling old man in filthy brown coat and unlaced boots, a glazed young woman with peach-colored hair and white skin, two moneyed types in gray suits as alike as freshly curried thoroughbreds.

'Wait,' I said, stopping at the corner. 'My brother's dead. What in hell did you do for him that was so great?'

K's eyes shifted. I thought he was avoiding my question. He stared east, into the hills. My nose twitched. I smelled smoke.

'Where *do* you live, Dr Cousins?' he asked.

I turned. A fire burned high and bright a few blocks below the Claremont. Flames rose seventy or eighty feet in the still air and cast a glow on the hotel's white façade like an early sunset.

A lazy column of smoke swung west, white and greasy, like – I could not avoid the comparison – the plume over a deep-sea vent.

'Nearby,' I said. 'Over there.'

'Let's make sure,' K said. His face became ruddy with an unexpected enthusiasm, and for an instant his appearance, more than ever, was pure Errol Flynn. 'It's possible they've already tagged your neighbors.'

We ran, then walked, then ran again, up the gentle slope around the campus, passing through alternating stretches of fine homes and streets with weedy lawns and houses in need of painting, not yet made over for the rich.

I was sick at heart – though nothing much of importance was in my apartment (I was certain now the smoke had to be from my apartment). I worried about the landlady and her artist friends, and about the houses nearby.

The actual scene still came as a shock. Fire trucks had

surrounded my short, narrow street, and thick gray hoses lay across the tar-patched old asphalt like snakes, fat with pressure. Firemen leaned into hoses and aimed nozzles. Arcs of white water danced back and forth over the flames.

I stood in sick horror. Three homes were ablaze, the half-timber with my garage apartment and one on each side. The smoke was mostly steam now, the houses collapsing shells. Banana trees within the old greenhouse had become charred sticks, and the iron frame had twisted in an agony of heat. Beyond junipers still burning like flambeaux, I could see the black skeleton of the garage's upper floor. It fell in with a rush of heat and roundels of flame that drove back a line of firemen.

A news helicopter churned the air with cocky *whup-whup*s. Its downdraft pushed some of the smoke toward the street in a wicked, enveloping gray spiral.

'Yours, I assume.' K gripped my shoulder.

'Mine,' I said.

'Pity. I was hoping you'd put me up tonight.' His tone was philosophical. 'It's a long, old war, Dr Cousins. I'm sorry.'

'Maybe it was an accident,' I said, folding my arms in what I hoped looked like cool resignation. I sat on a concrete car barricade and let out my breath in a long sigh. Before K could argue, my landlady and her two short-haired friends found us.

'Thank God, Mr Vincent, you're here!' the old woman exclaimed. Tears cut wet trails down her soot-smeared pink cheeks. 'We all made it out. I'm so relieved.' She touched her hair with a nervous, smoky hand. 'Did you see any-one?' she asked. 'Anyone suspicious? It happened so fast, the firemen say it must have been set. But why, oh, why here?'

She gazed up with dreaming blue eyes at the tall dogleg of white smoke.

'No accident,' K whispered in my ear. 'Let's go. You're known, *Mr Vincent. She* might have set the fire.'

I pulled away and stared at him in disbelief, then at my landlady. 'I have to fill out an accident report – don't I?'

'Do it from a pay phone,' K suggested with cavernous patience, as if explaining a simple game to an idiot.

I followed him like a robot through lines of gawping neighbors. The crowd thinned.

Just another day in Berkeley.

I felt light-headed from delayed shock.

A block and a half from the ash and smoke, I looked up at a rapid ticking, what I guessed was the spinning chain of a bicycle sneaking up behind us. K yanked me aside just as a big black-and-tan dog with a snoutful of busy teeth drew a long rip down the rear of my pants.

No bicycle – dog claws: two Dobermans on extensible leashes, held by a young, black-haired, black-clad Diana, her face a mottled peach pit of fury.

'Goddamn you!' she shrieked. 'Goddamn you rotten son of a bitch! *Chew him up*, Reno, Queenie!'

The dogs choked against their collars. K ran off a good distance, but to give him credit, whistled and stomped to divide their attention. I ran backwards, hands up in a gesture of both supplication and defense, using my brother's package as a shield.

The woman glared. Her lips were flecked with foam. I could not believe what I was seeing and hearing.

'You destroy our neighborhood, you stalk our children and drive your huge car over our lawn, you leer at us in the supermarkets and you sneak into our bedrooms!' The words caught in her throat.

The Dobermans danced in a white-eyed ecstasy of rage. Their hind legs wheeled and pumped like pistons, tendons taut as stretched wire. Front paws churned the air and knocked Rob's package to the ground. Nails swiped my palms, leaving blunt, bloody scrapes. The twin blurred arcs of their teeth snapped less than two feet from my throat. I could smell hot gamy whiffs of Alpo. They heaved and wheezed, hanging laterally from the white-nylon cords. The whites of their bugged eyes turned red as the veins in their necks were squeezed.

The Doberman on my right lunged and fanged the ball of my thumb. It lunged again and bit hard. I screamed even before the pain hit. The dogs' mistress chirped and crowed at the blood and gave her beasts more slack. The leftmost dog locked its paws into the hollows of my shoulders, twisted its head sideways, butting and poking through my weaving hands, then thrust its jaws home. As I went down, I felt its bloody cool nose on my Adam's apple, a wet flick of lips, the next ivory puncture, and another bright point of pain.

A hoarse, deep, 'Call off the goddamn dogs, lady!' followed by

Two shots like thunderclaps

And

I fell over a planter, slid along a bent sapling, tripped on a rope staked to the dirt. Some part of my attention saw the two dogs haul right and drop as if slammed by two big hammers. Blood sprayed the asphalt.

I finished my tumble and lay on my back, hands pressed to my shirt, sobbing in shock and to get back my wind. K moved in on short quick legs. He snatched up Rob's package and glared at the huntress with cold irritation. His eyes went dark.

The shooter ran down the steps from a shake-shingled house not ten yards away, a black .45 in one hand, the other bracing, ready to squeeze off a third shot. He wore red shorts and a white T-shirt that had tugged loose on his middle-aged paunch. His arms and legs were thick and hairy and his fat hands looked soft and pink. He stared at the dogs with a wrinkled brow and made sad noises. 'Ah, Jesus. I'm sorry.'

The slugs from the forty-five had struck the streamlined chests square, just behind their front shoulders. Good swift kills.

The woman's small breasts rose and fell under her thick black turtleneck. Skinny and ghostly, she belonged in a café filled with poets and cigarette smoke, not out siccing her dogs on strangers. She drew herself up with a toss of her short black hair and flung aside the leash reels. They raced over the asphalt, reclaiming their cords, tangled and spinning, until they clattered to a stop about a yard from where the Dobermans lay in parallel on the bloody sidewalk.

'Ah, Jesus,' the shooter repeated, and knelt by the dogs. I felt my stomach clench and bile rise in my throat, tainted by the Scotch I had drunk in the bar.

'We have no further business here, none at all,' K assured me. He helped me to my feet. 'They'll come to their senses in a bit, and there'll be more hell to pay.'

The huntress started to cry. Her cry inflated to a wail, then a shriek.

Only then did I notice a stench in the air. I thought it might have been the dogs. But I remembered Dave Press in the plastic sphere at the bottom of the sea.

It was the skinny woman in the turtleneck. She stank like a rotting jungle.

K tucked Rob's envelope back into his jacket, then wrapped my hand in his handkerchief, tying a deft knot around my wrist.

We ran.

To this day, I am surprised nobody followed. The woman became the center of attention. She laid into the man who had probably saved my life, beating at him with bony fists.

K jogged me, then walked me, and finally half carried me to an old brown Plymouth. I got in, feeling very woozy, and he drove me to the Alta Bates Hospital. As we pushed through the glass doors into the emergency room, I was white with shock and barely able to stand.

The receptionist performed her necessary rites of triage and asked about insurance.

'How long have you lived here?' K asked me as I fumbled for my wallet.

'I'm not badly hurt,' I insisted, then felt the blood on my neck.

'Don't touch that,' the receptionist said, grimacing as she wrote.

'How long have you been here?' K repeated.

'Just a few minutes. No insurance.'

'Not the hospital,' K said. 'In Berkeley.' He thrust a wad of bills on the counter, well over a thousand dollars. 'Is that enough? Get my friend to a doctor.'

K was full of surprises.

'Two months,' I said. Another nurse pushed me through a light but judgmental crowd of sniffles and bruises and sprained ankles. My shirt was soaked with blood. Someone was pushing a wheelchair my direction.

Just after I noticed how much blood, I got down on my knees, grabbed the arm of the chair, then toppled over in the hallway and felt the cold gritty press of linoleum on my cheek.

I worry about germs. I hate hospitals and their germs.

CHAPTER TWENTY-ONE
San Francisco

'I believe you now,' K said as we rode across the Oakland bridge. I wore K's threadbare suit coat over a green scrub shirt given to me at Alta Bates. My hand had been punctured in several places, but nothing had been torn, and there was no bone or nerve damage. My throat had been nipped, not ripped. I was lucky.

Rob's envelope pressed against my side. I leaned my head against the car window, queasy from pain – the Demerol was fading – and from my first intravenous dose of Integumycin.

'Thank you,' I said. 'But why should that matter?'

'You haven't been tagged,' he said. 'Or if you have, it hasn't taken.'

'I don't know what that means.'

'The woman with the dogs, and whoever set the fire, they were tagged.'

'Tag, you're it,' I said.

K gave this crack more than it deserved, a smirk and a wan smile. 'Nothing funny about it. If you were tagged, you could be a grave danger to yourself, to me, and perhaps to others.'

'All right,' I conceded. 'What is it, a psychotropic chemical? They spray the fruits and vegetables and the whole neighborhood goes crazy?'

Saying that took most of my energy, and I felt faint.

'As I said, I'm not a biologist. Your brother was beginning to understand when they tagged him. He fought back as best he could.' K stared grimly across the aisle of the half-empty bus. 'He offered me an explanation for my difficulties. He said I must have been tagged ten years ago. And now I'm very small potatoes. It's a truly paranoid vision.'

'Silk?' I asked.

He nodded.

'Sounds sinister,' I said. 'Like being strangled with a scarf.'

'We'll find a room in San Francisco, cheap and anonymous. I'm practiced at lying low. We have enough cash for the time being. I'm relieved, actually. From this point on, at least we know.'

K seemed familiar with all the fleabag hotels in San Francisco. We ended up in the Haight in a narrow little building called the Algonquin, squeezed between an Asian grocery and a store that specialized in posters, bongs, and Betty Boop dolls.

The hotel had ten rooms, a tiny lobby, and a small couch sagging and fading in front of a flyspecked window on the street. K rented a double with the air of an experienced, upper-crust European traveler, temporarily down on his luck while awaiting a draft from his London bank.

He paid cash.

The room was small, with two single beds, a dresser, a tiny closet, and an adjoining bathroom. The sink in the bathroom was chipped. I was too exhausted to care.

I took off the ugly green shirt, lay back on the bed, and thought about withdrawing my remaining three hundred dollars from the bank. Repaying K for my hospital tab.

Phoning my mother and asking for a loan.

K pulled the chair over to the window. He rubbed his temples with his hands, as if trying to focus psychic energy on the brick wall across the narrow shaft.

'Churchill forced him to do it,' he muttered. 'That isn't where it began, but it led to where we are now.'

I slipped in and out of his ramble.

'It was the Jews,' he continued. 'Krupp was a secret Jew, did you know that? Rockefeller. A Jew. They wanted the whole world to go to war. Read my last book if you disagree. Thoroughly annotated. We have lived a century of shams and deceptions.'

'I'm really tired,' I moaned, and curled up on the bed.

K turned his face toward me. Tears ran down his cheeks. 'I was the best there was at winnowing out the dark underside of contemporary history,' he said. 'The very, very best. I still am.'

'Then why are you so full of shit?' I asked, uncharitably, considering what he had done for me in the past few hours.

'Am I?' he asked with deep sadness. He pointed to his temple with a long, knobby finger. 'I've spent most of my life trying to understand the twentieth century. A hundred years of hobnail boots grinding human faces into hamburger. I've uncovered the darkest documents, the most heinous official papers ever concocted by human beings. It was my duty to read them, absorb motivations, plumb psychologies, to understand how such things could be. I imagined myself a doctor diagnosing a long and hideous disease. Perhaps my mistake was having an open mind. Ghosts got in. Bad and unhappy spirits.'

I rolled over and stared at him.

'Why did my brother ever come to you?' I asked.

He wiped sweat from his forehead. 'I wish I were a Jew myself. Then I would have the final answers. I would be given

111

access . . . if I knew the secret signs, the genetic identification. They wave a special . . . box . . . over your head, and it sways left and right if you carry the blood of Aaron, front to back if you're of the Levites. Then they tell you –'

I had had enough. I swung my legs over the side of the bed, sat up with an effort, feeling my bandaged neck bind and my hand throb, and fumbled for the shirt.

'Don't leave,' K said, a hitch in his voice. 'Please. I surely do miss your brother. He could see me as I really am.'

'What's your real name?' I demanded.

'Banning. Rudy Banning. My mother's maiden name was Katkowicz. She was Polish. I am Canadian by birth and British by nationality. I have written twenty-three books on the history of Germany and Eastern Europe, and for twelve years I was a respected professor at Harvard.'

He pulled himself together and stood, then went to his coat and drew forth a wrinkled pack of cigarettes. He tapped out a cigarette and stuck it in his mouth, patted all his pockets, but could not find matches. The cigarette dangled, its tip bobbing as he spoke. 'I was researching a Soviet program for the creation of artificial silk, in the 1930s. I located important documents. To make a very long story short, I came too close to the flame. They burned my wings.'

'What does this have to do with my brother? Or with Jews?' I asked.

His eyes glittered, and his lips squirmed as if they were fighting. '*They* saw how close I was.'

'The Jews?'

He shook his head, pointed his finger into his right ear, and lifted one eyebrow. 'No need to kill me . . . better to discredit me. I have a defect in my character, put there by my father and my grandparents. A little rip of tribal fear. We all have them. *They* pulled mine wide open.' He jerked the cigarette from his mouth. 'The subjects I studied became objectified. I began to hear them at night, whispering vast truths. Some people feel the touch of guardian angels. Mine is the monster I have studied most of my adult life.' His lips curled. 'A fine companion in the wee hours.'

Banning approached my bed, cigarette held in his bandaged left hand, filter squeezed flat between two tobacco-stained fingers. 'I am pariah,' he whispered. 'I am unclean, unemployable. The Jews have made sure I can't publish, can't teach. And *that* is the truth. But however hard I try to ignore my dark and hate-filled angels, they circle and strike like harpies. I have offended the gods.'

I didn't want to be in the same room with K, or Rudy Banning, any longer. I felt sick. 'I have to leave,' I said, and tried desperately to get to my feet. I slid to the floor.

'Don't be silly,' he said, and gently helped me back onto the bed. 'Where would you go? You need sleep.'

Despite anything I could will or do, my eyes closed.

'We'll try to make sense out of things tomorrow,' Banning said. 'I'll call Mrs Callas and make an appointment. And I'll tell you more about your brother.' His voice seemed to slide down a long slope. 'And about Lake Baikal.'

CHAPTER TWENTY-TWO

The brick red reflection of morning bounced across the air shaft into our room. I sat up in bed and reached for Rob's package. It was still on the nightstand. Dog claws had scraped through the paper and bent back a run of tape, but the contents were unharmed.

Banning slept on his side in the other bed, snoring. I went into the bathroom, blew my nose, and washed my face quietly, hoping to have some time alone with the package.

My back was a network of bruises and pulls. My throat hurt, and my hand felt as if it had gone through a meat grinder. I was clearly not cut out for adventure.

I examined my bandages delicately, then changed them using

113

the gauze and tape and disinfectant from Alta Bates. That done, I dropped the lid on the toilet and sat, then slid the blade of my pocketknife under the envelope's taped flap. Cutting through the hairs seemed significant, fresh from sleep as I was; had I dreamed about this? Rehearsed the moment?

The envelope had been hastily stuffed with papers, well over a hundred pages of typing paper, lined notebook paper, leaves ripped from a notepad, hotel stationery (the header in Cyrillic and Roman) from Intourist hotels in Irkutsk and Listvyanka. Pages of scribbled notes had been jammed between three slender manuscripts, two produced on a typewriter, one from an inkjet printer, the type smeared at the bottom by damp. All three manuscripts had been accented with yellow highlighter.

A postcard showed steam rising from Lake Baikal. It had no message, had never been mailed. On the back the caption read, 'World's deepest, largest, oldest: One Fifth of Earth's Fresh Water, Drink and You Are a Year Younger!'

I tried to remember what I knew about Lake Baikal. There was volcanism in the area – gases warming the lake and frequent earthquakes. Heated baths and healing waters.

At the bottom of the envelope I found a paperback book, an Auto Club map of California, and a small diary bound in black vinyl, all held together by a doubled and twisted rubber band. The book was *Uncommon Graves* by Benjamin Bridger, a history of the Soviet invasion of Germany near the end of World War II. I recognized the wrapper art, a hammer and sickle ripping through a Nazi flag. On the inside front cover, two names had been inked in precise, adolescent block letters: Hal and Rob Cousins. We had both read a lot of history in our early teens. Bridger had been one of our favorites.

The book had vanished from my shelves when we were fourteen, and I had accused Rob of stealing it. Now he was returning it to me. I put the book aside and opened the diary. It was filled with looping scribbles. I could hardly read my own handwriting, much less Rob's.

One last item was stuck in the bottom of the envelope. I

turned it upside down and shook it out. A ring of three keys clattered on the black-and-white tiles of the bathroom floor. Attached to the ring was a paper tag bearing an address in San Jose.

I rubbed the bridge of my nose. Did I want to learn what Rob was thinking before his death? I knew with that insight unique to twins that my brother had enjoyed making this selection, that the contents would lead me on a goose chase. Or worse, he had laid out a puzzle for me to solve, a challenge for arrogant Prince Hal.

I took my morning dose of Integumycin and two tablets of T3 – acetaminophen with codeine. I hated codeine, but a jagged buzz was better than a drumbeat of pain.

I heard Banning stir in the other room and pushed the bathroom door firmly shut.

Opened the diary to the middle.

Arrived Irkutsk this morning seven or eight hours from Moscow. Taxi. Fifty bucks and you're king for a day. Met with Ch. and Tur. in hotel restaurant and shared local salmon, very good. Took me to their little lake museum off newly paved and renamed ul K Yenisei (used to be ul K Dzerzhinskova). Jovial fellows. Tippled a bit, peppered vodka, toasted the Decembrists, then toured the old lake lab and museum. Shunned by folks from the Limnological Institute. The lab is filled with specimens from Baikal, baby freshwater seals (in jars) called Nerpas; small ancient lab filled with old equipment.

This was where G. did his early work.

Ch. and Tur. showed me aquarium with recently harvested freshwater xenos. Massive – thirty centimeters across. Water smells of sulfides. Fan blows continuously to clear the dark little room. Ch. confirms these xenos carry ur-kinetoplasts. Very primitive, some still free-living at lake bottom. Tur. explains: Waters thick with xenos and also with curtains of gelatinous semipermeable membranes haunted by clouds of bacteria. Baikal surface in northeast corner gelatinous with polysaccharide ribbons and oily with phospholipids at times, confused with bacterially polluted runoff from infamous pulp plant (six hundred miles south), but the slime is indigenous, from lake bottom around vents.

Rain here forms little fatty drops in water, protocells, that sink to bottom and get colonized by bacteria. Bacteria use polysacc. ribbons like dogs use trees, to establish communal centers and pass on local microbe 'gossip'. G. saw and studied all this in twenties and thirties (before pulp plant was in place).

Baikal is at most twenty-four million years old. But vent life here is hauntingly reminiscent of ocean communities. Like the Beginning Place, Eden?

I looked up from the diary and contemplated the wall, feeling chagrin that my brother had been on the same track, a spike of familial pride, then rank, face-flushing irritation that somebody had gotten there before either of us. And in the nineteen thirties, if I was reading correctly. What else did they know back then?

G. wanted to understand the causes of aging. Intuited that disease and aging are strongly related. Thought perhaps bacteria benefited most from both aging and all sorts of disease, dead bodies being such wonderful opportunities for bacterial orgies. His early theories begin with that premise.

G. studied parasitic control of hosts. Parasitized ant climbs to grass tip, eaten by bird, parasite's next stage is in bird. Rats with toxoplasmosis have cysts in brain, not afraid of cats, get eaten, cats carry toxo. Wolbachia, widespread bacteria, actually control reproduction of host insects and other arthropods. G. then moved on to studying mind-altering substances produced by parasites and compared them with bacterial products. Many gut bacteria talk to intestinal cells. They, too, alter host behavior, he found.

G. discovered 'vaults' in cells 1927–8!

After arrest, G. and wife threatened with deportation (Jewish problem?). Makes lemonade from lemons – G. went to Moscow and proposed to B. that mixes of altered bacteria in subject guts could make prisoners docile, talkative. Dosed in food. Beginning of Silk.

B. released G. and financed his project. Luvvy duvvy with Koba for twenty years.

None of the initials made sense, and who in hell was Koba? I turned a page and read on.

Useless day at Limnological Institute. Nobody will talk about G.

People at the university are more open. They say G. most interested in 'Little Mothers of the World.' That's what eastern microbiologists call bacteria when they're being sentimental. G. interested in germ networking, that's the word we use now, but it did not exist in that sense then. How do these bacterial societies cooperate? How do they communicate with their hosts? G. way ahead of his time. Might be ahead of some biologists even today. Can't find these papers in the library, but my guides Tur. and Ch. from the univ. say that's because B. took them back to Moscow. Wanted to use them to support naturalist view of Marxist theory!

Russian laughter is dark, hard. Siberian laughter is even darker.

I was so absorbed that when Banning knocked on the door I nearly fell off the toilet. I banged my knee on the edge of the shower stall, and the papers spilled on the floor.

'All right in there?' Banning asked.

'I'm fine,' I shouted, picking up the papers from the tiles. I had read just a fraction of the pages and my head swam with half-baked connections. Mind controlling bacteria, for Christ's sake! Rob and I had spent so much of our youth lying to each other about stupid things, especially girls. He might have been off on a tear, losing his sanity. Or he might have come under Banning's influence . . .

'Have a heart,' Banning suggested outside the door. 'My bladder's a balloon.'

Banning and I spent the late morning buying two new shirts and a pair of pants for me. I also picked up a cheap business valise to hold Rob's envelope. I refused to let Banning pay and drained my bank account writing checks.

That was it, I thought. I had become a pauper relying on the kindness of a homeless bigot. The extra time to think was not sufficient for me to reach any conclusion about the envelope's contents.

Our appointment with Mrs Callas drew near, and we took a taxi into South San Francisco.

The collar of the new shirt rubbed my bandaged neck as we climbed three flights of stairs to the top floor of a converted warehouse. The air was stifling, and sweat dripped from both of us when we finished.

A wide white door blocked the entrance beyond a small alcove. Banning pulled back a heavy iron knocker and slammed it down. Seconds later, a finger pushed aside the little brass cover from a peephole. A woman's dark brown eye peered at us. She let the cover swing back. The steel door slid open on small rubber wheels with a squeak like frightened mice.

Mrs Monroe Callas beckoned us into her sparely furnished waiting room. White plasterboard walls stood free within the larger space, open to the higher beams and corrugated tin roof above. Mrs Callas was built like a heron – everything about her was a little too long, legs and neck, nose and fingers. But her strength and assurance were obvious.

We took a seat before a stainless-steel desk, bare but for a tray and two sealed plastic bottles of water – Alpine Shiver. 'Have some,' she suggested. 'It's hot in here.'

The building was quiet. We seemed to be alone. Banning opened his bottle carefully and listened for the snap of the plastic protector and the hiss of escaping carbonation before drinking. I did the same.

Callas watched this ritual with some interest, then issued her pronouncement. 'I've looked into Mr Banning's references. I don't take on charity, and I don't do nutcases.' She looked at me. 'You seem to be one, and Mr Banning is certainly the other.'

Banning adjusted his jacket with nervous dignity. 'It's hardly charity,' he said. 'Dr Cousins is a respected researcher. He might even be able to teach you a thing or two about the life sciences. Think of it as an exchange.'

'Forget it,' I muttered. I felt like a fool, and Callas was only confirming it. Her evaluation was spot on. How much loyalty did I owe Banning because he had paid my bill at Alta Bates? How desperate was I in the first place?

Pretty desperate. And desperately confused. My brother's notes and manuscripts filled my head with disturbing and half-formed images, barely deserving the label of thoughts. The codeine was still active, but it wasn't cutting the pain completely. I gripped my wrist to stop the throbbing.

'I teach people how to avoid trouble,' she said. 'They pay me money.'

'Well, staying away from trouble is certainly what we need to learn,' Banning said with false cheer. 'Some months ago I tried to convince a young man to see you – perhaps you remember, we missed an appointment? Rob Cousins?'

Callas's face was impassive.

'He's dead,' Banning said sadly. 'This is his brother.'

'Sorry for your loss,' Callas said to me. She looked down at the steel table and tapped her fingers against her bare crossed arms. 'Gentlemen, I have work.'

'I am sure that if he remains alive, Dr Cousins could pay your fee . . . within a few months,' Banning said. I gave him a startled look.

'Not interested,' Callas said. 'Thought I'd tell you personally rather than blow you off on the phone. Besides, you didn't leave a number. Time to go, gentlemen.'

'What *did* you learn about us?' I asked. I thought she might enjoy a chance to show off a bit. Her eyes gleamed.

'Mr Banning is notorious,' she said. 'And you've got yourself into more trouble than I want to deal with right now.' She smiled; she had seen through my ploy.

We followed her out of the office, still clutching our bottles. Callas unlocked the door and leaned into it, making the wheels squeak again. She pointed. I went, my face hot.

Banning stood his ground. I thought he was about to get himself karate-chopped and pitched out on his ear.

'You will doubtless want to know –' Banning began.

'I'm sorry,' I said, coming between them. 'Mr Banning was mistaken to bring us here.'

'Right,' Callas said.

Banning looked stricken. 'I must –'

'Pleased to have met you, Mrs Callas,' I said, and pulled Banning away.

Footsteps echoed in the stairwell behind us. I let Banning go and swiveled and crouched.

'Banning, is that you?' a female voice called, breathless in the heat. A young woman in a white summer dress climbed the final step and turned the corner. Beneath a broad yellow sun hat, she wore dark glasses.

Callas gave a low, derisive snort. How loosy-goosy I had become. The woman was so unexpected, so out of place, I did not recognize her. She pulled off her glasses.

'I heard you on the stairs,' Lissa said. 'I'll pay, if money's the issue.' To me she said, 'Rob would have wanted it that way. How much?'

The women assessed each other. Callas seemed to like what she saw. 'Under the circumstances, and considering the students, thirteen-five for a thorough assessment and a four-week training session.'

'That seems reasonable,' Lissa said.

To me, it sounded outrageous.

With a long wave of her arm, Mrs Callas beckoned us back into her loft.

I took Banning aside as Callas brought out more bottled water and added sliced apples, crackers, and cheese. We stood in a side hallway leading to a partitioned, freestanding kitchen and two bathrooms. 'Eat nothing on that tray,' he warned me in an undertone.

'Do you know Lissa?' I asked.

'I've met her.'

'How did she know we were here?'

Banning looked uninformed, like a schoolboy accused of lifting candy from a classmate's desk.

'You called her, didn't you?'

He just stared.

I held up my hands in futility. My life was not my own. Owing anything to Lissa seemed worse than owing Banning. I still felt guilty for the thoughts she made me think. That sundress.

'I'm frankly surprised she came,' Banning said. 'Obviously, not for my sake. She doesn't like me. And I haven't attracted the attention of a woman since my mistress in Manchester left me ten years ago. A Jewish mistress, I might add.'

'I don't want Lissa paying for this!'

'You should have made your objections known earlier. I'm sure Callas has her signing a binding contract even now.'

I slapped the wall with my injured hand. They must have heard in the office.

'Look,' Banning said. 'I'd just as soon she go away, but we don't have much choice. You're as vulnerable as a fawn on a freeway. You need what Callas has.'

'Why am I letting you lead me around like a . . .'

'An aging bigot whose harpies are barely less formidable than your own?' Banning toshed, very British. He frowned as if tasting something bitter and rejoined Lissa and Callas.

My hand throbbed. I squeezed my wrist hard, gritted my teeth, and walked into the office. It was empty. Banning's footsteps echoed on the concrete floor in the open warehouse. I followed.

A wall of tall steel-framed windows opened east over more warehouses and industrial buildings. Whiffs of air pushed through the open lower windows, but it was as hot under the corrugated steel roof as it had been in the stairwell.

Lissa and Callas were seated at a spare old oak desk, heads bent over some papers. Sun baked the floor under the windows. I hated everything about this.

Lissa excused herself and walked over to me in a way that made the sundress look completely inappropriate. There was deliberation and no nonsense in her step, and her eyes bore into mine.

'What are you doing here, with Banning?' she whispered. Banning, about ten yards away, conspicuously stared through the windows. 'Do you know how crazy he is?'

'We met yesterday. He helped me.'

'He's a Holocaust denier. He's lectured to hate groups in California and Oregon. Jesus, it was bad enough that Rob consorted with him – now, why you?' Her jaw clenched and her cheeks turned pale.

'This isn't the place,' I said, trying to be mild and reasonable. 'Some unusual things have been happening. Banning –'

'How do you know he isn't *responsible*?'

I felt like a particularly stupid mooncalf.

'What do you know about Callas? *Mrs* Callas?' Lissa asked.

'Absolutely nothing.'

'Banning just leads you around like a goat?'

There was nothing I could say.

Lissa pulled back. 'I called friends in law enforcement. Callas is respected, but she's an equal-opportunity type. She's trained some really nasty customers. We're going to have a *long* talk,' she promised.

'Why are *you* helping?'

'Your mother and I had a heart-to-heart after the funeral. Remember?'

I remembered standing in the hall with a piss hard-on.

'She told me Rob was smart, but you are smarter. Well, maybe I'm smarter than either of you. I want to know who killed Rob, and why. I owe my husband that much.' She returned my unspoken skepticism with a 'spare me' grimace. 'I've explained that if you agree to her training, I'll pay. I think she wants to learn more about you and Rob. She already has the goods on Banning.'

Callas waited while we arranged our chairs. She propped her feet up on the desktop and wrapped her hands behind her head. All she needed was a matchstick between her teeth.

'I'm on your payroll now, thanks to Mrs Cousins. But we're in the early stages, and if I so choose, I'll cut loose. Fill me in.'

Lissa went first. She told what she knew about Rob's troubles and murder. I listened, trying to match the facts in her story to the papers I had been reading that morning. Rob's manuscripts had been filled with a sense of adventure and discovery, but paranoia might have been just around the corner.

I followed, with my tale of ships, submarines, harassment, arson, and dog attacks.

Callas took a deep breath and shook her head after I finished. 'I like our assailants quantifiable, our threats palpable and enumerable,' she said. 'I know a little about Mr Banning. The lurid parts. I meet a lot of weirdoes in my business, and I treat them professionally. Even paranoids have enemies. But you were once a respected historian. What happened?'

'I was discredited,' Banning said. 'Or I discredited myself. Let's leave it at that for now.'

'I can't,' Callas said, 'not if I'm going to grasp what we're up against.'

Banning straightened in his chair and gripped the arms. 'In 1991, I stumbled upon documents relating to a certain research program, top-secret at one time, dusty and almost forgotten by then. Russian file-keeping is notorious.'

'Go on,' Callas said.

'A campaign was begun to discredit me shortly after this discovery. And long before I met with Rob Cousins.'

'What sort of campaign?'

'I was subjected to mind-altering substances. My behavior changed.'

'Yes.'

'I lost all my money and my woman, and I was hounded out of academe. I became possessed.' Banning looked as battered and drained of life as an old mannequin.

'By what?'

He shrugged. 'Let's just say that this is my afterlife, and it's hell. To all intents and purposes, I am a dead man.'

Callas studied him like a zookeeper assessing a new animal. 'Do you think you were targeted by the KGB? The SVR?' she asked.

'They had no reason, after the Cold War.'

'The Jews?'

Banning twitched in the chair. 'I don't know,' he said.

'Do you know *what* you believe, Mr Banning?' Callas asked.

'What I believe isn't important,' Banning said. 'My head is filled with truths that are lies, and lies that are truths. I walk carefully and watch what I say.'

'Not all the time,' Callas said.

He swallowed and licked his lips, avoiding her gaze.

Callas returned her attention to Lissa. 'You've never been threatened?'

'No. But I watched my husband deteriorate. It could have been something like what Mr Banning describes.'

'Mr Banning worked with your husband?'

'He had some insights my husband thought could be useful.'

The interview continued for an hour. Callas asked us about our personal habits, whether we had ever had firearms, weapons, or martial-arts training, our political affiliations, fringe groups we might be associated with. She listened and took notes on a yellow legal pad. At the end of the hour, she flipped the pad over, and said, 'I can't make heads or tails out of this. What you're describing combines mind control with pointless violence or threats of violence from complete strangers.' She shuddered. 'I don't see how I can train you to protect yourselves against that kind of effort, if it's real. The woman with the Dobermans . . . chilling.

'Before I decide whether to proceed, I want to do more research. It could take a day or two.' She rapped her pencil sharply on the desk. Our first interview was over.

As we descended the stairs from Callas's gymnasium, Lissa told Banning to bug off. Just those words. Banning shrugged and said he would meet me back at the hotel room.

'What a Sad Sack,' she said when he had left. She walked me down several side streets and up an alley to a diner that served the industrial area. We sat in a back booth under a dusty and flyspecked window. A small bud vase decorated the table, but the carnation had long since given its all.

The waiter, a muscular young man with sideburns shaved into a Sony ad, ogled Lissa and honored me with a congratulatory smirk. I ordered two iced teas, and the waiter departed. Lissa tapped her serrated knife on the scarred tabletop.

'I am *really* angry,' she said. It was her turn to look vulnerable.

'At whom?' I asked.

'Rob. Myself. We screwed up, didn't we?'

'I don't know.'

'You both pretended you weren't close to each other.'

'We weren't.'

She shook her head and tapped the knife hard. I could see the glassy core of Lissa's direction now, and it made me uncomfortable.

'You and Julia are divorced, aren't you?'

'Yes.'

'What went wrong?'

'Julia stopped being interested in me or what I was doing. She started being more interested in other men. I don't share that way.'

Lissa's smile was a sad ghost. The way her face worked, I doubted she smiled often. Her kind of beauty almost precluded that emotion. 'I haven't been with another man since leaving Rob. Or since marrying him. I didn't lie to your mother. I wanted to get back together with Rob, but it was impossible. He was acting crazier than Banning.'

I remembered the phone call at Lindbergh Field. What a pair Rob and I were. What a lovely pair of failures, hoping to live for ever, but unable even to enjoy our allotted moment in the sun.

'I've been doing my own detective work. I checked up on Banning, and I checked up on Rob to see if he was involved in anything suspicious. Drugs, that sort of thing. My family's pretty well-off, so I can afford it. When we were still together, Rob went to Lake Baikal. After he got back, he read a book by Banning. I found a copy of the book in our house.'

'Rob mentioned an organization called Silk,' I said.

'*A clandestine organization, formed before the outbreak of the Second World War,*' Lissa singsonged. 'It's in Banning's book, self-published about ten years ago. Along with his belief that Winston Churchill forced Hitler to go to war against England, that the Nazi concentration camps were educational resorts, and the gas chambers were actually fashionable saunas.'

A silence over the table. 'Bastard,' she muttered. 'My grand-father lost his entire family at Dachau.'

'If you have any explanation that makes sense, I'd love to hear it,' I said. 'What did Banning do for Rob?'

'Banning was supposed to be a whiz at tracking down documents. Rob wanted corroboration. He didn't trust Banning very far, and Rob and I were . . .' She was having a hard time speaking, the emotion of a few seconds before still working through her. She swallowed hard. 'We'd separated. I didn't want to give him up, but he had this other life, this crazy search. Banning was helping him, and I couldn't go there.

'The last time he talked to me, he said he was taking samples from his skin and his nose. From his feces. Listening to his intestines. He said he was tracking down messages from some sort of supermind. Complete babble.' Lissa looked up from the gouge she was making with the knife. 'I hired a private detective to track you,' she said. 'I would have found you whether Banning called or not.'

'I'm flattered,' I said. That was true, but her words also made my stomach muscles tighten.

'You are so much like Rob,' she said, but it wasn't a criticism. Her eyes were more than windows. I put my hand on hers – to stop her from cutting the wood.

Then she turned away, and it was like throwing a switch. 'I'm a glutton for punishment,' she said. She released the knife with a clatter, reached into her purse, and draped six dollar bills on the table, covering the fresh scars. 'Where are you two staying?'

We left the diner, walked to Lissa's Toyota, and she drove me to the Haight.

I rode the tiny elevator to the hotel room.

Banning had just finished taking a shower and stood in his slacks and a T-shirt. He acknowledged my return with a curt nod, then reclined on the bed, inching down like an old man fearing a fall. He closed his eyes as if darkness were a delicious luxury and almost immediately began snoring. The worry lines around his lips and forehead softened.

Life was grinding him down to a nubbin, too.

I sat by the window looking out on the air shaft, feeling a roiling burn of dread. Banning wasn't telling us everything he knew, perhaps not even everything he had told Rob. Nor was I telling him everything. I didn't trust him, and he didn't trust me. We were at an impasse.

Lissa was caught up in our suspicion and confusion. I felt sorry for her.

The shaft outside the window darkened. Banning had become Sleeping Bigot, locked in eternal slumber. The air-conditioner was on the blink; a sticky, hot breeze poured through the heat exchange. I turned the machine off, opened the window, and leaned out, staring up at the twilight sky, a vagrant curl of cloud, a contrail savaged by high winds.

Banning had laid in some supplies, a bag filled with cans and bottled water in the bathroom. My throat was parched, and I needed some reward for the miseries of the day. I opened a can of peaches and drank down the nectar, started to suck my fingers to recover spilled juice, thought better of it, and washed my fingertips five times with soap, without wetting the bandage. Then I finished off the slices and sluiced my head with water from the tap. The dressing around my neck got damp, but that wasn't a problem. It felt good as it cooled.

Canned food and vitamin tablets. No way to live. I wanted desperately to get back to the laboratory, any laboratory, and perform work, however menial. That was my life, not this unending lunacy.

My stomach couldn't decide whether it liked the peaches. I could feel shadows gathering in the corners of the room. My hand and neck ached, and Banning's irregular snores allowed neither thought nor rest.

I tried to ignore the distractions. I carried the valise to the desk, unsure where to resume, pulled out the wobbly desk chair and sat.

Finally, my fingers opened the valise and worked through Rob's stack. I found a small airmail envelope and pulled out five strips of blue paper. Columns of three-letter nonsense words – abbreviations for the twenty common amino acids that make up proteins – filled both sides of each sheet. I laid them out on the desk. They could have made up one or more peptide sequences, running left to right, top to bottom, or in some other fashion, if arranged properly. A puzzle or a code. I rearranged them, and read them several different ways after each arrangement, trying to find something I recognized. No luck. I slid them back into the small envelope.

A letter in Russian, inked with a fountain pen, protruded halfway from one of the typed manuscripts. I tugged, and it fell out with an airmail envelope attached by paper clip. Inside the envelope was a Polaroid photo, yellow-brown and fuzzy. It showed my brother and me standing on a city street, perhaps somewhere in Europe, both of us smiling. Rob had evidently kept the photo as a keepsake – touching, but I could not remember where it had been taken.

Perhaps Banning could translate the letter.

But would I want him to? If he was holding something back from me, how could I trust him? And yet – if he had wanted to read the contents of the package, wouldn't he have done so already?

I set that conundrum aside for the moment and returned to where I had left off in the diary.

Parasite persuasion and bacterial communications with gut cells, skin cells. G. goes to Beria, Beria goes to Koba. Beria was much more than just boss of the secret police. Koba would later put him in charge of nuclear weapons research. But this – this would end up bigger even than atom bombs. Beria told Koba that Golokhov could give them a pipeline right into the human psyche

G. makes his case. Koba gets it instantly; G. gets funding, assistants, and a full-blown factory-lab in Irkutsk. This much is clear. Ch. and T. tacitly concur that's how it happened: The questions they won't answer – how did G. survive Lysenko? – , and the way they smile when I tell them my suppositions. They are hiding a lot but it's with a peculiar Russian guilt and shame. They don't want to hide anything, I'm thinking.

I tried to remember Russian history. Beria had been executed after Stalin's death. But what in hell did that have to do with our research? We were interested in life extension, not mind control.

Ch. and T. decided to take me to a place outside Irkutsk. Shame or truth or something compels them.

They drove me in a beat-up Opel truck fifty kilometers outside Irkutsk. Through a wire fence, past a pond, a forest of trees maybe sixty, seventy years old, a clay road flanked by torn-up asphalt and cobbles. Into a ghost city. Well-made stone and brick buildings, wooden houses, paved streets. All deserted, windows gaping.

'This is City of Dog Mothers,' T. told me in his broken English. I'm sure I missed half of the story. Do I believe?

Beria put this place together in '38–39, as testing ground for Silk. G. involved – to what extent, T. and Ch. don't know or won't tell. Modern power and water, an internal phone exchange, even a post office, comfortable, but isolated from Irkutsk and all surrounding villages.

Five thousand political prisoners were brought here – Jews, of course, military types and their families, intellectuals from Moscow and points as far west as Lithuania and Georgia. A fancy Gulag, I think, but T. and Ch. tell me not a Gulag, a research center. It never had a name just a number. 38-J.

I don't like this place. Nobody comes here, nobody lives here now. It doesn't feel right. We walk through the streets and it's still clean, but empty, not even cats or dogs or rats. T. and Ch. only allow me an hour or so to look around. They can't stand any more. They seem to want to say more, but at first they can't, they are ashamed in a way I have not seen in them before.

I gather from what they do say that everybody brought here was encouraged to believe this was a model city. A chance to redeem themselves and live out the purges. Then, bit by bit, the stores were supplied with foodstuffs prepared by Silk. Beria and Koba wanted to know how much and how long it would take.

Now T. finally opens up. He wasn't even born then but he weeps.

A few weeks after the special food arrived, the inhabitants of 38-J were walking naked in the streets, fornicating in public. Human meat – mostly children – was being sold in the butcher shops. Beria brought in truckloads of guns and gave them to every citizen. He showed off by walking unguarded through the streets in a town filled with armed dissidents and political prisoners who should have hated his guts.

Squads took instructions by phone, or from planted neighbors, and hunted down people who visited the library, who were bald or bow-legged, who carried their babies in public. Some were told to go out and whistle and others were told to go out and shoot all of those who whistled.

In 1940, Beria decided to shut it down, a big success and nearly everybody dead. The last women left alive in the town walked on all fours through the streets. A few who had been pregnant smiled and opened their blouses to nurse Beria's guard dog puppies while photographers made movies.

Koba laughed to see such fun.

They insisted I return to the truck. They had had enough, and so had I.

That evening, they gave me a video tape. The visual history of Silk.

There was no videocassette. I stuffed the diary and papers back in the envelope, and the envelope into the valise. I don't think I had ever read anything so ugly and disturbing. My head hurt. I had to get outside. I had to get some fresh air, no matter what the risk. But I didn't move. I needed a signal, something I could use as an excuse. A fly buzzing through the window would do it. A car horn. Anything.

An hour passed, two.

I lay down on my bed, wondering what was wrong with me. Cowardice, indecision, a head full of cotton. I tried to read more, but the letters swam on Rob's pages. Sleep would not come. The room got hotter and the air more still.

Outside, traffic seemed to recede, car engines grow softer, voices more distant.

The room phone rang, mechanical and shrill. I jumped, then turned to Banning. His snores continued. The phone rang again. I picked up the receiver.

'Yes?'

'This is Rob,' said the voice on the other end.

'Jesus,' I said.

'Wrong again. How's my lovely Prince Hal?' It *sounded* like Rob.

'Quit fucking with me,' I said.

'Listen close. You're tired and it's time to show me what you can do.' The voice began to read a long list of numbers.

'Wait,' I begged. 'I don't know what you're saying. Please slow down.'

'Got that?' the voice asked. 'Read me back the last three numbers.'

I tried to remember but couldn't. 'I saw Lissa today,' I said.

'Yeah? Listen again, and this time use your head. This is important.'

Was it Rob? I was convinced for a moment that it was. I had never seen him with his brains leaking out; the stupid funeral director who turned down tips had seen him that way, not me. I had to take my twin's death on faith, and that was certainly not enough.

It was good to believe he was still with us, so I could apologize. 'Are you nearby? Downstairs?' I asked. 'Rob, I am so sorry –'

'Please shut up.' The voice read me the list of numbers again. The air seemed thick as warm Jell-O. When I couldn't or wouldn't recite the last three numbers on the list, he swore under his breath and hung up.

I had disappointed my twin once more. I felt devastated. I so much wanted to please somebody, do what somebody expected me to do.

I lapsed into a low state of fugue. Remembered it was time for my tablets, to be taken with food. That would be all right. I opened another can, this time of kidney beans, swallowed my pills, and ate half of the contents. Then I leaned back in the chair and fell asleep.

When I awoke, I was stiff all over and it was nine in the morning. Banning was shaking my shoulder. He held a white-and-silver blur in front of my face. 'This isn't *our* can opener,' he said, his brow furrowed. 'I bought a cheap one. That one's gone. Someone's been in our room. Did you eat anything?'

I stared at him stupidly, then reached to the nightstand. The valise and Rob's papers were still there. 'I ate a can of peaches and half a can of beans,' I said.

'I did not *buy* a can of peaches,' Banning insisted. He backed off two paces, bumped up against the defunct air-conditioner, and stood with a rigid, military bearing that might have been comical in another circumstance. 'You might be tagged.'

I said, 'I'm fine. Bad dreams, though.'

His look changed to puzzlement. 'Did anybody call?'

'No,' I said.

'We have to find another place to stay.'

'All right,' I said.

Within half an hour, we had paid our bill and taken our belongings – pitifully few – down to Banning's car.

'What do you know about the City of the Dog Mothers?' I

asked him as we drove through downtown.

'Awful,' he said. 'But not the worst.'

CHAPTER TWENTY-THREE

Lissa, Banning, and I sat before Monroe Callas's desk at ten o'clock. We had stood for an hour outside the warehouse, saying little; our appointment had been for eight-thirty, and Callas had insisted we be there on time. The tension in the big room was thick, and it did not come from our being kept waiting.

Callas leaned back in her chair. 'My front door was spray-painted early this morning,' she announced, with an extra lilt in her voice that could have been mistaken for caffeine energy. 'I live in a good neighborhood. Vandalism is rare, graffiti unheard of. There's substantial security, three perimeters, two of my own design and under my control. Nobody who comes to this warehouse knows where I live.' She looked directly at Banning. 'You have no idea where I live, do you?'

'No,' he said.

'Can you guess what was spray-painted on my door?' Callas asked.

'No,' Banning said, brows lowered defensively.

'"Jew Bitch Whore."'

Banning's face hardened. 'Why,' he began, pausing to gather his words, 'would I do such an obvious and stupid thing?'

Callas shrugged. 'I'm not Jewish. I've never practiced the world's oldest profession. As for being a bitch – you bet. No argument.'

She let that sit for a while. I began to feel sorry for Banning.

'I doubt very much it was Mr Banning,' Callas finally said. 'It was probably one of our gardeners. I'm late because I traced his muddy footprints from the front porch to a garbage bin in the rear. I won't go into details, but he must have sprayed my door about five p.m. last night, just after he finished weeding the lawn. If I confront him . . . a gardener, a guy who hardly speaks English and who has no rational motive to do any such thing . . . What will I discover?'

'Confusion,' Banning said.

'That's what I was afraid of.' Lines appeared beside her lips – lines pointing down. 'Is my gardener being controlled by some top-secret Russian spy agency?'

None of us answered. Ridiculous, paranoid, too much to admit.

'Do they go door to door, "Avon calling"?' Callas reached into a desk drawer and pulled up a folder full of printouts and clippings. 'A Mr Hefner Thorgood was brought up on weapons charges yesterday for firing an unlicensed .45 in Berkeley city limits. The People's Republic doesn't like that. He shot two dogs he said were attacking a man. Sound familiar?'

I nodded.

'There's no police record of the dogs' owner filing a complaint, so I can't trace her. But there is an earlier report of a man who claims a woman set her pooches on him, then called them off and moved on.'

Banning nodded as if what she was saying fit some pattern.

'Did our pooch lady make a mistake? Run into someone about your size and age before she found you?' Callas asked. 'Next we have a Mr Alvarado Cunningham, transient. Mr Cunningham is a drunk. He's known to the police for urinating in public and tossing plastic bags full of his own excrement into the backyards of well-to-do citizens. A general nuisance. He's accused of setting a fire in Berkeley on August 8. Mr Banning, are we thinking that maybe somebody hypnotized him? Or is he a Russian agent in disguise?'

Banning did not answer.

'People just don't do things out of the clear blue sky, for no reason,' Callas said softly. 'Brainwashing isn't easy. But here's how I would work such a scheme. There's historical precedent. I'd find vulnerable people in the neighborhood, near my targets, and I would set them up and work them. However they do it. Drugs, hypnosis. Phone calls in the night.'

I clamped my teeth.

Callas flipped through more copies. 'Let's check my hypothesis. Dr Stanley Mauritz, accused of assault and murder in Washington state, is pleading not guilty by reason of insanity. His medical record, filed with the court by his attorney, includes treatment for bipolar disorder. And your submarine pilot, David Jackson Press . . . Treated in 1998 for depression. He became born-again shortly thereafter.'

'Rob was never treated for anything,' Lissa said. 'He had no mental disorders when I married him.'

Callas looked at me for confirmation. 'True?'

'We've never been diagnosed with any clinical mental conditions,' I said.

'Rob wasn't harassing or threatening to kill anybody, was he?'

'No.' Lissa shook her head. 'Not that I know.'

'Never,' Banning said.

I agreed.

'He was mostly a victim, a target – as Mr Banning claims to have been.'

'I was mentally clear of disorders before 1992,' Banning said, his voice thin.

'But since then . . . paranoia, anti-Semitism, obsessive racist thoughts, total collapse of your academic and writing career because of inappropriate behavior and associations,' Callas read from a list. 'Or is all that just character assassination?'

Banning took an interest in his knees.

Callas shuffled all the papers on her desk into a neat stack. 'I'd like Rudy and Lissa to step back into the office for a few minutes. I want to talk with Hal alone.'

Lissa stood and walked away at once. Banning got up more slowly, glancing forlornly between us.

After they had left, Callas said, 'People who kill people

usually want something, or they don't want something. What are you doing that someone would kill for?'

'My research.'

'Research on living longer.' She smiled dubiously. 'Are you competing with a major corporation to get a drug onto the market?'

'Not that I know of. No drugs.'

'Have you stolen secrets from somebody? Truth is important here, Hal.'

'No. Nobody rational would believe that, anyway.'

'Have you seen anybody you think might have been associated with these efforts – anybody suspicious?'

I told her about the man with the spray bottle in the market in Berkeley.

'What would anyone spray on lettuce?' she asked.

'Bacteria,' I said.

'To make you *sick*?'

'Not in the normal sense. To change behavior.'

'I don't follow that, Hal.'

'Neither do I.'

'Do you have a gun?'

'No.'

Callas mulled this over. 'A permanent place of residence?'

'Not now.'

'Gun laws being what they are, and with your name still circulating in the police system, it could take you several weeks to get a pistol and a concealed weapons permit. Maybe longer. Are you willing to buy a handgun illegally? It won't be cheap.'

'Do I need one?' I asked.

'Yes, you do.'

'How much?'

'A good nine millimeter, about seven hundred dollars, no questions asked. A reliable Saturday night special, maybe two, three hundred.'

'What about Banning and Lissa?' I asked softly.

136

'Is anyone trying to kill them?' Callas countered.

'I don't know.'

She shook her head. 'My guess is, either Mr Banning or Lissa Cousins, or both, could be a problem for you.'

I couldn't absorb that right away.

'They're both untrained and vulnerable. Mr Banning is a definite risk, and I'm always suspicious of female altruism, unless there's a romantic motive.'

I shook my head.

Callas flattened her hand on the desk as if for a game of mumblety-peg. She stared down at it. 'Lying could be fatal, Hal.'

'There's nothing between us.'

'What happened last night to make you abandon your hotel room?'

'Banning thinks someone broke in and planted a can opener and a can of peaches,' I said. 'I used the can opener and ate the peaches. He thinks I might have been tagged.' I explained what that meant.

Callas regarded me with morbid curiosity. 'Do you feel ill or out-of-sorts?'

'No.'

'Could you get the can opener analyzed?'

I thought that over. 'Yes,' I said.

'Why was your brother in New York?'

'I think he was putting together the last pieces of a puzzle,' I said.

Callas looked away and shook her head. 'You're claiming your enemies, whoever they are, work like the Shadow – they cloud men's minds. No?'

I felt like a bug under the tip of a huge and descending pushpin.

'Why couldn't they cloud your mind, too?'

I couldn't give that a comfortable answer.

'It's all up for grabs, isn't it?' Callas said. 'Everything we know about sanity and free will.' Her knuckles rapped the desktop lightly. She looked through the broad steel-frame windows. 'I eat a lot of fresh produce. They know where I live. What happens if they decide to cloud *my* mind? What good am I to you then?' She let out her breath. 'I'm returning Mrs Cousins's check.' She pushed Lissa's check across the desk. 'The detective work is gratis. Think of it as an exchange for alerting me to some interesting facts. And for what it's worth, from a professional who doesn't feel very smart anymore, some advice. Get a gun. Forget everything you think you know about life and decency and civilization. Stay away from your friends.

'And stay the hell away from *me*.'

CHAPTER TWENTY-FOUR

I joined Banning and Lissa in the street outside the warehouse. 'We're too weird for her,' I told them. I handed Lissa the check. 'She knows I don't trust Rudy, and Rudy doesn't trust me. And she thinks perhaps you shouldn't trust me, either.'

Banning nodded as if that only made good sense. 'I had a relationship with your brother,' he said. 'It takes me a long time to trust someone – I'm sure by now you can under-stand why.'

Lissa looked at me sadly. 'Whom should *I* trust?' she asked.

'I think Mrs Callas is right,' I said. 'We should all go our separate ways.'

'I've performed my duty to your brother, to the extent I was able,' Banning said. He sucked in his cheeks, making little hollows, before adding, 'Now I hope to return to obscurity and failure. Best of luck.'

We watched him walk down the street to his beat-up brown Plymouth, a diminishing figure in the perspective of the walls and windows of the warehouses.

'This is stupid,' Lissa said. 'Where will you go?'

'Wherever, I'll be on foot,' I said. I started walking south.

The engine of Banning's old Plymouth coughed. I smelled its blue smoke.

'Right!' Lissa shouted after me. 'No money, no car – just your goddamned shoes! You are so incredibly *stupid*!'

I stopped. Lissa stood on the broken sidewalk, wrists corded, fists clenched, face tight and splotched with red. She was furious and frightened. My resolve, not the strongest to begin with, weakened.

I had been alone for so long I had forgotten how much I despised it. But Banning could go and I would never for a moment miss him. Let's face it; I did not want to turn my back on Lissa. There's an instinct in most men that keeps us tied to beautiful women.

It's a real, honest-to-God weakness, and it's part of what makes us die younger.

'It cannot end here,' she said. 'I don't want it to end this way.'

I swore under my breath and jogged past her to the Plymouth. It took a while for the car to warm up. Banning rolled the window down a crack and gave me a wary, sideways look.

'Nothing funny, now,' he warned.

'Did you pack the can opener?' I asked. 'May I take it?'

He drummed his fingers on the wheel for a second, then said, 'It's in the box in the trunk. Just pull the wire poking out of the lock hole.'

I rummaged through the box of canned goods and found the can opener, then slipped it into the valise beside Rob's papers. I shut the trunk, slamming it twice before it caught.

'Found it,' I said. 'Thanks.'

He rolled up the window and pressed down on the accelerator. The Plymouth chugged north and turned the corner.

Lissa drove us past the airport, heading south, it didn't seem to matter where. For twenty minutes it was enough to be in the car and going. If we started asking questions, the tough decision would be, where to begin? Pull on this thread, would it come out short and loose, or would it unravel the whole mystery? So far, every pulled thread had revealed nothing but fuzz.

'Someone pretending to be Rob called me last night,' I said.

'Rob is definitely dead,' she intoned, as if repeating a mantra. 'They were messing with you.'

'Who?'

'Whoever.'

'That's why Banning was so glad to leave. He thinks I've been tagged.'

'All right, being *tagged*, what does that mean?'

'Slipping bacteria or something in your food. Mind control.'

'That's Banning's craziness. Banning drove Rob to think such things.'

'Did he? Rob wrote about what he learned in Siberia, and it's pretty damned scary.' I opened the valise and lifted the envelope. 'There was a Russian program in the 1930s to develop bacterial brainwashing. Certain kinds of special bacteria, laced in your food, could change your behavior or make you suggestible. Someone could then run you. Control your mind. You'd be tagged.'

'Do you think they control your mind now?'

'No.'

'Why not? They – whoever *they* are – sound ever so powerful. They scared Mrs Callas.'

'I'm on antibiotics,' I said. I'd been mulling that over for a couple of hours. As a hypothesis, it was definitely interesting, but it didn't cover any number of details – my trancelike state the night before – and it didn't explain how I'd escaped the madness on board the *Sea Messenger*.

'Antibiotics? That's all it takes to escape from the grip of Dr Mabuse?'

'Who?'

'Dr Mabuse,' Lissa said. 'Fritz Lang made a movie about an

evil criminal mastermind named Mabuse. Supposed to be a symbol for Adolf Hitler.'

'Oh.' Clearly, I had spent too much of my life buried in journals and lab manuals.

'Wouldn't these masters of the universe have thought about antibiotics?'

'There were very few antibiotics in the twenties and thirties. Just sulfa drugs.'

'So Dr Mabuse has this little trained flea circus of master spies, except they're bacteria,' Lissa said. 'And antibiotics knocks them for a loop-the-loop on their little trapeze. They shout *Mein Gott* and their eyes – do bacteria have eyes? – turn to little x's. How convenient.'

I smiled. '"*Bozhe moi*", if they're Russian. We'll see, after another eight days,' I said. 'I'll run out of pills by then.'

The conversation was so desperately loopy that it couldn't help but cut some ice. Lissa raised her arms and stretched as much as holding the wheel allowed, then yawned conspicuously, not tired, but to relieve stress.

'Rob gave the envelope to Banning, to give to you?' Lissa asked suspiciously.

'Yeah.'

'You're sure it's Rob's?'

'I know his handwriting. You can read the papers if you want.'

'You've decided to trust me?' Lissa asked, her expression somber. She kept her eyes on the road. The traffic was bunching up and getting herky-jerky, requiring her full attention. A red Honda with tiny tires carrying three young men in reversed ball caps zipped in front without signaling. She tapped the brakes and the horn at the same time.

'Trust doesn't amount to a hill of peanut shells,' I said. 'If what he wrote about happened, if I'm putting two and two together properly, if what Banning says makes any sense, or what AY said –'

'AY?' Lissa asked.

'Rob didn't tell you much about his work, did he?'

'Not at the end. I just couldn't stand watching him fall apart. What kind of antibiotic?' she asked.

'Integumycin. It's new.'

'I'm surprised any antibiotics work now. So many resistant germs. It's like they have it in for us.'

'Yeah,' I said. 'Where are we going?'

'Right now, it's eleven o'clock, we're stuck on the 101, and we're going nowhere,' she said.

'I have Rob's keys,' I said. 'And I have a map.' I slipped the map out of the envelope and unfolded it over my lap. A picture on ancient browned newsprint slipped from between the folds. It showed a line of smiling officials decked out in sashes, cutting a long ribbon with an outsize pair of scissors. Over their heads hung a banner:

Serving America the Very Best: Thuringia Nuts Fruits Pastries

The caption read, 'California's newest tourist town welcomes visitors.'

On the map, two circles had been marked in red pen, one around a small dot with no name east of Livermore, the other around San Jose.

'Do you know anything about a place called Thuringia?'

'No,' she said. 'Sounds like a sausage.'

'How much do you want to get involved?' I asked her.

She gripped the wheel tighter.

'Lissa?' I leaned forward to catch her eye and force her to answer.

'I want to feel at peace sometime in this life,' she murmured. 'If you're going to do what Rob did . . .' She glanced at me, and I knew instinctively that she was seeing Rob. My brother and I had diverged little in appearance in almost three decades. Rob had been dextro, I am levo – right-handed and left. Adroit and gauche. His hair had curled deasil, my hair curls widdershins. He put on his shoes first right, then left – me, the reverse. His left eye had been tilted a little, my right eye is tilted a little. Different fingerprints, retinal patterns, of course; embryos have some autonomy when they develop.

But the very same genes. The very same.

We had speculated, during our first and last run at cooperative dating, that disastrous eighteenth summer, that it wasn't technically unfaithful for one twin to sleep with the girlfriend of another. No difference in the old evolutionary game. We had learned otherwise.

Now I was the only one.

'There's something in Thuringia, and there's an address in San Jose,' I said. 'Shall we go open some doors?'

'Why?' Lissa asked.

'I think my brother's having one last joke on me. He gave me just enough evidence to tweak my interest, and he wanted me to follow in his footsteps and solve a mystery. I'm thinking if I succeed, I'll know why he was killed, and maybe I'll be able to recover my life.'

That didn't sound convincing even to me, but how could I explain a masculine game of chicken between a dead twin and a live one?

'Maybe he's warning you, stay away from these places.'

'By sending a map and a set of keys?'

She gripped the wheel even tighter. 'Hungry?' she asked.

'Famished.'

'Tell me where we should eat, and what,' she said with just a hint of tartness. 'You're the expert.'

I picked out a Denny's. We would be powerless against any organization that could control all the fast-food restaurants in California.

Lissa had a bowl of clam chowder. I had a cheese omelet with sausage. Everything was thoroughly cooked.

CHAPTER TWENTY-FIVE
Thuringia, California

We missed the turnoff twice. I looked at Rob's map and determined that Thuringia – if that was the unnamed dot in the red circle – lay between two little towns, Gillette Hot Springs and Cinnabar, about five miles off an old stretch of highway now used as frontage road and for backcountry access. But all we found east of Gillette Hot Springs were rolling brown hills and an abandoned restaurant complex with a decrepit green-and-white Dutch windmill.

We stopped for directions in Cinnabar, not much more than a gas station and a trailer park. The attendant at the station, a sixteen-year-old boy with long black hair and a torn LA RAMS T-shirt, had never heard of Thuringia.

'This is the most boring place on Earth,' he confided as he pumped gas into the Toyota. 'Nothing but old-timers. Even the dogs are old.'

Lissa was clearly unhappy but kept her mouth shut as I swore and fumbled with the map.

Finally I decided we should backtrack and stop at the old restaurant. We pulled into the weedy parking lot. I got out and peered through filthy and broken windows into a ruined interior, counters ripped up, trash on the floor. Around in back, in an angle of shade, I found a large, warped plywood sign leaning against two battered trash cans. I flipped it with my foot and it fell over. In faded green mock-Deutsche letters, outlined in powdery pink, the sign proclaimed:

Pea Soup Thuringia

I shaded my eyes against the sun and walked across the cracked asphalt. A barricade, splintered and bleached by the sun, blocked a side road that ran straight off into the hills.

'Bingo!' I called out to Lissa in the car.

She did not share my excitement.

The road to the hills had been turned into a washboard by years of sun and rain and neglect. Lissa pushed the Toyota along at about thirty miles per hour, our teeth rattling. 'What do you hope to find?' she asked.

'I don't *hope* to find anything,' I said. 'Except maybe that it's all a dream.' Utility poles lined the road. Power lines still served Thuringia, but it was no longer named on the map.

Lissa slowed to drive around a particularly deep pothole. 'You think there's something bad here?'

'I have no idea,' I said. But the words on the banner in the newspaper photo haunted me: SERVING AMERICA THE VERY BEST: NUTS FRUITS PASTRIES. I could picture ads in the back of *National Geographic* and *Sunset* in the 1950s: mail-order fruit and nut boxes from California.

'What if he made it all up?' Lissa asked hopefully.

'Then we'll just turn around and go on to San Jose. Confirm that Rob was wacko.'

Lissa seemed to take what I said as a cue. She spoke rapidly. 'The last trip we took, before we separated, Rob wanted to show me something in San Francisco. We drove all the way from Santa Monica to a salt farm in the South Bay. We took the Dumbarton Bridge and ended up on a dirt road on a levee. All around us were these big, square lagoons filled with *purple* water. They were drying ponds for salt. Rob told me they were filled with bacteria, halophiles, he called them.'

'Salt-loving,' I said.

'I *know* that.' She scowled but did not take her eyes off the road. 'We stood by the car on the levee and it stank and there were flies everywhere. I wondered if I'd ever be able to use salt again. You know what he asked me?'

I could have sworn that she was leading me on, as if cross-examining a witness; that she already knew. Perhaps Rob had told her more, and she was trying to gauge the depth of my own knowledge. I shook my head.

'He asked me if I ever wondered what was the oldest mind on Earth.'

'Oh, really?' I said.

'He pointed to the ponds. "There it is. I wonder what it's thinking right now," he said. "I wonder if it's mad at us?" That scared me. A long drive just to stare at some stinking ponds. We had a huge fight that night, and broke up a few weeks later. But I wasn't the one who filed for divorce. Rob did.'

'I'm sorry,' I said.

'What did he mean?' she asked.

'I suppose he meant that bacteria talk to each other.'

'That's stupid,' she said, then looked doubtful. 'Do they?'

'Yes,' I said. 'But not the way we're talking now. They swap genetic material, plasmids, chemicals.'

'Like in a brain?' Lissa asked.

'Maybe,' I said.

'Doesn't that scare you? It scares me. If they hate us, there are so many of them, they'll win.'

I shrugged. 'Too many things scare me now,' I said. 'I try not to think about all of them at once.'

Lissa braked the car abruptly and put the transmission into neutral. Ahead, in a flat stretch between the sun-yellowed hills, lay a low, brown, cornhusk of a town.

'Behold, the tourist mecca of Thuringia,' I said.

The engine and air-conditioner whined a precise Japanese chorus in the central valley heat.

'I don't want to do this,' Lissa said, and her face was pale, her upper lip damp with nervous sweat.

'You can stay here, I'll walk in,' I offered.

She thought that over. 'No,' she decided.

'We'll do it for Rob,' I said.

'I've done a lot for Rob,' she said, with a bitterness I hadn't heard before.

We both stared through the dusty windshield at the line of buildings, laid out in random clumps like a herd of drought-stricken cows.

Lissa put the Toyota back into drive and moved us slowly down the last hundred yards of rumpled asphalt. She pulled off and parked beside a chain-link fence held up by iron posts set in concrete and wrapped, for all we could tell, around the entire town. A sign clamped to the fence announced, in white letters on a red background, 'NATURAL POLLUTION SITE – OFF LIMITS'. The fence crossed the road. There was no gate.

'What's that mean?' Lissa asked.

I puzzled it over. 'The town east of here is called Cinnabar. That's an ore of mercury.'

'Mercury is poison,' Lissa said.

'Pretty nasty stuff,' I agreed. 'But I don't see how it could pollute a whole town. There's no factory or mine.'

'Are we sure of that? I think we should turn around and go back.'

It was a reasonable suggestion, but something told me the sign wasn't warning about mercury. 'You stay here. I'll go look,' I said. And added, 'I promise I'll wipe my shoes off when I get back.'

'The hell with that,' Lissa said. 'I'll go in with you.' She tried to put on a brave face.

It wasn't difficult pushing through the old chain-link. I found a rock and battered aside the link tension bar, then kicked it until there was a hole big enough to admit us. I slipped through without difficulty and decided to keep the rock, just in case. Lissa, in her dress, had an awkward moment that showed more thigh than either of us was comfortable with.

She straightened her clothes while I looked down the main drag of Thuringia. It resembled a ramshackle set for a cheap Frankenstein movie. Boarded-up buildings on either side had false fronts in European village style. The paint had been sunned down to a few hints of red and blue and green. The street was covered with dried mud and shallow gulleys from past rains and scattered with tumbleweeds.

'Tumbleweeds come from Russia,' I said to Lissa.

'So?' she asked.

'Nothing,' I said. We walked a few paces apart down the center of Saxony Boulevard. Some of the buildings had been marked with graffiti, but surprisingly few for this part of the country. To our left, down Bohemia Way, more ghostly shop fronts made old, phony promises.

We stood under a flaking golden kringle marking a Danish bakery. This shop had not been boarded, but the windows were long gone, and the interior was a dark, dusty ruin of bare shelves, exposed pipes, and electrical conduits poking out bare, dead wire.

Inside the display case lay a rain-wrinkled model of the town, all the color gone from the warped cardboard buildings. Next to a ripped-out void on the north side of the model, a curled paper label read, *THURINGIA BADEN BADEN: MINERAL SPRINGS AND SPA, Natural Healing Waters From Deep in the Earth*.

'Hot baths,' Lissa said. 'Bubbling death by fumes of mercury.'

'Not funny,' I said.

Two doors down, delaminating plywood covered a real estate office window. *Ye Olde Alpine Village Realty*, announced quaint chiseled letters above the plywood. Blue and red trim, gingerbread with edelweiss cutouts. White America, with so shallow a history, was always looking for affirmation from more rooted cultures. Anywhere else it would have been simply ludicrous. Here, it made me grit my teeth.

'Had enough?' Lissa asked.

'Four or five more streets,' I said.

For the next fifteen minutes, we walked through all the sad, desiccated dreams of a small and unsuccessful tourist town, reduced to bankruptcy and memories as bleached as the posters.

A bandstand stood in a small village square. It didn't take much to imagine oompah and polka music rising in the long summer nights.

The quiet was absolute. Not even a breeze blew through the old buildings. We passed a warehouse, doors yawning open, the concrete floor covered with broken pallets and mildewing heaps of burlap. In a narrow alley between two picturesque and thoroughly broken-down chalets lay an abandoned Ford sedan, stripped to body and frame. It had keeled over on a jack that had finally let go, after who knew how many decades.

Near the back of the town, separated from the other buildings, we found an office for the *Thuringia Courier-Journal*, a pretentious name for what I presumed was a one-sheet devoted to small-town flackery. Still, the door had not been boarded, and I thought it might be worth a look inside.

'Think the sheriff will mind?' I asked. I prepared to make a run at it with my shoulder.

'That's stupid,' Lissa said. 'You'll break something.'

I flexed my muscles. 'Man of steel,' I said.

The wood was old and weak, and the door gave with one slam. Dust flew everywhere. Pulling down a triumphant fist, I stepped into the darkness. As my eyes adjusted, I stared at stacks of posters, boxes filled with handouts, and a small gray desk.

I carried a poster and pamphlet into the sunlight.

'"Thuringia Farms, We ship everywhere,"' I read. '"Christmas, Thanksgiving, Any Holiday Occasion! World Famous Fruitcake, Walnut and Almond Baskets, Dried Fruit Samplers. Candified Oranges, Pineapple" –'

'"Candified"?' Lissa smirked.

'That's what it says. "Dates and Olives, Deluxe Pitted Prunes from California's Golden Hills. Satisfaction Guaranteed."'

'Keeps you regular,' Lissa said.

'Copyright 1950.'

I held up the poster:

WELCOME TO PARADISE THURINGIA!
SUN AND SPA, THERMAL SPRINGS
HEALTHY LIVING
AMERICA'S NEW VIGOR CAPITAL

Female bathers in polite Esther Williams suits posed on rock walls and dipped their feet into a steaming pool. All smiles. Vigor and white teeth and fifties-style pillar thighs everywhere.

'Let's find the bathhouse,' I suggested. 'Looks sociable.'

'Let's not and say we did,' Lissa said. But the light words did not cover her pallor. She didn't like the place one bit. To me, it seemed sad and stupid but so far, no cause for alarm.

The spa was a brick-and-stone blockhouse on the east end of town. Another run of chain-link surrounded it, this time with a locked gate, and an even larger sign announced 'NATURAL POLLUTION SITE.' There was more detail in fine print:

WARNING.
DO NOT BATHE OR DRINK FROM SPRINGS.
CALIFORNIA STATE DEPARTMENT OF HEALTH

And below that, in heavy block letters,

BACTERIAL CONTAMINATION.

'Curious?' I asked.

'No,' Lissa said.

I took the rock and whacked at the lock on the gate. It broke after three tries, and the gate opened with a shrill whine. Lissa followed a few steps behind.

The main entrance had been bricked up, but around the side, a service door sported another latch and lock. That one took five whacks. I grabbed the hanging lock and pulled the door wide, then peered into the darkness.

Inside, water dripped and rushed. Sunlight fell in narrow shafts from gaps in boarded-up clerestory windows. Lissa touched my shoulder but said nothing. After a minute, my eyes grew accustomed to the gloom. The air smelled sulfurous, as befitted a genuine hot spring.

'Phew,' I said, and waved my hand to dispel not just the stench, but a nervous reluctance to look any further.

A brick walkway led to three steaming pools, the biggest about twenty feet long, all filled with dark, rippling water. A nine-inch pipe thrusting from the far wall spilled a continuous stream of hot water into the largest pool. The smaller pools took the overflow, where the water cooled to a temperature more comfortable for the uninitiated.

I knelt beside the smallest pool. A thick film coated the surface, forming yellow islands in the middle and scummy coastlines around the sloshing gutters. I swirled the film with my rock and lifted it to examine and smell. Foul, not algae but bacteria, probably distantly related to the floc at the bottom of the sea, and dying upon exposure to the air in the bathhouse.

I held the rock up to show it to Lissa, but she was no longer behind me. I stood and squinted into the shadows. Someone moved on the other side of the blockhouse. A ticking rose above the rush from the pipe: machinery, and still in working order. I thought I heard someone say something, broken syllables over the noise.

'Lissa?'

No answer. I walked around the pools and saw a large black box and a complex of pipes. Several of the pipes dropped into the big pool. All were painted red. They looked newer than the bathhouse and were well maintained, dusted, polished.

Lissa came around the box and passed through a shaft of sun. Despite myself, I jumped.

'What?' she said.

I waved my hand feebly.

'It's steel,' she said. 'There's something inside, but I don't think you'll be able to burgle this one.'

I walked around the box, about five feet square and seven feet high. The steel door resonated with strength. It was at least half an inch thick, like armor plate. A deep-set key lock was the only access.

'Department of Health station?' I speculated.

'Earthquake detection,' Lissa guessed. 'You know, like in that movie, the water gets hotter if there's going to be an eruption.'

I hadn't seen that one, either.

We spent five minutes in the bathhouse until the smell drove us outside. I was no more enlightened than before we had entered. We retraced our path through the sad streets, and stood once more on Saxony Boulevard.

Footsteps tapped behind us. Lissa and I spun around toward what turned out to be an echo, and saw a Highway Patrol car parked in the shadows behind a storage shed. We swiveled our necks as one to the right. A tall man in tight khaki uniform and Sam Browne belt, holstered forty five on his hip, approached with one thumb hooked into a belt loop and his gun hand swinging free. He wore a rakish Tom of Finland biker's cap.

I dropped the foul-smelling rock.

'Hello!' Lissa greeted him bravely. Good cover, I thought. Safe white couple out for a drive in the back country. Nothing wrong here, ossifer. 'What a wonderful old town! Is anything still open?'

The uniformed man tipped his cap to her. His hand was ancient, with an odd little pucker between the tendons of each finger. Behind MacArthur sunglasses, his face resembled an apple dried in a hot oven. Feathery white hair poked from under his ridiculous cap.

I couldn't tell how old he was. Too old to be a cop.

'Town's off-limits,' he said, his voice like a scratchy 78. 'Don't drink the water.' He reached around behind his back and unhooked a holder for a big plastic bottle of Evian. 'Days are hot. Bring my own. Truly, folks, you're trespassing. People forget about private property. Found a door busted in. Nothing to steal.'

At the end of the street, I could have sworn a gray figure watched from the inky shadow of a storefront awning. But it might have been an afterimage of the glint off the old man's silver badge.

'Nothing here, not even ghosts,' he said. 'Most boring place on Earth. Nobody around but boring old farts. Even the dogs are old. Can I help you find your way back to the main road?'

Lissa shook as we drove down the asphalt washboard to the old highway. 'He's following us,' she said, glancing in the rearview mirror.

By then, I was shaking, too. 'Christ, that car is *vintage*. And he is *geriatric*. Pretending to be a police officer.'

'He has a gun,' Lissa said.

A crazy old coot in a deserted town, driving behind us in a black-and-white straight out of the old *Highway Patrol* TV show my dad had watched in reruns when I was a toddler. Sunglasses. Clipped and polite.

'Bacteria,' I said. 'Hot springs full of bacteria, and not just from dirty diapers, I'll bet. A natural source, right out of the Earth. No wonder Rob was interested.'

She said *um* and pointed to the backseat. 'Get my purse.' I reached back, stretching my shoulder muscles, and tugged up the soft brown-leather handbag. It hung heavy in my grasp.

She took the bag into her lap and pulled out an angular black pistol.

'My father gave me some lessons, but that was years ago.' She poked the grip at me, and I took it from her. 'Do you know how to shoot?' she asked.

'No,' I said.

'You know how to pull a trigger, don't you?'

'I suppose.' I felt the gun's weight, its balance, like a piece of fine lab equipment, but simpler and more earnest. Death is easier than science. 'Do you trust me?'

'If you have to ask,' she said, 'when I've just accompanied you into Fruitcake Hell, we're being followed by a weird old geezer, and you're holding my gun . . .'

I twisted the pistol carefully. A Glock, just what Mrs Callas had recommended. 'It's not loaded,' I guessed.

'Yes, it is. It's a law-enforcement model. It has a fifteen-round clip, and three more clips in the purse.'

I checked.

'He's stopping,' Lissa said. She let out her breath. 'No, he's starting up again.'

I spun my head around. The black-and-white was churning

153

up dust at the side of the road. The clouds lay thick between us, and for a moment I couldn't see what he was up to.

Lissa accelerated gently, as if trying to outdistance a wary predator.

The dust blew aside. The black-and-white had turned around and was heading back to Thuringia.

'He's gone,' I said.

'Thank God,' Lissa said.

It was then that I had that weird outland hunch that had been lurking for hours, a swooping revelation that chilled me right to the bone. Fruitcake, dried fruits and nuts, shipped all over the USA, straight out of one little California town, a commercial front for . . . what?

Silk?

Spraying mind control germs on every little prune, over every holiday fruitcake, injecting them into packages of shelled almonds and walnuts. And all the while, collecting samples from hot springs that bubbled up stinking white clouds of the Little Mothers of the World.

Rob could have come across something almost beyond belief. Screw the almost. I had to know more to even begin to believe. 'Had enough?' I asked.

'Have you?' she said.

'San Jose,' I said, and shoved my finger down the rutted road.

'Aren't you tired?'

'Let's stop someplace for coffee,' I said.

Lissa rubbed the back of her neck.

'For Rob,' I said, and knew too late that I had pushed that button once too often.

Her face turned to marble.

'Where did you get the gun?' I asked.

'None of your business,' she said. 'And don't you tell me one more time that we're doing anything for Rob. You're doing it because you're curious, that's all. He was curious too, and he left me, remember? He was the one acting like an asshole

154

and traveling all over the world. He wouldn't listen, and now, neither will you.'

I dropped the Glock into her purse. It made me nervous just looking at it. 'I'm sorry,' I said.

She lifted her chin and rubbed her nose. 'Forget it.'

'Maybe we should stop and get some coffee.'

'No,' she said. 'I'm fine. Let's go to San Jose and get this over with. Where's that goddamned key ring?'

CHAPTER TWENTY-SIX
San Jose, California

Lissa looked up at the glass-fronted stairwell of the Creighton Building, an early-seventies office cube on a nondescript front-age road adjoining 280, surrounded by used-car lots. Banners flapped enthusiastically at Choosy Chan's, just a few dozen yards south, but at six-thirty, with dinner on and dusk falling, there were no customers. A tall, skinny salesman in a tight-fitting herringbone suit lounged against a Ford Explorer, picking his teeth. He ignored us.

I held the small steel ring with a paper tag on which Rob had neatly printed this address. The ring held three keys, two of the common brass variety that would fit any number of doors, and one steel, new, square, and shiny.

We pushed open the glass door and entered the lobby. Fluorescent lights came on and made us jump, but it was just a building timer. The makeshift security desk was deserted and dusty. We looked at the list of tenants in a glass case on the wall, columns of white-plastic letters against ribbed black velvet. None of the names suggested Rob.

'Maybe he moved out,' I said.

'He would have thrown away the keys,' Lissa said. 'He hated old keys.'

I threw away old keys, too. The first floor was occupied by

an investment firm, the third floor by a law firm. That left the second.

All but one of the twelve doors on the second floor were closed and locked. Most sported engraved Formica plates slipped into cheap aluminum mounts. Beyond the open door, a lone receptionist sat at a cheap desk, talking on the phone. 'All right, Mother. I'll work it out. Let me see,' I heard her say. 'That would be four hundred and twenty-six oranges. Right? I'm sorry. Five hundred and two.' She did not look up as we walked past.

After first checking to make sure the corridor was empty, we tried the brass keys on each of the three doors that had no name plates.

No go. We paused. Lissa wanted to use the water fountain at the end of the hall, but I suggested that could be a bad idea.

'How would they know about this place?' she asked. I shook my head.

'It's hot,' she complained, but did not drink.

I scanned the name plates, trying to get in touch with my brother's sense of humor, his quirkiness. It took me two strolls up and down the hall, and a glance from the receptionist as I passed for the third time, before I stopped in front of a door with a plaque engraved *Richard Escher Industries*.

Escher, Richard. *Escherichia coli*, *E. coli*, had been discovered by a German named Escherich.

The second brass key worked, and the door opened. The office was dark. The door bumped halfway through its swing against something heavy. I made out shadowy piles of boxes. A musty smell, something old and spoiled, drifted out with the cool air; not big, not a body, I thought, but mildew or mold. Old magazines or books.

I was suddenly very reluctant to go in.

Lissa sneezed. 'How did you know it was this one?' she asked as she took a Kleenex from her purse.

I explained. 'Much too obvious,' I concluded under my breath.

'Obvious to whom?'

Someone spoke at the end of the hall. We both leaped into the office. I closed the door and fumbled for the light switch. Fluorescents flickered to stark white brilliance over the small lobby and down the hall.

Lissa let out her breath and laughed. 'We're acting like burglars,' she whispered.

'Not as long as the rent's paid up,' I said.

'It's been a month and a half,' Lissa said.

We were just talking to break the quiet. What we saw did not make much sense. Cardboard file boxes lined the wall behind the door. Two had toppled from a corner stack. We stepped over a slide of old issues of *Friday*, *Colliers*, *Time* and *Life* magazines.

I slid open a balky closet door and found heaps of newspapers, a box full of clippings, another box packed with offprints from web sites.

'What was he doing?' Lissa asked.

'Research,' I guessed. I picked up a magazine. Two pages had had clippings removed. Nearly all the magazines in the stacks were from the late nineteen forties and early fifties. A few dated back to the thirties.

The carpet – what we could see beneath the boxes – was worn and gray.

'What *is* that smell?' Lissa asked, and tried to hold in another sneeze. It backed up on her, and she snorked delicately into the Kleenex.

'Old newspapers,' I guessed.

'Smells like stale beer.'

We looked into the second room, a small office space about ten feet on each side, and found a folding cot covered by a single wool blanket. Around the cot, books and newspapers filled cheap pine-and-cinder-block shelves, overflowed boxes, or tumbled out of another small closet. The books were paperbacks, mostly, narratives and histories of World Wars I and II, the Russian Revolution. I recognized a few Rob and I had read as kids.

I spotted three hardcover books by Rudy Banning and pulled them carefully from the middle of a stack. *Between Two Devils*, a history of the Hitler/Stalin alliance, was labeled 'NY TIMES BEST-SELLER FOR FIVE WEEKS.' It had been published in 1985. The second, *We Knew Nothing*, compared German civilian complicity in the Holocaust with Russian civilian complicity in the expulsion of Jews to Siberia in the 1950s. Published in 1992, it was not labeled as a best-seller. Each of these was heavily underlined and annotated, with lavender, yellow, and pink highlighting spread across many pages.

The third, slender and outsized – *Blondi, Dog of Destiny* – had been published in 1997 by the White Truth Press in Ojai, California. On the title page, in bold fountain-pen strokes, it was signed, 'To Rob and any future children – a legacy of fact, sworn to by Rudolph B.'

I passed *Blondi* to Lissa, who studied the simple illustrations with a wrinkled brow. 'Hitler had a dog?' she asked.

'I guess so.'

I placed the valise, never out of my sight, on the floor and piled Banning's two other books on top, then dug through the closet. A small safe, bolted to the floor, stood open beside accumulations of the San Jose *Mercury News*.

My brother had never been a pack rat. He had always traveled light, just like me. This clutter was totally unlike him and pointed to either a hasty and unfinished project or a true change in personality.

I stooped and looked into the safe. Empty.

Through the thin walls, I heard the mechanical chuckle of a small compressor turning on – a refrigerator, I guessed. The sound came from the third room, at the end of the hall.

That room was the largest, about twenty feet long and twelve wide. A small conference table in the center supported at one end a small, cubic white refrigerator. A medical-quality microscope occupied a cleared space at the opposite end. Bottles of chemicals and boxes of lab supplies shared the middle with a loaf of bread and some cheese, a wilted head of lettuce, an open jar of dried yellow mayonnaise, and a package of Oscar Mayer lunch meat. The cheese, bread, and lunch meat had long since been covered by a lush growth of mold.

A pan perched on a small cookstove on the floor held a cracked sheen of agar.

A six-foot freezer chest thrust out into the room from the right wall. White, spotless but for a thin layer of dust, and conspicuously padlocked, the freezer hummed efficiently to itself. I glanced quickly at two big maps pinned on a corkboard above: Russia and North America.

'Bachelor apartment,' Lissa said blandly. She opened the refrigerator and took out a petri dish. 'Mosquitoes,' she said, holding it up. She picked out others. 'Flower petals, I think. More lettuce. Apple slices. Lots of mold.' She held up a rack of test tubes filled with milky fluid.

'Bacterial samples,' I said.

She paused, lifted a small plastic tray of six more dishes, and said, 'Meat. I think.' She replaced the tray and carefully wiped her fingers on her dress.

I stood before the freezer chest and looked more closely at the two maps. Red and blue pushpins marked locations on both. I leaned forward. In Siberia, a red pushpin had been stabbed into the northern end of Lake Baikal. Red pins also marked parts of Southern California, Utah – the Great Salt Lake – and Yellowstone. Three blue pins punched a line off the coasts of Oregon and Washington. A red pin almost obscured the southern end of San Francisco Bay. That could be the salt lagoons Lissa had told me about. A blue pin rose out of New York City. The other pins could mark bacterial concentrations of interest – but New York City?

I rested my hand on the freezer, looked down, and tugged at the heavy padlock.

'Should we?' Lissa asked.

'Of course,' I said. If anyone had a right, I thought, it was I. Lissa stood behind me, curious despite herself. I used the shiny steel key. The padlock snicked and fell open. I lifted the lid. A small cloud of vapor rose from the interior and quickly settled.

Lissa gave a shrill yelp and retreated.

I have seen dead human bodies before, in medical supply houses, on dissecting tables. I know what they look like. But I never get over the shock of seeing another. For me, a dead body means defeat. I bent over to look more closely.

I had no doubt there was a reason for this particular body to be here, in my brother's rented office, frozen, still wearing black socks and a rucked-up T-shirt and blue bikini briefs. There was also certain to be an explanation for why it had been autopsied. The top of the head had been sliced through and the skullcap removed, leaving most of the brain and peeled-back scalp to rest on a square of thick black-plastic sheeting. The torso had been opened in a single neat slice front to back, from the upper abdomen to the kidneys.

But this was no supply-house cadaver. Its flesh was pale blue and mottled green. I doubted that I would find lividity, blood pooled in the lower tissues, if I turned it over. It had probably been frozen after being dead less than a few hours.

I closed the lid and stepped back, bumping against the crowded central table. Took a deep breath to keep my stomach steady.

'We have to leave,' Lissa insisted.

'Stand by the door and listen,' I said, swallowing hard.

'I *want to leave.*'

'Wait for me in the car, then,' I said. 'Keep an eye out.'

'You can't touch anything!' she said in a muffled cry, knotting her fingers. 'We should call the police *now.*'

'Quiet, please!' I said between gritted teeth. I pulled up a chair to sit and think. I stared at the freezer, heard Lissa march away on the old gray carpeting in the hall.

Her footsteps returned.

'Did Rob do it?' she asked.

I shook my head, no way of knowing.

'If so, why?'

'Please, let me think.'

Lissa pulled out a second chair and sat.

'Fingerprints,' I warned. She took a fresh Kleenex from her purse and wiped where she had touched the chair.

'It's a lab, obviously,' I said. 'Maybe the body is someone who tried to hurt him. Kill him.'

'Why cut it up?' Then, in a small but steady voice, Lissa added, 'You should try thinking like your brother.'

I straightened and walked around the room. Something nagged, some awareness fogged by more immediate shocks and events. I looked through the clutter of slides, trays, plastic bags, dishes, bottles of chemicals, and found a box of disposable synthetic lab gloves. Rob and I were allergic to latex. I pulled a pair from the box and slipped them over my hands.

Lissa handed me another Kleenex and I wiped the freezer handle. 'Take those with us,' I said. She stuffed them into the purse.

'Do you think someone's searched here already?' she asked. 'It looks that way.'

'Shh,' I said, hoping to kindle that elusive spark of memory. I tried to look at the room through other eyes than my own, similar eyes, windows to a similar brain. I opened the small refrigerator. Thirty or so petri dishes had been stacked on the upper shelves. I slipped the cover off one dish and sniffed the pinkish, pudding-like contents.

'Yogurt,' I said. Behind the dishes, in the back of the refrigerator, stood a small, apparently unopened cup of piña colada Yoplait, one of my favorites.

One of Rob's favorites.

We looked at each other.

'He was trying to learn how they doped his food,' I said. 'He was culturing samples from things he might have eaten, or things he knew had been tampered with.'

I closed the refrigerator and looked around with a slow

pirouette, as if to catch a shadow off guard. My head hurt with the effort of trying to remember.

A file box about two feet long had been tucked in the corner beside the freezer. I pried up the lid with one finger. Inside were stuffed a pair of gray slacks, a soft knit shirt, pointy-toed black Italian shoes, a black-leather belt, and on top of them, an eelskin wallet, some keys, and a pair of wire-rim sunglasses with small oval lenses.

I picked up the glasses. It all clicked. I opened the freezer and shoved my face and hands down into the cold mist.

'Don't!' Lissa said, her voice high. 'You'll drop a hair or something.' She must read mysteries, I thought. Could forensic specialists detect the difference between the hair from one twin and the hair from another? I strongly doubted it. Genetically, I *was* my brother.

I stared at the face, locked in a corpse's zazen, its frosted eyes indolent. The scalp, like a loose toupee, was covered with thick black hair.

'I've seen this guy before,' I said. I lowered the sunglasses over the face, working one temple piece past a stiff fold of scalp and hair. With the top of his head removed, it should have been difficult to recognize him, but I focused on the sharp nose, the lean features, the glasses. Bingo.

A glance and poke in the ribs between two fit, wiry men standing at a bus stop in Berkeley. Not far from the market on Claremont Avenue, before the incident of the little man with the spray bottle.

The corpse in the freezer was one of those two men, alive more than a month after Rob's murder in New York.

'Rob couldn't have done this,' I said, and dropped the lid. 'Somebody else is involved.'

'Banning?' Lissa asked.

I couldn't see Banning performing any kind of crude autopsy. 'I don't think so. He's a book, not a knife.'

It was very, very important that we get the hell out of the room, the building. With my gloves still on, I opened the door and looked up and down the hall. Empty. We stepped out and I closed and locked the door behind us.

We had to walk by the receptionist to reach the stairs. As we passed, she looked up and called out, 'Are you from Mr Escher's office? I have something for you.'

Numbers. She had been reading numbers to her mother.

'Shit!' I grunted. I grabbed Lissa's hand and pulled her down the hall.

The receptionist popped from her doorway like a cuckoo out of a clock. She carried a big cardboard box. 'Wait!' she shouted. 'Someone left this!'

I pushed Lissa into the stairwell. She screamed and half jumped, half stumbled down the first flight, fetching up hard against the cinder-block wall.

I was mostly shielded by the corner when the explosion threw a ragged hammer of flame and debris down the hall. Nails, bolts, jagged splinters of glass and scraps of metal ripped the backs of my shoes and my shirt and shotgunned through the large window. The shock wave kicked me down the steps and I rolled beside Lissa. Smoke filled the stairwell, black and harsh like burning rubber. The valise dug into my diaphragm. I could hardly move, could not breathe.

An alarm went off and the sprinkler system opened up.

Lissa dragged me down the next flight of stairs. She was strong. At the bottom, I recovered enough to grab a rail and get to my feet. I lurched after her into the twilight.

The sidewalk and street were covered with glass and shrapnel. We looked up to see flames and steam blow out of the second floor in hot, eager rhythm, like the breath of a panting dragon .

The skinny salesman in the tight herringbone suit leaned against Lissa's car as if he had been waiting patiently all this time. 'You all right?' he asked. He tossed a well-used toothpick onto the lawn and pulled a pistol from his coat pocket, as casually as if it were a sales contract. Pointed the gun at me, not Lissa, and dressed his weasel face in a cool smile. A blob of spittle glinted on his chin. We backed away. 'Goddamn it, just stay right here,' he said, facing me. 'You're making me lose some sales.'

I flinched at the crack of a gun. *That's it.* I clutched my stomach. Nothing. No blood, no pain. I looked up from my belt just in time to see the man drop back a couple of steps, as if punched. A small black hole opened in his suit.

He still had enough blood in his brain to try to aim, but when he realized what had happened, the gun was the last thing he cared about. His legs gave way and he hit the ground with a grunt. He lay there kicking and making rough husking sounds.

'Oh, Jesus, oh, *Mother*,' he said.

His face went empty but his foot kept twitching.

I had never seen a man die before.

Lissa was putting her pistol away in her purse when I spun around to look at her. Her face was white as a full moon in the light from the car dealership. Her blond hair and shoulders reflected orange from the puffing flames in the window above.

'Fucking amateur,' she said. 'Let's get out of here.' She looked furious, and she scared the last dregs of hell right out of me.

part two

BEN BRIDGER

CHAPTER TWENTY-SEVEN
El Cajon, California
June 6

I was a mess when Rob Cousins called.

The coffee machine had burned through a gasket and spouted hot water from all its joints. The house was a national park for dust bunnies. Our old white cat had skipped out to play pinochle with the coyotes and the coyotes had won. He had preferred Janie anyway.

About the only joy in my life was going to used bookstores, and most of my favorites had closed down to sell on-line. Janie haunted the kitchen so I rarely cooked. The lawn was so high I didn't dare push a mower through it. I spent mornings in such a goddamned funk I could hardly get out of bed.

Evenings were the best. At dusk, the summer heat dropped to a dull furnace glow and a sea breeze glided in through the canyons like angel's breath. The swamp cooler shut off at seven-thirty or eight and the house became quiet. Outside, the stars rose over the black hills and the crickets started their thermometer chirrups.

I was sixty-three years old. My book on guerrilla submarine operations in the Philippines was an inch deep and dead in the water. After all my research, I still couldn't find the story. I was tired of writing about brave young men fighting a good war sixty years ago. Writing seemed to be through with me.

I couldn't see any future, and that made the past useless.

I sat in my overstuffed chair with the cat-frayed leather arms and sipped a martini. I don't like gin, but Janie did. After the martini, I planned to have a beer, then, an hour later, a Scotch. I'm not suicidal, so I always stopped at three.

Three drinks sufficed to make me feel sad rather than frantic.

The windows were shiny black and the shaded lamp by the chair cast a warm glow over everything. By nine o'clock, grief was starting to feel almost comfortable.

My daughter lived in Minneapolis. Always a chameleon, she had acquired the distinctive Minne-sooa-tah Norwegian-Chippewa accent after six years and seldom called. My son in Baltimore couldn't even be at his mom's funeral. He had claimed to be sick with seafood poisoning. Maybe he was.

Janie and I had just sent off the kids' unclaimed stuff to Goodwill and started thinking about our second honeymoon when the stroke felled her. The hell with relationships. I would never again fall in love, never again trust a woman not to get up and walk into another room and die on me.

I would haunt the dark like the lone white barn owl I saw at night in the backyard, scissoring mice in the tall grass.

There is nothing sadder than a rugged son of a bitch minus his life partner.

The phone rang. Janie had bought one of the cordless kind but I kept an old Bakelite Ma Bell special by my chair. It had once been used by Admiral Halsey. I answered and a young man's voice said, 'Is this Ben Bridger? The author of *Uncommon Graves*?'

'It is,' I said, and pushed my chair forward so I could lower my voice to a dignified baritone. 'Who's this?'

'My name is Rob Cousins. I'm a biologist.'

'That's nice,' I said.

'I read your books when I was a kid. The old Ballantine and Bantam paperbacks. I think I may still have a few somewhere. They were great.'

'Thank you,' I said. 'What can I do for you?'

'You wrote a book with Beria's aide, the one who escaped getting shot, right?'

'Yeah.' *Waltzing with the Beast*, Houghton Mifflin, 1982. Four printings in hardback and a couple of paperback editions.

'Do you know a writer named Rudy Banning?'

'Used to outsell me four to one.'

'And now?'

'Can't get published to save his life. He's a crank.'

'Totally unreliable?'

'I guess he pulls up some papers at the National Archives now and then.'

'What do you think happened to him?'

'Not my business, Mister . . .'

'Cousins. I'm in El Cajon now. On Broadway, I think. If it's not too late, I'd like to bring some dinner and talk with you.'

Little warning bells. 'It *is* late,' I said. 'How do you know I haven't had dinner?'

'I don't. I haven't eaten since breakfast, though. I could bring dessert.'

'Cheesecake?'

'Sure.'

'What do you want to know, Mr Cousins?'

'I have to confirm some things Rudy Banning told me. They could be important . . . to me. Also, to a historian like you.'

If he was one of Banning's little goose-stepping admirers, if he came over with a Luger or a Mauser, I could tick him off with the lyric about Hitler's lone testicle, and he'd freak and blow my brains out. That wouldn't be a bad way to go. Quick, with my name in the paper. The Laphroaig was getting low, anyway.

'I actually haven't had dinner,' I said.

'I'm near a Vietnamese takeout. What can I get for you?'

'Some of those things like egg rolls or lumpia,' I said. 'Pho, with tendon and sausage and cooked beef. Lots of basil and jalapeño slices. Forget the bean sprouts.'

I gave him directions to the house.

Outside, I heard the big barn owl hunting in the tall grass, wings whispering like little geishas.

Cousins arrived about an hour later and we ate on the back

porch, with the yellow bug lights on. He was a slightly built fellow, not quite thirty, handsome, mousy brown hair thinning at the temples, but it looked good on him. Pale, a little sickly, his forehead damp, but no goose-stepper. Eyes intense and dark green, the left eyelid angled down a little, speech quick, hands with long fingers like a piano player's.

'What do you know about Lydia Timashuk?' he asked after I had finished my Sara Lee cheesecake.

'Timashuk,' I said. 'Caught Stalin's ear in the thirties. Said all the best scientists and doctors in the Soviet Union should work together to make Comrade Stalin live longer. Stalin liked that, but Timashuk was a fraud. She informed on the Jewish doctors in 1952. Most of them were shot.'

Cousins nodded and smiled. I had the feeling I had passed the first test. 'She *was* a fraud. But have you ever heard of a researcher named Golokhov? Maxim Golokhov?'

'Maxim Gorky, yes. Golokhov, no.'

'How about a project called Silk? Started before the war.'

I knew which war he meant. 'No . . . Unless it was one of the projects to make artificial silk. For parachutes and stuff.'

'Anything involving Stalin, research on mind control, Lake Baikal, and Irkutsk University? Starting in the 1920s?'

'Nope. But that's hardly authoritative. They're still uncovering tons of paper every month over there, files on this or that. Not as organized as Nazi files, but every bit as damning. Stalin was some piece of work.'

'What can you tell me about Rudy Banning?'

'He was the best.'

Cousins smiled. 'That's what he says.'

'You're working with him?'

'I don't know what the relationship is, exactly.'

Cousins seemed nervous but stable. The crickets had fallen silent. The house timbers creaked as they shrank. I thought I heard footsteps in the kitchen. I often hear footsteps in the kitchen at that time of night.

It was good to have somebody to talk to.

'Rudy's books were pretty good once,' I said. 'He had a knack for sniffing out rare documents. But something happens after you dig into the thousandth official archive of intolerable brutality. Spiritual evil, as they say. But it's not demons, it's flesh-and-blood people doing the unimaginable, then recording it like you and I balance our checkbooks. You come to mistrust everyone, and finally the paranoia kicks in. It can always happen again, you know. Ordinary people are out there waiting for the orgy to start. They lick their lips, waiting for the hate to flow. You study the twentieth century long enough, you want to pack a gun.'

I stretched out my arms and flicked off a mosquito. The neighbors had a stagnant koi pond about three hundred yards down the road, and old folks have thin skin. 'Anyway,' I said, reaching my point, 'Banning is possessed by the specter of Adolf Hitler. Figuratively speaking.'

'I think he'd agree with you,' Cousins said. He had brought in a blue backpack stuffed full. He reached into it.

I looked at the backpack with vague longing, but I already knew he wasn't the type to put an end to my troubles. He removed not a Luger but a picture book, *Blondi: Dog of Destiny*. I had seen it before – in the bargain bin of Wahrenbrock's in San Diego, marked down to twenty-five cents.

'This is what Silk did to Banning,' Cousins said. 'He doesn't know how crazy he actually is. Neither do I.'

I read the publisher's address. 'White Truth Press, Ojai, California. UFO abductees and would-be-Aryans. Pitiful.'

'But what I'm after is serious,' Cousins said. 'Banning found some files in the National Archives in the 1990s, and when he read about my research in a magazine, he got in touch with me. His material was interesting, so I went to see him. Ever since, a lot of peculiar stuff has been happening.'

I stared at him for a few seconds, long enough to make him feel uncomfortable.

'Look,' I said. 'I've read *The Odessa File*. I wish I had written it, this house would be a lot nicer.' *And maybe I could have gotten better medical care for Janie.* 'But I'm not much for Nazi conspiracies. I don't believe in trivializing real horror with skinhead fantasies.'

Cousins looked dismayed, but he was resilient. He said, 'It's not Nazis and it's not just Communists. It's biologists, some of the smartest people in the world. Pioneers, in their way. And it's really important to me, Mr Bridger.'

'Ben,' I said.

'I need confirmation. That's all I'm asking. A little help from someone who taught me history when I was a kid.'

He was so sincere, and his voice so level. I didn't want to be in the house alone. The kitchen was definitely haunted. Maybe I was the crazy one here. Besides, Cousins reminded me of my son. I really missed my son.

'Okay,' I said with a sigh. 'We got half an hour, then it's my bedtime.'

Cousins told me he was doing research on life extension – indefinite life span. He had published a few papers and had contracts with two pharmaceutical companies to develop drugs that replenished skin collagen. It sounded legitimate. Biology is sexy, I hear.

Then Rudy Banning came into his life. Banning sent Cousins a letter asking if he had heard about research conducted in the Soviet Union in the 1930s.

'I wrote Banning and asked him what he knew. He said that scientists in Russia had stumbled onto a kind of human immortality, using substances extracted from primitive organisms. Coincidentally, they discovered some very effective methods of controlling human behavior. All this before we had more than an inkling about DNA and genes.'

That was too large to swallow all at once. I took a chunk and chewed it: 'How could immortality lead to mind control?' I asked.

'Let's concentrate on mind control,' Cousins said. 'Bacteria are wonderful little factories. They can make almost any substance you program them to. And you program them by providing them with the appropriate genes. In the early 1930s, at Irkutsk University, a biologist named Maxim Golokhov was studying huge, primitive, single-celled organisms he had found in Lake Baikal. To his astonishment, he discovered that the big cells had recruited an unknown type of bacteria to help create a primordial immune system. Even more amazing, Golokhov discovered that the system was *adaptive* – ingenious and flexible. The bacteria sensed the presence of invading organisms and made negative peptide molds that precisely matched a target molecule, immobilizing and killing the invader.'

My eyes must have looked sleepy. Cousins's response was to talk faster and wave his hands.

'But when their work was finished and they cleaned up the leftovers, these same bacteria could also make molds of the molds, re-creating a positive with the same qualities as the original. They could reverse-engineer almost any organic substance and encode a gene to reproduce it. Theoretically, that was fantastic – Nobel prize material. But Golokhov was more interested in surviving in his own harsh political world – neutralizing the forces that were targeting him and his wife. If he wanted to make something useful to the human monsters of his time, he had to think of a practical application for his discovery. He came up with an astonishing scheme . . . something really dreadful. He decided he would reprogram bacteria commonly found in humans. His first problem was to transfer the necessary genes. He used phages –'

I asked what 'phages' were.

'Viruses that attack only bacteria.'

'Make them sneeze?' I asked.

Cousins did not smile. This was his stuff, his meat and drink, and it wasn't funny. 'Some phages ferry host genes from one bacteria to another. Golokhov infected *E. coli* –'

'Like in the wells out here?' I asked.

Cousins did not enjoy being interrupted. 'Ordinary gut bacteria. Yeah, sometimes they're a sign of sewer pollution. Using phages, Golokhov gave the *E. coli* new genes reverse-engineered from psychotropic chemicals in hallucinogenic mushrooms. He sprayed the altered bacteria on vegetables and served them raw to student volunteers. About a week later, the students got high. They stayed high for months.'

'So in the sixties he moved to California and turned into Timothy Leary,' I said.

This time Cousins gave me a weak and tolerant smirk, about what my crack deserved. In fact, so far, he had my attention. 'Before we go any farther, I'd like to see what kind of documents you have. No sense wasting our time if Banning's put together a farrago.'

'I beg your pardon?' Cousins said.

'Just show me your stuff.'

He pulled out three fat envelopes. With all the deliberation of a young stripper feeling the shys, he spread their contents on the wrought-iron patio table beside a citronella candle.

The bug lights gave everything a jaundiced glow.

I read a fair amount of Russian. It took me about ten minutes to come wide-awake. The imprimaturs and typewriter fonts, the stamps and signatures (I saw 'Beria' about thirty times in as many pages), all looked very, very correct. I had never known Banning to fake documents, nor had anybody else, to my knowledge. It was the conclusions he had been drawing since the early 1990s that sank his career, not the validity of his sources.

'Where did he say he got these?' I asked.

'Actually, we've both been digging in old archives,' Cousins said. 'I went to Irkutsk last year.'

'So . . . it isn't just Banning, it's you, too?'

He nodded nervously.

'A lot of stuff from Irkutsk University,' I said.

'They're opening old files,' Cousins said. 'Glasnost still lives.'

'All right. I see the names Golokhov and Beria on a whole

bunch of documents having to do with a secret research project. What's the context?'

'Golokhov started off as an idealist, like so many of us. But he and his fiancée were Jewish. There was trouble, we don't know what kind exactly. They were going to be arrested and deported even farther east. In 1934, Golokhov approached Beria, the future head of the NKVD, the Soviet secret police, and told him what he had learned. Beria saw it as his ticket to bigger things.' Cousins pulled out a copy of a letter requesting that meeting. 'Beria handed the matter up to Stalin a week later. Golokhov made his pitch and showed Stalin some movies. Comrade Stalin financed Silk right then and there, and Beria gave it a cover story, hiding it behind a program to discover –'

'How to synthesize silk.'

'Yeah. The operation had two components. First, Golokhov had to alter gut bacteria to accept genes from his phages. He gave them the equivalent of standard electrical outlets that new genes could plug into. Then, he had to make sure everyone – and I do mean *everyone* – had the new bacteria in their bodies. Silk began with Golokhov releasing altered *E. coli* into the general population. There are lots of ways to do that – spraying fruits and vegetables, in the air, doorknobs, money, clothing . . . handshakes. Bird droppings. Even animal feed. No doubt he had the assistance of agents who thought they were engaging in some sort of Communist subversion. Some might have even guessed at germ warfare.'

'When was that?'

'The first phase started in 1935. Golokhov began experimental operations first in Russia, then in Germany, Japan, and China. He wanted to create a firm foundation for later plans. Some populations took up the new coliforms quicker than others, especially where sanitation was spotty. The altered coliforms had spread across Russia by 1939, I would guess, and worldwide by the end of the Second World War.'

'We're born with them, now?'

'No, but we acquire them a short time later from our parents, animals, the environment,' Cousins said. 'You have to understand – Golokhov chose hardy strains likely to dominate. Now, they're all over the Earth. Every one of us carries bacteria that can be programmed from outside. Programmed to make chemicals that change how we think.'

'Like a bomb in two parts,' I said. 'We carry one half, they carry the other.'

'Exactly,' Cousins said.

'Why stay in Irkutsk? Why not just move straight to Moscow?'

'It was isolated. It was his home. And besides, Irkutsk was on the main rail line to Siberia,' Cousins said. 'Beria supplied the lab with trainloads of political prisoners. Golokhov picked out those who were mentally ill, took samples of blood and lymph, stomach fluids, chyme, and so on. After they were shot, he ground up their brains. Using all his samples, he isolated peptides and enzymes and other fractions he suspected could alter human behavior, and fed them to his reverse-engineering bacteria. The bacteria were then programmed to induce a variety of psychotic states.'

By eleven-thirty, after I had ventured into the kitchen twice to make coffee and didn't even think about Janie, we had worked our way up to Lydia Timashuk and the Doctors' Plot of 1952, followed by the 'expatriation' of two million Jews to Siberia, then the death – some called it murder – of old Joe Stalin. I was more than hooked, and we hadn't reached the end of 1953.

It was the biggest thing I had ever encountered in all my days of doing history. The documentation was exquisite – copy after copy of state papers, memos, letters. There must have been quite a hemorrhage from the old University of Irkutsk.

And it was pure nightmare.

'No wonder Banning went cuckoo,' I said. 'Makes me sick just thinking about it.'

'It gets worse,' Cousins said. 'By the late nineteen thirties, Golokhov had established centers in Moscow, Paris, and London. He even managed to get around Lysenko's destruction of genetics in Russia. Beria probably protected him, and I guess he knew where to be successful, and where to just shut up. By 1950, it's possible he was conducting secret research in the United States. There are five towns across the continental U.S. where he may have set up operations. I've been to one of them, in the hills east of Livermore.

'In 1953, Rudy thinks Golokhov opened a laboratory in Manhattan, under the guise of an international organization trying to create vaccines for polio, malaria, and dengue fever.'

I'd had dengue – we called it breakbone fever – in Laos in 1970. I had nearly died and couldn't remember most of those weeks. 'False front?'

Cousins nodded. 'They were creating Manhattan Candidates, all over the U.S.'

'Jesus,' I said. I felt goose bumps go up my arms. 'And because we all have the altered germs . . . we're all potential Manhattan Candidates?'

Cousins nodded. 'My guess is that in the thirties and forties, only about a third the people in the world could be reliably programmed by Silk. Their operations were pretty fragmented. Thank God for that. Orwell might never have finished *1984*.'

I let out a whoosh of breath. 'Why just a third?' I asked.

'Because we're all custom built. We don't use our hormones, enzymes, peptides, neurotransmitters, all the necessary chemicals in our bodies and brains, quite the same way. That puts a roadblock in the path of creating new operatives. But I'm sure they've refined their techniques. My guess is they now have eighty or ninety, possibly even one hundred per cent success, especially if they choose their people carefully. And of course it all depends on the dose you can deliver. When you start an operation, you send three or four handpicked people, with the necessary supplies, into the target area. They lay down some phages in nearby supermarkets, or deliver them right to the home, and wait a couple of days. How often do salesmen come knocking? Seventh Day Adventists?'

'Not very often, where I live,' I said. But I took his point.

'How safe are the fresh vegetables in supermarkets?' he asked.

I cocked my head. 'You could run this sort of thing on a shoestring. Free labor, free resources, skim off the top. Jee . . . zusss. What about the Internet?'

'I think you see the problem,' Cousins said.

At twelve-thirty, I asked Cousins to stay over and we'd continue later in the morning. He nervously declined.

'I don't want to put you in any danger,' he said. 'I'm a Jonah, you know.'

He piled together the papers, stuck them in their envelopes, and slid the envelopes into the blue backpack. 'I have a place to stay. I'll be safe,' he said. 'I'll call you tomorrow. Please don't think I'm being paranoid.'

'Oh, no,' I said. 'Paranoid' was not the word.

'But I *would* like your opinion.' He was like a jumpy doe with a newborn fawn. 'Is this stuff legit? Banning isn't crazy?'

'It looks promising,' I said.

'I'm going to Manhattan soon to visit an old building,' Cousins said. 'It may have been Golokhov's main lab in the fifties. I'm looking for proof – and for samples to test. Would you like to come along?'

That shook me. I had learned to prefer a desktop to the field. I said I'd give it some thought.

'There's one more thing,' he said. 'You have a VCR?'

'Yeah. Janie – my wife – loved movies.'

'Seeing is believing, right?' He reached into the backpack and handed me a videocassette. 'From Russia,' he said. 'From Irkutsk. We can talk about it tomorrow.'

After Cousins left, I ignored my fatigue and plugged the tape into our VCR. The tape jumped a lot. I doubted very much that it was the original. Russians use the SECAM video system. We use NTSC.

With my rusty grasp of Russian, I translated the white Cyrillic letters flashing over the screen.

University of Irkutsk
New Student Inquiry for Truth and Justice, Anthology Number
5, Secret Indoctrination Camp Films, 1935–1950.

It was one in the morning, and as the grainy old films played, the living room filled with ghosts.

A woman in the long black dress stood smiling on the prow of a yacht, mist shrouding the lake behind her. Mrs Golokhova? She gave the photographer a somber little wave, then turned left, squinting into the sun.

Next came a wedding in an industrial-looking warehouse surrounded by hundreds of men in uniform. Mr Golokhov (I presumed) and his new bride stood under crossed rifles with mounted bayonets and were toasted by a small, dapper man drinking champagne from a lab beaker. Quick shot of Joe Stalin, his smile frozen, turning this way, then that, as if looking for escape from the jolly crowds.

The flesh on my neck started to crawl.

A lean, handsome man with aristocratic features, a short sharp nose, and thin but very black hair, stood over a bathtub and smiled awkwardly into the lens. Swift cut to an emaciated, naked little man walking in circles around a small cell, then jumping up and down, genitals flopping, shaking out his hands and smiling broadly. The aristocratic man watched and directed the naked man, taking notes in a little black book with that serious and awkward expression people wore in the 1930s when they knew they were being put on film.

The film had not been well preserved. There were scratches and blotches, and in the hiss of the vacant sound track could easily be heard the aching whispers of the dead.

I watched Mrs Golokhova and her husband relaxing at play, or hard at work, studying the details of architectural drawings, preparing their empire in the deadly and unlikely world of prewar Soviet Russia.

Then, there were no more scenes of Mrs Golokhova. Just Maxim, looking older and more serious. Supervising workmen on a brick blockhouse, standing by a steaming hot spring, surveying pools filled with milky-looking fluid stirred with long paddles held by hollow-eyed women in nondescript uniforms. Golokhov's clothes changed little with the years, but his eyes became more vague, his features more drawn.

Long lines of haggard prisoners in shabby street clothes, some carrying tattered bags filled with their worldly goods, stood in a train yard, being examined by dour guards in cinematic quick time.

Sudden cut to mounds of heads in big tin basins outside a wooden lab building, jaws slack, tongues protruding, hair matted with blood, waiting to be processed.

That was not the worst of it.

The next title card read,

CITY OF DOG MOTHERS
1938–1939

I could not turn away. I watched dozens of whistling men, marching about, lips puckered and cheeks puffing in cheerful, silent tunes. Their methodic executioners walked down the streets like marionettes, clutching pistols at the end of stiff, straight arms. The arms jerked up with each methodical shot.

I watched starving women clasping fat, squirming puppies to their shriveled bosoms, smiling for the photographer.

The last few seconds of film showed Lavrenti Beria strutting up and down the cobbled streets. He waved at the lifeless buildings, grinned proudly at the camera, nudged a woman's headless corpse with his boot, then lifted a hand in victorious thumbs-up.

Happy, happy man.

As I shut off the tape, I wondered about the photographers. How long had these horrors stuck in their minds like dirty pins and needles? I vowed I would never read a history book again.

I fell asleep on the couch wrapped in Janie's last afghan.

And woke less than two hours later. Rolled off the couch and made a sound I had not heard come from my mouth in over sixty years, the frightened whine of a child. I could not stand being human. My skin was too filthy to wear. I moaned as I pissed, handling myself, thinking that these organs of generation had given rise to children not so different from the shadows on the old films. I washed my hands and face over and over, then took a shower. The hot water did a little trick for a few minutes, lulling me into warm blankness, but when I toweled myself dry, standing on the thin, ragged bathroom rug, the sense of oppression rushed back like a cloud shadow.

I walked around the house with my privates hidden by the towel and my hair sticking up like a grizzled Kewpie doll. I couldn't get the pictures out of my head. I cursed Rob Cousins.

Then I asked myself, what if it was all a ripe, royal fake? Assembled from old files, altered copies of documents, forgeries, sure, that was it, wasn't it?

Much easier to accept than a world controlled by monsters.

Rob Cousins had pulled a fast one on old, gullible Ben Bridger, setting me up for another crazy Rudy Banning book, this one guaranteed to be a huge best seller – and all of it a lie.

But I knew better.

The sun was coming up over the hills. It was going to be a bright, pretty day.

Using some of my old mental tricks, learned back in Vietnam and Laos, I had 'photographed' a couple of the documents Cousins had shown me, and I wanted advice on names and dates. I got on the Internet and sent a coded inquiry to five of my friends. They had all served, some in the CIA, some, like

181

me, in Naval Intelligence. We were all retired and we had set up a kind of Old Boy's Internet Tom-Tom club to alert each other to stuff, mostly new history books and web sites with good photos of naked ladies.

Some of the guys on the Tom-Tom were pretty old – they had trained and run the rest of us – and they had been around back in 1953.

I had responses in a couple of hours. Two drew blanks. Two said they couldn't tell me anything and their messages winkled away before my eyes. Clever trick. One didn't reply.

I can never leave a wasp nest well enough alone. What Cousins had shown me was ugly beyond measure, and frightening; it was also the most important historical revelation of my life.

I was just a stupid, lonely old man who wanted to be important again.

I dressed, poured my fourth cup of coffee and stood in the kitchen, trying to think what would be the best course to follow, when I heard trucks and cars turn up the long concrete driveway. I opened the front door to the sun and heat, and saw three white Tahoes and two San Diego County Sheriff Crown Victorias. Guys in black, dressed in bulletproofs and combat helmets, poured out of the trucks with assault weapons and automatic pistols in plain view, safeties off and fingers resting on the trigger guards.

The deputies stayed in their cars, heads bobbing, mikes pressed close to their mouths. They seemed confused.

I pushed open the screen door and the guys in black assumed the necessary positions to turn me into hamburger. I had to admire the choreography, but thought it a tad ironic that just as I had a reason to live, this was going down.

I slowly stooped over and placed my cup of coffee on the ground, then held out my hands with all fingers showing. I had been busted for possession upon returning stateside in 1973. I knew the drill.

'Good morning,' I said.

'DEA,' said the lead guy. 'We have a federal warrant to search the domicile of Benjamin Bridger.'

'That's me. What are you looking for?' I asked. 'Maybe I can save you some time.'

The man gave me the same hard stare I had once given the Pathet Lao. He flashed papers as his team moved into my house, doing their dance of dash, take cover, inspect, present weapons, move in, all very Foxtrot Tango Delta. I would have been impressed if my blood hadn't taken a chill.

'Anybody inside?' he asked.

'Just me. My wife died –'

'Shut up,' he said.

Agents lifted two happy beagles from the back of one truck. The dogs had their own little black bulletproof vests. They lolled their tongues and whined while their boss turned the handle on my garden spigot and filled two red plastic bowls marked 'DEA.' The dogs lapped eagerly, spun about, and went to work.

They were looking for cocaine, heroin, marijuana. Whatever. The sheriff's deputies were looking for child porn. They had a warrant, too, though they were surprised and a little awed by the presence of the feds.

Not one of them was polite.

CHAPTER TWENTY-EIGHT
San Diego/El Cajon
June 10–11

My sense of irony doesn't run very deep.

I was in the Metropolitan Correctional Center in downtown San Diego for three days before all the charges were dropped. No explanation, and nobody apologized.

My lawyer, a large woman in a dark green suit, cost me a good half of my savings, money from Janie's retirement account that I had not wanted to violate. She explained that she had me out on a writ of habeas corpus but there wasn't going to be any case. Informants had waffled, sources had literally gone south, a bunch of solid leads had turned into string cheese rather than a rope, and they can't hang you with string cheese.

I was lucky they hadn't seized everything I owned. The county still had my computer. They could take weeks to analyze what I had peeped at on the World Wide Web.

I had overnight become a suspected drug dealer and child molester. My neighbors had probably picked up the story, and the local press, too. Nobody is careful with reputations these days, especially the reputation of an ex-Marine, a Vietnam vet, retired on disability and probably addled with Agent Orange. Who knows how many kids he bayoneted?

I felt filthy and guilty without having broken a single law.

I went home and stared in numb admiration at the mess they had made. Walls had been kicked in, holes punched in the ceiling, and old brown insulation pulled down. Family photos had been dumped in the living room and walked over with dusty boots. All my electronic equipment – VCR, old Kenwood stereo, Sony Trinitron, Akai tape deck, CD player – was piled by the door, cases roughly unscrewed and pulled back.

The videotape was gone.

They had even taken a backhoe, dug up my fiberglass septic tank, and bashed it open. The whole property smelled of sun-ripened shit. Yellow police tape lay in curls along the drive and all around the house.

At least they had locked the doors when they were done.

I picked up broken furniture and a shattered toilet in the front yard and piled it in the garage to sort out later.

They hadn't even left me a pot to piss in.

Janie had made me sell my Colt and my shotgun and all my knives years ago. I was grateful for that. A: I had gotten some money for them and B: I hadn't posed an immediate threat to the guys in armor and jackboots. I could have died.

Imagine my surprise when I found a Smith & Wesson thirty-ought-six planted conspicuously on top of a stack of four of my books. My own books, in hardcover, author's copies, sitting in the middle of my small office. Something I would be sure to look for.

The rest of my library had been dragged from the shelves and tossed around the room.

I tried to make sense of the pistol. It was old. Its grip was wrapped in what looked like white medical tape, gone gray with use. Someone had left it behind, just in case I might need it. I considered calling the sheriff's department, then decided that doing anything without a good think was sure to be counterproductive.

I had been staring at that damned gun for maybe five minutes when the first phone call came. I picked up but heard only a click, then a long and faraway silence. One of those operations, I assumed, that computer-dials a hundred folks at once but can only respond to ten or fifteen.

The second call was from Janie. A cloud seemed to drift over and the house got darker. She asked how I was doing.

'Not too well,' I said, and began to cry, hearing her voice, missing her so and feeling utterly and devastatingly useless, empty as a discarded doll.

Janie's words began to fill me up.

I took a pee in the side yard and catnapped in the chair. The sea breezes came and went, then the stars. The canyon air was still and I heard the owl in the backyard but couldn't see it. Finally, I pulled the slashed queen-size mattress outside, shoved it onto the stiff high grass, flung a sheet over it, and lay down.

The next morning, I sat on the front porch again, this time with a beer in one hand and the tape-wrapped Smith & Wesson in the other. I was entertaining the notion of checking out of this shitty old motel called life. I could be with Janie in the flash of a muzzle.

I didn't think about Rob Cousins until he turned up at eight with another man. I recognized Banning from his dust-jacket photos, foppishly handsome. They cast long shadows as they walked up the driveway.

'You all right, Ben?' Cousins asked.

Banning stepped over a strip of yellow police tape and waved at me like a professor on holiday.

My first thought, when I saw them, was that Cousins had abandoned me just like my real son. I felt the heat build. 'Fuck you,' I said. 'You lied. You set me up. Where were you when they busted me?'

'I believe you've been tagged,' Banning said with a prissy British accent. He didn't come any closer.

'Did you bring dinner?' I asked. 'Or was that all a setup, so you could plant some coke?'

Cousins spoke to me as if I was a child. 'Did they find any coke?' he asked.

'Would I be here?' I played with the pistol, sighted along the barrel, and pointed it in their general direction, to show them how useful I could be. 'No,' I said. 'But not for lack of trying.'

'What a mess,' Cousins said. 'You must be really angry.'

'I roll with the punches,' I said.

'We should get you out of here,' Banning said.

'Why would I want to go anywhere with a couple of fuckheads?'

'Who called you?' Cousins asked, dripping reason and calm.

I aimed the pistol straight at him. Janie had explained a lot, how I had been set up, how I was too old to get respect. She wanted to come back and help me put my life together, but Cousins wouldn't let her. Banning was probably in on it, too.

Cousins stood close enough I could blow a hole in his chest the size of my fist. He was sweating like a stuck pig. 'I'm going to do something a little odd now,' he said. 'I'm going to read you some numbers and see if you remember them.' He took out a small strip of paper like a grocery receipt.

'Why?' I asked. I didn't know the pull on the Smith &

Wesson. It might go off with a tap. I jerked the pistol right and squeezed for practice. The gunshot sent Banning running like a rabbit.

Short, light pull, but not hair-trigger.

Cousins flinched but held his ground. 'Seven five two four,' he read from the paper.

'Yeah,' I said. 'Now spin the dial on the old combo lock right two turns –' I stopped babbling. His number made sense. It was perfectly reasonable. 'Okay.' I listened.

'Repeat it back to me.'

'Seven five two four.'

'Three seven eight one. Again, repeat it back to me.'

'Three seven eight one.'

'And the *last* one, I promise, two six nine eight.'

'Two six nine eight.'

'Dear old Ben, I have some news,' Rob said. 'Shall we visit Doctor Seuss?'

I cringed at a flash of green that seemed to pass right over my head.

'How do you feel now?'

'All right,' I said, and lowered the pistol.

'What color did you see?'

'Green.' I sniffed the air. 'Jesus,' I said. 'Who cut the cheese?' I tried to place the stink. Bodies and rotting vegetation, like a day-old battleground upcountry.

Banning retraced his steps up the driveway on short, mincing legs. He wrinkled his nose. 'They really got you,' he said.

'Who?'

I felt calm but very sad. The phone call from Janie had been a dream. I started to cry and Cousins put his arm around my shoulder. He took the gun and passed it to Banning, who dangled it from two fingers like a dead rat.

'That's better,' Cousins said. 'Let's pack up and get you the hell out of here. It isn't safe.'

'What's going on?' I asked. My nose was running and sweat

beaded off my chin and soaked my shirt. My stomach and bowels were in a riot. 'Christ, I need a shower.'

'There really isn't time,' Banning said.

We picked through the mess and stuffed a travel bag with clothes. I scooped some pictures into a grocery sack and filled a box with my favorite books. Banning took a sledge from the garage and smashed the Smith & Wesson. We didn't want to be caught with a cop's drop piece, probably stolen and unregistered.

Then we left the house, the ghost, twenty years of memories, my whole goddamned life, and I haven't been back since.

CHAPTER TWENTY-NINE
San Diego/Los Angeles

'I wanted to thank you for confirming I'm an honest man,' Banning said. Cousins rode shotgun and I sat in the backseat of Banning's beat-up Plymouth with my boxes. The trunk was latched with baling wire and he thought it might spring open.

'I didn't state anything of the kind,' I said.

We slowed in the commute heading north on 5. There was some chance we'd be pulled over at the San Onofre checkpoint, but we had to get to LA to meet some people Cousins knew and there's no quick way around *la Migra*. We were all white, I was no longer a suspect. We took the chance.

They did pull us out of the line at the checkpoint. They searched the car and gave us the long stare. We were fugitives from something or somebody, they could see it in our eyes. Cousins talked pleasantly. They had nothing on us, so they let us go.

I hate the law.

*   *   *

I snoozed most of the way to LA. We were deep in Laurel Canyon when I awoke. Banning drove up a twisting private road to the ridgeline. Late in the afternoon, the tree-filled hollows were sunk in shadow. Quail darted across the cracked asphalt behind us. The air blew sweet with eucalyptus and sage.

Banning stopped the car before a heavy steel gate. Cousins got out and spoke a few words into a box on a long, curving pole.

'Our safe house,' Cousins explained, climbing back in and slamming the car door. 'This will take a minute. Lots of security to disarm.'

I was alert after my long nap. Now seemed the time, before we had to deal with anyone new. I could not explain my behavior back in El Cajon. I wanted to apologize, but that wasn't appropriate, either. Maybe *they* were the ones who should apologize.

'What happened to me?' I asked.

Cousins looked over his shoulder. 'Jail cuisine,' he said. 'Someone doped your food when you were in the Metropolitan Correctional Center. They wanted you to kill Rudy and me. That's why they left the gun in your house.'

It seemed suddenly hard to breathe, sitting in the back seat, even with the windows rolled down. 'Thanks for warning me,' I said.

'Did you get a phone call from someone you love?' Cousins asked.

'Yeah,' I said.

'Your dead wife?'

'Yeah . . .'

Cousins turned his focus on me like a teacher with a problem pupil. 'I'm not sure who actually called, or who doped your food in the jail,' he said. 'We suspect there are a number of agents in California, and elsewhere, working to intimidate us or kill us.'

'So why didn't I shoot you?'

'Do you remember, you answered once and got an empty line?'

'Yeah.'

'That was me,' Cousins said. 'The night before, when I brought dinner and dessert, I sprayed some bacteria on your cheesecake, harmless, but infected by my own special phages. I hoped they would give you at least partial immunity against later attacks.'

'Jesus H. Christ,' I said. I folded my arms over my stomach and felt like curling up and pulling a blanket over my head.

'Ideally, I would have given them forty-eight hours,' Cousins said, so matter-of-factly my fists clenched. I had to hold back from striking him. 'By the time you were in jail, you were less than half-protected. When I learned you had been released, I phoned until I caught you at home. You were suggestible, but you weren't their zombie yet, so I turned the tables. I ran you, in a way – gave you a list of numbers and asked you to describe the colors each one evoked. Then I told you this would take priority over everything else.'

'You called me first, made me jump through some hoops – and I forgot all about it?'

Cousins nodded. He didn't seem to find any of this very funny, or even unusual. I had to put a shine on this shit and make it pretty. 'You vaccinated me against mind control. Is that it?'

'Mostly,' Cousins said. 'It still needs work.'

'And that stopped me from shooting you?'

'It was a little dicey,' Banning said with a sniff. He took out a handkerchief and blew his nose.

'You *did* set me up. I was a guinea pig.'

'We're all guinea pigs,' Cousins said. 'It was for your own protection, and ours, too. We don't know what Silk is capable of, the size of their operations now, but at one time they had thousands of agents around the world.'

I rubbed the door handle, seriously considering just getting out and walking away. But Cousins threw his arm over the back of the seat. His eyes tracked my arm to the door, and he looked straight at me and shook his head.

I released my grip on the handle. 'Tell me again, what we're doing here,' I said.

'Let's wait till we get to the house,' Cousins said. 'Tammy's laying out dinner. *Clean* food.'

'It's quite a story,' Banning said.

The gate swung open. In the road ahead, a spiked caltrops rolled into its iron sheath.

'All clear,' Cousins said with a sigh.

Up the long drive, over a cattle barricade with big green transformer boxes on either side, past video cameras mounted on tall steel poles, through a no-man's land surrounded by barbed wire, Banning drove the old Plymouth as if it were a limousine carrying heads of state.

A dark, tubby, cheerful-looking fellow met us at the Spanish-style double door, under the deep overhang of the front porch. Cousins introduced me to Joseph Marquez, our host. He wore silk pajama bottoms over a tight potbelly, had a thick-pelted chest and arms, a flowing Maharishi beard, and long, curly, jet-black hair topped by a little embroidered yarmulke. He looked a lot like Jerry Garcia. His eyes were small, amber, and shrewd, and he had expressive lips and perfect teeth.

Marquez circled suspiciously. 'You check him over?'

'He's okay,' Cousins said. Marquez scowled and repeated my name, enunciating every syllable, until I wanted to curse. Then he lifted his arms in the air and shook them like a preacher getting his daily revelation.

'Damn, I *know* you. I've read your books. *Uncommon Graves*, right? Shit, a veteran! The final member of the team. Munitions, *all right*! Cambodia? Special Forces?'

I stared around the room with a new sense of dread.

'Welcome to the inner sanctum! Everyone's safe here. Tammy's laying out a feast.'

Marquez was a director and producer who hadn't made a movie in over fifteen years. Still, he had invested wisely. His beautiful house covered three acres of leveled ridgeline above Mulholland and looked out over Laurel Canyon.

I gathered quickly that Marquez had given Cousins some money and let him set up a laboratory in the basement. But there was something else in the mix. A squib in my éclair, as it were.

Tammy joined us in the limestone-walled foyer. She was young, in her late teens or early twenties, with chocolate skin, high forehead, pulled-back Titian hair, broad hips, a slight tummy, and ample breasts. I hadn't seen her like outside of *Playboy*. She wore silk pajama bottoms and a bikini top that hid nada, and she hugged us all with childlike innocence and asked if we preferred basmati or wild rice.

'We're having a curry,' she explained, favoring Cousins with a smile. 'Joe loves curry.'

'Kills germs,' Marquez said with a little-boy grin.

He enjoyed my expression as I watched Tammy depart.

'No movies in development,' he said, 'but there's a son and heir tucked inside that *amazing* incubator.'

'Stop it,' Tammy called back.

'She's half-French and half-Brazilian. I'm half-Irish and half-Spanish, a *marrano*. Wow, huh? A month and a half along. How about a tour?'

'Maybe they'd like to clean up first,' Tammy suggested from two rooms away.

'That'd be good,' Cousins said.

I washed off the grime of our trip in a marble-walled shower bigger than my whole bathroom in El Cajon. Two rows of adjustable nozzles switched on as I turned, stinging hot needles of water causing such a good pain I had to groan out loud. I could have stayed in there for days.

As I switched off the water, I heard a knock on the bathroom door. Cousins tossed a small plastic bottle of pinkish cream over the top of the cloudy glass enclosure. I caught it after a slippery fumble.

'Rub this on your skin when you're done,' he said.

'What is it?'

'Part of being immunized,' he said. 'Lanolin and my own special brew.'

I sniffed the cream as I dried myself. Smelled like fresh bread. I rubbed it on my arms and calves, then on the back of my neck, wherever my skin felt dry and stretched. I got dressed and joined Cousins, Banning, and Marquez in the living room.

Tammy took our drink orders as we walked through the stainless-steel, copper, and granite kitchen. Overflowing flagons of India Pale Ale were recommended. I did not disagree. I walked around in a daze, clutching my glass, shoulders slumped and wearing a stupid grin. A tornado had whisked me straight to Oz.

'You did special ops, right?' Marquez asked. He put his arm around my shoulders. I don't like being touched. My comfort zone is about two meters for anyone but Janie. 'So tell me,' he said. 'How would you get through all my defenses, you know, just to take me out?'

I clenched my jaw muscles and told him I'd think it over.

The house was a split-level ranch design with sweeping views on all sides – through bulletproof glass. In the den – bigger than my whole lot in El Cajon – Marquez dragged the sheet off a model of his estate and swore me to secrecy, not that it mattered, he said – he was adding stuff every month. 'Need to keep a jump ahead.'

Marquez was a certified California paranoid.

The only entrance from the front was through a narrow defile blocked by the steel gate and protected by three razor-wire fences, a staked moat, and a ten-foot-wide electrified barrier of ankle-breaking rolling pipes. Down the cliff behind the main lot, he had laid in steel beams and sprayed concrete to protect against landslides, then studded the concrete with trip wires and motion sensors. Later, he had dug an emergency elevator shaft to the bottom of the cliff, with its own power supply and an exit in the house below, which he also owned. 'Having just one exit bugged me,' he said. 'What if they mounted a full-scale assault from the west? Couldn't sleep nights. So I purchased the lower house and made an escape route. I store my memorabilia down there.'

Video cameras swept the grounds. Two fulltime bodyguards patrolled, armed with Beretta semiautomatic weapons.

Marquez took us outside to show us his garden and the dogs. He bred Rottweilers as a sideline. Some of his favorites waited their chance in kennels in the backyard. We met them near the end of the tour. With Marquez present, they were happy puppies. 'If I'm not here, they go for the throat,' he said, grinning like a boy with a train set. 'But they respect Tammy. They roll over for her, show their tummies. Smart dogs, right?'

Marquez turned shy as he took us back into the house and led us through his hobby room. His manly center was Tammy, he explained, but this was his 'boyish heartwood,' the place where he buried a million regrets and found true peace. I have never seen so many plastic models in all my life. Walls and ceiling were covered with glittering steel-and-plastic cases. Airplanes everywhere, armor, aircraft carriers, dioramas of land and sea battles. And they were accurate, too. Among the aircraft I recognized Shithooks, Spads, Thuds, and Willy Fudds with all the right markings and colors, none of them bigger than my fist.

A few spaces were left open between the cases for framed posters, lobby cards, and photos from his movies. He had written and directed three: *White Lion*, about a software engineer who imagines he's Tarzan; *Garbage Masters*, a nasty suburban comedy; and his epic, *The Big Stick*, a historical fantasy about early German U-boats challenging Teddy Roosevelt's Great White Fleet.

'Not one of them was a smash hit,' he said proudly. 'I kept

my place in this fucking town by force of will alone. And all it ever gave me back was Tammy. All right.' He smiled wickedly. 'Fair exchange.'

Seemed to me he had made a lot of money as well as Tammy. We sat down to dinner at a rosewood table as big as my kitchen, covered with heaping bowls of sumptuous food. Marquez passed around a lamb vindaloo that easily explained all the hair on his chest. Tammy carried a tray stacked with chutneys and sauces. I hadn't eaten so well in months.

'Rob says there have been adventures,' Marquez said. 'Tell me. We don't get out of the house often.'

Cousins began. 'First, I'd like to apologize to Ben. I didn't think they'd get to him so fast.'

'Silk?' Marquez asked eagerly.

'Mr Bridger spent some time in jail,' Banning said.

'Jail!' Marquez crowed. 'Wow. A setup?'

Cousins nodded. 'Joe knows everything,' Cousins said to me. 'And so does Tammy.' Tammy looked down at the table. From the way he said it, I suspected we would eventually focus on her, and I could see she wasn't looking forward to it.

'But Dr Cousins turned the tables and immunized Mr Bridger ahead of time,' Banning said.

'As a precaution,' Cousins added. 'And, of course, to protect Mr Bridger. He knows his history, and that's important.'

'You didn't trust me,' Banning said, eyes darting around the table. 'You wanted confirmation from another source.'

'Because you're a fucking wacko,' Marquez said. Banning looked resigned and settled into his chair. He had been hit with this particular bladder many times.

'We needed confirmation,' Cousins agreed. 'Ben had the expertise.'

'But that isn't all of it, right?' Marquez said, eyes glittering. 'He understands deadly force. Explosives. He's our power guy.'

'Not so fast,' I said. 'I know little or nothing about the rest of you.'

'There's nothing fair about any of this,' Cousins said.

Tammy nodded as if with special knowledge. Marquez reached over and put his arm around her. 'Rudy could have used some immunizing ten years ago,' he said. 'Silk turned him into a bigoted Nazi.'

'I wish you wouldn't use that phrase.' Banning's lips worked as if trying to clean a scrap of food from his front teeth.

'They didn't really change you,' Marquez said. 'They just brought your hatred of Jews out in the open. If Jews are so inferior, how do you explain Golokhov?' The two men stared at each other, Marquez with the wide-eyed triumph of having scored a point.

Banning's face emptied.

'Back up a bit,' I said. 'Who in hell was Golokhov? How did he manage to do all this?'

'He was the most brilliant biologist of the twentieth century,' Cousins said.

'The Svengali of germs,' Marquez said. 'That's how I'd pitch it.' He stood up from the table. 'Everybody eat their fill? Wonderful curry.'

Tammy looked nervous, as if her performance were about to begin.

'Time for some videos,' Marquez said. 'I'll bring a tray of drinks.'

'I'm a pig, and I know it,' Marquez said. We sat in his lavish theater, four rows of plush seats flanked by dark red velvet curtains. A video projector hung from the ceiling, its cooling fan a soft whisper in the hush. In the wall behind us, slits opened for the peering rodent eyes of three film projectors. Marquez pushed a button and a short length of front curtain pulled aside, revealing racked towers of expensive electronics. He slipped a disk into a player. 'Banning's a loon, but I'm a platinum-plated swine. I got where I am all by myself, with no help from anybody. I locked myself up in this paranoid's castle, and . . . lo and behold!' He made a biblical sweep with one hand, as if unveiling a new Golden Calf. 'I'm just what the poor girl needs.'

Banning marched across the front before taking his seat. He waved his arms like a professor giving a lecture. 'In 1948,' he said, 'Stalin and Golokhov seemed to have had a massive falling-out. Stalin may have felt that Golokhov was trying to control everyone around him. Stalin gave orders to purge Golokhov and all the specialists involved in Silk. He instructed Beria to deport all . . .' His lips worked. '. . . the Jewish medical researchers who might have been associated with Silk. The so-called Doctors' Plot of 1952. Ultimately, millions of Jews were banished to Siberia. You must agree, there was a measure of poetic justice.'

Marquez sat straight up in his seat. 'You are a guest,' he muttered. 'But you will not provoke me.'

Banning's eyes seemed to glaze. He sat.

'Rudy, we aren't concerned here with who was Jewish and who wasn't,' Cousins said calmly.

'No, of course not,' Banning said, and looked away.

'Golokhov escaped and went to New York,' Cousins continued. 'He, and what remained of Silk, kept a low profile. Beyond that, it's sketchy. We're going to New York to fit in the final pieces and look at the whole puzzle. Then . . . we're off to Florida and Exuma Cays.'

Marquez leaned forward. 'That's where Tammy comes in.'

'Tammy?' I asked. 'She's part of this?'

'Tangentially,' Cousins said, and looked to Marquez.

Marquez raised his hands. 'What can I say? It's all amazing.'

I was getting punchy with too much information and too many gaps. The silence lengthened.

'So?' I said.

'Tammy flew to LA from the Bahamas with her boyfriend,' Marquez said. 'They were at an awards ceremony for Themed Entertainment at the Beverly Wilshire. You know, Disneyland, Sea World, casino shows, that sort of thing. Have you ever heard of *Cirque Fantôme*?' Marquez punched a button and another curtain parted. The projector threw a gorgeous, sharp picture of an amphitheater onto the screen. People were filing down the rows to reach their seats. Long, filmy, white drapes obscured several layered stages at the center. Lights inside the drapes played like butterflies.

'Yeah, I suppose,' I said. 'Some sort of Vegas show, isn't it?'

'Mostly European,' Marquez said. 'Best circus in the world, really. Incredible acts, staging, unbelievable stunts.' Marquez gazed at Tammy with little-boy worship, marked by a small eyebrow twitch of concern.

'It is my story, I will tell it,' she said, drawing her shoulders up. 'Fantôme is more than a circus. They send recruiters into the city, the slums. When they found me, I was orphaned, a slum girl in Rio. What did I know? I was fourteen. If I did not leave, I would end up selling my body, taking drugs, and soon I would die. Tending bar or working dates was the best I could hope for. My guardian – he would have been my pimp, maybe – signed me over and the recruiters got me a visa, a work permit. They took me to Lee Stocking Island.'

'Exuma Cays,' Marquez said. 'In the Bahamas.'

Titles played over the screen: 'Cirque Fantôme, Fin de Siècle, L'Ombre et la Lumière.' The translucent drapes drew back to show three empty platforms. Steel columns rose on all sides, six in all, supporting lights and ropes, platforms and wires.

'Fantôme taught me English and Russian and French and high wire, juggling, and dance. I try with the boleadoras. You become part of a family. Everybody contributes, everybody works together. They train you day in, day out. The food is wonderful. You eat all you want but you don't get heavy. You work it off. I had never known fresh sheets, soft bed, people caring. It was heaven.'

A male clown at least twelve feet high from toe to crown, with very long legs, walked onto the largest platform. Though he must have been wearing stilts, they were like nothing I had seen before. One half of his face was painted white, the other black, and he wore a formal suit of charcoal gray. He bowed at the waist, then got down on his knees, if they were knees. Eerie music rose in the background, and above the platforms, another drape lifted to reveal a rock band of men and women wearing what looked like concentration-camp uniforms.

'I was sixteen, youngest in our group, the child,' Tammy continued, her eyes fixed on the screen. 'I was a pretty good juggler, but not good on the wire. I lacked concentration. So my family took me to visit Dr Goncourt at his house on the beach. There, I met Philippe Cabal. Philippe is top performer, close to Dr Goncourt. He liked me.'

The tall clown spread wide his arms and spun about. Old-fashioned bicyclists in turn-of-the-century clothes wheeled around all the stages, juggling armloads of small antiques – clocks, jewelry, lamps. On the next turn, they were tossing pistols and rifles. How they switched, I could not tell. The music became cockeyed martial.

Tammy turned her golden brown eyes on me. 'At sixteen, I became Philippe's mistress. He was both lover and father. My master.'

Marquez held his hands behind his head and stared up at the screen. 'You're leaving out the ship,' he gently reminded her. He touched a button on a large remote control. The picture sped up, clowns and bicyclists racing, music rushing past at a cheerful jog.

'Oh, yes. They have built it for five years now. They call it *Lemuria*. Big.'

'The floating skyscraper – condominiums?' I asked. 'I read about it in the papers.'

'Two thousand feet long,' Marquez said. 'Tax haven for rich bastards like me.' He froze the picture just as the tall clown was leaving the main stage.

'That is Philippe,' Tammy said softly.

'Fucker,' Marquez said. He fast-forwarded until the clown was off the stage, then froze the picture again.

Tammy's eyes were astonishing, irises like gold-flecked chest-nuts. 'On the ship, they did not sell all the units. They have money problems. Goncourt, director of Fantôme, our doctor, our father, suggested the circus rent space on *Lemuria*. We would provide entertainment and publicity. The *Lemuria* stockholders agreed, so that is where Dr Goncourt moved his training and medical center, from Lee Stocking Island to *Lemuria*. I go aboard *Lemuria* last year to live with Philippe and take Dr Goncourt's treatments. He wants to make us the finest athletes, the most disciplined performers the world has ever known. We never get sick, we are always strong, always of the right temper. We are the best.'

Marquez started the video again. Five golden women climbed the steel columns to their ropes and began a high-wire act.

Tammy's eyes took on a dreaming quality, remembering marvelous days, commitment and faith. 'Philippe said Dr Goncourt was a genius. To me, he was God. He chose our foods, supervised our training. He gave us special baths, smell very bad, like sulfur. Swabbed our skins. But he never gave us drugs. I never felt so good. I learn the *boleadoras*. I am topnotch, excellent even on the high wire. Philippe was proud. They told me I can travel now.'

The high-wire act was amazing. Strength and agility I had never seen before, and grace as well as ingenuity. The young women seemed to dance in the air, or sometimes just to fly.

'I learned from Philippe that a few of the family did more than just circus. They went places and did favors for Dr Goncourt. He asked me if I wanted this. Everything was grand, exciting, I loved Philippe so, I would do anything. I agreed. He nominated me – took me before the Committee, older people who had been with Dr Goncourt since long before Fantôme. Olympic athletes, performers from Russia.'

'Fucking Communists,' Marquez muttered. He hid his eyes behind his hands, then leaned his head back again to stare at the ceiling.

'Damn the Jews,' Banning shot back, as if in spasm.

Tammy held her hand to her mouth and bit a knuckle, blinking. 'The Committee adopted me, with Philippe –'

Marquez boiled over. He stood and pointed his finger at Banning. 'I'll tell you about Jews,' he shouted. 'I'll fucking tell you about victims and crimes!'

Banning's eyes went wide and his brows pushed up his forehead in furrows. 'Marx, Trotsky, Sinoviev, Kamenev . . . The Communists were empowered by world Jewry, by Jews who hated themselves and their race!'

Marquez almost leaped over the chairs to get at Banning. Tammy held him back.

Banning was into it completely. He couldn't stop. 'The Jews orchestrated their own demise, bit by bit – and blamed it on Hitler, but it was also Stalin who killed so many, who killed all but one of the Jews around him, sent them to Siberia, and *who* put *him* in power? Jews. Who spied for him? Communist Jews. The Rosenbergs, Ted Hall . . . Jews! *Damn the Jews!*'

Marquez let out an anguished war cry. 'I'll *kill* you!' He pushed Tammy aside. Banning leaned back over a row of seats and braced to receive Marquez's assault. Marquez wrapped his hands around Banning's neck, shaking him like a chicken.

Cousins nodded to me as if we had always been beat partners, cops on patrol. While Tammy shouted, 'Stop it! Stop it!' we grabbed the two men and pulled them apart. Banning slipped through my arms, tripped in the aisle, and fell with a loud thump.

Tammy whispered in her lover's ear. Marquez screamed his curses but stopped trying to break free. 'Goddamn that bastard, I don't care what he knows –'

'He's sick, shhh, he is a sick man,' Tammy soothed.

Banning stood, brushed his jacket and pants with as much dignity as he could muster. He inclined his head and extended his gloved hand as if politely requesting permission to leave, and minced out of the theater.

'I don't care if his brain has got filthy Nazi syphilitic worms all through it, that's enough, that's more than I can stand!' Tears streamed down Marquez's face.

Tammy started to sob. '*I can't bring a child into this!*'

Marquez's anger blew out like a candle in an open window. 'Oh, shit,' he said.

Tammy fell back in her seat. 'I can't leave the house, I have to act brave, my head is like a hurricane. I have to keep it all inside, all day long! I don't know who or what I am, or where I belong, I don't know anything!'

'We're sorry, honey,' Marquez said. 'We are all so sorry.' He looked sick with remorse. Tammy tried to push him away, but he clutched her tightly and stroked her hair. It was a sad and scary moment and I didn't know what to do. I wanted to slink off down the road.

We stood in silence while Marquez tried to placate the mother of his coming child. 'I wish we could take it all back,' he murmured to her. 'I surely do.'

Cousins had an odd look. Analytical, like watching fish in a bowl. It seemed out of character, and maybe I was just seeing his way of coping with emotional scenes.

From the entry, I heard the sound of a big piece of glass breaking. Cousins and I ran into the hall. Banning stood before a tall decorative arrangement of silk flowers rising from a marble table. He had shattered the gold-framed mirror behind the flowers, picked out a piece of glass as long as a dagger, and was shoving it by inches through his left palm. Blood fell in a thin red ribbon on the tiles, his shoes, his pant legs.

'I am such a wreck,' he said, then his eyes rolled up and he toppled like a sack of rice.

Together, we hauled him into the bathroom. Tammy told us we would find a first-aid kit under the bathroom counter. Marquez shook his head and clenched his fists and marched back and forth outside the door as we pulled out the shard, stanched the bleeding, and bound the wound.

'We have to get him to a doctor,' Cousins said. 'He could have nerve damage. He'll certainly need stitches.'

'I have my own doctor,' Marquez said through the bathroom door.

I opened the door. Banning was just coming to. Marquez

backed off. Two of his bodyguards, brutes in black T-shirts and silk suits, heads shaven down to fuzz, flanked him, frowning mightily.

'Tammy,' Marquez said, 'call Dr Franks.' He rubbed his palms on his pajama bottoms.

Tammy made the phone call. Cousins and I carried Banning, groggy and disoriented, past the bodyguards, through the back door, and across the side yard to the guesthouse next door. Tammy unlocked the French doors and we laid him out on a bed.

'My apologies,' Banning said, his speech slurred. Then he rolled over and passed out again.

Cousins wiped his hands on a towel from the guesthouse bathroom. His face was pale and the underarms of his shirt dark. 'What a day!' he said.

The doctor arrived just after ten. The guards drove him up from the front gate. He examined Banning's hand in the guesthouse and said he would much prefer to take the man to the hospital. The wound was serious enough, but he was more concerned about Banning's state of mind.

Marquez stood out in the yard doing stretches. The dogs in the kennels were going crazy, barking and leaping in their chain-link runs.

Banning glanced up at me, groggy, as they helped him walk to the waiting ambulance. I gave him a little wave. He shook his head. He didn't need to say it again: *I am such a wreck.*

The ambulance drove off into the darkness.

Cousins had dragged me into a world of nightmare and no sense. I had had my house turned upside down and spent three nights in jail. I had been drugged – I think – twice, and did not know whether I would ever again be the master of my own soul.

They wanted my help, but what could I do? What were they up against? How could they possibly win? It all was piling up on my shoulders and I did not know what my final decision should be.

The Rottweilers were still leaping and barking. 'It's all the fuss and the people,' Marquez said. 'They'll get over it. They always do.' He walked over to the cage and tried to calm them, but all three dogs went into a spinning frenzy. Two of them, hefty bitches, chewed at the wire, spit flying through the links onto the concrete. Marquez backed off with a dismayed smirk and stuck his hands in his pajama pockets.

Cousins approached from behind. The dogs caught his scent. The male started rolling around in his separate cage, gnawing at his paws, eyes rolling. I tried to get one of the bitches to come to the wire, but she ignored me and barked madly at Cousins.

'Who feeds the dogs?' I asked.

'Why?' Marquez said with a defensive look.

Cousins suddenly got it. 'Oh, my God,' he said. 'Joe, who feeds them?'

'Sometimes Tammy or me, sometimes the bodyguards.'

'Where do the bodyguards come from?' I asked, kicking myself for not seeing it earlier.

'A security firm in Van Nuys. They rotate out every other day,' Marquez said.

Cousins took Marquez's arm and they backed away from the cages. The dogs settled down a little but watched them with keen interest. 'Let's go into the house,' Cousins said.

Inside, Cousins told Marquez the bodyguards would have to leave the compound. We couldn't trust them. Marquez paced around the living room, orating one long and monotonous apology, flinging his arms, swearing at his stupidity.

Watching him was the final straw.

I approached Cousins and said quietly, 'This isn't Oz, this is Kafkaville. Banning isn't the only loon here.'

The guards made Marquez sign a special form that their firm would not be held responsible, then piled into a black Nissan SUV and rolled off down the road, through the main gate.

Tammy took Marquez off to bed.

I peered into the theater, waiting for Cousins. The circus was still frozen on the big screen. The room was quiet and peaceful. None of it, on the screen or off, seemed real.

Cousins came back and closed the theater door.

'Looks hopeless, doesn't it?' he said.

'When did you guys meet?'

'Six months ago. Marquez had worked with Banning on an idea for a war movie, before Banning was tagged. When Tammy showed up last year, Marquez called Banning to get his opinion. Not long after that, Banning called me.'

'That is a remarkable string of coincidences,' I said.

'All roads lead to people who make movies,' Cousins said mildly. 'Believe me, in Los Angeles, there are very few genuine coincidences. Before you go, let me show you what we've got on our side. What I'm working on. Might change your mind.'

'I really don't think I want to see any more,' I muttered, a little ashamed. 'I might compromise your operation.'

Cousins sighed. 'Look at us,' he said. 'We're amateurs. If you can't help us, it's time to give up. And that means . . . well, you can guess. But I'll understand if you want to just get the hell out. Give me ten more minutes of your time, then I'll escort you down to the gate myself.'

I followed him around the east side of the house, down a flight of steps and through a side entrance, below the level of the lawn, into the basement.

Cousins flicked on a light switch. There was a bright white room down there, like something in a hospital, with expensive-looking equipment, microscopes, refrigerators, incubators. Equations and sketches of molecules covered a whiteboard on the wall. Off to one side stood a sunlamp, in the corner a small bath and shower stall, and beyond the benches, several stools and an easy chair.

'Is this where you made the stuff you fed me?'

'It is,' he said.

'And you?' I asked. 'Are you susceptible?'

'Yes. But I've been experimenting with myself over the last few years, in the interests of living longer. Before I knew about Silk, I altered my own gut bacteria and some of my cellular characteristics. Unwittingly, I gave myself some immunity. Now it's all I can do to stay just one step ahead of Silk.'

'They know where you are,' I said.

Cousins made a wry face. 'I thought Marquez's paranoia made this place ideal.'

I let that pass without comment. Civilians rarely know the best places to hide or whom to trust with their lives. 'What about Banning? What do you know about him? He brings you all together, he provides the catalyst that unites all these people who could be dangerous to Silk. Have you ever considered the possibility that he's some sort of henchman or decoy?'

'I've thought about it,' Cousins said. 'It's not impossible. But I don't think it's him.' His face loosened a little, sad, then thoughtful. 'My wife, maybe.'

'You're afraid of *your wife?*'

'We're getting divorced. I got suspicious. Lots of little things.'

'Shit.' Nastier and nastier. I rubbed the back of my neck and stretched, looking around the setup in the basement. 'How long have you been working on your vaccines?' I asked.

'Six months.'

'And how long has Silk been out there?' I had already done the math, I was making a point.

'Seventy years, maybe.'

I held up my hands as if surrendering. 'These guys have been scouring channels and making contacts, creating their little operatives, breaking trails of subversion, for *seventy years*. That's way outside my league. No, thanks. Pardon me, boys, but that's the fucking Chattanooga Choo-Choo.'

Cousins stared at me sadly. 'I know we have a chance,' he persisted. 'We can't just let it all go!'

Tammy opened the basement door and poked her head in. 'Interrupting?' she asked.

'Not at all,' I said, dropping my hands and walking off.

I did not want that woman in the room, not when I had made my decision, when my instincts told me to get the hell out and fast. Something melted in me when she was near. Not even Janie had evoked such a reaction, and that made me angry.

'I put Joe to bed. He sleeps like a baby.' She sighed and closed the door behind her. She had put on a blockprint caftan, warmer and almost able to conceal her shape. 'He is sensitive about Jews, especially with Mr Banning. He does not understand.'

'Tammy didn't finish her story,' Cousins said. 'Maybe now's the time?'

'I can guess,' I said.

Tammy stood beside Cousins. They both looked at me expectantly.

'Tammy saw Golokhov,' I said. 'That's what this is all about. He's Goncourt, isn't he?'

Tammy rewarded me with a sad, lovely smile.

'We're pretty sure,' Cousins said.

'He'd have to be, what, a hundred years old by now?'

'Closer to a hundred and five.'

'And you want me to help you do something in the Bahamas.'

Cousins looked me straight in the eye. 'Eventually. If you're up to it.'

'I tell why I leave Philippe?' Tammy inquired.

Cousins nodded.

'Yeah,' I said, giving up. It had been a very long day. Surely there was a point to it all.

'I was ill in Los Angeles just after Philippe and I arrived. Something inside, *turistas*.'

'Theme of the day,' I said dryly.

'There was a banquet. Fancy hotel, beautiful people, from Canada, Venezuela, Brazil, China, Puerto Rico, Las Vegas, Bahamas, Disneyland. I became sick in our big room. Philippe was angry, he wanted to show me off, but what can he do?' Her voice was so exotic, a touch sad, with unpredictable upbeats and downbeats. Just achingly beautiful. 'I don't know it, but I am coming out of their control.'

'Hardy constitution, tough on out-of-town bacteria like Goncourt's,' Cousins said. 'From living in the slums. That's my guess.'

Tammy rubbed her eyes and peered dramatically, demonstrating new insight. 'I suddenly see the room, the city, all different. It is like suddenly losing faith in God, you know? But it is a big city, I am afraid, I know nobody and nothing. I go with Philippe to another hotel, the Beverly Hilton. He introduces me to a woman. The woman is blond, beautiful, tall. She is with two shorter men I do not know, but they also have look of circus performers. I think of them as the Gray Men. Philippe says they represent Goncourt in California and the West Coast.'

'Runners,' Cousins said.

'He tells me he is going to leave me with the Gray Men, and they will train me.' Her face wrinkled in revulsion. 'Leave *me*! In a strange town, away from my family!'

'The bastard,' I said.

'The two men ask Philippe how *obedient* I am. The blond woman acts as if I am a dog or a cat. *Obedience* is essential, Philippe tells me. We are a *cell* in LA, and we do important work for Dr Goncourt. It is a fabulous life, he says, you go everywhere, sneak around in the dark. The Gray Men say I will become like them, masters of being inconspicuous.'

I wondered how she could ever be inconspicuous.

'They will teach me all the necessary skills, even how to kill without touching.'

I heard a low, choppy rumble outside. Not like thunder. No windows in the basement. My neck hairs twitched.

'I escape the next morning,' Tammy said. 'I hang out on the streets, at YWCA, until I am picked up by Beverly Hills police. I tell them my story. I tell them it is about drugs, and maybe it is. Then, two, three people help me, I am lucky. One of them is a psychiatrist, she knows Joe. Joe's house is isolated. Secure. Nobody bad will find me.'

She dropped her shoulders and her chin, then looked at the far wall, the whiteboard with the cryptic writing. 'I remember the codes,' she said. Before she could explain that, Cousins interrupted.

'There's no escape, really,' Cousins said. The hollowness in his voice was startling. He sounded like a ghost. 'Think about it. What can they force people to do? Anything. Who can they touch? Anybody, anywhere. Jesus, I'd like to make them know how it feels.' He lifted his fist and swung at empty air. 'Smash them right in the fucking nose.'

The low-level noise – a harsh, distant whickering – was at first familiar and even welcome. My heart thumped in unison with the slicing blades, so like the rush of angels' wings to an old jungle warrior. But that hope didn't last for more than a couple of seconds.

I wasn't in the bush.

'What is it?' Cousins asked.

I had been working over Marquez's challenge some more. How would I breach his security, invade his fortress? Like most civilians, he had made the basic assumption that there are boundaries in life, that what you've never experienced and can't imagine just won't happen.

Marquez had neglected air superiority. I pointed my finger up. 'Listen.'

Tammy cocked her head.

'It's just a helicopter,' Cousins said. 'Probably on its way to LAX.'

By then, the sound of two, maybe three choppers, blades laying down rhythm to a steady turbine roar, would have drowned out my voice anywhere but in the basement.

'They're too close,' I said. 'Flying formation.'

'Police?' Cousins said, but he didn't believe it.

I opened the outside door. Cousins stood with me in the doorway in the early-morning coolness. Behind us, Tammy busied herself moving things around. I knew without looking what she was doing. She was piling up furniture and hiding.

Cousins and I started up the steps, me first. Without thinking, at the grind of a new and terrible noise, like Satan clearing his throat, I dropped into a crouch. Cousins nearly fell over me.

My body recognized that awesome roar. I hadn't heard it in over thirty years, and it was still supreme: the air-ripping, saurian bawl of the gun that kills a village.

I lifted my head over the edge of the concrete retaining wall. Three AH-1 SuperCobras, Marine Corps jobs, little more than silhouettes in the deep gray dawn, snooted their floods down on the next house along the ridge. The first chopper's thirty-millimeter cannon bawled again, followed by the second, then all three opened up on the house and the grounds. *Braaaappp-Roarrr-hum-buzz-ROARRR* and red tiles flew up in spinning fragments. Hundreds of shells per second carved away the roof. Walls flapped and curled like surgically sliced tissue. The swimming pool erupted in a thousand geysers.

A figure in a white nightgown ran over the grass and just turned red. She seemed to disappear, like a chicken leg down a garbage disposal.

I said something to Cousins, I don't remember what. Even in Vietnam the damn gunships chopping up the paddies and hamlets had made me cry, and these were infinitely worse. Here I was, thirty years later, sobbing like a child.

The third Cobra pushed back a few dozen yards and went to work on the house below the cliff. I could not see the destruction but I could hear it.

The floodlights on our lawn went dark.

'Not now,' I said. *Don't let them know you're here.*

The guns stopped. Cousins poked his head up next to mine. We squatted in the well outside the door.

Marquez ran out on the grass in his pajamas, a gnomish shadow against the glow from the valley. 'What the fuck?' I heard him shout.

The house on the next lot had caught fire. A flare of natural gas shot up like a giant Bic lighter.

Marquez straightened and held out his arms, mesmerized by the spectacle. Not good to live a life of movies. Everything is special effects, nothing seems real.

'It's a mistake,' Cousins said. I knew what he meant. The pilots had screwed up.

Just as he spoke, all three of the gunships backed off, hesitated for a few long, loud seconds, as if checking their maps, *Aw shit.*

They yawed right like three toys on sticks, pitched their noses down, and flew right at us.

part three

HAL COUSINS

CHAPTER THIRTY
Imperial Valley, California
August 10

Lissa drove. We didn't speak until we were on 5 heading south through the long valley.

'Don't look at me that way,' she said. 'He would have shot you.'

'Who in hell was he?'

'He had a gun.'

I was still in shock.

'I couldn't stand seeing you both get shot,' Lissa said.

We stopped at the Spanish Baron's Ranch House Inn to eat. We hadn't had dinner and it was ten p.m. Rain left big clean splatters on the windshield. The air smelled wet off the asphalt in the parking lot and I realized I was happy just to be alive.

'Thank you,' I said.

'*De nada*,' Lissa said. We made our way to the restaurant past a big antique steel-tired steam tractor, displays of old plows, and barn-plank paneled walls hung with oxbows, yokes, draped leather harnesses, and collections of brass hondos. The waitress guided us to a booth.

Lissa looked tired but not one whit less beautiful. She fumbled in her purse, could not find what she was poking for. 'I would love a cigarette,' she said. 'And I don't give a shit who knows it.'

'Tough lady,' I said.

'Tough lady,' she echoed with a decisive tilt of her head. 'He would have killed you.'

'No question,' I said.

'He had that look.'

'He was smiling,' I said.

'He had that look.'

'He looked stoned,' I said.

'He was tagged,' Lissa said.

'Almost certainly.'

'He wore the most godawful suit, did you notice?' Her breath hitched, and I thought she was about to cry. She wiped her eyes. 'Do you think anyone saw us?'

'I don't know.'

'I don't think so,' she said.

The waitress brought our drink order. I swallowed my Integumycin tablets. Lissa chased two Tums with a swallow of milk.

'Stomachache?' I asked.

'Calcium,' she said. 'I don't want to get brittle bones.'

'A proper mix of male and female sex hormones is the key,' I said. 'You should also begin probiotic therapy for better calcium uptake.'

'I know,' she said. 'Rob told me the same thing.'

Now the tears came, and silent but shaking sobs. 'I don't want to do this,' she said, her voice a trembling squeak. 'I don't want to be here, I really don't.'

I changed seats to put my arm around her.

We ate our sandwiches.

She paid with cash, and I drove for a few hours.

'Numbers,' I said, 'seem to be important to them.'

But she was asleep. It was two in the morning when I stopped at a blocky, beige, eighties-style motel, another Homeaway, rising alone in the central valley, outlined by big orange lights in the dead of early morning. I walked into the lobby to rent two rooms.

'You want them adjacent?' the desk clerk asked.

Lissa walked in brushing her hair and said one room would do just fine. 'They're suites, right?' she asked

'Sure are,' the clerk said, and smiled encouragement.

*　　*　　*

Once again, death had smoked out all my reason. We curled up on the queen-size bed, still in our clothes, and slept for four hours. When daylight peeped in through the curtains, I woke up to the sound of my brother's widow taking a shower. It was a pleasant, reasonable sound, and the steam coming through the open bathroom door made me bold.

I walked into the bathroom and stood there in my stocking feet, feeling the tile under my toes.

She pulled back the curtain. 'You smell like him when you sleep,' she said as she stepped out onto the mat. The hot water had pinked her all over. She looked delicious, raspberries and cream, wet hair the color of butterscotch with vanilla bean streaks. 'Oh,' she said. 'You surely do.' She was completely unself-conscious. She wrapped her hair in a towel and used another to dry, working from the shoulders down, rational and thorough.

I couldn't smell any soap. Just the steam. The bars and shampoo in the little wicker basket hadn't been touched.

She bent over in the small bathroom, butt pointed toward me, and toweled off her hair. She backed up a few inches into my hips and left two damp marks on my pants. She straightened, turned, and said, 'We should be on the road soon.'

All perfectly pleasant and reasonable, but with that lingering of sight lines that told me I would not be rebuffed. She took a small bottle of white skin cream – her own, not from the hotel – and rubbed it on her arms, her legs, across her breasts, then on her face.

'Where are we going?' I asked.

'Los Angeles,' she said, and toweled for the second time between her thighs.

'What's down *there*?'

'I'm sorry?' She stopped rubbing.

'In LA.'

'Okay,' she said.

'I'm confused.'

'And now I'm ready,' she said, and held out her towel. She rubbed it gently on my face.

The sex was wonderful and awful. I could not get Rob's privilege out of my thoughts, no matter how much I reasoned that they had separated and he was dead, and that she had saved my life and I owed her something. I knew she felt as if she was going to bed with Rob again, and that creeped me out even as it excited the hell out of me.

'Don't tell me I make love like Rob,' I said.

It was eight-thirty.

'You don't,' she said.

'Don't tell me I'm better,' I said, angrier still.

'I'm sorry,' Lissa said. She lay on her side, head propped up on one arm. Her breasts were close to perfection, one in repose on the stretched white sheet, the second draped so slightly above it a feather would have escaped. I wanted her again, now.

'You haven't had a woman in how long?' she asked.

'Long,' I said.

'Poor man. Well, you have certainly done justice by me.'

I did not know what to say. I was out of my league and had been for several hundred million years.

She made coffee, using the room machine, and brought me a foam cup. 'I boiled it,' she said. 'The water's a little salty, but this *is* the Imperial Valley.'

We drank from our cups in silence, trying to discover what we added up to in this new arithmetic. Lissa had a loose, relaxed way of moving when she was naked. She smelled like hay and Lipton tea, with a rich base of beef broth and lemons. She fluffed the pillow to cushion her back, then lay against the headboard. Her toenails were perfect, unpainted, carefully but not, I judged, professionally manicured, skin without blemish. Fine little blond hairs rose from her arms, the small of her back. She did not shave her legs, and it did not matter.

The coffee tasted pretty salty, and I only drank half. She took my cup and threw the rest down the sink. We got dressed and went downstairs.

Lissa bought a copy of the *Los Angeles Times* from a stand in the lobby and tossed it at me as I got in the car. In the headlines: three Marine helicopters, ditched off Malibu, had been recovered by a Navy diving team. The helicopters had flown from Camp Pendleton and strafed a neighborhood in Los Angeles almost two months ago, killing four, including a Hollywood director. No motive, no explanation. The bodies of six aviators had been recovered, still strapped into their aircraft.

'Anybody we know?' she asked. The look in her eyes – distant and cold – startled me.

'Sounds like a drug thing,' I offered.

'That's it,' she said, jerking the car into gear. 'Ace Marine pilots slam a house for a drug deal gone bad.'

She gunned us out of the parking lot and back onto the road. We were twenty miles down the freeway when she started talking again. 'Have you ever thought that looking for eternal youth is just crazy?'

'It isn't,' I said.

'But isn't believing that crazy in itself, in a way? Such confidence?'

'Not if it's based in science,' I said.

'Have you got it in your grasp?' she asked, holding up a hand and squeezing as if her fingers held a juicy orange.

'Not yet. Soon, if I can just get back to work.'

'I watched Rob disintegrate. It started with Rudy Banning, but what if it was in Rob to begin with? A gene for insanity. The capacity to just break up at a touch.'

'Rob wasn't crazy,' I said. I looked out the window at fields of cotton, mottled green in the late-morning sun. The glare hurt my eyes. 'Neither am I.'

'You and Rob have the same genes. What if it's all a circle of deluded people –' she took a deep breath, '– chasing around, killing and getting killed, for nothing?'

'Granted, it's hard to believe any of this is happening,' I said. 'But you've seen the results.'

'I've seen the *craziness*,' she said, her voice rising in pitch. 'I can't see anything that makes sense. Can't you at least acknowledge the possibility?'

'As a hypothesis, sure. Now it needs to be supported by facts. Am I *acting* crazy?'

'Your life is a mess. You said it yourself.'

'Even paranoids have enemies,' I said, echoing Mrs Callas.

'But what if Rob contracted some sort of communicable disease, a virus, in Russia, something that screws up your brain, before he even knew about Silk?'

'Now *that* sounds paranoid,' I said.

'Is it really any different from what you say is happening, any harder to believe?'

I acknowledged that it was not. 'I still don't see the point.'

'I want to tell you what happened between Rob and me.'

That was not high on my list of things I wanted to hear. The whole conversation was going south rapidly.

'I don't want to cause pain,' she began. 'But I think you should take it into account. To support my hypothesis, you would say.'

'I'm listening,' I said. But in fact something was wrong with my hearing. I scrubbed my ears with the tips of my little fingers, and still the sound in the car seemed muffled.

'He started losing his bearings after he went to Siberia. It got worse when he met Banning. He wouldn't shut up at night. He was amazed that someone had got there ahead of him. He became obsessed, then, he started agreeing with whatever Banning would say –'

'The Nazi crap?'

'No,' she admitted. 'He didn't go that far. But he started to avoid me, stay away on any excuse. I loved him, and I tried to stick with him, but he wouldn't accept my help. He accused me of holding him back. How could I? He wouldn't even tell me what he was doing! Then he left.'

I tapped my jaw to dislodge whatever was blocking my ears.

She nodded grimly. 'And to tell the truth, I was fed up, too. I couldn't stand it any more . . .'

The next few words I didn't catch. I heard a humming and watched the windshield turn white as a sheet of ice. Lissa kept driving, but all the sound had been turned down. I leaned against the cool glass of the side window. Through the corner of my eyes, I watched her lips move.

I was perfectly calm. How nice that I didn't have to listen. But I would have to come up with suitable responses. 'Probably they got to him, by then,' I said, just to stay in the conversation. 'Induced madness. That's likely.'

She pulled over and stopped the car. In silence, she opened my door and helped me out. I saw fields of dark green strawberry plants all around. We were on a dirt road some distance off the freeway. She waved a hand in front of my face. I think she was saying, Hal, are you all right, but I wasn't paying much attention. The calmness was wonderful. After all I had been through, to have this benison delivered to me was a real treat.

She put me in the backseat. I imagined that she took off her clothes, then my clothes, and rubbed her body all over me, going through graceful contortions between the seats. She carefully rubbed her thighs, her labia and pubic hair, on my face, my mouth and nose, and over my own hair, scenting me with hay and roses. She gently inserted her finger up both my nostrils, then into my ears. I felt vividly the press of her smoothly manicured and painted fingernails. Then, as if it were an afterthought, she got me hard and slid down over me, made me come, and went through the process all over again. When she was done, she pulled me from the backseat and dressed me.

It was all interesting and diverting, but it did not break my extraordinary and welcome calm.

'You are a horny bastard,' she said coolly when we were back on the road. I checked my clothes. Shirt all buttoned up. I could hear again. That was nice.

'Did we just make love by the roadside?' I asked.

'We did,' she said. 'Thank you for remembering.' She smiled at me, beautiful but chilly.

'Wonderful,' I said. 'When are you going to let me drive?'

'Not now,' she said, and shook her head primly. 'A freshly fucked male has no sense of danger.'

I could not disagree.

CHAPTER THIRTY-ONE
South-Central California

My memory of events for the next few hours is muddled. I can revive images of small two-lane highways and dusty towns, and they all seem to bring me like a wash of gravel to a brown strip motel in a small town dotted with drooping, dusty green trees. I think we were somewhere east of Los Angeles.

The calmness had filled me like a transfusion of chicken soup, healing most of my pains and making the rest seem unimportant. I wanted Lissa to rub me again, and on what I believe was our first evening in the motel, she did. She rolled me around on the bed like a happy puppy, inspecting me with sad deliberation.

She rubbed her skin with her hands, spit on her palms, then rubbed her hands on me. Again she inserted fingers into my nose and mouth and ears.

She did not have sex with me. And that was okay. I was just being rewarded for being a good puppy.

She allowed me to sit in a chair on the concrete walkway outside as we waited for the balky air-conditioner to cool the room. Just to make small talk, I told her about the air-conditioner in the hotel in San Francisco. That made her even more sad.

She sat beside me on the rusted metal chairs and watched the sun go down over reddish mountains. The hotel was empty except for us, a broken-down wreck on a dying old highway. Maybe that was why she had chosen it.

A small white Toyota Celica drove into the parking lot, skirting a deep pothole. The other fellow I had seen in Berkeley, companion to the corpse in the freezer, got out, walked over, took off his Fedora, and waved it at his face to stay cool. He stood in front of my chair, watching me with fixed black eyes.

Lissa spoke with him in a language I did not understand. I smiled at them both. Then he got back into the Toyota and sat in the driver's seat with the door open, paying no attention to either of us. Arrogant son of a bitch, I thought.

'You know him?' I asked Lissa.

'He's my trainer,' she said.

'Like a lion tamer?'

'No. Training for the Olympics. But I broke my ankle.'

'Sorry.'

She shook her head. That was long past and very far away.

At some point I thought it was appropriate to ask, 'What next?'

'You're going to stay here,' she answered.

'All right.'

She looked at me. 'You know what's happening?' she asked.

'No.'

'Do you care?'

'Not really. Not yet, anyway.'

'You should care.'

'Why don't you just plug me?' I pointed my finger and clucked my tongue.

'That isn't the way we do things. Nobody enjoys just killing people, not if there's another way.' That sounded funny, coming from a woman who had so coldly and quickly blown away the guy in the herringbone suit.

'Making other people kill people, that's better, cleaner,' I said, just to keep up the conversation. 'No doubt about it.'

She lifted her eyes to the horizon. Sun going down fast, rocks all around.

'If somebody's going to shoot me, I'd rather you do it,' I said.

'You really haven't a clue what's happening, do you?'

'Well,' I said, and stared at the last of the sun, then at her, also luminous and beautiful, 'you've rubbed me with something from your skin and body. Your oils and juices. They probably have special bacteria mixed in, from the skin cream in the bottle . . . a heavy-duty dose. You didn't use soap.' Too bad I hadn't assembled all these observations earlier. A freshly fucked man, etc. 'They're putting out their special peptides and such, keeping me happy, but . . . somehow I'm still protected against being made into a zombie. Maybe it's the treatment I gave myself. Or the antibiotics. I really don't know.'

'Integumycin is designed to stay in the body and not leak out through the skin,' Lissa said.

'Is that a fact?'

'So you *are* vulnerable, more than you know. But I won't make you kill somebody else, if that's any consolation,' she said. 'Whom do you think I work for?'

'Nobody,' I said, lying with a smile. 'I think you're beautiful.'

'I belong, heart and soul, to Silk, and so does my trainer.'

'Not surprising,' I said.

'Why isn't it surprising?'

I thought it over, trying to round up all my free-range thoughts. 'I suppose they find it useful to track people doing research in, you know, longevity, and those in the forefront merit special attention. A wife, maybe, to keep tabs on them, report on progress, work them if need be.' I frowned. 'But I'm not clear on one thing. How do they program *you*?'

'They don't, not that way,' she said. 'I'm an orphan. They found me in Budapest.' She pronounced it *Booda-pesht*.

'What about the parents you introduced to Rob and me?'

She shook her head.

'They're Silk, too? Wow. Must be pretty widespread.'

224

'Bigger than you want to imagine,' she said.

The evening was getting on nicely. The air, easily a hundred degrees in the late afternoon, was now cooling into the low eighties. We were having a very nice chat.

The man in gray must have been sweltering in the Toyota, but he didn't move.

'Could you take me back into our room and rub me some more?'

'You don't need it,' she said.

'Why don't the bacteria affect you the same way?'

'I carry cultures tailored to make Rob happy,' she said. 'What he was doing, his research, blocked some of their effects, and after a while he got suspicious. He wouldn't make love anymore. Then he left me.'

'You really are very, very attractive.'

'In a few more hours, you'll want to be around me all the time, like a lover or a wife,' Lissa said.

'Puppy obsession,' I said.

'Don't get me wrong. I *will* let you die.'

'I don't doubt it for a moment.'

'Don't think you're James Bond and I'm going to fall in love with you, too.'

'I won't think that, I promise. Not if it makes you unhappy.'

She got up and took my face in her hands. 'You aren't half the man your brother was. I won't be sad when you die.'

'You had to be in love with Rob to do your job convincingly,' I said.

'It was something like love,' Lissa said.

'Maybe you inspired him,' I said.

'You each had half the secret, but you never put the two halves together,' she said. 'You were stupid, quarreling brothers. It's a *nasty* little secret, anyway, you know? You have no idea how nasty.'

'So tell me,' I said. 'Why doesn't Silk target drug dealers? Tyrants? Serial killers? Really bad people. You should work to improve society, rather than going after arrogant scientists.'

'I don't know,' Lissa said.

'Was *my* wife part of Silk?'

'No.' Then she added, 'I don't think so.'

'I don't think she was, either. She wasn't like you at all. Not nearly so beautiful.'

'Silk gives that to us. Not that I was an unpretty child.'

An unpretty child. I rolled that around, savoring it. 'You swallow Mudd's little sparkly pills and you're suddenly lovely?' I asked.

She brought her brows together, narrowed one eye. She didn't get the reference. A woman marries a scientist but doesn't watch *Star Trek*? No wonder Rob had become suspicious. 'We are very healthy,' she said. 'No diseases.'

'Still, you're going to get old and die,' I said, and suddenly wished I could take it back. A horrible thought. Beauty fading.

'The other way is madness.'

'What about Golokhov?' I asked, innocently enough. 'Is he going to live for ever?'

Lissa slapped me hard. She grabbed me under my arms and dragged me into the motel room, which was still hot, and pushed me back on the bed. 'I won't allow someone to come in here and hurt you,' she said. I saw tears on her cheeks. 'But it will make me happy if you hurt yourself. It will make me *very* happy. I have to leave now. Go to sleep.'

I plumped a pillow and tried to do as she asked, but it was too hot. Through slitted eyes, I watched her gather up her luggage, go outside, and close the door.

Heard the lock click.

Lissa and the man in gray engaged in a heated exchange outside the room. Something about 'transition' and 'all finished.' They were really going at it, but after the first couple of sentences, I didn't understand a word. They were speaking Hungarian, maybe, or Russian.

I tried hard to sleep. Glanced at the alarm clock by the bed: Ten p.m. I had slept a little. My body felt as if it was coming down with something. Shivery warmth. Could be a gross bacterial infection. Maybe Lissa had pathogenic bacteria in her mix, as well as persuasive ones. Little flesh-eaters. Wouldn't that be a kick?

'What kind of retirement plan do you have, sweetie?' I shouted into the dark, hoping she would hear and come in and slap me. All sorts of little concerns drifted through my head, especially when I saw that another hour had passed and I still hadn't heard a peep outside. Was it okay if I got off the bed?

'Do you sleep in dormitories, communally?' I called out. 'Or is it a little, you know, Shaker village sort of thing? Not celibate, that's for sure. Are you celibate with your family? You did say you have family, but you're an orphan, from *Booda-Pesht*. All sorts of beautiful women back there. In the former Soviet Union and Hungary and Romania and Czechoslovakia. They want to come here and find rich husbands.'

The door did not open. Perhaps I could make her pay attention if I did something rash. I looked around the room, got up, and switched on all the lights. Peeled off my clothes except for my briefs. Examined the electrical cords to the lamps. One was frayed. I applied the bare wire to some white stuffing creeping out of the cheap quilted bedcover. Nothing happened.

I wandered around restlessly, thinking about what Lissa had said. She wouldn't make me hurt someone else. Maybe she couldn't. I had felt the touch of Silk's bacterial persuasion in the DSV, in the hotel room with Banning in San Francisco. I was feeling it now. But I could not be turned into an assassin. That made me glad. The saucy little widow of my twin could not make me kill somebody else. That was significant.

You both have half the secret.

I looked on the dresser, then on the nightstand in the corner. Lissa had left little matchbooks around the room with their covers open. How accommodating. She would probably return to the room and check on me if I started a fire. At any rate, she would approve.

I pulled a match from the nearest book and struck it, then dropped it into a metal wastebasket. The little doily at the bottom of the basket caught fire and started smoking. Curious, I looked up at the smoke detector. Not a peep. Batteries dead, probably. Cheap hotel. Frame and wallboard, with a continuous attic, great for sucking air and spreading flames. Burn fast and hot like a cracker box.

I pulled out bathroom tissues and set them around the room, wondering all the while what little areas of my brain Silk's bacteria were activating. Through my skin. In my nose. On my cock? Up in my urethra? The salty coffee. In my gut again. Something to do with dopamine and adenylate cyclase inhibitors, activated G proteins, cyclic AMP. A little symphony orchestra of subtle effects, direct and indirect.

The urge to join mob action? More likely the urge to please a powerful woman, to please my mother, my wife. Women have such a strong influence on young men. Pyro boy locked in hotel room pining for a good rubdown, baby won't you light my fire.

The tissues I arranged on the worn carpet burned like little campfires. I imagined myself looking down on Sherman's troops camped around Atlanta, waiting to torch the whole city. The city, of course, would have to be the *bed*. I set to work ripping the mattress, impressed by my cleverness.

I have half, Rob had half. Put them together ... All the little pathways line up, and we're in it for the Long Haul.

The doorknob turned. I stood back from my labors, curious about the noise. I was wearing only jockey shorts and my watch. I was ready for Lissa if she wanted another session.

A little swearing, a low deep voice, barely audible. Scratching. All right, this was the guy who was coming to kill me. If Lissa had lied, had actually gone out to arrange for my murder, rather than let me burn up in a fire, that was fine. Less cruel, actually.

The door burst open with a bang and the old heater behind it rattled and dropped some screws internally. A big shadow

228

stood there against the night, six feet at least, bulky, with a glint of streetlight on a balding head.

'Hal Cousins?'

'That's me,' I said, turning to make a better target.

'You look just like him.' The silhouette's shoulders drooped, and I heard him let out his breath. 'You're a mess.'

'I am in proper attire.'

'We're hauling your ass out of here, understand?'

'Not unless that's what Lissa wants.'

'Fuck Lissa.'

It was beneath me to discuss such things.

'Who are you?' I asked, dropping back seductively on the bed. Everything was so sexy.

The big guy stomped out the little tissue campfires. He pulled me off the bed and stood me up. 'You stink,' he said.

'I smell like tea and sandalwood, don't you think?'

'Hell no. You smell like water-buffalo shit.'

He propelled me by the shoulders into the bathroom and opened the shower-stall door. I stepped in, smiling. Without closing the door, he turned on the water – a blast of cold, quickly turning hot – and grabbed a couple of toy bottles of shampoo from the counter. Then he palmed a wet washcloth and lathered me all over, scrubbing me in quite intimate ways, which I enjoyed.

My skin felt scalded. He shut off the water with a bang of old pipes and pulled me out of the stall. I turned coyly for his inspection.

'Where's your stuff?' he asked. I had brought nothing with me, not even Rob's papers. They might have been in Lissa's car, but they certainly weren't in the hotel room. Or had we left them in the office building to burn?

I could not remember.

'The papers,' I said, with sudden concern.

'Put on your clothes,' he ordered.

'I'm wet.'

'Do it.'

I dressed, pulling sleeves and pant legs over wet skin, jerking them into place seductively. While I was buttoning my shirt, he slung me over his shoulder and hauled me roughly through the narrow door to the parking lot.

The lot glowed an unreal orange under the streetlights. The whole neighborhood was quiet, waiting. 'It sure is spooky,' I said, looking up and around from my slumped vantage.

The car was a Mercedes S-class, very nice, dark red that looked black.

He put me down on my feet on the asphalt beside the car. Someone opened the driver's side door and stepped out as if to help.

It was Banning.

'Rudy!' I said.

'That,' said Banning, without a touch of humor, 'is a disgustingly sloppy grin.'

'What are *you* doing here?'

'Saving your life,' Banning said. 'Please hurry.'

I wove back and forth like a drunk to get a closer look at the big guy. He was in his early sixties, with big round shoulders and hairy hands. He lugged a solid beer belly.

The big guy opened the back door and pushed me in. I sat.

'How wonderful for you, Rudy,' I said. 'Nice German car.'

Banning stared fixedly through the front windshield.

The big guy sat in front and passed me a gallon plastic milk container. 'Drink this,' he said. 'Drink all of it. It will make you sicker than a dog and you'll spew from both ends. Let us know when the rumbling starts.' He looked at his watch. 'Might take an hour.'

'I'll warn you,' I said earnestly.

I started drinking. It was not milk. It tasted awful, like very sour yogurt laced with Angostura. I did what they told me, not because I was compelled to, but because a fresh, frightened, but still-small voice told me that I had almost killed myself, and that these were friends.

The big guy watched me drink. 'Let's go before they come back to check on you.'

Rudy swung a quick look around the parking lot, put the Mercedes in gear, and drove away from the strip motel with old-world ease.

'We're taking you to a plane,' the big guy said. 'Then we're going to New York. I've already been there.'

'I know Rudy, but who are you?' I asked between gulps.

'I'm the bastard who shot your brother,' he said, with a bitter twist of his face.

part four
BEN BRIDGER

CHAPTER THIRTY-TWO
Manhattan
June 20

'It's got to be like moving chess pieces by walkie-talkie with someone wearing kitchen mitts,' Rob said as the Amtrak pulled into Penn Station. He had just come out of a heavy snooze, with loud and liquid snoring. His eyes were dreamy as he goggled at the stone and brick walls outside the train. He looked terrible. 'Hands-off, three and four removed, waiting, hiding out . . .'

I asked him what he was talking about.

'Silk,' he said.

'They've stomped us so far,' I said. We stepped off the Amtrak, crossed the platform, and hauled our two bags – LA thrift-store cheapies – up the stairs to Pennsylvania Avenue. I looked for a taxi.

'Don't take a cab that's waiting,' Rob said. 'Don't take a cab if they seem to be looking for us. In fact, let's walk a few blocks.'

It was a sensible precaution. 'You sure you're okay?'

Rob was pastier than ever and unsteady on his feet. 'We're two-footed lab rats,' he murmured, weaving through the crowds, trying to avoid any physical contact. 'I'm okay. Just walk, all right?' This, in reaction to my trying to carry his suitcase. 'I've got it, really,' he insisted. 'God, I feel so stupid. I thought there were limits. I should have read your books more closely.'

'You should rest. We'll sit in a hotel lobby, have some bottled water.'

'Did you hear? Someone's spiking bottled water all over the three boroughs.'

'Yeah, but it's ammonia and bleach,' I said. 'Garden-variety sicko.'

'How do we know it isn't a cover?'

I shook my head. We didn't. We didn't know anything. We had been working and traveling for a week. We were half-dead from exhaustion, Rob's left arm was bandaged from a flying splinter, I had cuts on my scalp – covered by a baseball cap.

I looked up at the Empire State Building. Still impressive, still New York. I had a sudden shivering sense of place. This was the real world; out west it was twilight crazy-time, bugfuck nonsense.

But bugfuck kills. We had been the lucky ones.

The basement had partially fallen in, trapping Rob and me for a while. Tammy crawled out through a hole in the floor. We heard her walking overhead, shouting, then another round of cannon fire.

While I pulled aside rubble and used a two-by-four to prop up a piece of floor blocking the exit, Rob grabbed an ice chest from under a fallen beam and went through what was left of the lab. He filled the chest with jars and little plastic dishes.

We found Tammy bleeding and screaming and walking around the front yard, stretching out a mangled hand. I did what I could, holding pressure points, scrounging through a first-aid kit to put together a bandage.

Rob searched through the leaning walls and collapsed rooms and found Marquez in the shambles of the den. There was blood and glass and broken model airplanes all over and Elvis had very obviously left the building.

The dogs in the kennels had fallen silent, lying on their tummies, ears laid back, eyes big.

The house was burning fiercely. There wasn't much time.

Police cars, ambulances started rolling in. We helped Tammy get to the paramedics and decided we couldn't do any more there. We rode the elevator down to the second house, which had only been lightly damaged. There we found a red Mercedes

S320 with the key in the ignition. The garage door opened and we departed the scene before fire trucks and other vehicles could block off the lower streets.

Marquez had thought of everything. A second set of plates in the trunk, and the car was registered in Nevada.

We took a chance and visited Tammy in the hospital. Four new bodyguards watched us enter the door to her room. No police protection.

She was groggy but she could talk. 'Tell Dr Goncourt he kills good people,' she said, and stroked my hand. 'He killed my man. He killed my son.'

Then she gave us the keys to Joe's kingdom. Bank-account numbers and passwords that Marquez had made her memorize. Security codes to lockboxes in seven cities, with phone numbers where we could hide out if things got impossible on the street.

And the crown jewels: maps and key codes for sections of the *Lemuria* and the Goncourt estate on Lee Stocking Island. She did not know whether the key codes were current.

I hated to abandon Tammy, but there was nothing we could do for her. We had work to finish.

I had changed my mind during the gunship slaughter. The cowardly masters pulled puppet strings, but the puppets had fucked up. The masters were vulnerable. And they had killed a whole lot of innocents. They had tried to kill a pregnant woman.

Janie would never let me into our heavenly condo if I didn't do something to square that angle.

We drove to San Jose and stored Rob's samples in an office he had rented with Rudy Banning, half repository for Rudy's crazy piles of research and half makeshift lab. Rob had kept paying the rent even after Marquez lent him his basement.

It was a kind of safe house, just in case.

There, he worked feverishly for several days, then gave us the latest version of his vaccine. While he worked, I made a phone call.

I was eager to fight, but if I could arrange for some special help, I thought we'd have a better chance.

New York became Rob's holy grail. I swear he acted as if we were going to visit a shrine. I thought we were too obvious, too open. He did not care. 'I need to get some specimens,' he had said. 'I can put it all together if I just get a few specimens.'

We must have looked like two bums in a bad New York comedy.

Rob suddenly pulled up short in the middle of the sidewalk, staring at clouds dropping specks of rain, then fixed his eyes on me.

'Are *you* all right?' he asked with real concern. 'It's a witch's brew, I know it is. I didn't have time. I need those last few surface proteins. I can make antisense RNA and block the gene expression –'

'Hold it.' I pulled him up close. Our suitcases bumped. A dark green Ford Crown Victoria, no marks, passed us for the third time. An old guy wearing a brown-leather bomber jacket hung his arm out the window and watched us. He caught my eye and nodded amiably, then motioned for the driver to pull over.

Rob and I stood like two jacklighted deer.

The guy in the bomber jacket stepped out on the curb and waved his arm. 'Damn it, Ben, get over here!' he shouted. 'We're your ride.'

Rob shivered. I thought he might pass out. I squinted at the man. 'Stuart?' I called, and smiled. I immediately straightened my face. No reason to smile, no reason to trust anyone.

'Yeah, get in,' Stuart said.

'Who's that?' Rob asked, ready to bolt.

'Some of my spook friends. We have a last-resort help line with an answering machine. I didn't think anybody would believe me. If you're crazy, you're on your own.'

Rob followed a few steps behind as I approached the car. Stuart Garvey had been in the CIA before retiring in the early eighties. I hadn't seen him in person since 1985, at an old spook reunion, but he was part of the Tom-Tom club. He had been the second man I had fired off my question to, back in El Cajon, the one who had not replied – and the last person I had thought might meet us in New York.

'You need transportation, don't you?' Stuart asked casually, and opened up the rear door. He eyeballed Rob critically. 'Your friend could take a header, he doesn't get to sit down.'

'I'm fine,' Rob said. I doubt anyone believed him.

We got into the backseat and Stuart introduced us to the driver. 'You remember Norton, don't you?'

I did, vaguely, from sessions at the Marine base in Quantico. Norton Crenshaw, younger than Stuart, in his sixties and quite heavy even in his younger years. We had called him Melon. He wore a windbreaker and a faded *E.T.* cap. 'I'm a silent partner,' Norton said with an easy smile. His face was pleasant but I remembered he enjoyed being trained to kill.

Stuart took us to a quiet diner where the owner knew him. We passed through an airport-style metal detector just inside the front door. Stuart held out his arms and pirouetted through. The machine gave a small *wheep* – just change and keys. The rest of us passed with as little fuss. The owner, a small Asian man, wrinkled and solemn, gave us a booth way in the back.

Stuart and I went to the men's room. He glanced at me over the marble divider between two urinals. His flow got going quick and easy, mine took a while; that meant he thought he had the upper hand. 'Do you know what you're into here?' he asked quietly, shaking himself and zipping up.

'Hell, no,' I said.

'That's all you have to say?' Stuart washed his hands first in the sink. Toy-dolly strawberry smell wafted up from the basin. He wrinkled his nose.

'Convenient to check us for guns going in,' I said.

'Yeah. Mr Chung's had some problems with punks *packing heat*, as the old cliché has it. Do you know all there is to know about Dr Cousins?'

'You tell me,' I said, washing my hands next. He rattled down a length of cotton towel and wiped vigorously.

'The wind is up. Shit is flying loose that we thought we'd glued down forty years ago. Dr Cousins is right at the eye of the storm.'

He pushed through the swinging door and left me standing in the rest room. My bush-sense was ringing some bad bells.

Back in the booth, Rob picked at his pastrami on rye with a fork and hadn't touched his glass of iced tea. His look suggested he did not want to either eat or drink there. 'How did you know which train we'd be on?' Rob was asking as I rejoined the group.

Stuart tapped his temple with his middle finger. 'Once a spook,' he said. 'Where are you staying?'

'We're not,' I said. 'We want to visit a building and get the hell out of here.'

'Which building?' Stuart asked.

Rob looked at me for advice. I nodded. 'The Jenner Building,' he said, and showed them the address on a slip of paper.

'Christ.' Stuart lowered his voice and leaned over the table. 'Anthrax Central? It's closed. They can't even tear the bastard down, it's so contaminated.'

I could not tell what Stuart was up to. Then it dawned on me. Chemical and Bacteriological Warfare had been Stuart's specialty. 'That's right,' I said. 'You covered CBW way back when.'

'There's no anthrax,' Rob said. 'It's just a cover.'

'That's not what *I* heard,' Stuart said. He was playing with Rob and I did not enjoy it, but I needed to learn which way the water was going to rush when the dam burst, which would be soon.

Stuart and Norton had known all along where we were going. They were still on active duty. They had been assigned to find us.

'It's not anthrax,' Rob insisted. His brow was covered with

240

sweat. He jerked his head and looked at me. 'We should take a cab.'

'Your friend's not feeling well,' Stuart stated categorically.

'I'm fine,' Rob said.

'He knows what he's talking about,' I said defensively. 'Now, Stuart, explain.'

'Ben, how could you let yourself get involved in this? You of all people. You don't know jack about CBW. Being kind to stray puppies?'

'When someone's trying to kick the shit out of them,' I said. Norton snorted and tapped his lip with a pudgy finger.

Stuart made a sour face. 'The hell with waiting,' he said. 'Finished?'

Rob waved a dismissive hand over the sandwich. 'I'm not hungry.'

'Let's help you do this thing.'

We went back to the car. Norton whistled a jaunty little tune as he started the motor. Rob looked worse than ever.

'Manhattan used to be a hotbed for biological research, a lot of it secret,' Stuart said as we drove through the crowded, rainy streets. I touched the left-rear door handle. It flopped back and forth, attached to nothing important.

'They put up three special buildings here, beginning in the late 1930s. The most modern laboratories of their day. Some of them housed researchers working to cure smallpox, malaria, polio. They used the best isolation procedures available. Even so, it's a miracle something didn't escape and kill thousands. Maybe millions. The last building was finished and occupied in 1954.' He pointed up the street. 'It housed Silk until the early sixties.'

Rob leaned forward, his cheeks pinking. 'What do you know about Silk?'

'A lot more than Rudy Banning,' Stuart said. 'My last job was to help get Rudy discredited. Wasn't hard. The man's a loon.'

'I thought you retired in the eighties,' I said to Stuart.

Stuart stared out the window, annoyed by so many pointless

words floating through the air. You learn nothing from a spook by watching his eyes, but this time he wanted me to see how he felt: impatient. 'Ben, this is not for you. You should have smelled it early on and jumped clear.'

Rob looked around like a neck-jerking pigeon at the rest of us in the big old Crown Victoria. 'I wasn't nearly paranoid enough, was I?'

The car slid into a loading zone across the street from a large, gray, stone-fronted cube, wet with steady drizzle.

'Here we are,' Norton announced. He reached under the dash and handed Stuart something I could not see. I was pretty sure it was a gun.

The lower floors had no windows and the entrance doors had been boarded over, with boards nailed over the boards. Graffiti covered it at ground level, protecting the building with an air of disuse like a fence made of spray paint.

'Prime real estate,' Stuart said. 'Doesn't that tell you something?'

'Stuart, why are you here, and what do you know?'

'I'll tell it straight, Ben, for old times' sake,' Stuart said.

Norton gave him a disapproving glance, then lifted his hands, so be it. 'Nobody will believe it, of course,' Norton said. 'It's crazy shit. Like Area 51.'

'Retirement sucks,' Stuart said. He lifted the pistol into our view. A SIG-Sauer, I couldn't tell the model number, but it was dark and shiny, strictly new-millennium government issue. 'After the end of the Cold War, the best of the old guard were called back to put the whole espionage thing on a new footing. Industrial, corporate.'

'They didn't ask me,' I said.

'Right,' Stuart said.

'We're fried,' Rob said, and held up his hands like a bad guy giving up to the sheriff.

'Shut up,' Stuart told him. 'You're responsible for a lot of hard work coming to grief.'

I put a hand on Rob's arm: maintain.

'I worked Silk in the late fifties and early sixties, as a youngster,' Stuart said. 'I heard things in the briefings you wouldn't believe. OSS and MI6 had tracked them intermittently through the forties. Nobody knows the real history of the war. But that was before my time. I do know that Silk started cooperating with us in the late forties. They saw the approach of Stalin's final madness, and, over three years, they dismantled their operations in the Soviet Union, sabotaged their stockpiles and labs, and disassociated themselves from the next generation of biowar researchers. It was all very ingenious. Essentially, to the Russians after Stalin, Silk became a bunch of crackpot has-beens, on a par with Lysenko.

'In 1953, when I was still a kid, we were ordered to help them find a safe zone in the United States. They had peculiar needs. So we outbid some drug companies and bought Anthrax Central before it was finished.' He pointed to the gray cube across the street. 'We handed it over to Silk in exchange for certain activities in Latin America, Southeast Asia, and China. Political sculpture, it was called. I took over the day-to-day operations in 1961. It was a funny relationship. Half the time, they didn't do what we wanted them to. I always thought they were working other streets, maybe financial, in Europe or in China, even in Russia again, but that was outside our scope. The Agency told me to let it go, so I let it go. Hands off, don't provoke them, those were our prime instructions.'

'You were afraid,' Rob said.

'You bet your ass we were afraid. The more I knew, the less I slept nights. I'm pretty sure they called the shots from the very beginning. Nobody knew who they were running – in the State Department, the FBI, the military. The Oval Office. Even the Agency. Whenever we tried to authorize countermeasures, we were squelched at a very high level. In 1970, I was assigned elsewhere. Silk went offshore, to the Bahamas, and stopped its activities. I had a long and easier career and retired. The Soviet Union fell apart. Happy days. Then I got word I was needed again. Surprise, Silk had actually come to us with a proposal. They wanted a new and safer haven in a changing world. Someone decided that American industry could benefit from what Silk knew. Contracts were drawn up. I helped make sure the secrets were kept, even when some folks were eager to tell all. That was when I was ordered to discredit Banning.'

Stuart leaned his head to one side and massaged his neck. '*They* worked out a *deal* – not me, personally, you understand. It was a good deal, as far as it went. Now it's falling apart, and it looks like Dr Cousins here is responsible.'

'Shit, shit, shit,' Rob said. He grabbed his door handle, discovered what I already knew, then pounded the armrest and slumped back in his seat. He focused on Stuart. 'You helped them go after AY3000 and me, too?' Rob took on the look of someone realizing he has been gut shot. 'Have you gone after my brother?'

Stuart shook his head. 'I don't know anything about that, and I don't want to know. But it's obvious you've pissed off someone who should never have been pissed off. And that makes a lot more work for the rest of us.'

'This stinks, Stuart,' I said. 'What if you just let us walk away? The Tom-Tom club knows.'

Stuart looked peeved. 'You wanted to come here, Ben. We brought you here. We've done everything you asked, right?' The rain on the side window drew sliding beads of shadow over his face. 'Nobody in the Tom-Tom will believe you. You were never the brightest member. You were a grunt in the bush, Ben.'

It was an old slur. *What do you get from a grunt in the bush*? *A pile of shit.*

'Fuck you,' I said to Stuart. To Norton, 'You too.'

Stuart let me see that his eyes could go cold if he wanted them to. 'The dead don't fuck. They are beyond fucking and being fucked with. *I don't know what they're going to tell you.* Believe me. But I suggest you listen close. It may be your only way out of this mess. You, too, Dr Cousins. You sure look like hell.'

The car pulled around to a broad alley behind the building.

Norton squeezed out and opened my door. He, too, held a pistol, another SIG-Sauer. Stuart opened Rob's door.

Guttering streams fell in a thin curtain from the parapet at the top of the square gray mass. A big steel door covered with graffiti – eyeballs, grasping hands with thick splintered fingernails, thorn crowns on bleeding heads – opened to receive us.

'I thought it was shut down,' Rob said. I could see the last of his starch going. 'We were going to break in and get some samples.'

'Don't say we didn't warn you,' Stuart said.

Two earnest, tired-looking young men with short hair, wearing wrinkled business suits that had been sweated in for hours, stepped out of the shadows inside the door and stood at parade rest, waiting.

The building's breath smelled dry and warm and clean.

The young agents greeted Stuart and Norton. Stuart whispered something to the one on the left. Norton walked right on through.

'Let's go,' he said.

Rob entered Anthrax Central. I followed, looking for places to duck, pull things down, get some confusion going. There wasn't much. We walked over a concrete floor. The concrete walls had been painted gray and red, and a raised loading platform crossed the rear. Big glass tanks filled with murky water stood along one side of the platform. It could have been a receiving area for a big metropolitan aquarium, but the tanks didn't seem to have any fish, just lumpy shadows like coral and pipes going in and out at the top.

Two boys and two girls, late teens, dressed in denim overalls, supple as sea lions and alert as terriers, emerged from the shadows between the water tanks. They squatted on the edge of the platform as if waiting for a rock concert to begin.

'We stay here until the caretaker arrives,' Norton said.

'I wouldn't go any farther without an escort for all the sin in Singapore,' Stuart said, and winked at me as if we were still buddies.

Out of the corner of my eye, I saw a little gray wisp emerge from the dark between the tanks. It walked with a quick, shuffling step along the platform. I craned my neck. At first I thought it was an old man, head small and wrinkled, eyes large, frame shrunken, walking along the upper ramp, skirting the aquariums. But something about the way the wisp moved, a sway of the shoulders with each step, made me think again about its sex.

Rob watched with feverish interest.

'There she is,' Stuart said.

'That's the caretaker?' I asked.

Stuart nodded. His Adam's apple bobbed. He did not look happy to see her.

The caretaker wore a calf-length black shift and a cloth cap like the ones they give newborns. The kids stood out of the way as the specter passed. She nodded to all and patted a slender boy of sixteen or seventeen on the head, folding her lips into a ghost of affection.

She glided down a flight of steel steps in a blur of tiny feet.

Stuart and Norton stepped back as she passed, as if they might catch something that would steal away their souls. She ignored them.

The caretaker walked around Rob and me, inspecting us with a patient, gray gaze, her head tilting left, then right. She smelled like wine left in a glass after a party.

'Rob Cousins,' she said in a youthful tenor voice that could have been either male or female. She reached out and pulled Rob's hand close to her eyes. 'You've made some mistakes, I see.'

Despite his resistance, she thrust out the hand for our inspection. Between the tendons on the back, the skin had folded and puckered into tight little furrows. I had noticed the marks before and thought they might be scars from an operation.

'Gross mistakes,' the caretaker said.

'What about you?' Rob said, his voice gravelly.

The caretaker held up her own hand: the same puckers,

though smoothed over by the years. 'How old do you think I am?' she asked Rob.

Rob snatched back his hand. 'You're suffering from progeria,' he said. 'Premature aging. You're forty, tops.'

The expression on her face hardened. 'No reason to be petty.' She was not used to being judged. 'Once I was the *future*, Dr Cousins.'

She walked back toward the ramp, shoulders undulating slowly, wrists hanging. When we held back, she turned and blinked like a thin old monkey at Stuart and Norton. They urged us to follow with a couple of shoves. To Stuart, it was just part of the day. Norton enjoyed shoving.

The agents in wrinkled suits stayed by the door, foreheads damp. The kids vanished into the shadows.

For some time now I had been looking for a way to start a mad minute, to provoke some hasty action from our captors – without getting killed ourselves. Nothing. They were tight and observant.

The caretaker walked ahead of us down a dark, tomb-quiet hallway. The polished floor shone in the milky fluorescence of a far-off ceiling fixture. Rob caught up with our guide. 'You said I did something wrong. How wrong? How do you know?'

She looked up. 'Your chemistry runs like a spinning top first this way, then that. You cut too many channels between the Little Mothers. The puckers show me you will have the disease in a few months, perhaps sooner. Yes, you could live a long time. Maybe centuries. But you will spend years in rabid madness.'

Rob looked like a dog about to throw up. He hung back, and Norton gave him an encouraging tap on the ankle with the tip of his hard black shoe.

'We're going to be killed,' Rob told me, as if this was news.

I looked back at Stuart and Norton. 'You're going to let this happen?'

Stuart shrugged.

I just wanted to see who was paying more attention. I knew how these guys thought, the exercises they went through at the end of a hard day to put away in drawers the things they had done and seen. Maybe this was all I deserved. Christ, I had gotten slow the last few years.

All the corners, the edges between walls and floor, walls and ceiling, were covered over with curved runnels of ceramic. The linoleum was not linoleum, I realized, as we walked a few steps, but long sheets of blue tile sealed with a vitreous sheen. The walls were also tile, fitted and treated to eliminate seams.

Not a breath of air in the hall. Age showed here and there in the star pattern of an impact fracture or cracks from building settling. Some of them had been repaired – glazed over with another vitreous layer.

The caretaker touched the wall with a finger. 'Once a day, they used to go through the corridors outside the labs with steam hoses and sterilize, in the evenings. The whole building smelled like a Chinese laundry. It was a lovely smell.' She turned. 'You keep looking at me, Mr Bridger. You have obvious questions. I am Maxim's wife.'

'Maxim Golokhov?' Rob asked.

'Yes,' the caretaker said, so softly we could barely hear. She turned to the left and Norton pushed us again.

'We're going to ask you some questions,' he said.

I tried to match this wrinkled stick with the woman in the video, lean but handsome, smiling. I couldn't.

Stuart took a position by the turn in the corridor and crossed his arms. One last pleading look didn't faze him.

Norton pointed to an open doorway. Inside a small office was a bare wooden desk and an old, scarred filing cabinet with labels in Cyrillic. Photos lined the walls. Norton pushed two chairs up to the desk. Rob and I sat. The caretaker stood by the wall of photos. I swept my eyes over the ranks of small black frames and their black-and-white contents. I recognized none of the people in the photos on sight, except for one – in the lower left-hand corner, Joseph Stalin, standing beside another, younger man, both in military dress, both smiling. Stalin looked to be in his sixties. A war photo.

'Let's get going,' Norton said. 'We don't want to be here too long.'

The caretaker gave him a pinched look. 'Dr Cousins,' she said, 'your research is interesting, what you allowed to be published.'

Norton kept his eye on us with as much intellectual engagement as a guard dog.

'My question for you is, will you stop your research?'

Rob looked up. 'Would that do me any good? I'm a dead man already.'

'We are at that crossroads, yes. But there is a way. We bring stability, not greed. Tell us what you have done that blocks our controls.'

Norton nodded. The conversation was following the proper form now.

'I'd like to know what my mistakes were,' Rob said.

The caretaker moved closer. Her eyes inspected him with a surprising heat and her voice rose almost an octave.

'When you seek to live for ever, you cut yourself away from the Little Mothers and their ministrations. That can make it difficult for others to control you, yes. But not impossible. It just takes more, much more, over time, as a *wife* or lover might deliver, or all at once, a mix of product and maker, the pure form, then you can be run for several hours, even days, sometimes weeks.'

'Why do I have wrinkles on the backs of my hands?' Rob asked.

I watched Norton – Melon – carefully. Stupid men always leave themselves open, but I was not at all sure Melon was stupid. He just knew what to pay attention to and what to ignore. And he seemed less ill at ease than Stuart.

He knew the place. *It was Melon's assignment.*

'You have cut off signaling paths used by both the body and the Little Mothers.'

That phrase kept popping up and it was bugging the hell out of me. 'What are these Little Mothers?' I asked.

'She means bacteria,' Rob said, his eyes on the caretaker, as if they were playing a game of chess and he wanted to psych her out. Another bad move. Don't stare at the beast.

'The body feels lonely without guidance,' the caretaker said. 'It turns in on itself. You lose your connections to other humans. What you hate and fear becomes magnified.'

She looked at Melon again. I could not read her expression, and clearly Melon did not want to try. Who was in charge here? Who was running whom?

'Dr Golokhov – treated you first?' Rob asked.

'Skip it,' Melon said.

'I was the first. I volunteered,' she said. She wanted to talk. Rob was providing a sympathetic ear. A fellow traveler. I was back in Kafkaville with a vengeance.

'And it didn't work?'

'I am still here. I will be here a hundred years from now, barring accidents . . . or losing control.'

'But you said you went insane.'

'You pass through the most horrible gates to escape death.' The caretaker sighed like a little girl. 'I remember the days we worked together, how he tended to me during my transition, and learned from my example to change his treatments, to avoid the most obvious side effects. He was wrong to leave me here. I could have helped him listen to the Little Mothers. That's the important thing, isn't it?'

'Listen to them – where?'

'Downstairs. In the tanks. Everything else we did was wrong. He drove me to this. Maxim was wrong.'

Melon's eyebrow twitched. 'Time's a-wasting,' he said.

'Tell me about my errors,' Rob insisted, his face as intensely focused as a cat's over a bowl of cream. 'He must have done more work, more research. How can we avoid making his early mistakes?'

The caretaker looked up at Melon.

'Fuck this,' Melon said. He pushed his gun against Rob's neck. 'How do you block the tagging?'

Rob blinked. We were on a knife edge and he was discovering courage.

'How?' Melon insisted.

The caretaker held up her hand. However small, this gesture made Melon back down – but only for a moment. 'Will you work with us?' she asked. 'It is obvious we have so much information to share.'

Rob looked pained and shook his head adamantly. 'Never,' he said.

'Give them what they want!' I shouted.

'They don't need me,' Rob said. 'This is a charade.'

'We had to try,' the caretaker said. 'We are not monsters, you know.' She faced the wall of pictures, head tilted to the right, then the left. She seemed to have tuned us all out.

'Tell them,' I said to Rob. 'Give them something!'

Melon waved his little gun. 'Let's do it,' he said. The caretaker swung around on her tiny feet and glided out of the small office.

We got up from our chairs and returned to the main corridor, where Stuart was waiting.

'Ready?' he asked me.

We all came to a wide doorway and stopped. Beyond lay a room that might have been an abandoned Turkish bath, slick gray surfaces rising into long benches against the walls. Seven blue-gray tile basins, as big as double-wide bathtubs, held the center in two rows of three, and one in the middle, forming an H. Dark, pudding-thick liquid spiraled in the tubs, stirred by hidden paddles. Long hoses connected to aerators hung off the far sides of each tub. I could hear small bubbling sounds. The room was mostly in shadow.

'Take off your clothes,' the caretaker said.

The air smelled faintly of jungle. Seawater in an old tide pool. Fresh sweat on Janie's arms on a sunny day. I could not identify all the odors rising from the tubs, but they scared me more than the mephitis of rotting corpses or the gravy-tang of spilled blood.

I watched for a lapse of attention and put on an act – not much acting needed, really – that would suggest a mark about to lose his cool. A mark is someone who is all too aware he will soon be meat. Lieutenant JG Mark Wasserman changed his name as we flew into Laos because that was how we used to designate those who would soon be dead. *'Look at all those marks.'*

'How old are you?' Rob asked the caretaker. 'Why am I like you? Which receptors did I screw up?' Curious to the end. Like a young steer in the chute.

Stuart and Norton took their positions. I started taking off my clothes, but slowly. Prolong the inevitable.

The caretaker walked to one of the aerators and picked up a black wand with a brass nozzle. Two hoses hung from the wand, I saw, one going into the tub, the other snaking around to a row of brass nipples mounted in the back wall.

She inspected the nozzle. It resembled a showerhead and seemed to meet her approval. She turned the valve and a small dollop of goop smeared her palm. She approached Rob. Melon held his arms. Even with the difference in ages, it was no contest.

Rob drew his head back. Delicately, like a cosmetologist applying makeup, the caretaker dabbed her finger in the goop, then painted it beneath and around his eyes, under his lips. He jerked his head aside and Melon tugged at his elbows until he gasped. She applied greenish streaks to his gums, his cheeks, his temple, under his chin, with swiping jabs, her arms quick as wasp wings.

'Greed and stupidity,' she said. 'It is old history.'

Melon let Rob go, leaving him to scrub at his face vigorously.

I had taken off my shirt.

The caretaker aimed the brass nozzle in my direction. 'That is enough,' she said. She turned the valve all the way. The stuff stung as it hit, like paint out of a spray gun. I felt the tingle over my skin, involuntarily sucked some of it into my nose and mouth, choked and heaved, tried to spit it out. I fell on my back and wiped my eyes, flung strands of the slime against the floor, the side of a tub.

'I was Maxim Golokhov's student and assistant in 1924. I became his wife in 1936. Beria and Stalin were at our wedding. We spent long years in Irkutsk and in Moscow, learning, always learning.'

Through the haze, watching for her next move, I saw that she could still cry. 'I helped him build this facility after we were finished in Russia, after we fled. The Politburo wanted nothing to do with us, even though we had saved them. Maxim, he was the brave man, but he had other concerns than our marriage. He went to the islands in 1965 and left me here, and I became a caretaker. I *earned* my keep.'

The stinging subsided. I started to enjoy the sound of her voice. She checked my eyes and nose and lips, like a vet looking over a dog. 'Your friend has treated you with something, an antidote maybe?' she said confidentially.

I nodded. The slime dripped off my chin.

'But not expertly. Do you like me?'

I did, actually.

'Rob Cousins is a dead man. Do you see this? Do you see and feel why?'

Her voice was really something. I felt like a tree about to topple from its stump, but somehow stayed on my feet.

'You are covered with Little Mothers making a palette of persuasive chemicals, all over your outside, soon inside, too. Insinuating. It's not unpleasant, is it?'

It wasn't. I was feeling pretty good now. Confident.

'Listen to me, Mr Bridger. I tell you the truth, then I tell you what to do.'

'Let's hurry it up,' Stuart said. 'How do you know they're under? Silk couldn't work them.'

'I could teach my husband a few things,' the caretaker said.

'But I don't think Maxim's heart is in it anymore. Maybe he's learned all he wants to know.' I could have sworn that pruned, wrinkled face was sneering. She looked at me. 'You are not a rich man, are you?'

I shook my head. 'Far from it.'

'Rob Cousins asks the rich and powerful for money. He would make them immortal. But would you trust these plutocrats with your most precious things? Would you leave your *children* and grandchildren, for ten, a hundred generations, with them? *Would you make that mistake again?* These rich and greedy and ignorant people, tyrants, robbers of *all* the resources, *all* the money, *for all time*? *Do you trust them with that power, for all time?'*

As if for good measure, she sprayed Rob full in the face with the wand. He fell over on his hands, choking and gasping. She lifted the wand and turned. She stared at Stuart and Melon – Norton, I corrected myself. Best to be respectful.

They dropped back. They were distracted, their guard was down. But it was far too late to make my move. I was on the deck myself, writhing, feeling little orgasms work up my spine. The skin on my back sucked along the slick floor.

I wondered how Rob was doing. The caretaker leaned over him and showed him the back of her right hand, as if she might slap him.

'Do you know how old I am?' she asked in a shrill tenor. 'I am a hundred and seven. I will not age. I will be ugly for ever and ever. Do you know how many years I was mad?'

I rolled over to see Rob's reaction. I was starting to feel pissed off at him for causing all this trouble, and for going to all those rich people.

'Ten years. Maxim watched over me,' she said. 'I was kept in a cage. He took notes and made improvements on the treatment. He wanted to live a long time so he could decipher the voice of all the Little Mothers, from the deeps and the salt seas, but Beria and Stalin were more practical. They insisted they be treated next or we would *all* be executed. They had killed so many and yet they were such cowards. They did not go *quite* so mad.' Another dead smile.

'Just shoot us!' I shouted at Stuart, with the last of my will to resist.

Stuart actually leveled his gun at me. There was a scrap of decency still in him.

'What can she learn from that?' Melon asked him. Stuart lowered the gun.

The caretaker turned one last time to Rob. 'There is always your brother.'

Rob tried to grab her. Melon batted his arm down and kicked him in the stomach. He curled up, retching.

The caretaker leaned over me and pouched out her lips like a wizened little gibbon. 'Here are some numbers,' she said, and pulled a small sheet of paper from the pocket of her overalls. 'Tell me what they mean to you.'

part five

HAL COUSINS

CHAPTER THIRTY-THREE
Arizona
August 13

We were still driving east in the blood-red Mercedes, through desert caught up by morning. Bridger and I had been talking for hours, telling our stories. Banning spoke only rarely and kept checking his maps.

Bridger's story was coming to the conclusion I did not want to hear.

'The kids sprayed us down with water to get the slime off,' Ben said. 'We were both pretty limp by then. I was having visions. I was able to fly, I thought. I was in touch with powerful people all over the world. I could hear my intestines talking to me – as if they were stuffed with angels.

'They took us out to the loading dock and pushed us into that goddamned Crown Victoria. We got the seats wet, I remember. Rob was talking a mile a minute about cells and channels and receptors, about how he could feel the pathways opening up inside him. He said he could identify the ones he'd missed, the ones he'd got wrong. He seemed happy as a clam, eager to get back to work. "They're letting us go!" he said. "We're getting off easy!"'

'Did he tell you what the receptors were?' I asked Ben.

Ben gave me a look, as if I were some kind of curious and disgusting insect. He faced front, squinting at the long two-lane highway. 'No, fuck it, I'm *sorry*, Hal, he *didn't*. Not in so many words, and how in hell would I know, anyway?'

'Rob had the other half of the secret. That's what Lissa said. If I get that list, I could finish the work. I would know everything Golokhov knows. Maybe more.'

'I'm sure,' Ben said with a sigh. He had finally realized I was incurable, so he was giving up the moral tone.

This angered me. 'Don't you see it could be important? Rob asked, didn't he?'

Ben nodded. 'It was the most important thing in the world to him,' he said, his voice seeming to come from outside the car.

'They've tried to kill us, they've murdered innocent civilians, just to stop us from knowing.' I held off for a second, face hot, before adding, 'And my brother.'

'Yeah,' Ben said

We were five minutes down the road when Ben resumed.

'We were dropped off near Times Square, soaking wet. In an alley. Stuart stuffed a pistol into my hand, and said, "I'm sorry". He looked genuinely disgusted at what they had to do. Then he and Norton went to the end of the alley to wait. I honest to God tried to aim the gun at them, but I couldn't. I was focused on Rob.'

I felt my breath take a hitch. 'You shot him,' I said, hoping he would end his story now.

'It wasn't that simple,' Ben said. 'First, I had to get mad. So I punched him, right there in the alley. I broke his nose, I think. There was this awful voice in my head, it kept telling me "Go for the snot locker. That'll get him angry and that will make you angry". His face was covered with blood. But Rob danced and sang a song about which genes he'd work on next, which proteins he would block. He said we'd all live for ever.'

'Shit,' I said, and covered my ears.

'Goddamn it, listen to me!' Ben shrieked over the back of the seat, pounding it with his fist. 'Listen to me and, Jesus, give me some sort of absolution! Your brother *came to me*, he *dragged me* into this! You two stirred up the hornets, and *they all used me!*'

We were both crying. I reached out and tried to touch his arm. He flicked my hand aside.

'Then something changed. The flag went down and Rob got frightened. He wasn't reacting the same way I was. He didn't want to kill me, he wanted to talk. But I wasn't having any of it. He backed off and said he knew something. He told me to pass on something to his brother. He wanted me to tell you what he knew, if I survived. He said, "Tell Hal I know why it works on Ben and not on me". Then he rattled off some names, didn't make sense. Peace keeper or peace maker or something was the first.'

'Piecework?'

'That's it. Then . . . Revolver or regulator.'

'Regulus?'

Ben nodded. 'I told him to shut up. He found a chunk of wood from a crate. He was pitiful. I had the gun but he was waving that stick of wood. The last word was *chopper*. I remember that, because he was chopping at me with the wood. He wanted to get away, but I blocked the alley. He kept shouting that if I just remembered who I was and what we were doing, we could get out of here. "There's so much life, there's so much more to see," he said. But I couldn't stop.'

Piecework, regulus, chopper. I was familiar with two of them. *Piecework* was a common bacterial gene that regulated the creation of adhesins. Toothpaste companies were interested in it because it stopped *Streptococcus* and *Actinomyces* from binding in the human mouth and reduced plaque on teeth. *Regulus* was a human nuclear gene that coordinated mitochondrial functions. Mess with *regulus* in the wrong way and you could end up with Parkinson's. That's why I had avoided it, though it was a clear candidate for my work. *Our* work. *Chopper* wasn't a gene. I couldn't immediately place where I had heard the name.

I dropped my face into my hands.

'Rob couldn't take it anymore,' Ben said. 'He made a run at me, and I shot him. Then I threw away the pistol and ran out of the alley. Stuart and Norton were gone. I was all alone on the street. It was four in the morning.'

Ben spoke this last quickly, his cheeks shining.

We pulled into a service station. I leaned out of the door, thought about vomiting, decided it wasn't strictly necessary, and stood beside the car. 'I have to go,' I said, for the sixth or seventh time. The elixir was still having a strong effect.

Banning bought gas. I got the key from the young man behind the counter, went to the rest room, and leaned over the dirty sink. Despite the nausea, I couldn't bring up anything.

I had just listened to a man confess to shooting my twin, my shadow. My essential shadow. And I did not know how to react, whether to hate or pity. I was angry, not at Ben Bridger, but at Rob and myself. We had screwed it up so badly. We could have beaten the world. Or saved it. Instead, I had stolen his girls, then bits and pieces of his dignity. Rob had done things to me, in return. So many little disputes I should have been willing to concede. His science, that I didn't steal, because by then we had kept secrets and stayed away from each other.

We could have done it together. We would have had the Long Haul in our hot little hands right now. We really would have, I kept telling myself, staring into the scratched and filthy mirror.

I was my twin, right down to the suicidal arrogance.

The elixir's diarrhea came and went. I spent ten minutes on the toilet, totally absorbed in misery.

Back in the car, Ben was drinking a Dr Pepper. I climbed gingerly into the backseat. He blew his nose into a blue wind-shield wipe and avoided looking at me.

Banning sipped coffee from an orange 76 mug and studied another fold in the map.

'You probably haven't been following the news,' Ben said.

'No.' I felt my stomach turn, tried to stop my voice from shaking.

'The director of the CIA just resigned. He's under suspicion of downloading classified files, but that's just a cover. There's more going on, much more. Cracks in the Silk network in Washington. A little war. Anyway, something did the trick,' Ben said. 'Some agents reported back to their bosses – maybe the two that were in Anthrax Central, assigned to help Stuart and Norton. The bosses discovered something pretty special, a little late. They discovered they had done enough kowtowing and cringing. "It's a new millennium, gentlemen,"' Ben pontificated, swinging out his right arm and waving it at the night air. '"Time to clear the slate and set things right. Time to get a new compass." Maybe Rob's death wasn't in vain.

'Some cops found me an hour later outside the alley. I was pretty strung out. The next day, three agents I had never seen before sprung me from Rikers and took me in from the cold. Put me in hiding, gave me a physical and detox, then debriefed me about everything since Rob first showed up at my house. I thought at first they were just going to kill me after they'd got what they wanted. But no. There were two agencies, a cover agency either tagged into treason or defending its mistakes, and a special investigation team with almost no support and no money.

'I accompanied a group of them back to San Jose and we opened up Rob's secret office. They assigned their own lab guys to look over Banning's papers and what Rob had put together. They inventoried all his cultures and chemistries.'

'Before Lissa took me there,' I said.

'Yeah. They modified the elixir based on Rob's work. By the time they had their act together, and set out to find you, it was a couple of weeks after Rob's funeral in Florida. You had gone underground. Banning got to you first, but he was acting on his own, as usual.'

'Sometimes that's best,' Banning said.

'We're in a small operation, so far, deliberately – they don't know who might be tagged, and who might not, and they want it to look to Silk like we're still rogues. The operation may not even be officially sanctioned. I think they're still making some tough discoveries and decisions back in Washington.'

'What about the body in the freezer?' I asked.

'There was a dust-up in San Francisco. We almost got shot – and caught two runners. One was killed, the other got away.'

'A man in gray?' I thought of the man who had argued with Lissa in front of the strip motel.

'Yeah. The Agency did a quick autopsy of the dead fellow,

took samples to see what Silk might be doing to control runners. Then they hauled the body in a refrigerated truck down to San Jose. Left him in Rob's freezer in case Silk decided to come looking. It was convenient, and there was an element of payback. A little psychological warfare.'

Lissa had certainly been surprised. 'They put a sentry out in the used-car lot, in case I showed up,' I said. 'The skinny guy in a herringbone suit. The one Lissa shot.'

'We don't know who that was,' Ben said. 'Maybe just a good citizen, hoping to arrest a bomber.'

Fucking amateur. 'I doubt that,' I said. 'Something went wrong – some lack of coordination at the top. The bomb scared Lissa. Maybe she took it out on one of their own. Maybe a taggee . . . maybe an inept runner.' Or maybe – the thought came and went – we didn't understand anything yet.

Ben shrugged. 'They make mistakes. That's something in our favor. Our team started tracking you after Mrs Callas illegally logged on to NCIC2000.'

'What the hell is that?'

'The FBI's on-line database of criminal activity in the United States. It's available only to law enforcement. A real hacker's target.'

'Callas refused to have anything to do with us,' I said.

'Smart woman,' Ben said. 'We caught up with you after they spotted Lissa Cousins's car east of LA.'

We rolled out on the road again.

'Those three names,' I said. 'Let's make sure. They were *piecework*, *regulus*, and *chopper*?'

'I think so,' Ben said.

'They could be important,' I warned.

'The first could have been *peacekeeper* or *peacemaker*,' Ben said.

'There are no such genes.'

'They're names for genes?'

'Two of them are genes,' I confirmed. *Chopper* was coming back to me. Not a gene, but a glycoprotein often created during phage infection. It was part of a bacterial ID system.

'Make you live for ever?'

I shook my head. 'That wasn't what Rob was telling us. They're part of the complex of pathways that allow bacteria to coordinate their activities on our skin and in our gut. Pumping in antisense RNA with a shuttle vector could block the gene products. Phage-infected bacteria, without *chopper*, could get picked out as "foreigners" and targeted by other bacteria. Rob must have worked them into his treatment early on, but not into yours. That made the difference in your tagged behavior. He came out from under faster.'

'*Piecework, chopper, regulus,*' Banning said. 'It is nice to be among fellow crazies, to have some acknowledgment of my efforts, and to finally, after all these years, have a government job.'

'Sure,' Ben said. 'Drive.'

'I hope, gentlemen, that when this is over, one of you will lend me a pistol. I would like to kill these *idiot* voices once and for all.'

'Gladly,' Ben said.

Banning's lips started working. He couldn't help it. 'My first love was a beautiful young Jewess, you know,' he confessed, eyes darting.

'Just *shut up*,' Ben said wearily.

Banning was quiet the rest of the way.

Our rendezvous point was a small civilian airport in the desert. A group of ten or so earnest-looking men in suits waited inside a big tin hangar. They seemed surprised to see us.

'You did it,' said a pleasant-looking fellow a little older than me and wearing jeans and a white dress shirt with the sleeves rolled up. He introduced himself as an FBI agent named Condon. 'Good to see you. Our other outside expert didn't get through. We're to accompany you to New York. Do you know where we're going?'

'Near where they shot my brother,' I said.

'Sorry about that,' Condon said, and ran his hands through his sandy hair.

'Don't apologize to me,' I said tightly. 'Apologize to Ben. You're the bastards who did this.'

It wasn't a fair assessment, but no one tried to set me straight. Three doctors came out of the back of an unmarked van and checked us over, then gave us some injections. I made one last visit to the bathroom, and, when I came out, I felt as empty as I've ever been in my life.

Ben and I and three others climbed into an Air Force Learjet, and a few minutes later we took off into a clear morning sky.

They left Banning with the car. He waved at us from beside the hangar. Rudy Banning, whether he wanted to be or not, was a survivor.

Once we were at altitude, the oldest of the three agents unbelted and walked forward, hunched over in the low cabin. He had a square, tanned face topped with a thatch of graying brown hair, black eyes, and well-formed Levantine lips. He clamped his hand on the blue fabric of my seat back to steady himself while he spoke.

'My name is David Breaker,' he said. 'We want to thank you for all you're doing.' I heard his stomach grumble. 'Ben might have described our operation.'

'A little,' I said.

'I've been put in charge of this part of the effort. We're taking you to New York. To Manhattan. As you can see, I don't feel good, and it isn't because of airsickness. We're pretty ashamed, but we're doing all we can to make up for it, including a little intestinal penance.'

'Fine,' I said tonelessly. I still did not know whom to believe, whom to be nice to, and certainly not whom I would trust with my life.

'I, personally, did not know about Silk until a month ago. But that's neither here nor there, and after the death of your brother, with the collusion of a portion of the Agency, I just wanted to . . .'

'Apologize,' I said, feeling another brutal cut of anger. 'The hell with it.'

'You need to know some things about this operation. One, it is not sanctioned by the President. The President tests positive as a recent taggee. We've disengaged two of the people we think are running him, but there could easily be backups. Some of my colleagues are monitoring all the President's phone calls. I don't know what more we can do, practically or constitutionally, at this point. So we're ultimately on our own, illegal as it may be. First we need to weed out the center of Silk activity in North America. That effort requires your help, Dr Cousins. This afternoon, if all goes well, we're putting an armed team, everyone we can muster, Army, CIA, NSA, FBI, maybe twenty people, into the Jenner Building in New York. You know the one I'm talking about?'

'Ben told me,' I said. 'Anthrax Central.'

'That was its cover for years. We hope to have it under our control by the time our plane lands. You'll go in with a security team. We want to give you a chance to evaluate their facilities. Think of it as a kind of dress rehearsal for the big show in Florida.'

'*Lemuria*?'

Breaker nodded.

'I can help you right now, possibly,' I said. I looked at Ben, sitting across the aisle from me, partially hidden by Breaker. Ben leaned forward and our eyes made contact. For no good reason whatsoever, I trusted the very man who had pulled the trigger on Rob.

Rob would have appreciated that. It would have amused him greatly.

'How?' Breaker asked.

'Tell your scientists to antisense *piecework*, that's piece with an i-e, *regulus*, and *chopper*. It was my brother's last message to me.'

'Antisense?'

'They'll know what I mean. Add them to the list in your elixir. Immunize all of us again, if there's time.'

Breaker seemed doubtful. 'If there's time,' he said. An agent seated behind us shifted an assault rifle to one side and recorded the names on a paper notepad. I spelled them all several times to make sure.

Breaker plugged a small DVD player into a screen mounted in the seat back. 'This is from a security camera in the cafeteria at the J. Edgar Hoover Building in Washington, D.C.,' he said. 'Two weeks ago.' A title card came up: 'TAPS HOOVER July 29.'

The segment, shot from a security camera at a high angle, showed two skinny boys and two matronly women working in the kitchen and food line. All wore aprons and plastic snoods. They worked a number of serving stations, cleaning up and replacing food.

One by one, they used little plastic bottles to spray a salad bar, steam tables, and, finally, racks of Jell-O cups, puddings, and other desserts. Men and women filling their trays paid no attention. Just part of the routine.

Then, more segments with titles like 'TAPS CIA ARL VA July 30,' 'TAPS FBI ACDY Aug 2.'

'It's the beginning, or the resumption, of a general massive assault on our institutions, conducted by perhaps fifty Silk runners,' Breaker said. 'They're aware of our activity, apparently are frightened by it, and are taking measures to counter it.'

Sound recordings followed, several phone calls from outside the FBI headquarters to offices within.

'The callers claim to be relatives,' Breaker said. 'Often dead relatives. They read through lists of numbers and ask them to be repeated. Nearly everyone repeats the numbers. Afterward, the agents remember only receiving blank phone calls.'

'I'm familiar with the routine,' I said.

'You can see the size of our problem,' Breaker said.

'It's huge,' I agreed. 'I think you've waited too long.'

Breaker lifted his eyebrow. 'Possibly.'

'Any word on Garvey and Crenshaw?' Ben asked.

'None,' Breaker said. 'We won't take any action against collusive agents until we have the situation well in hand. And until we know whether or not they were tagged.'

'Give me a crack at them. I'll take action,' Ben said in a low rumble.

'You are not essential to this operation, Mr Bridger,' Breaker warned. 'I will remove you if necessary.'

'Is there any food on board?' I asked, feeling particularly contrary.

'None,' Breaker said. 'There's hot coffee. Very hot.'

This army, I saw, would not be running on its stomach. The stomach and everything south could no longer be trusted.

CHAPTER THIRTY-FOUR
Manhattan
The Jenner Building, 'Anthrax Central'
8:00 P.M. August 14

We drove down the wide alley behind the gray cube. I saw the steel door Ben had described, covered with acid swaths of graffiti. At a honk, the door was pushed open from the inside. Breaker and two other agents got out of our cars and conferred with figures from inside the building, wearing white decontamination suits. They gestured and talked for some time.

I looked through the window at the blank expanse of stone and concrete rising to a sunny morning sky. New York was putting on its best face. It was going to be a beautiful day.

My entire self had shrunk to a little point. Exhausted, wrung out, the point was vaguely aware of the past, intensely connected with the present, unwilling to consider the future. It was only loosely related to the former Prince Hal and all his desires.

I was an animal, a cat, a bear, a rabbit. I did not want to be human.

Breaker returned to the car and tapped the glass. The driver rolled my window down, and Breaker leaned over. 'We're clear, but our opposition within the Agency and the rest of the government could join the party at any minute, so we have to move fast. Offense has finished, security is in, and a technical team will be here soon to back you up. Ready?'

I nodded, lying.

Breaker opened the door. Ben got out on the other side and puffed his cheeks, sucking in some courage from the air. 'I do not want to go back in there,' he said. 'That means I have to.'

'Right,' Breaker said. Not a smile between them. A rigor and honor thing I certainly did not feel.

I was terrified, but I would do it for Rob.

We walked through the steel door. Immediately inside, four men in white-plastic suits with clear flexible helmets helped us put on similar outfits and attached our tanks. We had three hours of air, assuming moderate exertion.

I looked around the loading dock as the men adjusted my straps. Directly ahead, the big aquariums Ben had described had been shot up and drained, leaving the dock floor wet and smelling of salt water. To the right, I counted twenty bodies arranged in rows under white sheets. A man in a transparent plastic outfit was dousing them with antiseptic from a pump cylinder, like a gardener spraying lilies.

I was ready. One of the white-plastic suits gave me a gloved thumbs-up.

'Can you hear me?' Ben asked. His voice was a little muffled, but carried clearly enough.

Everyone I saw looked pasty and unhappy, and no wonder. We rely on our little bacterial allies. They do a lot of work for us. They are vigilant defenders as well as, at times, harsh judges. Now we were trying to get along without these support systems. We had turned our guts into war zones.

Breaker took us up the steel steps to the platform. I looked through the shattered glass of the nearest aquarium. Slime and big black lumps rose from a thin slick of water.

'What was this?' Breaker asked, too loud, like someone speaking while wearing headphones. He pointed at the slime.

'Little Mothers of the World?' I guessed, and shrugged my shoulders.

'I still don't get the crap about "Little Mothers",' Ben said.

'Bacterial colonies from the sea – those black lumps could be stromatolites. Golokhov wanted to study how bacteria form communities. Maybe it was mystical, like keeping the bones of a saint. Maybe he thought we're all just evolved super-colonies of bacteria, spaceships for bacteria, with no will of our own. That sort of crap.'

A formal young woman with an experienced no-nonsense face and buzz-trimmed inch-long hair met with our group. She carried an assault rifle with a prominent clip. 'Secret Service, Nancy Delbarco,' she said through her plastic hood. 'Follow me.' Her eyes were focused and unemotional, but her lips, tight and grim, betrayed her. She was scared, too.

'We've restored some power,' she told us, as we marched behind the shattered aquariums. 'The elevators are still out. Each floor has its own power supply, but some cables were cut and generators sabotaged. Right here' – she pointed at the concrete floor – 'we're above three levels of basement, going down about fifty feet. We haven't explored the lowest level, but it seems to be mostly storage and infrastructure – air-conditioning, steam plant, water, the pumps that maintained the aquariums. There are subway tunnels below that, so we've had trains halted until we certify the building is not rigged to blow.'

'How many died?' I asked.

'Enough,' Delbarco said in a tone that implied it was a rude question. 'I don't know how long we can stay. There could be an opposition team arriving any minute, and we certainly don't want to get involved in another firefight.'

'We're still not in complete control either at the top or locally,' Breaker said.

'Garvey?' Ben asked.

'His bosses have influence,' Breaker conceded.

Delbarco led us up a long flight of stairs. The lighting was dismal. The painted steel stair treads showed shiny wear patterns. Peering up past the center railing, I could see all the way to the top of the building – sixteen stories.

'The first four floors are vats and steel culture tanks, like a brewery,' Delbarco said. 'Most haven't been used for a long time. It's difficult to conceive why they would need so much tagging material, but we could be making a bad guess. The techs will get samples when they arrive.'

'That was what my brother wanted,' I said absently.

Three floors. It was tough getting enough air in the hood, but I was doing okay. Ben was working to conceal his condition, or lack of it.

Delbarco pushed open the door on the fourth floor. We walked over a shiny, vitreous blue-gray floor between shadowed rows of steel vats, the largest twenty feet high and ten feet wide, surrounded by cooling coils and forests and arches of color-coded piping. At the opposite end, a glass-walled laboratory stood empty, its benches sparkling clean and cabinets bare. Two of the wide panes of glass had been shot out and lay in jagged shards all over the floor.

A body lay slumped against the only intact pane: a slender young woman in her late teens, a small hole dimpling her forehead and a puddle of blood under her thighs. She had once had the intense, lean beauty of an Eastern Bloc gymnast. She wore denim overalls and a red T-shirt.

Delbarco walked past the corpse. 'We've got some children, live children, quite a few of them, on the eighth floor,' she said. 'They don't have weapons, none we can see at any rate, so we're just . . . working around them for the moment.'

I thought of Nicolae Ceausescu, former dictator of Romania, recruiting his core bodyguards from orphanages, raising kids from childhood to serve in a kind of Praetorian Guard. He had been deposed and executed in 1989. His kids had supported him fanatically to the very end. They had had to be put down like rabid dogs.

'I'd like to see the children,' I said. 'Are they under super-vision?'

'No. As I said, we're leaving them alone for now. They could be booby-trapped or contaminated.' She was eager to change the subject. 'We don't think there's been any real activity in most of the building for some time. Even most of the lighting fixtures have had their bulbs pulled out.'

'I need to see the kids,' I insisted. 'I want to know how they were being used.'

Delbarco reluctantly agreed. I was the expert, and she had her orders, even though it could be her funeral as well. So I was actually in charge. I didn't like it.

We all followed Breaker to the next floor. In the stairwell, we walked around another body, a young man no more than twenty years old, sprawled faceup and studying the next flight of stairs with relaxed dismay. He had made random finger-twitch scrawls, then started to write two letters in a river of his own blood as it dripped from tread to tread. The letters were Cyrillic, K and A. Perhaps he was writing his name, perhaps a farewell to friends.

'Where are the defense troops?' Ben asked.

'We pulled them out once the building was secure. We're shorthanded everywhere,' Breaker said.

The eighth floor looked like a state hospital suddenly fallen on hard times. A deserted reception desk stood at the center of a semicircular room. Six hallways radiated outward like a sunburst in the surrounding square of the floor plan. At the end of one corridor, in the blinking glare of a single fluorescent light, I saw a gymnasium: pommel horse, stacked play mats, parallel bars, hanging rings.

'We don't want to be here too long,' Delbarco said.

No sunshine. No windows. *Never a chance to go outdoors.*

I turned left and walked down a hall, stopped, looked into the first open door. Lights flickered in broken ceiling fixtures.

Scattered papers, a kicked-in television, blood tracked and smeared by boots. A *Come to Middle Earth* poster from the nineteen sixties competed with kids' drawings of dragons, a hook-nosed witch, airplanes. Below them, a white-enameled iron bed frame supported a bare mattress, the sheets torn off and coiled on the floor. In one corner, someone had left a small pile of yellow turds. Broken glass everywhere.

From the end of the hall came singing, thin but lovely – a young boy or girl. It sounded like a Russian folk song. Closer, I heard crying. I walked past two closed doors, half-expecting a teenager with an Uzi to come leering out and spray us with bullets. Or for the ceiling to crack open and pour down gallons of tagging solution mixed with needles, piercing our suits. Anything was possible. I had been through too much to disbelieve.

The door to my right opened on a room full of steel bathtubs – hydrotherapy, I guessed, but then I saw the tubs were crusted with a dry yellow paste. I was glad to be in the suit and unable to smell the outside air.

This was what Tammy had described to Ben and Rob – a training area. A bathhouse of bacterial indoctrination. Mrs Golokhova had had to make do, however; she wasn't able to afford space on the world's biggest cruise ship. Did she keep up any contact at all with her husband?

I couldn't picture them lingering over long phone calls like separated lovers.

I slowed at the sound of footsteps. A black girl in a long white gown emerged from a door in the middle of the hall. She was accompanied by a toddler with a thin face and long, silky blond hair, clinging with white fists to her ragged nightgown. They stared at me with suspicious, puffy eyes.

The older girl barked something in Russian. I looked at Ben, a few paces behind me. He shook his head.

I waved my hands at the girl, no savvy, and stared at her bare forearms. Long pink scars reached from her wrists to at least her elbows, where they vanished beneath wide, flopping sleeves. In her long brown fingers she clutched a plastic ampoule with a dangling tube attached to an IV needle.

Three more children emerged from other doors in the hall and walked forward, wary but curious.

The black girl shook her head, then pointed her fingers into her mouth, eyes staring defiantly: *Food, you son of a bitch, get it?*

A boy of eight or nine padded across the floor in rubber-soled slippers. Yellow strips like plasterboard patches crisscrossed his shaven crown. His eyes were angelically calm, and he grinned as his slippers alternately slapped and squeaked on the hard blue floor.

Ben touched my elbow, giving me a start. 'Let's go,' he said. 'Nothing we can do, and no sense taking risks. We don't know what was going on here.'

I could hazard a guess. The older children, Mrs Golokhova's assistants, the same ones who had come out to see Ben and Rob in the loading dock, must have tried to protect the younger. The first team in had killed everyone on the lower floors. Not that many, I guessed; a small operation.

'Mrs Golokhova was still doing research. She maintained her own runners and subjects,' I said. I shouted to Breaker and Delbarco, 'Can you get some food for these kids?'

The black girl glared at us critically from a distance of ten feet. She seemed reluctant to come closer, as reluctant as I was to have her so near. I studied her skin, finely wrinkled, her knowing, weary eyes, and was suddenly not at all certain of her age.

She tried me again with another imperative string of Russian. I could only lift my shoulders in ignorance. Disgusted, she flung her ampoule, needle swinging. It bounced off my plastic-sleeved arm and rolled on the floor. I searched the arm frantically for tears as she laughed.

'Let's go,' Ben said, pulling me back.

The children darted into their rooms. I heard giggles and small, frightened voices whispering, whimpering.

We climbed past nine, ten, eleven, stopping to briefly examine each floor. More vats, steel-walled isolation cubicles, huge but stripped labs, their doors welded shut, their shadowy interiors visible only through dusty acrylic windows. Storerooms full of hundreds of filing cabinets toppled over and cleaned out, steel drums filled with old ashes, plastic barrels, empty chemical bottles and glassware stacked high in Dumpsters, martial rows of old black typewriters, an IBM 360 half-covered by a ripped and age-browned plastic tarp, broken crates.

On twelve, a dark storage room had been piled high with empty plastic coffins. An obese male in a black windbreaker lay facedown in the middle of the nested coffins. He had been shot in the back.

Ben walked around the darkening pond of blood – an awful lot of blood – and rolled the body over with one foot. It was wearing green loose-fit Dockers, and under the unzipped jacket, a blue golf shirt.

'Norton Crenshaw,' Ben said. 'Hello, Melon.'

'Satisfied?' Delbarco asked.

'Fuck, no,' Ben said. He made a quick reconnaissance of the rest of the room, pulled over a stack of coffins with hollow, reverberating booms, no joy. We walked quickly back to the stairs.

'Learning anything?' I asked Ben.

'Too damned much,' he said.

Forty years ago, the Jenner Building had held one of the biggest CBW operations in the entire United States. Right in the middle of Manhattan.

Creating Manhattan Candidates.

'You're going to have to rewrite all your books,' I told Ben as we climbed.

'No joke,' he said. 'This makes Enigma look like a wet firecracker.'

The door to the fifteenth floor had been blasted wide open. Scorch marks and smoke decorated the walls around the door and the ceiling at the top of the stairwell. Beyond the blasted door stood another, smaller door, intact, made of blond fir or spruce and decorated with carved flowers and bas-relief saplings. Two spotlights guttered in the cove ceiling over the door. The carvings cast alternating, lopsided shadows.

Ben pushed the wooden door. It creaked open, and we entered a room about forty feet square, filled with toppled chairs, rucked and twisted rugs, off-kilter paintings of landscapes – a beautiful lake (Baikal?), mountains, quaint log cabins in forests. Bookshelves, some upright and some pulled over, books piled between an intervening chair and the inlaid parquet floor. A long oak dining table was covered with thick, leather-bound photo albums, some lying open, others in stacks. One stack had toppled and upset a silver candelabra.

'It's an apartment,' Breaker said. 'Someone lived here.'

A gallery of life-size heroic painted portraits glowered down from the rear wall, draped in velvet curtains and hung with pulls of tasseled gold cord. It could have been the living room of a well-off Russian expatriate, a personal shrine to a glorious past.

Ben flipped through one of the open albums. He spun it around and studied a few pages of mounted photos, then whistled in amazement. 'Let's take these,' he said. 'All of them.'

Breaker gave him a quizzical look. 'I thought we were here for biological specimens.'

'I had a maiden aunt who kept our family's photographs,' Ben said. 'She pasted them in albums and typed up labels with names and dates and places. Everyone sent her copies. She worked at it until she died. She was our archivist.'

Breaker was still not convinced.

'Just take them,' Ben insisted. 'If we don't, we may never understand what happened.'

Breaker looked at me. 'Take them,' I said.

Three technicians in isolation suits finally arrived, out of breath, lugging aluminum cases. Delbarco spoke with them in low tones in the living room while Ben, Breaker, and I explored further.

Ben found a bathroom. He opened the heavy white-painted door, peered around it, then advanced to a claw-foot tub. The tub was surrounded by a daisy-print shower curtain. He gripped the curtain and gave me a sad, reluctant look through his plastic hood.

'Time's a-wasting,' I said.

'Fuck that,' he said. 'That's what Melon said.'

Ben pulled back the curtain with a *shing* of steel rings. A body lay in the white-enamel tub, curled in a frail, angular tangle of arms and legs. The wizened face appeared to float, like a lolling puppet's, above one end of an ill-fitting, calf-length black dress. Wide milky eyes stared up at the tiled ceiling with a squirrel-monkey expression of disappointment and surprise.

'Mrs Golokhova, I presume,' Ben said. 'Come pay your respects,' he insisted. Breaker and I stepped forward. 'The wife of our secret master. I guess she didn't want to be kicked out of her home.'

She had apparently shot herself in the temple with a small, ivory-handled revolver, still clutched in one gnarled hand. The hand rested against the side of the tub, pistol hanging from stiff white fingers.

She was supposed to live for ever. Perhaps her husband had promised her that much as a reward for being a guinea pig, for years of madness.

Ben backed away. 'There's nothing here for me,' he told Delbarco on the way out of the bathroom. 'But let's get those photos.'

'I'd like tissue samples from her,' I told Delbarco. She passed the request to the technicians. They went to work quickly, pulling the body from the tub and laying it out on the tile floor.

I left the bathroom before I could see more.

Breaker took two albums. I grabbed three. Ben carried four. That was less than a third of them, but they were thick and heavy, and Delbarco warned us we didn't want to be too burdened in case we had to move fast.

'One more floor,' Delbarco said, eyelids heavy, as if she had already seen far too much. 'Prepare yourselves, gentlemen. This one takes the cake.'

We climbed to sixteen, the topmost floor in Anthrax Central. There, Delbarco applied her shoulder to what looked like a medium-security bank-vault door, heaved it wide, and motioned us through. The door made a hydraulic sigh as it tried to close. She jammed a screwdriver in the locking wheel before it could throw its bolts home.

Beyond the vault door, a hundred or more horizontal steel cylinders, about the size of antique iron lungs, stretched in five long rows to the opposite wall, separated only by square support columns and, at the center of the room, two small, glass-walled laboratories or monitoring stations.

The cylinders had been mounted on cement platforms. Two thin copper pipes, no wider than a pinky, and a stiff white electrical cable emerged from the end of each cylinder.

'We're going to need some help understanding this.' Delbarco blinked rapidly behind her plastic hood. 'Not that I'm keen to know,' she added.

I gripped a steel handrail, climbed a set of concrete steps, and looked over the top of the first tank on my right. A long, narrow glass window provided a clear view of the contents. Inside, bathed in a few inches of reddish fluid more like thin jam or ketchup than blood, lay the naked body of a man. Slight, balding, in late middle age, he seemed to be trapped in light but troubled sleep. His facial muscles and fingers twitched, and his eyes jerked beneath their lids. Thick ripples spread across the red fluid.

Above the man's head, something clicked, and a silvery blue light came on inside the tank. Full spectrum, I thought, and looked up with spots swimming in front of my eyes.

A faint electrical hum filled the chamber. Lights had switched on in all the tanks, throwing ranks of fuzzy blue bars on the ceiling.

Once my eyes adjusted to the new brightness, I could see the man more clearly. Filaments rose from the red liquid and crawled over his fingers, his naked arms, his face, leaving oily trails on the pale, beardless skin.

With a sense of fascinated dread, I examined the back of his hand. Between the tendons, the skin had formed puckered slits.

Throat dry, legs wobbly, I climbed down, braced myself, and moved on to four other tanks. Four more men, all naked, two elderly, two middle-aged or perhaps younger, their faces sallow in the silvery glow, all lay in the same red bath, locked in uneasy sleep.

Ben tapped the end of the fifth tank and pointed to a stamped tin ID plate, the size of a file card, slipped into a holder. Following a twelve-digit string of numbers was a hyphen or dash and what might have been a date: 9/3/61.

'Maybe they sealed him up in 1961,' Ben suggested. 'Like canned tuna.'

'Self-contained,' I said, and immediately doubted that was possible. With such tiny pipes, there couldn't have been much in the way of fluids going in and waste going out; maybe only a little fresh water. No pumps, no oxygen. Just the lights. Nothing so simple, whatever the ecological balance, could keep these people alive . . . yet they *were* alive. Twitching. Troubled. 'Failed experiments?' I guessed.

'Maybe they went crazy from Golokhov's treatment,' Ben said. 'Too crazy to take a chance and let them go out into the world.'

'Should we breach a tank?' Breaker asked.

'I wouldn't dare,' I said. 'I wouldn't know what to look for.' We were in unknown territory.

'Let's move on,' Delbarco insisted. Her voice echoed over the rows of tanks. 'There may not be much time.'

We ignored her. Ben and I simultaneously turned to look down the long rows of buzzing steel tanks. The horror had gripped us, and we needed to shake loose, to find answers.

With a staccato series of clicks, up and down the rows, the tank lights went out in sequence.

We were like kids in a carnival, determined to see the next freak. Delbarco sensed our giddiness. 'Shape up, gentlemen,' she warned. Then, with a pale, tightly controlled expression, she added, 'The last thing I want is to know what's actually going on here. I like to sleep nights.'

'Too late,' Breaker said.

Ben raised his hand and snapped his fingers. Within his plastic glove, the sound was not much louder than the plop of a raindrop. 'I've just had a horrible idea,' he said. 'The gallery in her office. There were about a hundred people in the pictures. Count the tanks.'

'About a hundred,' I said. 'If they're all occupied.'

Ben stooped and laid his albums on the floor. I stacked mine beside them.

Breaker took a call on a small walkie-talkie as Ben stalked purposefully between two rows, peering in the murky light at the stamped tin labels. 'Maybe we can find a catalog,' he said. 'Some ID for these bastards.'

I followed Ben, wondering what he was up to. 'What's your idea?' I asked.

'It's too weird,' he murmured.

The doors to the monitoring stations in the center of the room were open, but the glassed-in rooms were completely bare. Dust lay in a thin gray film on the floor. Ben left tracks.

The lights switched on again. The tanks buzzed like electric hives. Instant sunlight every few minutes, regular as clock-work.

'Think Russian,' Ben called over his shoulder. 'Golokhov was playing every side, pitting them against each other, supposedly doing services for everybody, with secret shenanigans as insurance. Who was taking advantage of whom? I can't believe these are failed experiments. It doesn't make sense they would keep them lying around, sucking up resources. They would just dispose of them. And I don't think they were friends. Who would treat their friends this way? Wouldn't you put them out of their misery?'

He looped back and marched up another aisle, pausing to read the tags one by one. 'I think we're in a Gulag. A steel Gulag.'

He stopped and held his finger on a tag, jiggling it experimentally. He had found what he was looking for. 'This could be it. Dear, sweet Jesus.' He adjusted the plastic leggings on his suit with muttered curses and clomped up the concrete steps.

The date on the tag, following the long serial number, was 3/7/53. That would have been a year before the Jenner Building had been handed over to Silk.

Ben waved for me to climb up beside him. Together, we leaned over the rectangular window in the cylinder.

The man stretched out in the bath of red fluid had bushy eyebrows, a distinctive thick nose, and a long, back-slung shock of what had probably once been white hair, slicked now and stained pink. Spatters and purposeful ribbons of red gelatin clung to his lined cheeks and his ragged mustache, worked along parted lips.

I wondered if the red fluid dissolved the lengthening hair, took care of the waste products, kept the confined individuals fed and alive. *Self-contained.* I still wasn't convinced, but the dust between the rows of tanks, marred only by our footprints, showed that few if any people had been there for years, perhaps decades.

'Doesn't look happy, does he?' Ben asked. 'Maybe he's having bad dreams.'

'So?'

'Granted, he isn't in the best shape. After all, he's over a hundred and, what, twenty-five, twenty-six years old?' Ben seemed in awe. 'Christ. Who had a stroke in the Kuntsevo dacha? Who was leeched but denied access to doctors? Who pointed up at the print on the wall of a boy and a girl bottle-feeding a lamb? Who died on the bed while Svetlana was watching? It was all a sham. Did Beria know?' Ben looked at me almost cross-eyed with a weird excitement.

'Know what?'

'Don't you recognize *him*? Didn't they teach you history in school?' Ben paused, then asked plaintively, 'Or am I just going crazy?'

'Could be,' I said.

Ben shook his head as if to scare away flies, but he could not stop staring at the old man in the cylinder.

'Hell, I'm sure of it! He's a wreck, but I've studied pictures of him since I was a kid. This is *him*. Banning was right, Golokhov treated him, kept him going way past a normal lifetime. But not the way he would have wanted.' Ben let out a barking laugh that echoed from the far walls of the chamber. 'Golokhov was in exile, but he must have helped the Politburo bring him down. Fake an illness. Incapacitate him. Maybe they slipped in a double. Or maybe Svetlana and the others were tagged or brainwashed.' Ben was working up enthusiasm for this unlikely tale. 'It *has* to be! They shipped him out of Russia when Silk set up shop in New York. Installed him here in the new building, along with his fellow monsters, architects of the old regime. Then they hung their pictures on the wall downstairs.' Ben squinted at the rows of cylinders. 'Jesus, do you think Beria is in here, too? Packed away for old times' sake?'

'I'm still lost, Ben.'

'It's *Koba*, Hal!' Ben cried out, exasperated. 'Iosip Dzugashvhili. Say hello to Papa Joe Stalin.'

I looked down on the shrunken, pocked, red-beribboned face and could not see a resemblance, but then, I hadn't pored over as many old photos as Ben.

The eyes of the man within the tank opened suddenly and stared up through the glass, then fixed on me. His sclera were tinted pink and reddish spittle bubbled from his mouth. I was sure he could see me. His gaze chilled me: dim, but still electric. Charged with pure hate.

'You're imagining things,' I said, with an awful, hollow feeling that he was not, that I was standing only a couple of feet away from the worst mass murderer in human history.

'*Gentlemen!*' Delbarco called.

'Am I?' Ben shot back, ignoring her. 'Look at those *peepers*. Gorky described him as a flea blown up to human size. Didn't give a damn about the human race, just wanted to suck out all its blood. Looks like a real vampire now, doesn't he?'

'We've got to go *immediately*!' Breaker shouted from the vault door.

The man's purple tongue poked out obscenely and his lips were drawn back, uncovering yellow teeth. He seemed to be trying to speak, or to scream. His head canted over, and waves of red fluid slapped against the sides of the tank. Some flowed into his mouth and he swallowed, gagged, weakly pursed his lips as if to spit, but could not. Then he writhed like an eel in a jar, thumping against the walls of the cylinder.

'It's not *possible*,' I said.

Ben slapped my shoulder and laughed. 'Hal, that's the stupidest thing I've ever heard you say. Fuck, man, *look around you*.'

'There's trouble on one!' Delbarco shouted.

Mercifully, the light in the tank clicked off, but the thumping continued, then a long, thin shriek.

Ben jerked his head to one side, breaking the spell, and shuddered as he descended the steps. I lingered by the cylinder even as Breaker stalked down the aisle to pull us out of there.

'It's nuts!' I said as I joined Ben. We reclaimed our load and ran awkwardly to the vault door in our plastic suits, the albums heavy as bricks. Ben managed to hold on to his stack and touch his plastic-sheathed cranium with a finger, screwing his hand back and forth. 'The whole damned century was nuts, Hal!'

We descended sixteen floors. Delbarco went first, scouting the platform overlooking the loading dock, then waved us through the door. We walked between the shattered aquariums and looked down over a milling crowd of NYPD officers and firemen. Through the doors, I saw fire engines and police cars in broken echelon, lights blinking.

Someone – probably on our side – had called out all the city watchdogs.

'Just play it cool,' Delbarco said, as we stripped off our isolation suits. 'Let Agent Breaker do the talking.'

'Friends, you need to get out of here,' Breaker called out over the crowd. 'This building is still contaminated.' Wearing a plastic isolation suit gave him some authority. A few broke for the door. The firemen donned their oxygen masks.

'Follow me,' Delbarco said. 'I don't think they'll shoot with the City's Finest watching.'

'I wouldn't count on it,' Ben muttered.

We walked through the crowd. Halfway out the door, I grabbed a fireman's arm. 'There are kids on the eighth floor,' I told him. 'They're hungry, and they need medical attention. You can go in there – we did. Please go get them.'

The fireman stared at my suit. 'Easy for you to say. It's contaminated, buddy.'

'They're just kids!' I shouted.

He waved me off.

Mingling with the men and women in police uniforms and emergency gear, I spotted a few men in casual clothes, no more than six or seven. They watched us closely. Some carried pistols, others, small boxes.

Ben froze.

'Come on,' I said, and tugged at him, but he was unshakable. I followed his line of sight and saw a trim man in his middle seventies, wearing Dockers, a black windbreaker, and a stoic expression. He folded his arms and stood in the middle of the crowd as if no one else mattered.

'Forget him,' Breaker said to Ben in a harsh whisper. 'We need to get out of here before they cut through the confusion and bring up reinforcements.'

The man in the black windbreaker stared Ben down, then spat on the concrete.

We were hustled with our photographic treasures into the cars waiting in the wide alley. Weaving through the fire trucks and police cruisers, we drove down the alley.

No one followed.

'Was that Stuart Garvey?' I asked Ben, as the flashing and blinking lights grew small behind us.

He nodded, then leaned his head back and closed his eyes.

Delbarco made a call on a satellite phone. She did not sound happy with what she was told. When the call was finished, she, too, closed her eyes and rested her head on the window.

We left the city and transferred to a caravan of Suburbans in New Jersey.

Ben switched on his seat light an hour or so later and lifted one of Mrs Golokhova's albums into his lap. The truck's big tires hummed on the highway. 'We should have taken all of them,' he said. 'It would have been worth the risk. Christ, the history she must have pasted in here.' He flipped a few pages, squinting at the snapshots.

I pictured Mrs Golokhova in her husband's special asylum, living out her madness, with plenty of time on her hands, and these albums as her special task.

A few minutes later, Ben whistled. 'Jackpot,' he said.

He held the page up for my inspection. A crinkle-cut black-and-white photograph – a home snapshot, judging by the trimmed edges and lighting – showed a middle-aged Joe Stalin, easily recognizable, hair graying with dignity. He stood with his arm around the shoulder of a doctor in a white lab coat, wearing pince-nez. Stalin smiled broadly, contemplating a brave future. The date neatly penned below was 4.vi.38.

He *did* resemble the man in the tank.

'He'd already killed millions,' Ben said, voice tinged with that odd wonder that comes over male historians when they contemplate vast atrocities. 'He wiped out the Soviet military leadership. He's going to make a pact with Hitler to gain some time, then Hitler will invade Russia. In the next ten years, almost *thirty million people* will die, some say fifty million, some say more. Do you think he was undergoing Golokhov's treatments by then?'

I had no answer. I just stared at the picture, memorizing the second man's features. Pleasant, mousy even, with soft eyes and a beaky nose.

Two middle-aged guys being chummy.

Most of the trip to Florida is a blur. I don't know what finally happened to the steel Gulag. I'll probably never know whether Ben was simply imagining things.

But the man in the tank, if he had any mind left at all, was suffering. If the stamped tag was any guide, he had been suffering for more than fifty years.

CHAPTER THIRTY-FIVE
Port Canaveral, Florida
August 17

We could see the *Lemuria* from the balcony of our hotel suite. It was hard to miss, four gleaming high-rise towers arranged from bow to stern on a white cruise ship almost two thousand feet long. In the deep-water port, the ship had come about over the last ten minutes, using bow and stern thrusters, making ready to put out to sea. Through a small pair of stabilized binoculars I could peer a little ways into the shaded entrance to the marina deployed between the ship's massive twin hulls. Yachts drifted in and out of this portal like little butterflies flitting through a house's open back door.

In its presumptive way, the *Lemuria* was about as ugly as anything I had ever seen go to sea. No doubt the views from the seven hundred condos were spectacular. Rich folks, I thought with a twinge. All with enough money and not enough time to spend it. Lots of potential investors.

Perhaps Golokhov had struck a real gold mine.

Beyond the long entrance to Port Canaveral, I could make out the towers of a launchpad. I spun my map around on the table. Cape Canaveral Launch Complex 39. Squeezed into a few square miles around the hotel were some of the greatest technological endeavors in human history. Why didn't I feel a surge of pride?

We were on the fifth floor of the Westin Tropicale, under the guise of attending a Wade Cook investment seminar. There had been some talk of moving us into the Coast Guard station, but that had been nixed just before we arrived, hence our new cover. We had badges and bags full of pamphlets and everything we needed. As the highlight of our seminar, we were scheduled to take a tour of the *Lemuria*.

Breaker returned to the room accompanied by a man and woman unknown to me. Ben followed. I stayed by the window, a prepackaged ham sandwich in one hand, binoculars in the other.

Breaker formally waved his arms. 'Hal Cousins, I'd like to introduce Nate Carson, from the National Institutes of Health.'

'Pleased to meet you,' Carson said. He was in his early thirties, with shoulder-length brown hair and a long, pale, patrician face. He held out his hand, but I shook my head, sorry. He withdrew the hand with a glance at Breaker, then a sheepish grin. 'Right,' he said.

'And this is Dr Val Candle. She's from NSA, we dare not speak its name, a specialist in security bioinformatics.'

Candle appeared to be in her late thirties. She had strong Middle Eastern features – long, thick black hair curled into a loose bun, elegant sad eyebrows, large black eyes faintly underscored by marks of shadow, prominent but classic nose. Depending on my mood, I could have found her homely or strikingly beautiful, but it was clear she didn't much care what anyone thought. She was professional and clipped in her speech, with a deep voice and a defiant Brooklyn accent. 'You don't look so good, Dr Cousins,' Candle said.

'I don't feel so good,' I said. 'What was in that elixir besides Ex-Lax and ipecac?'

'Desperation and hope,' Candle said. 'We're learning a lot. I wish they'd put us on the case years earlier.'

'Let's go over this thing now,' Breaker said. 'You've been briefed about Washington. The President may be in remission, but he still refuses to sign the necessary papers. That limits us. The Vice President is in Israel, the Speaker is God knows where, so the Secretary of Defense is in charge of our operation for the time being. Everyone else in the White House is sicker than dogs. The director of the FBI committed suicide this afternoon at three p.m. The new director of the CIA has sanctioned our operation, but substantial portions of the Agency are still resistant and may be considered either turncoat or thoroughly tagged. Emergency review is under way at the Pentagon, but we're going to take some initiative and make our move on *Lemuria* before it's finished.' Breaker turned to me. 'Here's the serving suggestion. You'll go with them into the *Lemuria* to provide expertise. Mr Bridger will accompany you. You've both had lots of experience with Silk operations. Someone will be assigned to protect you.'

'How do you know whether or not they'll be tagged?' I asked.

Ben clutched the single album from Mrs Golokhova's collection and approached the broad window.

'I appreciate your concern, Dr Cousins,' Breaker said. 'I am going to spend the next few hours smoothing the way with the reluctant folks in Washington. A few old-guard agents and politicos, *not* tagged or run by Silk, still hate to think we're going to dredge up all this carefully buried toxic waste. I've argued that you should be part of the cleanup, because you know what to look for.'

'We hope he does,' Candle said.

'There'll be two marine architects with ship plans here before midnight. That's all we're going to tell you about the operation until you're under way,' Breaker said. 'But be assured, there *is* more.'

'We could take her in port, now,' Ben said, looking wistfully through the plate glass.

'We'll follow procedures,' Breaker said.

'Just like in Nam,' Ben said. 'Your procedures could cost a lot of lives.'

'I couldn't agree more,' Breaker said. 'But that's the way it's going to be. You can opt out now if you want.' He left the room. Ben went to the refrigerator to drag out a six-pack of Cokes, pulled one from its plastic circle, and fell back into a chair. He tapped the album with a row of fingers and lifted an eyebrow my way. Something to show me.

Candle and Carson folded their arms and stood staring at me as if I were some curious bug. 'Why immortality?' Carson asked critically.

'We'll discuss that later,' Candle said. 'We need to know all the receptors you've blocked. We've searched your papers, but you never published all the details.'

We sat around a glass-top table in the middle of the suite's living room. They opened their valises and pulled out stacks of paper, all stamped TOP SECRET HIGHEST, all edged with finger-zip incendiary strips.

'You're going to learn some things here that go beyond top secret,' Candle said. 'I'll personally track you and claim your testicles if you ever reveal this, *ever*, to any one, in any way.'

I held back a wisecrack. She was in no mood for flippancy, and I was tired. 'All right,' I said.

She delivered her speech crisply, with no discernible emotion. 'NSA has been studying the potential for biological encryption. Our division is tasked to learn whether genomically coded messages can be or are being sent into our country in birds, insects, plants, or bacteria. We analyzed bacterial genomes in samples sent from major metropolitan centers and detected non-aleatory genomic alteration, which we prefer not to call mutations, in three hundred different varieties of common gut bacteria. We determined these alterations involved intelligent intervention. In twenty-five of thirty alterations, an internal self-modification scheme was mathematically demonstrated. We eliminated outside intelligence as the cause and invoked the possibility of interior genomic intelligence.'

'You can do that, I mean, confirm that?' I asked.

'I can't, personally,' she said with regret.

'But you know what it means?'

'It implies that bacteria can modify themselves worldwide in less than ten years. Call it evidence of coordinated genomic shift, call it microbial "thought", call it whatever you want, but people I trust, brilliant people, tell me it's real.'

The Little Mothers of the World, I thought.

'The other alterations we reluctantly interpreted as human intervention, by potentially unfriendly forces, on a huge scale. In addition, we determined that the outside changes were not done to encrypt language-based signals, but to alter gene function in common human microbes, with the aim of having them produce novel substances, either to cause illness in targeted military or civilian populations, or to induce large-scale psychoses. A lot of grumpy biologists in our employ huffed and puffed and tried to blow our house down. We survived their assault, but just barely. When all of *your* shit hit the fan' – she gave me a cold grin – 'our stock rose in the Agency.'

'Many thanks,' Carson said wryly.

'How long ago was the work done?' I asked.

'That's not important,' Candle said.

'It is to me,' I said.

'Five months ago, we brought it to the attention of the director of NSA. She passed it on to appropriate agencies. It lingered in their in-baskets, too obscure and crazy to act on, until two months ago.' Candle kept her dark eyes on me, one eyelid twitching. 'Three Marine helicopters blew up some houses in Los Angeles. Someone decided it was time to find out what in hell was going on and put a stop to it. Now it's your turn. Tell us what you've done.'

I told them most of what I knew about the secrets of bacterial/gut interaction, how to immunize or reshape the major varieties, how to adjust one's interior ecology to thwart or subvert seventy years of human mischief. I did not mention the insertion of altered genes into my intestinal cells. I doubted

291

that would be useful to them; and I did not want to have them experimenting on those who might not be informed, who might not even be volunteers.

Candle made notes on special sheets of paper equipped with genome maps for several types of bacteria, and a highly condensed chart of the human genome. When we were done, she called a well-deserved break.

Ben sat in an overstuffed chair, slurping back his third Coke and listening, brows knit, as if he might be planning another book.

'Watch your testicles,' I warned him.

'She's a tiger,' he agreed. The hotel suite was temporarily empty except for Ben and me. He had inserted his finger into a specific page in the album. Now he let it flop open on his lap.

'How much do we really know, Hal?' he asked, and tapped a photo in the upper corner of the right-hand page.

I leaned over. The picture showed five people in suits posed stiffly in front of a curtain.

'So?' I said.

'This must have been taken by a Russian photographer and passed on to Golokhov's people. Mrs Golokhova pasted it in with all these other photos, but this is the last album she compiled, I think. There was a big Communist Party sponsored conference in New York in 1949, the "Cultural and Scientific Congress for World Peace". Also known as the Waldorf Conference. Bigwigs and celebrities came from all over the world to attend. Pre-McCarthy, of course. I think there was coverage in *Life* magazine.'

'So who are they?'

He ran his finger over the photo. 'The fellow on the left is a novelist, Alexander Fadeyev. He was head of the Soviet Writers' Union. Just another Colonel Klink in Stalin's zoo – "I see nothing, I hear nothing!" Next to him is Norman Mailer, the original Stormin' Norman, and Jewish of course. This guy is Arthur Miller, also Jewish. Married Marilyn Monroe, who some say slept with John F. Kennedy. Between them is Dmitri

Shostakovich. Pretty good composer, struggled with Stalin for years. But this guy on the right, with the Windsor hairdo – who do you think that is?'

'I don't know,' I said, irritated. But the profile of the fifth man in the picture had already caught my eye. I picked up the album, held it closer. The nose, the eyebrows, the stance . . .

I felt my hands get sweaty, instant anxiety.

'What do we *really* know, Hal?' Ben asked. 'Who's running whom around here? You tell me.'

The fifth man looked a lot like Rudy Banning. A few years younger, but otherwise unmistakable.

'Nineteen forty-nine,' I said. 'You sure?'

'Look at Mailer,' Ben said. 'Just an ambitious sprout. And Miller, all that black hair. Absolutely, that picture is from New York in 1949.'

'They could have retouched it.'

'Hal, she glued that picture into the album in 1949 or 1950. It's part of a sequence from the conference. I'll bet Maxim Golokhov was there, making plans with his American contacts.'

'It could be a fake.'

'I don't think so.'

I met Ben's gaze. 'Still going in?'

'Wouldn't miss it,' Ben answered, and clapped the album shut.

Outside, Florida's balmy night brought out constellations of mercury and sodium lamps over all the shopping centers, parking lots, apartment complexes, and restaurants that served Port Canaveral and the cruise ships, and in particular, the *Lemuria*. The big ship's display and running lights came on last. She looked like a row of ziggurats dressed up as Christmas trees. A bare dozen of the windows in the four towers were illuminated; only a few of the ship's condos had been sold and occupied.

At nine, Breaker returned with the marine architects. They spread rolled sheets of plans on the table. Each of us would carry a small map showing our proposed routes through the ship. They judged Tammy's key codes to be unreliable. We would find other ways of getting into Golokhov's sanctuary. Still, Ben handed me a copy of Tammy's sketch map and the codes. I folded it and stuffed it in my pocket.

We were still operating with a hodgepodge of assets and personnel. We would 'borrow' a cabin cruiser from Port Canaveral's private marina. Ten Marines would accompany us. Others would board *Lemuria* from at least two and possibly four Coast Guard helicopters. In addition, if the details could be worked out, two cutters from the Coast Guard station would join in the fun.

Ben listened with a long, sober expression. Rob's original crazy scheme was going to be carried out, but on a grander scale than any of us had hoped.

I was getting pumped – a kind of delayed shock reaction. Something was going on deep in my head but I couldn't drag it out into daylight. To compensate, to find some solid ground, I fantasized about confronting Maxim Golokhov. I wanted to rifle his clandestine laboratories and maybe grab a few clues. He owed me.

Everyone there owed me. I blamed their ignorance and intransigence for all I had been through, and for Rob's death. I would carry on for the both of us. Rob's memory deserved that much.

Despite all I had seen and survived, I was still a fool for the Long Haul.

Delbarco and Breaker brought in sleeping bags still in plastic wrappers, more white towels for the bathroom, stinking of fresh disinfectant, and a box of MREs – Meals Ready to Eat, not gourmet and not fresh, packaged in 1997.

Carson caught me studying the back of my hand.

'Any puckering, Dr Cousins?' he asked.

I closed the hand into a fist. 'No,' I said.

CHAPTER THIRTY-SIX
The Atlantic Ocean/*Lemuria*
August 18

The sixty-foot cabin cruiser bounced through three- and four-foot waves, following the *Lemuria* on the open Atlantic. Dawn was a faraway glow as yellow as lemon ice cream over the dark gray sea.

'The Eagle has landed,' Breaker said. He walked forward, bracing his hand against the stained walnut burl bulkhead of the forward bunk room, and sat on a padded bench next to Delbarco and across from me and Ben. 'The President has finished detagging. He is with us.'

Candle and Carson sat slumped against the rear bulkhead, behind a small table. Three of our ten Marines, two young men and a woman, sat stiffly on luxurious leather swivel chairs, dressed in desert-style camouflage that I doubted would be effective on a cruise ship. They steadied their helmets in their laps and listened closely to all we said, with a focus and intensity that impressed me.

I was working on my third cup of black coffee. I had felt like hell since waking up, dizzy and disoriented, over four hours ago.

Breaker watched the distance close between our boat and the giant cruise ship. 'We're not going to get everything we asked for. Washington's in more of an uproar than ever. Secrecy is shot; some senator went to the ship's owners and told them we're on our way. By the time we get there, we're hoping Coast Guard contingents will have already secured cooperation from the captain and crew. We'll board after they've taken control.'

Nobody commented on appearances. We were all marked by the singular effects of both the ocean chop and another round of elixir, incorporating yet more modified bacteria, incubating phages eager to express antisense messenger RNA. We were high-tech seasick in a bad way, cranky and touchy, and nobody could tell us what we would find in the bowels of the floating city.

Lemuria was now five miles ahead and cruising south-southeast at about fifteen knots. Carson and Candle grew more tense as the day brightened.

Ben and I went out on deck to get some fresh air. The biologists followed a few moments later. Spray from whitecaps and the bow wash put a salty chill into our bones, but to me it felt good. My stomach stopped its dog-settling turns and I began to believe I might not disgrace myself in the next few hours.

Carson and Candle stuck with me as if they had a score to settle. Wanting some time alone, and sensing trouble in the air, Ben went forward.

I did not appreciate being abandoned and outnumbered.

'Damn, she's big,' Carson said. He pulled a real estate prospectus from his jacket pocket and spread it out against the wind. A cutaway of *Lemuria* covered three large panels. 'Got this in Port Canaveral. Bel Canto Lines and American Sea Life Corporation . . . Isn't she pretty? Cheapest condo available, one point five mil.'

Lemuria's stern towered almost ninety feet above her water line, not counting four terraced observation, restaurant, and exercise decks that added an additional seventy feet. Beyond the canted decks, swept by a stray wisp from a pearly bank of low cloud, rose the fourth tower, named Elite, a sea-going skyscraper topped by the spread jade green wings and ivory white dome of the aft concourse and Olympic gymnasium.

'No servant quarters?' Candle sniffed. 'Why bother.'

'A crew of seven hundred, plus a population of one thousand three hundred live-aboard wage slaves, waiting to attend to your every need.'

'The other half,' Candle said. 'Don't you just love 'em?' She faced me with dark, critical eyes. 'Your kind of people, Dr Cousins.'

'How's that?'

'You've been going around hat in hand, promising immortality to every billionaire you meet. Should be rich pickings in *that* crowd.' She jutted her chin toward the giant ship, jaw underslung in anger like a bulldog.

'Yeah,' Carson said. 'Just what the world needs – immortal plutocrats.'

'My work is for everyone,' I said.

Candle shook her head. 'How noble. How incredibly naive. I *know* how powerful men work. At NSA, we listen to their nasty little secrets all day long.'

'It's our right,' I insisted. My palms started to sweat again. They were provoking that unfinished thought, that raw hypothesis I could barely make out. 'Who's going to tell us we can't live as long as we want?'

'They are,' Candle said, pointing to the *Lemuria*. 'Every rich son of a bitch, fat cat, church leader, yammering populist, self-righteous fascist, Communist, nationalist. They'll call it a sin. They'll make it illegal. But what they'll really be saying is' – she pointed a tense finger into the breeze – '*it's wrong for everyone but me.*'

'We'll fight them,' I said.

'No, you won't,' Candle said. She held on to the rail with one hand as the sea got heavier. '*You*'ll have lots of clients. *You*'ll charge them a fortune. *I*'ll lose, my children will lose. Everyone I know and care about. The same people who pay off the politicians will pay *billions* to stay alive. How much is life worth? To them it will be chump change. A hundred years of compound interest, and they'll buy up the whole planet.'

'Just like they suck up all the money and the IPOs and the beautiful women,' Carson added.

'Careful,' Candle said, striking a pose. 'They don't get *all* the beautiful women.'

I could not tell whether they were genuinely pissed off or just ragging me. 'We should stick to our task,' I said, but it came out as a mumble.

'You lanced this boil, and now we're all going in to clean it out,' Carson said.

'Courage,' Candle said, to Carson, not to me.

'What I want to know is, what did you do to provoke them? Is this Golokhov jealous of you, or does he want to hog all the glory for himself?'

'I don't know,' I said.

'Think he knows something you don't?'

'I've done nothing wrong,' I said, too loudly. 'I do research in life extension. I go to private citizens who have money because the medical community closes ranks on the issue, and government refuses to consider the possibility –'

'Social security,' Carson muttered.

Candle gave me a pitying glance.

'How long *do* you want to live?' I asked. 'Forty years? As long as someone in Bangladesh?'

'Chronovores,' Carson said in disgust. 'Plutocrats gobbling the feast and leaving scraps for the rest of us.'

I knew it was hopeless, but I tried a new tack. 'Would the government have ever done anything if we hadn't been targeted? They've been pulling strings for decades, and maybe you've been helping them. Did you think about that? Maybe I did all of you a favor.'

Carson snorted. 'Thank you for caring.'

Candle turned away with that same twist Julia had once used, assuming the same final, feminine posture that told me I was unworthy of any more fuss.

Once more I was a Jonah. I was to blame for everything. Why did this always happen when I took a cruise?

Suddenly, the tension broke. I had to laugh. The laugh was genuine, the best I had had since I was a kid watching cartoons on TV.

Candle and Carson stared at me pityingly.

What I felt was the fanciest kind of foolish, too foolish to be cynical. I knew I was wearing the ultimate bright-boy defense, a shit-eating grin. It was the only armor I had left, the only armor I had ever really owned.

I walked forward, wiping my eyes with my shirt cuff, relishing the wind from our passage. Ben squatted like a gray-blown Buddha near the bow, behind a windlass cover, contemplating a neatly coiled rope. An orange-and-white Coast Guard Sea King helicopter roared overhead, bearing down on *Lemuria*. Ben looked up and shielded his eyes against the eastern brightness. A second helicopter followed.

'Right on time,' he said. We watched them weave beside the ziggurat towers like mosquitoes around Madonna.

'Am I a bloody monster, Ben?' I asked, kneeling beside him.

He folded his pointing fingers and lifted them to his upper lip, making Dracula fangs.

My laugh turned into a lone hiccup and fled. 'Was Rob a monster? Would we both have ended up like Golokhov, slaves to the Stalins and Berias?'

'Listen to Orwell, Grasshopper,' Ben said sententiously.

'What about Orwell?'

'The true and authentic voice of the twentieth century.' Ben drew quote marks in the air. ' "If you want a vision of the future, imagine a boot stamping on a human face – for ever." '

'You too, huh?' I said.

'I'm just an aging son of a bitch who's done questionable things,' Ben said. 'I don't want to live for ever, not without Janie. Being with her took away the bad memories. Now, I'll spend the next few years climbing in and out of a box filled with fewer and fewer bottles of Jim Beam. Or I can die sometime in the next couple of hours. I prefer the latter. History's a joke, and it was the last passion I had left.'

'I *cannot* feel that way,' I said, my throat tight. 'There's too much left to see and learn. History does not repeat itself.'

'It can't,' Ben said. 'It stutters too badly. Truth is, history can't even remember its lines.'

'Goddammit, I'm serious.'

'Was that you cackling a few minutes ago? *There*'s the true spirit. Smoke a goddamned reefer and sling your rifle. Suck up some ganja fortitude and get ready to meet the Man.' He swung out his arm, wagons ho, and imitated John Wayne. 'Laugh in their faces, pilgrim.'

I fell back on my butt beside him, letting my breath out in a whoosh. My thoughts were like a skim of oil blown around a puddle.

Ben took off his cap and ran his hand through his thin gray hair. 'Fuck it. It's all war talk. I hung out with Rob – I swear, Hal, it was not much different from hanging out with you. I watched him work. I admired his brains and how he stood up to going nuts. Christ, he was a brave, crazy bastard, and maybe he was just the type to deserve another fifty or a hundred years, or a thousand, to think things through.'

This left me even more confused.

Ben leaned forward. 'Life is for those who still have illusions. Fix up your clinic and watch them beat a path to your door. Maybe I'll join them. We're all hypocrites about dying, and old age is scary, too.'

'It's not for sissies,' I said.

It scares the hell out of me. My father had been as strong as a goddamned tree, an eternal fixture in my little boy mind, profane and often angry, but liable to turn around when he was sober and buy you a bicycle (which Rob and I had fought over) or haul us around on his shoulders.

Dad. Poppa. Mon père. Not a tree, but a vegetable, rotting away from the inside and turning into a blood-soaked clump of God's potting soil.

'I think after this is over we should compare notes,' Ben said. 'I have a hunch we've got something all wrong here.'

For a moment I felt defensive and did not know why. Then I put on a reasonable face. 'What makes you say that?'

'We've been trying not to think about Rudy Banning, haven't we?'

So true. Too much else to worry about. Screw that enigmatic picture. It was a mistake.

Ben focused on the ship. The helicopters had landed and disembarked their teams. *Lemuria* slowed. We watched it glide over the sea, coasting for a couple of miles before coming to a dead stop.

The cabin cruiser zagged east a quarter mile or so. A ribbon of smoke rose from a louvered vent on *Lemuria,* just above the main deck and forward of the second tower. It might have been a kitchen grease fire. Alarms sounded thin and frantic over the choppy water.

'I do not like this,' Ben said with a doggish shake of his head. 'We're going in without coordination at the top and with damn few resources. I don't think we have any idea what we're in for. It's going to be like squeezing a huge zit.'

Our cabin cruiser put on a burst of speed, her twin diesels growling like huge lions. The ship loomed, shining white and jade green, her thousands of ports and windows glinting in the fresh yellow light of the new morning, a steel-and-glass mountain plowing a nervous sea.

'Looks like Purgatory,' Ben said. 'Let's go join the others.'

Breaker got off the radio in the main cabin and told us we were next. 'Doesn't sound like everything's optimal,' he said, walking past me with a frown. 'But we've been told to board and move forward to the first tower.'

We climbed out of the cabin and arranged ourselves as if for a group photo shoot, on and below the bridge. Delbarco handed each of us an orange armband and gave the civilians a pistol. We had all been issued a bulletproof vest and holster earlier. 'Keep it on safety. Don't shoot without orders, unless you're away from your team and in imminent danger.' Breaker grabbed a walkie-talkie from Delbarco and stepped away to talk in a low voice. His frown deepened.

I took little comfort from the gun.

Lemuria's stern cut off the blue sky above. Inside, between the walls of the split hull, the dock had been lowered like the jaw of a prehistoric fish. The space between the hulls, now a gigantic portable marina, was quiet, an iron mouth waiting patiently to swallow.

Breaker handed the walkie-talkie to Delbarco. Delbarco spoke rapidly behind a cupped hand. The cabin cruiser churned water just aft of a barricade of wide-weave, Day-Glo orange canvas strips, blocking the entrance. Voices shouted in several languages inside the cavern, and were finally dominated by a husky male speaking American with a Texas accent.

Lights burned brightly within the marina, like orange and blue stars in a Cyclops's cave. Through my binoculars I could make out four yachts winched out of the water on slings. They rocked gently in the westerly breeze blowing between the hulls, waiting for their owners should they wish to escape the humdrum world of the biggest luxury liner on Earth. Excursion launches clung to the inner hulls like larvae in a hive.

A horn sounded and bells rang as the canvas barricade rolled back on a motorized pole. Our boat grumbled out of the daylight and into the banked blue glow of mercury vapor lamps. The marina appeared even bigger from the inside. Two of *Lemuria*'s emergency rescue Zodiacs, manned by men in wet suits – probably not part of the ship's crew – helped guide us to a mooring about a hundred feet inside the starboard pier.

Marines in fatigues greeted us on the dock. In French, Spanish, Portuguese, and broken English, a surrounded mob of uncooperative deckhands promised us new orifices for what I loosely translated, using my high-school Spanish, as piracy on the high seas. They were afraid for their jobs, the money they sent their families back in Jamaica, Tobago, Acapulco, Miami, Corpus Christi, Port au Prince.

Breaker grimly pushed us through, our Marine escort acting as a wedge. They were now fully decked out in lightweight armor, combat helmets, and the requisite orange armbands.

'It's going to get better,' Breaker told us, as we entered a wide glass elevator. 'C Team is moving aft to join us. They're carrying our isolation suits. B Team has gone to the bridge. *Lemuria*'s captain thinks we're conducting a Coast Guard drug search. He says he has instructions from the ship's owners in Florida to cooperate. But he also claims there are about a thousand guests onboard, rich investors and potential buyers.'

Candle caught my eye but said nothing.

'That's contrary to our intelligence. We'll have to watch out for them,' Breaker said. 'No weapons fire without a direct command.'

Ben stayed close. Carson and Candle clutched their aluminum cases close to their chests and stared straight ahead, toward the elevator door, despite the view opening behind them as the elevator rose out its black well and climbed the side of the ship.

We got out on the first deck of Tower Four and walked through a carpeted but unfurnished lobby – real marble and fake gold, very Las Vegas – to the glassed-in promenade. Escalators rose and fell all around us. Our camouflaged Marines stood out like muddy smears in a Greek temple.

Going to the rail and looking forward, I surveyed the curved glass along most of the starboard length of *Lemuria*, protecting five levels of walkways, cafes, and lounges.

'Looks like South Coast Plaza,' Ben told me in a low voice. 'But I think this is bigger.'

Workmen gave us puzzled and partisan glances but continued bolting down tables, laying out massive rolls of precut carpet, and hauling stacks of cushiony chairs draped in streaming sheets of plastic. The room smelled of glue and fresh carpet and fabric. Large fans, like those used on movie soundstages, vented the odors through open segments in the promenade cover.

Breaker fidgeted with his folding map. 'C Team should be here to escort us forward,' he said. Delbarco pointed.

A tall woman in a clinging blue gown stalked through a wide door and pushed ahead of four Coast Guard officers and two Marines. Her voice carried out over the unfinished lobby and echoed from the far walls like a harsh bell. Fortyish, tanned a coppery chocolate, eyes large and with prominent gleaming whites, adorned in plum lipstick and blue eye shadow, she looked ready to spit.

'I don't believe I have any reason to cooperate. I don't care what Captain Moustakis says. The passengers are upset, nobody's said anything that makes a lick of sense, and –'

The woman clapped her mouth shut as the two groups squared off. She scanned the new invaders with leonine annoyance.

'Lieutenant,' Breaker said to a young Coast Guard officer. 'Where are our suits?'

'They didn't arrive, sir,' the lieutenant said. 'Commander thought they were superfluous.'

'How in hell was that his call to make?'

'Don't know, sir.'

'Shit,' Delbarco said. 'Was he tagged?'

'Don't know, ma'am.'

For the first time, Delbarco seemed on the edge of losing it. She stared at the floor, clenching her jaw muscles spasmodically. Breaker watched her closely. She shook her head. 'I'm all right.'

'We can't stop now,' Breaker said, but his shoulders dropped, and he looked for a moment like a whipped kid.

'You,' the woman said, focusing on Breaker. 'What in hell are we supposed to do, hand over all the passports and green cards and stand aside? This is a privately owned and funded ship . . .'

'Registered in Liberia and full of sin,' Breaker said, his patience coming to an end. 'Just show us the way forward to Aristos Tower.'

'I have better things to do, believe me. We have a thousand guests who are unwell, in the banquet hall –'

'Unwell?' Candle asked, raising her head as if at some stage cue.

'I'll say. There was a fire alarm and the sprinklers soaked everything. An awful smell. Now they're throwing up and fainting and blaming it on bad food and seasickness. That's utterly ridiculous – this ship has the world's best chefs, seventy-eight stabilizers, and premium steel-and-aluminum construction. It's the strongest and steadiest ship ever built. I need to get back there and do my job!'

Delbarco moved in, with Breaker's tacit permission: woman to woman. 'Ma'am, we have maybe an hour to finish what we came here to do,' the Secret Service agent said. 'You haven't a bat's chance in a bonfire of understanding why we're here, and we couldn't tell you anyway. Enough to say that unless you want a lot of death and destruction, *you will shut your fucking trap and take us forward!*'

The woman absorbed the outburst with some resilience, obviously used to playing the lightning rod for tough customers. 'I have a *name*,' she said. 'I hope you will use it and treat me with respect. I am Mrs Holloway.'

Delbarco rolled her eyes. 'Fine. Mrs Holloway. *Please* take us forward.'

Ben looked over the small crowd like a lighthouse keeper judging the weather, his face painted with a stiff, clownish grin. 'Is that your war face?' I asked in an undertone.

'No suits. We're fucked,' Ben said. 'It's a regular Philips head screwup.'

'Why?'

'*Food poisoning*, Hal?' he asked.

'Anything you'd like to contribute?' Delbarco shouted. Breaker jumped at her voice, as did Mrs Holloway in her tight blue gown. 'Tell us how to get there!' Delbarco ordered her.

'The trains are in working order,' Mrs Holloway said, blinking rapidly. 'They follow the inside gallery. It runs the length of the ship, dividing the first seven floors of each tower. The Executive Express is the quickest way to travel on *Lemuria*. Are there others . . . of your party, expecting you?'

If she couldn't make us go away, perhaps it was time to treat us like difficult guests.

'There are,' Delbarco said.

'Then I will help you get in touch with them.' Mrs Holloway tugged at the waist of her gown, drawing it down over a disciplined Nancy Reagan figure. She shivered for an instant, throwing off her pique, and adjusted her hair with patting hands as she led us up an escalator. 'If there's anything else you need to know about *Lemuria*, please ask.'

We boarded the express, a full-fledged airport-style train running on a single track and rubber wheels. It rolled with absolute smoothness through the central gallery.

Even to someone who has been to Las Vegas, the gallery of *Lemuria* was stunning, over fifteen hundred feet long, a straight shot down the centerline of the ship. I could almost feel the overarching weight of the four huge towers interrupting long stretches of skylight. The express whisked us through blue grottos of layered decks, glass walls shot through with mosaics lit by neon and fiber optics, escalators made of what looked like crystal and studded with sea-glow lanterns. As we passed signs announcing we had arrived at the base of Aristos Tower, we rolled through a sunny golden Cretan palace that would have made Minos faint with envy. A giant robot Minotaur straddled the train platform, raising and lowering a golden double-bladed ax.

We were now about a thousand feet closer to the bow.

As the train's doors slid wide, we heard shouting and gunshots echo from above. A clutch of workmen in denim overalls frantically hauled red tool chests and a compressor down a spacious marbled hall, babbling in German, getting out of the way as fast as they could.

A broad sliding glass door on our left, etched with sea horses, opened with a click. A Marine staggered through and tossed aside his rifle. He held out his arms, fingers wriggling, as if he couldn't see, but his eyes jerked this way and that, tracking the walls, the ceiling. He broke into a run and caromed off a brushed steel pillar onto a stack of carpet rolls, then clung to the rolls like a baby monkey on a terry-cloth mommy. Three of our Marines rushed forward to help.

'*Keep the fuck away from him!* Stay together! Stay on objective!' Breaker ordered. 'He might be contaminated. Call for a medic. What the hell deck are we on? Where is this?'

The panicked Marine whimpered and tried to climb the rolls and hide.

Mrs Holloway finally seemed to realize that Delbarco was not prone to exaggeration. 'My God.' She scratched her cheek with a manicured nail, leaving a white streak. 'That poor man.'

'Where are we?' Breaker shouted. Delbarco tapped her map and held it up for Holloway to see.

'You're just below Aristos Tower,' Holloway answered feebly. 'B Deck, adjacent to Shell Crescent Residential.' She fumbled for words as her body conveyed more clearly its animal opinions. 'Aristos is the premier tower for midpriced living, with the best sports facilities on the ship. Somebody should help that poor man.'

'There's a hospital in this tower. Where?' Breaker asked.

'We have four hospitals on *Lemuria*,' Mrs Holloway explained, 'and seventeen clinics, with one hundred and fifty-seven licensed –'

'We want the first tower hospital,' Delbarco said. 'Goncourt's medical center.'

The Coast Guard lieutenant answered his walkie-talkie.

'That's a private facility, the Goncourt Training Center,' Mrs Holloway said. 'Sports medicine. Not yet open, and not really a public hospital.'

'We're being ordered to break off,' the lieutenant interrupted. 'It's over. The operation is canceled. We're to rejoin our chopper team on the helipad, or head toward the bow platform, whichever is closer.'

'It's split command. Ignore it,' Ben advised.

The lieutenant stared at him. 'There's something wrong, and I have my orders,' he insisted.

'Go,' Breaker told him. 'We'll keep the Marines.'

'Sir, with all respect, we will –'

'Just go!' Breaker shouted, and Delbarco moved up to lend her sandpaper stare.

The Coast Guard officers reluctantly broke away. The Marines stayed.

'Should I leave, too?' Mrs Holloway inquired hopefully.

'Hospital,' Delbarco insisted, taking her by the elbow.

It did not matter how often we had studied the charts and maps – within ten minutes we were lost. The ship's decks were a labyrinth of staggered passageways, promenades, galleries, multilevel ventilation shafts, sitting rooms, lounges, bars, restaurants, shops – all in different degrees of finish. We ascended one long escalator inboard and stared up at a huge stained-glass skylight. Turned left in the atrium, spun around to another escalator . . .

Mrs Holloway began to look pale.

Came out on the starboard promenade, looking along a row of doors opening into empty condos.

We were not where we wanted to be.

Barricades of equipment and construction materials had left Mrs Holloway as confused as the rest of us. After half an hour of twists and turns and doubling back, only to arrive at where we had been earlier, she started crying. 'They haven't posted the deck signs yet. We're going too fast,' she said. 'I want to know, *please*, are we in danger? I can't help you now. We're out of my area.'

Ben and Delbarco walked in lockstep to the nearest wide port. Delbarco raised her rifle and fired a burst. The safety glass erupted in a million flying jewels. Mrs Holloway cringed and covered her eyes.

Ben leaned through and looked up, sideways, down. 'That way,' he concluded, and pointed at a forty-five-degree angle. Delbarco agreed.

We approached a ribbed-steel fire door blocking a broad walkway. 'What's that smell?' a Marine asked, lifting his nose. Something did indeed smell rich and foul.

'The alarm has been turned off,' Mrs Holloway said. 'This door should be open.' She took a key from her wrist bag and inserted it into a red box. The door obediently slid aside. Fluid slopped and spilled across the deck.

We drew back, repelled by an unbelievable stench, like ten thousand rotting skunks. A flow of puslike liquid, pink and green and filled with congealed yellow streamers, pooled at our feet.

Mrs Holloway dissolved in hysterics.

'Let her go,' Delbarco said. Breaker took Mrs Holloway by the shoulders and pointed her aft. She ran off in quick jerking steps, lifting her gown to free her legs and not looking back.

'Tell us what this is,' Breaker asked Candle and Carson.

'Looks like, smells like, contaminated fluid,' Carson said.

Breaker gave him a disappointed sneer. They turned to me.

'It's a culture,' I said. I pointed to a strand of slime hanging from a sprinkler head. 'Someone connected a vat to the fire control sprinklers.'

That explained the grease fire, the thin ribbon of smoke; the emergency water flow had been deliberately triggered, and not by our teams.

Breaker closed his eyes. 'No suits.'

Delbarco asked, 'Aren't we immunized?'

'Someone had loose lips,' Ben said. 'What do you want to bet Golokhov is trying something new?'

Four of the Marines started coughing, waved their hands, coughing harder, excused themselves, then doubled over and fell to their knees. Through their gasps, I saw they were smiling; coughs were giving way to laughter.

Two others shook their heads and unslung their rifles, holding them out as if to keep them clean should they throw up.

Candle looked ready to turn to stone. Carson backed away from the troops, pushing the safety off his pistol.

'Hysteria,' Delbarco said in disbelief. 'There's nothing here!'

'Aerosol,' I said. 'There could be a mist in the air throughout the ship. Bacteria, phages . . . We've been breathing it for some time now. Right into our lungs.'

Delbarco looked as if she had just been kicked in the stomach. 'Goddammit,' she said. She raised her rifle again. 'Get up off your knees. We need to move forward.'

Breaker put his hand on the barrel. She jerked it aside and glared at him.

'Fuck it,' Breaker said.

'Let's go,' Ben whispered to me. 'We don't want to be here.' He took me by the arm and we walked away. One of the prone Marines looked up, saw our departure, and reached for his rifle. 'Ma'am,' he said.

Delbarco ignored him. She had locked eyes with Breaker.

'We are being influenced,' Breaker said. 'We have no choice but to head back to the boat.'

'I do not agree,' Delbarco said.

'I am in command.'

'And I will not abandon this mission because of a bucket of pus, Goddammit!'

'Move it,' Ben ordered me under his breath.

'Put down your weapon, Agent Delbarco,' Breaker ordered.

'The entire country is in jeopardy here!'

'Put down your gun.'

I looked over my shoulder. Breaker had a reasonable, even a pleasant look on his face. He held out his hand, cleared his throat.

Delbarco opened fire. Breaker slammed back against a bulkhead and bullets whinged and sighed around the deck. One of the ricochets took a Marine in the nose. He bent backwards and his weapon discharged. I felt the wind as a round buzzed past my ear.

Ben had been right. Trying to take *Lemuria* and confront Maxim Golokhov was indeed like squeezing a giant zit. We had not progressed as far as we had hoped with our elixir. But then, Ben had known, I suppose I had known; anyone could have guessed. Golokhov had been studying his microbes for over seventy years.

We ran to the escalator and took the moving steps three at a time.

Ben and I split up when we encountered a group of four Marines, all sporting blue armbands, using light fixtures for target practice.

'Chickenshit!' one of them shouted. Ben went right, down a corridor, and I took a narrow stairwell.

I'm working to remember in some linear sequence what happened on board *Lemuria* in the next few hours. I'd like to tell the truth, but even at the time, truth was a rare commodity, all too easily squandered. I was better off than some I saw, but in fifteen or twenty minutes, I was sweating like a glass of ice water in a swamp. At my heart I felt glacial, but my skin was hot and damp, and my breath smelled – so I thought – like the fumes off a bucket of hot tar.

I felt happy enough, but not so happy I could laugh at my condition.

At first I wasn't afraid. I had a kind of wanderlust. I was like an ant hosting a parasite, looking for my bird. I just didn't know what my bird looked like.

I did know that a troop of Marines, their uniforms soaked and stinking, mingling with kitchen crew in chef's caps and goop-stained whites, was not my bird. They were to be avoided. They were happily shooting up a huge hanging sculpture in a high-ceilinged bar area, dodging the long, falling glass stilettos.

Red and green and blue shards covered the oak dance floor. One Marine had not dodged fast enough. A long blue knife of glass had entered his upper thigh and pinned him to the wood. He looked down in dismay at his predicament, then laughed with the rest of them, twisting in hobbled jerks, straining at the flesh of his calf like a closely staked dog. 'Anyone want to bet how long before it breaks?' he called out.

Gunfire and happy shouting rose from a tropical garden

below another skylight. Marines and Coast Guard had taken sides and were using each other for target practice. Points were being awarded, and even as I listened, bursts of rifle fire reduced the number of voices. Best to avoid that area entirely. I pushed forward and across the ship to the starboard side of A deck, I think.

I made my way down a carpeted passageway with granite walls studded with gold fasteners. It was beautiful, but my head was clearing and I felt a little anxious. I was thinking about *piecework* and *chopper* and *regulus*. Perhaps my brother had not been as good as everyone had thought, Lissa included. Maybe these alterations had unwittingly primed us for the defenses on *Lemuria*.

Or perhaps he had known that they would protect me, with my gene modifications . . . but would not protect the others.

I came out on a balcony (I hadn't the foggiest idea what the nautical term was) pushing out below a huge jutting wing that I presumed was part of the bridge. That positioned me just forward of Aristos.

The balcony overlooked the starboard side of the bow, a long sloping hill spaced with lines of windows, gleaming like a knife blade against the gray sea. God, it was getting late. The eastern sky was dark and the western was suffused with the last of a flaming sunset. How time had darted and distorted. I stood there for a while, enjoying the fresh air, then decided I would not try to escape. I would find Goncourt's hospital for myself.

I did have a few questions to ask of the Master. I would deliver my respects in person, then surrender. History had won. That was it, really, in a nutshell. Maxim Golokhov *was* the twentieth century. He *was* my history. And he had definitely won this war, a war I had never wanted to fight in the first place.

Just as I turned to go back inside, I heard a rapid succession of cracks, like popcorn in a steel drum. I looked aft and saw several columns of smoke, black and worried by sea breezes, rising from the starboard side. Another puff joined them, and more cracks.

They might have been unchambered rounds going off in a bag of clips, some Marine's body cooking. Or firecrackers. I wasn't a soldier, and I did not want to know.

I encountered Ben standing by himself near a bank of pay phones. He was just hanging up, rubbing his chin's stubble and smiling like a kid with a full sack of chocolate bars. He looked surprised to see me.

'Hey,' I said.

He puzzled for a moment. 'I thought we'd made our farewells.'

'Not formally,' I said.

He had tucked his pistol in his waistband. He took it out, and I backed away. He put on a simple, concerned face. 'No worries,' he said reassuringly, and handed it to me like a gift. 'I've thought it over and you'd better take this,' he said. 'Janie will be here any minute and she doesn't like guns.'

I took the pistol. Relieved, he raised his arms and did a slow, ecstatic jig. 'It's been so *goddamned* long, I miss her so much. I don't care how long it takes, I'll wait for her.'

'I think you should come with me,' I said. 'Think hard, Ben.' I tried to be gentle. Ben had been a pillar in this muck and confusion, and now they had reduced him to a hopeful child. 'Is Janie really coming?'

He didn't seem to hear me. He did another turn and smiled.

'Ben?'

'Go away. I'll be fine.'

'Right,' I said. For the moment at least, Golokhov would make him happier than I ever could. 'I'll give you two some privacy.'

'Yeah, thanks, bud. When she gets here, we'll need it, we certainly will. I'll introduce you later.' He clapped his big hand on my arm. 'And make sure to say good-bye to Prince Hal. Janie would have liked him, too.'

'Will do,' I said, and walked off with all due speed.

Even my tears stung and stank of creosote.

I did not trust myself with Ben's gun or any other. I threw

his pistol over the rail into the ocean, along with my own. Getting rid of them made me feel a lot less apprehensive. At least I would not be compelled to put on a wide grin, happy as a clam at high tide, and blow my own brains out.

I started climbing the emergency stairs. The safety doors had been hammered open on seven decks. The helicopter teams had made it that far before succumbing. On what I guessed was the ninth or tenth floor, I found a brass plaque propped against a bulkhead, waiting to be bolted at eye level. I bent over to examine the plaque. It showed the plan of the tenth floor of Aristos tower. I traced my finger along the etched lines: Olympic-sized pool, left, a small pressroom for circus interviews, right, a gymnasium and physical-therapy clinic. Most of the spaces on the plaque had been enameled in shiny black: no public access.

I mused that the *Lemuria* was probably the closest thing I would ever experience to Montoya's starship, hauling rich immortals across the universe. Clean (at least when finished and mopped up) and well lighted, smelling of plastics and paint and filtered air, spanking white sheets rolling across acres of California king-size beds, beautiful women sprawling before ageless studs, for ever young, willing and fertile, and outside, terrific views of the Horsehead Nebula and Orion's Belt. Each planet a challenge, every day an adventure.

'Is that what I'm after?' I asked myself. 'Forgiveness and a few bits of charity from the Master?'

Gloom descended, and I had no way of knowing whether it was genuine or a bacterially induced fake. 'Travel to the stars. Fill the universe with human flesh. *White* human flesh. White-boy dreams, Imperial destiny. All clean and healthy and Spin and Marty and . . . *shit*.'

I heard voices. I wasn't alone. I looked around the corner, tripped over a gap in the tile, and stumbled into the open.

In the corridor beyond, three stewards and a Coast Guard enlisted man were going through the pockets of a body. They rolled it over, swearing monotonously under their breaths.

Beyond them, five big guys in business suits caromed down the hall like drunks, but their eyes were steady and predatory. The enlisted man and one steward saw them coming, spun about to abandon their catch, and noticed me. They hunched and didn't even signal each other, but as a team brandished a pistol and a fancy hunting rifle covered with scrollwork. The enlisted man got off a round before I could do anything more than flinch. The shot creased my cheek. I shouted and turned, somehow ended up on my hands and knees, and picked myself off the deck. Another slug went through my pant leg. I ran, skidding on tile as I rounded the corner.

Adrenaline cleared my head like a blast of stinging cold water. Screw the Long Haul. I wanted to live another few seconds, please God, please Mother. I hid in a fire-station alcove, shivering, until I heard someone coming, then burst from my cover like a stupid pheasant. The steward, less than ten yards away, had aimed his rifle in anticipation, but before he could fire again, I was through a passageway feed, into the opposite spaces.

Somehow, I had ended up back by the unmounted brass plaque. I touched my cheek, brought my fingers away bloody, and looked into the corridor where I had seen the hunters and their kill. The body remained, its face a red mass. It had been joined by two others. I picked up the plaque to use as a weapon, or a shield, and studied the engraved map. Left. I was sure of it; the hospital was on this floor and inboard, to my left.

The first heavy door to the private spaces was intact and locked. I shivered at the sound of voices, a rifle butt rhythmically tapping the walls. A painful crack and ricochet.

I took Tammy's papers from my pocket, read them quickly, punched in an entry code, and waited for the little LED to flash red, red, *no luck*. I was sure that would happen, and I would be dead soon.

It flashed red. I tried another number. The voices were in the passageway.

'Did you see that bastard go down? Christ, got him right through the spine.'

'Better than paintballs.'

'Yeah, more splash.'

Laughter. Two guys out in the woods, hunting for me and whatever else they could flush from cover.

Red, red.

I lifted the paper to my eyes, studied the blurry copy of Tammy's diagram. This was a rear door, I guessed, used by staff in the medical center. I found the door on her crude map and tried to make out the combination. She had been writing with her left hand. The scrawl of fourteen numbers was hard to understand, but I took a guess and punched it in, the buttons clicking into place above each integer. The buttons popped out on the tenth number. Confused, I angrily slapped the frame, then punched in four more.

'Whoops! Gotcha,' someone called with ringing cheer.

The light flashed green.

I fumbled the handle. Grabbed it again. Something snicked and clacked behind me: well-oiled gunmetal. The door was heavy and opened slowly. I pushed through the gap. Saw at the end of the short hall a white steward's jacket and a pasty damp face with a five o'clock shadow, glint of ornately decorated rifle swinging down.

Click.

'Ah, fuck. Wait up, stupid!'

A hand clutching a pistol poked around the corner and fired. The slug caught me in my side, glanced off the bulletproof vest over my ribs, blasted paint and metal from the bulkhead, and shoved me like a bully's big hard fist through the door.

I tugged the door shut and pushed the lock home, then jerked at the pound of a rifle butt. In one frantic turn, as I stood away from the door, I saw what could have been a gray-carpeted hallway in any well-funded modern hospital or university building: closed office doors, cork bulletin boards (still virginal and bare) mounted on freshly painted beige walls, and at the

316

end, a sitting or waiting room with two utilitarian blue couches, two red chairs, a table, and a wall-spanning mural.

I caught my breath. Touched the vest through the hole in my jacket, felt the compressed groove beneath the fabric, poked my finger through the exit hole.

One one thousand, two one thousand, three . . .

Inspected the pattern of gray-and-black marks on the back of my sleeve, from the bullet's near impact and the spray of paint chips.

Five one thousand, six one thousand, seven . . .

Lifted my calf to inspect the hole in my pants.

'*Fucking amateur*,' I said, and giggled harshly.

Nothing outside.

Then, against the door, five staccato bangs, loud as horse kicks – bullets. They were trying to shoot through the door. No marks on the inside, not even a reverse dimple. Thick and armored. The back of my head hurt. I had slammed it back against the wall in surprise.

Another thump on the door, soft and frustrated.

Eight one thousand, nine.

The room was silent but for the ticking of a clock on the wall. I stood with my back to the wall for several minutes, listening, waiting for my heart to slow, and that was all I heard. My heart, and the soft ticking of the big clock. Time passing. I couldn't believe I was still alive. I could feel the pain in my cheek like a small, hot brand.

In the waiting room, I washed my face in a water fountain, sluicing away the blood. The crease wasn't very big, little more than a bad shaving cut. It was already clotting.

I wiped my hands on my pant legs. Swallowed hard.

Belly of the beast again, but the safest place on the ship.

The mural showed the Earth in a Dymaxion projection, the globe according to Buckminster Fuller, covered with wide irregular patches of green, red, and shades of blue, chiefly in the oceans. I found Lake Baikal – intense red. Another red patch surrounded the Bahamas, the waters where the *Lemuria* would commonly be sailing on better, more peaceful days. Small red dots in the Mediterranean, the Dead Sea, western Canada, around the Galapagos and Peru, off the coast of Japan. A large kitty scratch of red lines hugged the northeast coast of Australia – encompassing the Great Barrier Reef, I guessed. Smaller patches and points near Sri Lanka, Borneo, and New Zealand. The map was void of words or labels.

I was sure that the colors signified bacterial hotspots. Phone exchanges for the Little Mothers of the World. Ever since the 1920s, Maxim Golokhov had been listening for his message from the oldest minds on Earth.

Right of the map stood a simple windowless double door and another combination lock. I used Tammy's list once more, with some confidence. I twisted the handle, gathered what little genuine courage I had left, and walked through.

Beyond lay an Olympic-sized pool, deserted. Crazy quilt patterns of tiny waves reverberated across the opal blue surface. I walked along the pool's edge, shoes squeaking on antislip coating like rubbery sandpaper. I sniffed, then leaned over the pool and sniffed again. No pervasive smell of chlorine. I dipped and tasted. Not salt water, but I spat anyway. The pool was filled with untreated fresh water.

Wouldn't want to discourage our microbial friends.

Tammy's codes worked for all of the spaces forward of the pool. The clinic held massage and chiropractic tables, acupuncture and moxibustion stations with little chrome buckets filled with incense cones, exercise and recovery equipment, coordination test benches, hydrotherapy tubs, most of which could have been found in any good sports stadium. (The moxibustion seemed over the top, but who was I to judge?)

A glass cabinet on the wall enclosed neat lines of opaque jars marked SKIN, NASAL PASSAGES, SCALP, RECTUM. Smaller labels on some narrowed their use: PRE-PUBESCENT, MENARCHE, >30. A tampon dispenser beside the cabinet bore the red label ATHLETIC REHAB ONLY.

Open shelves supported tidy stacks of plastic-bagged and

serial-numbered white-cotton panties, sports bras, jockstraps, and briefs. All very egalitarian and unisex. Post-Cold War, more up-to-date than Anthrax Central, and perhaps reflecting a new approach to a younger generation of recruits.

Preparations were in place for a long stay with a select group of adapted and highly trained young bodyguards, runners, and circus performers. Golokhov's Praetorians. I noted the room's pleasant colors but saw no personal marks, no patterns of use or wear. The rooms had yet to be broken in.

Large plastic beakers in the middle cultured a churning white-and-yellow ooze. A fan of pipes ascended from the beakers to the ceiling, then dropped to connect with soft-drink dispensers, a shower stall, a curtained colonics station.

I pulled aside another long curtain and found a row of stainless-steel toilets. The bowls held the same milky fluid. Excreted germs must be reunited with their fellows, not sacrificed to a shipboard sewage-treatment plant.

Or perhaps Dr Goncourt did not want to unnecessarily pollute the waters around *Lemuria*.

Against the back wall, inboard – I was trying to keep myself oriented – I saw the first signs of disorder, human habitation. Blue, green, and red backpacks had been tossed on the floor with some carelessness. I strolled along the line of packs, hands in my pockets. Smiling at the thought, I removed my jacket and bulletproof vest and laid them down at the end of the line. One of the team, now. Less obvious.

The forward doors opened. I looked for a place to hide, but it was too late. Three young women entered and saw me. In their late teens or early twenties, cheerful, lithe, vivid with health, they wore orange-and-silver exercise togs, hair tied up with blue, red, and green stretchies. They walked briskly by with sidewise looks of puzzled recognition, smiled politely, then went to the benches.

Chatting in low voices in accented English, with just a hint of self-conscious reserve, they taped sensor pads to each other's arms and legs and shoulders, read the meters, and made notes on small clipboards. It seemed part of a familiar routine. No concern, no alarm at my presence.

Another ordinary day, isolated from the chaos and death on the rest of the ship.

I watched for a moment, feeling like a voyeur, then stepped toward the door through which they had entered. According to Tammy's map, beyond were the makeup and prep rooms for the amphitheater, and a relatively large circular space, labeled 'Listeners 1.'

In the curving corridor outside, behind a half-open utility hatch with ventilation slats on the bottom, I heard sounds of water pumping and a low electrical hum. I opened the hatch.

I was in some sort of long, high-ceilinged pump room. The inner arc of the circular space was a steel-walled tank at least forty feet in diameter. A male in his early thirties, big-shouldered, pug-nosed, dressed in orange togs with blue leggings, came around the tank's curve, passed briefly behind a forest of feed pipes, then emerged into view again, penciling notes on a clipboard.

He stopped when he saw me. Smiled shyly. Turned. Walked back the way he had come.

The feeling of unreality intensified. In the heart of Golokhov's new headquarters, I was unchallenged, maybe even welcome.

I took a deep breath to steady my nerves, now jangling like a curtain of off-key wind chimes. A steep ladder ahead gave access to a catwalk over the steel tank. I climbed, dropping cautious glances down at the pump room. The tank was filled with shadow too deep to penetrate. Its black expanse yawned beneath a concave cap hanging by thick chains from the upper deck I-beams. Out of the darkness came a periodic slop and the tang of seawater, fresh not stagnant. An aquarium, possibly; I thought of the shattered glass tanks in Anthrax Central.

My unfinished hypothesis poked me, like a knitting needle jamming a sensitive nerve. Little sparks of ideas, suspicions, fears. *What the hell do I want to learn here?*

Delbarco had said she didn't really want to know. She wanted to sleep nights. Too late, Breaker had said.

Right.

I came to a control panel mounted in the middle of the catwalk. I could make out vague labels, again in English: *Lights. Microphone. Music.*

I flicked the switch marked *Lights.*

The tank came alive with a deep blue-green glow. It wasn't as deep as I had thought, shallow in fact, about shoulder high at the center, if the light wasn't playing tricks. A sandy bottom supported mushroomlike black-and-green lumps, furry with strands of algae. The lumps resembled old heads of coral or overgrown tree stumps, jutting up around the perimeter like eroded snags in a drowned forest.

No doubt about it. Golokhov liked to culture stromatolites. Colonies of cyanobacteria, eucaryotes, algae, building up thick layers over the centuries, making towheads in shallow water. Trunk lines for the Little Mothers.

No fish. No sharks. No octopi, no seaweed or stylish rocks with serpentine moray eels. Not much of an aquarium, actually, hardly worth anyone's notice, but the opposite side of the tank had been set with long observation windows. With a jerk of surprise, I saw people beyond those windows, distorted by refraction and blurred by the ripples, wrapped in purple twilight and doubled up like loving couples.

As my eyes adjusted to the twilight glow beyond the main tank, I could discern that they wore dark hats or helmets, from which jutted white tubes and short, black pipes. I stepped to the opposite side of the catwalk, gripping the iron rails, and leaned to stare down into an adjoining tank, a narrow, rectangular pool filled with lavender liquid.

The people facing the windows were fully immersed. More puzzling, they were naked. They weren't lovers; they were Siamese twins, seven pairs. Three were united at the abdomen, three at the hip. One pair joined at the temple required a special mask and goggles with three lenses. Their arms hung from rubber straps, the straps hooked to black, motorized levers that slowly exercised their limbs, up and down, in and out, like the long black fingers of a puppeteer.

I watched in horror, thinking they must be drowned corpses, arranged in an awful parody of modern art. No hoses supplied air to their noses and mouths. No bubbles rose from their masks. But their fingers twitched. Their limbs flexed weakly against the straps. They could not breathe, but they were alive.

The lavender pool smelled like a nursery, milky-sour and as nitrogenous as a soaked diaper. But these were adults, not children, chests hairy or breasts prominent, genitalia fully formed and flossed. I shaded my eyes to make out more detail. Regular rows of fleshy bumps studded their shoulders and backs. Each bump had a tiny dimple with one or two central black pits. Far too small to function as gills. Still, I thought I could see the pits opening and closing like little mouths.

In the main tank, pipes stretched from the black mounds to the steel wall below the windows. Small valves at the ends of the pipes sucked in clouds of white curds, like the floc surrounding the deep-sea vents. The curds flushed into the lavender pool, where they swirled around the twins like snow in a glass paperweight.

'Listeners 1,' Tammy's map said. If these were the Listeners, what in hell could they possibly be listening to? How many others were there, on the ship or elsewhere? I tried to imagine Golokhov collecting unwanted children from around the globe, taking in the handicapped along with the firm, selecting with strange acuity for special talents, extraordinary patience. Creating a biological Shangri-la, a preserve where everyone had his or her (or its) place, doing something basically incomprehensible to the rest of the world, and certainly to me. An empire based on microbes.

Then it struck me. Golokhov had isolated the doubled figures from respiration. They did not suck oxygen from the water like fish; they did not use oxygen at all. They no longer relied on mitochondria to fuel their cells and tissues.

The Siamese twins had become anaerobes.

I can't actually recall my thoughts at that moment. I imagine that I felt anger, indignation, even jealousy, but shock may have topped the list and blanked all the others.

The problem of our ancient reliance on mitochondria had been solved. But the solution seemed to be a passive, motionless slavery. Or the awful, endless hell of the prisoners on the top floor of Anthrax Central. Or the shriveled eccentricity of Mrs Golokhova, who had suffered years of madness.

Lissa had warned me that what Rob and I were searching for was nasty. How right she was.

I straightened and looked for a ladder at the opposite end of the catwalk. There wasn't one. A blind bulkhead blocked the way. I walked back to the middle, swiveled, my shoes grabbing at the grating, and knelt to peer through the blue water, into the lavender pool, at a steeper angle, to see if there was a gallery, a viewing area, on the other side of the conjoined twins. Between the water and the thick windows, I discerned a ribbon of some lighter color that might have been a floor. Then I made out a flat, ghostly figure like a damp paper cutout stuck to the glass, barely evident through the ripples and optical compression, the squeezing of sight lines.

It stood with arms folded.

I dropped to all fours on the catwalk.

A face steadied between two long waves in the main tank. It had a down-angled left eye, and its lips bent into an interested gape as it examined the twins. I had seen that face in a mirror so often, I thought I was catching an impossible reflection. But the image moved out of sight, walking or simply rippling away.

It was Rob.

It *was* Rob. I couldn't believe my luck. He was still alive. I could speak to him and apologize. I felt a surge of something approaching ecstasy.

Then I remembered Ben waiting for Janie.

I got to my feet and wiped my eyes, ashamed at giving in so easily to this swindle of emotion.

'Who's there?' a female voice called out behind me.

I turned and grabbed both handrails, fully expecting to feel another slug, the one that would blow through my ribs and kill me.

A woman with dark hair climbed onto the catwalk and stood in the dim blue light. I recognized Betty Shun, once again wearing an abbreviated black-knit dress and running shoes. A fire ax swung from one hand. For a moment, she seemed to know me. She relaxed and smiled, then studied my clothes, the cut on my cheek. She tensed.

'You!' she said. 'How did you get this far?'

'Someone gave me a key,' I answered, smiling, but my armpits dripped. 'How's Owen?' I watched the ax head slow in its pendulum motion.

'I hope he rots in hell,' Betty said. 'Come with me. You shouldn't be up here.'

CHAPTER THIRTY-SEVEN

She waited for me at the bottom of the steep stairs, lips tight, ax held in a bloodless grip.

'I'm okay,' I said. 'I'm not crazy.'

Shun nodded but did not seem to believe me. She pointed for me to go around the tank, around the forest of piping, opposite the way I had entered.

'I'd like to see Dr Golokhov,' I said. 'I've come through hell. I deserve at least that much.'

'Dr Goncourt left the ship a week ago,' Betty said. She led me out of the tank room into the inner sanctum of the main lab, big clinical spaces with stainless-steel counters and sinks, incubators, sequencers, a phalanx of proteomizers linked to connection machines. All these rooms were deserted, but I saw unpacked crates waiting in a corner, stacks of DVD-RW disks in plastic drawers, journals, cardboard boxes full of textbooks.

'I'm really not sure how much you know,' Shun said. 'I've just arrived here myself.'

'I know it all,' I said, my throat threatening to close.

'Well,' she said. 'Many of the others have left. Dr Goncourt paroled a lot of them as soon as Irina died in New York. No need to be so vigilant now.'

'Mrs Golokhova?'

Betty nodded.

'I didn't know her first name.'

Shun smiled. I had lied. There was a lot I did not know. 'Dr Goncourt has always planned to retire and pass on his operations to others. It's important that there be continuity.'

'Where is he?'

'Dr Goncourt?'

'Golokhov.'

She shook her head. 'He no longer uses that name. It brings back bad memories.'

'He put up quite a fight . . . didn't he?'

'You should know,' she said.

'Who won?'

'You did, of course,' Betty Shun said.

'Of course. Who are the Siamese twins?'

'They are Listeners. They were Dr Goncourt's main concern in the negotiations.'

'Negotiations? You call all of that *negotiations?*'

'Now they will stay and continue their work. The circus will go on, too.'

'What are they listening for?'

'The voice of the Little Mothers, so we've been told. But the Little Mothers speak slowly. Dr Goncourt investigated life extension so he could live long enough to understand what they were saying.' She looked at me with a sad expression, as if to add, *and look at all the trouble*.

'They're listening to bacteria?'

Betty Shun lifted one eyebrow. 'Don't we all, in our way? Isn't that what you were telling Owen?'

Out on the black ocean, rescue boats, fishing smacks, yachts, Coast Guard cutters, tugboats, even a big container ship, all converged on *Lemuria* with floodlights waving, outlining the huge hulk in the early dawn.

Betty Shun left me in a flight lounge on the top deck of Aristos Tower, in the charge of two strong, tall young men in sweaters. They were polite but said little. When she returned, she took me aside, and whispered, 'You are leaving now.'

'What about the others?'

'I don't know anything about them.'

'What about Ben Bridger?'

She shook her head. 'Maybe the boats will take them all away. You will use the helicopter.'

'Where am I going?'

'To meet with Dr Goncourt,' Betty said. 'It's an honor, don't you think?'

I watched from the side window of the small business helicopter as it lifted off the pad. The two young men in gray accompanied me. I was leaving behind Delbarco, Breaker, Ben, Carson, Candle, and all the others, alive or dead, probably dead.

I was sure I was being taken somewhere to die. The only consolation I had was that I would meet the greatest man of the twentieth century. My brother's real murderer.

I would be able to ask a few questions, and maybe, if he was kind, and if I was lucky, I would get a few answers.

Part of me said it was a betrayal of all my past principles not to scream and shout and claw and hang on to every second of life, but a larger self had control now, and it was calm.

And curious. Not even flying scared me. Do lambs count the butterflies as they're tugged to the knife?

No one noticed our departure. Everyone was too busy trying to figure out what in hell had happened aboard the world's most sophisticated and expensive cruise ship. Why so many had died. I doubted anyone would ever get to see the hospital, the clinic, the labs, and the Listeners. Somehow the investigators would all be distracted, faked out, sent elsewhere. Or mysteriously killed.

Silk would live on.

The helicopter flew east. I asked the pilot where we were going.

'Exuma Cays. Lee Stocking Island,' he said with a Russian accent. 'A resort. Nice. You'll like it.'

'I'm sure I will.'

'Pity you can't stay for too long,' he added. 'There's a tropical depression brewing. Might even get a name soon.'

CHAPTER THIRTY-EIGHT
Lee Stocking Island, The Bahamas
August 20

I walked in late-morning brilliance toward the white-sand beach. A cool, moist breeze luffed at my hair and my fresh white shirt. A mass of towering gray clouds walled off the eastern ocean, and it was from the east that the wind blew.

I had eaten a light breakfast of oatmeal in the resort restaurant, lubricating it with hot coffee, then had asked where the estate of Dr Goncourt was located. The staff all knew of it. It was a mile away, a bellhop said, down a paved road toward the Atlantic side of Lee Stocking Island and through a private gate that was always open.

I was free to do what I pleased, to leave the island – the men in gray had dropped me off with several thousand dollars in my pocket – or to stay and accept the invitation. Apparently, I was no longer a threat to anybody.

On the island, Dr Goncourt's estate was famous for having the only private beach with its own stromatolites. Stromatolites made up one of the prime attractions on Lee Stocking Island.

The house was medium in size, wood frame, concrete foundation, large windows with wooden shutters, mostly open. It blended in with the rustling palm trees. I avoided the house and walked straight toward the beach, as I had been instructed. It was ten o'clock.

A blond woman in a swimsuit with a turquoise shawl draped over her legs sat in a lounge chair away from the driftwood and sea wrack of the high-water mark. A sun cap hid her face. As I approached, she heard the slap of my sandals, shaded her eyes, and half rolled in the chair to look back at me. She stood to meet me, without a touch of embarrassment or selfconsciousness.

'Hello, Hal,' she said.

'Lissa,' I said. 'Surprised?'

'No,' she said. 'Should I be?'

'You did your best to kill me.'

'Not my very best, obviously,' she said. 'But now it's over. A request was made, and Dr Goncourt is waiting for you. I doubt you want to stay and chat with me.'

'I've been thinking about you a lot, actually.'

'I've been thinking about you not at all,' she said.

'Rob would have loved to see this,' I said.

'How considerate of you to think of your brother.'

'We went through a lot of misery because of you. I hear somebody's replacing Golokhov after all these years.'

'Dr Goncourt. Indeed.'

'Are you guarding him?' I asked.

'He doesn't have long to live. We decided it would be best to let him work and save his dignity, away from the mess.'

'Is it finished? The control, the tagging, the runners? The government is shivering like a big dog now, throwing it all off, don't you think?'

'Of course, Hal,' she said, as if humoring a child. 'You can just walk out there, through the water. The waves are light. No more than a few minutes, though. He tires quickly, and we're leaving soon for the mainland. We won't stay for the storm.'

'Moving to another estate? More hidden riches?'

Lissa shrugged.

I wanted to reach out and strangle her, or just touch her face, to discover whether she was a phantom. I could not be sure anything I saw was real.

'Why am I here?' I asked.

'I don't know,' she said. 'But don't do anything rash.' She lifted her arm and crooked it, then pointed her finger into the trees beside the house. I turned and saw four men in gray suits. Three of the men were young and athletic. The fourth was much older, in his seventies. He wore a Hawaiian shirt and Dockers. He was the man Ben had stared at in Anthrax Central.

Stuart Garvey.

I turned away then, hating the thought that Lissa would see me so confused. I stalked over the dry sand, onto the hard wet sand, then into the blue water. Stromatolites are not pretty, just stunted forests of little brown lumps in the water, surrounded by shifting sand. The brown towheads broke the gentle waves for thirty or forty feet before the ocean overtopped them.

A thin old man with a shock of white hair knelt in the water, a canvas bag slung around one shoulder. He looked up as I sloshed closer. His face was pale, heavily wrinkled, but his eyes were bright. He did not seem to have suffered from the same affliction as Irina Golokhova, and in fact he looked at least a hundred years old, though still spry. His wrinkled, spotted, but otherwise normal hands stroked the damp upper round of a stromatolite. Algae clung to his fingers.

He looked up. 'Hello,' he greeted. 'Are you a student of things biological? Do you know of these marvels?'

'Dr Golokhov?'

He looked at me more critically. 'Goncourt, please. Golokhov should have died decades ago.'

'I'm Hal Cousins. You killed my brother,' I said.

'Did I?' He made a regretful face. '*I am* sorry. I *hope* you will forgive me.'

This reaction brought all the blood to my face, but it also took me by surprise. 'You damned near killed me.'

'How good that I failed,' he said with false gallantry.

'Don't tell me it was war. It was vicious stupidity.'

'Perhaps it was,' he said. 'Engendered by fear. Unimaginable, so much fear. You are one of the little human tumors, aren't you? You and your brother. You both wanted to live for ever.'

'I still do.'

'The Little Mothers watch over us all,' the old man said, and wiped his hands on his pants, leaving dark smears. 'Sever the connections between the body and their ministrations, and you block far more than the path to old age. Have you ever felt fit and in tune? Life is good? Perhaps you have a mystical feeling of connection with Nature, with something higher? That is the voice of the Little Mothers. All the stresses and rewards of life are balanced, you are doing well, and they approve. To be judged and found wanting, that is painful. But take those voices away, and you soon lose all balance. We are far more than just brains encased in bone. Larger and older minds live inside our bodies and all around us, speaking in languages I have worked all my life to interpret.' He trailed his fingers in the water. 'Perhaps we are only a dream the bacteria are having.'

I couldn't just let the arrogant old bastard babble. I wanted answers. For Rob, for Ben.

'Did you make a deal with Stalin? *How many people did you torture and kill?*'

Golokhov stuck out his jaw and looked down at the water.

'You experimented with your wife, then you abandoned her!'

'Yes. Irina.' He rubbed his nose, then his forehead, leaving a streak of slime on the pale, wrinkled skin. 'I made her into a new kind of woman. I watched her for ten years. She was full of hatred and guile, uncaring, a cruel and unrepentant thief. I tried to fix my mistakes, and in time I reversed her ill effects . . .

but I should have stopped there and destroyed my records. Too late. I had attracted the attention of beasts who were already hatred and greed made flesh. What will *you* do, Mr Faust, who still wants to know so much? What beasts will you unleash when you cut all the strings?'

'You still want me dead, don't you?' I asked. 'Why not just tell them to shoot me?'

'Ah,' he said, and lifted his hands to the air, shaking them as if invoking a higher power.

My anger flashed over. 'You're a coward,' I shouted. 'You'd never just grab a gun and pull the trigger. You're too *fastidious*.' I lifted my hand, targeting the back of his frail old neck. I didn't care about the men on the beach.

Golokhov looked up. A line of spit hung from the corner of his mouth. 'I *was* a coward. I feared torture and death. I watched blood flow in rivers and corpses stack like cordwood. To save myself, I gave the monsters even more power . . . and the rivers became oceans. I set myself to bringing them down, and when they were defeated, I made it my duty to watch and guard, with the few resources left to me, to spare the world even more slaughter. How do you think this painfully cruel and inept species survived to see a new millennium? But I was a fool to think I could stop so many curious and immoral children.' He wiped his mouth and washed his hands in the sea. 'I hope your generation will do better.'

'No, you don't,' I said.

He knelt in the lapping waves and returned his attention to the stromatolite. 'You're no better than Stalin or Beria,' I added. 'You try to kill our brightest dreams. I want to enhance human life. But you gave us the City of the Dog Mothers.'

He shuddered. For a moment I thought he was having a fit, but he flung aside his canvas bag, spun about in the blue water, and glared at me, the fiercest and most hate-filled look I ever hope to see.

The face of a wrathful God as Blake might have drawn him before he tore up the paper and burned the pieces.

'Yes, and there will be punishment!' he said. 'Do you know what the message is? What little I have intercepted and translated over seven decades, the sum of all my good work on this Earth, in this forsaken century?' He reached down and patted the stromatolite between his knees. 'All the Little Mothers whispering in our bowels and in the forests and jungles and in the oceans we are working so hard to destroy. They are not happy. They are not happy with us at all. *We are a bitter disappointment to them.* They wage all-out war against us now. It is a judgment none of us can withstand. Not those on the ship, not those on the shore. None. None.'

He faced the gray wall of storm across the water.

'How long do you think we have, young monster?' he asked, still trembling. 'How long?'

EPILOG
Southern California (no addresses, please)

It's been a little more than four months and I'm still alive. Still sane – I think. Ben is alive. They must have gotten him off the ship. I wonder how he felt about not seeing Janie again.

He sent me a copy of *Life* magazine; it came in the mail last Friday. From 1949, photos of the Waldorf Conference in New York. Communists for world peace. (How did he get my address? Once a spook.)

I read the magazine wearing plastic gloves. There's another picture of Rudy Banning. He's standing next to Arthur Miller, and Miller is chuckling at something Rudy has just finished saying. It's definitely Rudy.

On a little Post-it, stuck next to the picture, Ben wrote, 'No way they can fake this. Rethink everything. What Banning was doing, what Rob was doing. Who did I shoot?'

And I am rethinking. I've tried to assemble a sequence of events and figure out who was running whom, and when.

Here's what I've got so far:

Year Before Last
   June: Rob has treated himself to block bacterial connections, but I am ahead in my research at this point.
   August: Desperate, Rob takes a long shot, goes to Siberia.
   October: Rob contacts Banning, or does Banning go to him?
   December: Begins to be harassed (by Stuart Garvey and Irina, or Maxim?). Tagging effects only partly successful because of his self-treatment and altered gut bacteria. He appears to be getting more and more eccentric.

Last Year

Late January: Rob on the outs with Lissa. (Lissa sent to stop Rob – or to convert him, recruit him?)

Who is trying to tag Rob? Is it Lissa, working for Maxim Golokhov, or is it Irina Golokhova? Banning tries to get Rob to go to Callas and be trained. Rob refuses.

February: Rob begins concerted research program to block Silk. At his lowest point . . . (Opens lab in office building in San Jose?)

April: Tammy flees to Marquez. Marquez contacts Banning about Tammy's story. Banning puts Rob in touch with Marquez and Tammy in Los Angeles. Rob builds lab in Marquez's basement. Marquez likes the longevity angle, but is paranoid about government mind control – and Tammy's story only makes his fears worse.

May 28 Rob calls me in San Diego Airport. Gives me a warning.

May 30 I visit Montoya, make my pitch, get approval for sub dive.

June 6 Rob visits Ben Bridger.

June 7 Bridger is arrested and taken to Metropolitan.

June 8 Dr Mauritz kills his wife.

June 10 Bridger released.

June 11 Bridger, Rob, and Banning go to Los Angeles.

June 12 Marquez house is attacked. (Newspapers with story appear while I am at sea. Lissa shows me the story later, crashed Marine Corps helicopters – why? Is she asking me if I know, or does she know?)

THE DIVE: On June 18, I go down in DSV. Sea Messenger food dosed. Dave Press tries to kill us both. Three die on Sea Messenger.

June 19 Sea Messenger pulls into port in Seattle.

June 20 Breakfast with Bloom and Shun, 9-10:30 a.m. Investigate specimens 11:30 a.m.-8 p.m. Dinner at Canlis 10-11:30 p.m.

June 20 <Noon, EST. Rob calls my cell-phone from public phone in New Jersey. (Guessing at place and time.)

2 p.m. EST, Ben and Rob meet Stuart Garvey outside Penn Station. Have lunch. Garvey takes them to Anthrax Central in downtown Manhattan 4:00 p.m. Irina tries to turn Rob. Recruit him? Ben shoots Rob in New York alley (2-3:00 a.m.?).

June 21 12:30 a.m. PST Lissa calls on cell-phone to leave message about Rob's death.

June 21: 1 a.m. PST Last meeting with Montoya. I walk around Lake Union to Genetron lab, discover trashed specimens 2:30 a.m. PST.

June 21 3:20 a.m. PST I turn on my cell-phones, take message from Rob, Lissa, learn Rob is dead.

June 27 Funeral in Coral Gables, Florida.

June 29-August 8 I am in Berkeley.

August 8 Promethean Conference. I meet Banning. Apartment fire and dog attack, hospital visit. Banning pays.

August 8-9 Haight hotel room.

August 9 I buy clothes, Banning and I meet with Callas, Lissa returns. I read several of Rob's papers; City of Dog Mothers. Tagging attempt (can opener) partially successful that evening, late.

Never got to test can opener.

August 10 Second meeting with Callas, who turns us down. Smart lady.

August 10 Thuringia – crazy old fake cop with signs of Golokhov's immortality treatments – and trip to San Jose with Lissa to open Rob's office/lab. It's a trap. Lissa shoots car salesman.

August 10-13 Lissa gives me supreme tagging and drives me out to desert hotel. Tells me to kill myself. Sounds like a good idea at the time.

August 13 Ben Bridger and Rudy Banning rescue me, give me gallon of elixir, then haul me shitting and puking to airport in Arizona.

August 13-14 Back to Anthrax Central. (My first time.)

August 18 Assault on Lemuria.

August 20 Meeting with Golokhov/Goncourt. Bad news about the Little Mothers.

August 21 Return to Miami from Bahamas. Not much news about Lemuria. *Go into hiding.*

I've worked out some of the history. Here it is, as far as I've gone. Open up the sealed brown paper envelope (hairs taped over the flap for security) and read. Wear gloves, though, ha-ha. Feel free to add your own details or correct me. It's all up in the air, little or no documentation.

I can't trace all the threads and who is pulling them and when. It still doesn't add up. Something's missing, something itches at the back of my head.

Why did Lissa shoot the skinny man in the herringbone suit?

Why didn't they change the combinations in Goncourt's hospital aboard the *Lemuria* after Tammy went missing? I'm thinking maybe they didn't know she was betraying them. *Tammy was there to foil Banning and Rob.*

Why didn't she? Who turned her? Rob?

Was he working for Mrs Golokhova and the government?

Who ordered the gunship attack in LA? Probably Golokhov – but why? Why provoke his former allies? Was he that worried about Rob and Banning?

Weird election this November, wasn't it?

Maxim Golokhov cooperated with the United States after the war. Everything else about him is murky until 1954, when he shows up in New York, but he must have been there to set up Thuringia and the other towns. Shipping tagged fruitcake all over the world.

Irina Golokhova was cooperating with some branches of the federal government, and had been since at least the 1960s, after Maxim left her in Manhattan. To keep things secret, Stuart Garvey and his cohorts at the CIA destroyed Rudy's reputation in 1992. Supposedly that's when Rudy's career falls apart.

But Rudy is clearly not who he says he is.

The picture that fell out of Rob's envelope, me and Rob somewhere in Europe, maybe, I don't remember the occasion. Just a simple memory lapse?

Why would Golokhov distract himself from studying the Little Mothers? Did Golokhov think we would upset the balance of nature so badly? He already believed the bacteria had passed judgment and had it in for us.

Do I believe that?

Do you?

My first instinct is to fight back. Cut all the strings. Time for us to grow up and go it alone. If the Little Mothers want to be abusive, I say we can play that game, too.

But the fact is, I'm tired.

I'm not sleeping well. I'm living in a crummy apartment in

Los Angeles, Culver City actually. So now you know. The air-conditioner is broken and I live out of Safeway cans. I shop for them in different stores, and I clean the can opener with boiling water and soap each time I use it.

I still have my incomplete list of proteins, still think now and then of the shining path to the Long Haul. I remember the blue strips of paper in the package from Rob, slipped into the airmail envelope. Maybe they were the other half of the secret – Rob's half. Maybe he was willing them to me in case he failed.

Doesn't matter. They're gone now.

I still convince myself I have the dream, that history hasn't stolen my life from me. But I can't work, can't get work, and Mom has run out of money, she says.

Then, last week, her phone was disconnected. I don't have the cash to go see where she is or what she's doing. I think she's probably fine, but I don't know why I think that.

Owen Montoya is in the hospital. I read the headlines at a newspaper stand. A nervous breakdown. He tried to stab a visiting scientist.

I keep waking up late at night. I'm having dreams about Rob, frequent and nasty. He's chasing me. He blames me for his death. He's mad that Lissa had sex with me. I try to tell him it wasn't my fault, and he just gives me his most infuriating smile.

My phone bills scare me. (I can't pay them, but someone is paying them, because the phone hasn't been cut off.) I'm making long-distance calls to numbers I don't know, and if I try calling them again, I'm not recognized, or I get answering machines, or a modem line and all I hear is an electronic raspberry.

The last few weeks I've been answering so many dead calls. I pick up, and nobody's there. Just silence, or a hum from another galaxy.

I can't just let it ring.

Maybe it's part of this election, thousands of political phone banks, they dial hundreds of numbers at once, I answer, my voice triggers the computer to bring in an operator, but all of the operators are busy . . .

That sort of thing. Common, really. Nothing to worry about.

But eighty or ninety a day? To a guy with an unlisted number, who isn't registered to vote and has a lousy credit rating? I forget who I am some days, the phone cuts away so many chunks of my time.

Last night around midnight I answered on the third ring. This time there *was* a voice on the line, but I can't remember whether I was awake or asleep.

It was Rob. He said he was calling from Lee Stocking Island. He said, 'Hal, old boy, I've got some news. Do you have the final clues? *Shall we visit Dr Seuss?'*

'Goddamn it,' I said. 'Leave me alone.' But I couldn't hang up the phone. After he made sure I was still on the line, he read me a list of numbers.

I still remember those numbers. Every damned one of them.

We kept the coffin closed. I never saw the body. Rob was running Ben, had control of him even at the last, made him see what Rob wanted him to see.

Rob's list – *chopper, piecework, regulus* – did not stop the others from being tagged on *Lemuria*. But it could have protected me. Maybe, in his way, he loves me. He wants to keep me around, especially if I'm under his thumb.

Is this crazy thinking or have I finally figured it out?

Rob found a way to turn the tables. He finished his work while everyone thought he was dead, even his brother. After all the different factions had exhausted themselves, he moved in. Cut deals, made promises. Took over. Replaced Golokhov.

But his hands have the puckering, Irina's disease, Stalin's madness.

This morning, I found a pistol under the mat on my front

porch. A Glock with a fifteen-shot law-enforcement clip. Lissa's gun.

Do I use it on someone else, or on myself?

History is my brother's fist smashing into my face for ever.

My stomach hurts.

Learn to live well, or fairly make your will;
You've played, and loved, and ate, and drunk your fill:
Walk sober off; before a sprightlier age
Comes tittering on, and shoves you from the stage:
Leave such to trifle with more grace and ease,
Whom Folly pleases, and whose Follies please.

Alexander Pope, Imitations of Horace

ACKNOWLEDGMENTS

Many thanks to Special Agent Carl Jensen, FBI; Juliann Brunzell, Special Agent, Minnesota Bureau of Criminal Apprehension; Ed Ueber, NOAA; David and Diane Clarke; Yoshihisa Shirayama, Director and Professor of the Seto Marine Biological Laboratory in Kyoto, Japan; Mark E. Minie and Rose James; David Thaler, microbiologist at Rockefeller University; Dr Karl and Sylvia Anders; Karen Anderson; Ron Drummond; copy-editors Bob and Sara Schwager; and to my English-language editors, Shelly Shapiro, Jane Johnson, and Joy Chamberlain. And special thanks indeed to the Extropians, and to Max More and Natasha Vita-More.

The theory of aging described in this book is speculative. The concept of bacterial cooperation, however, is firmly established in scientific papers and books, including *Bacteria as Multicellular Organisms,* edited by James A. Shapiro and Martin Dworkin.

Eshel Ben-Jacob of Tel-Aviv University has an excellent website devoted to his ground-breaking explorations of bacterial cooperation:

http://star.tau.ac.il/~inon/baccyber0.html

The notion of a distributed bacterial network – a bacterial mind, if you will – is far from fantasy.

Speculations on the ultimate description and relationship of xenophyophores and the Vendobionts are my own. Dr Mark A. S. McMenamin's *The Garden of Ediacara* is an excellent personal examination of the Vendobiont fossils and their possible relationships to modern life forms.

Almost needless to say, I owe a great debt to the work of Lynn Margulis.

None of these fine people, of course, are responsible for any blunders or misconceptions.

*　　*　　*